W9-BUR-062

"Shayla Black creates emotional, searingly sexy stories
that always leave me wanting more."
—Maya Banks, *New York Times* bestselling author

"Sizzling, romantic, and edgy, a Shayla
Black book never disappoints."
—Sylvia Day, #1 *New York Times* bestselling author

PRAISE FOR THE NOVELS OF SHAYLA BLACK

Mine to Hold

"Ms. Black is the master at writing a steamy, smokin'-hot, can-I-have-more-please sex scene."
—*Fiction Vixen*

"The perfect combination of excitement, adventure, romance, and really hot sex . . . this book has it all!"
—*Smexy Books*

Belong to Me

"I couldn't put the book down until the last page in the wee hours in the morning. *Belong to Me* is a fabulous read."
—*Fresh Fiction*

"This book is HOT!"
—*Smexy Books*

Surrender to Me

"Full of steam, erotic love, and nonstop, page-turning action, this was one of those books you read in one sitting."
—*Night Owl Reviews*

"Delicious and entertaining, the scenes are unforgettable, and the characters are to die for. Fabulous read!"
—*Fresh Fiction*

continued . . .

Delicious

"Too *Delicious* to put down . . . a book to be savored over and over."
—*Romance Junkies*

"This one is a scorcher."
—*The Romance Readers Connection*

Decadent

"Wickedly seductive from start to finish."
—Jaci Burton, *New York Times* bestselling author

"A lusty page turner from the get-go."
—*TwoLips Reviews*

Wicked Ties

"A wicked, sensual thrill from first page to last. I loved it!"
—Lora Leigh, #1 *New York Times* bestselling author

"Not a book to be missed."
—*A Romance Review*

"Absolutely took my breath away . . . Full of passion and erotic love scenes."
—*Romance Junkies*

Strip Search
(writing as Shelley Bradley)

"Packs a hell of a wallop . . . an exciting, steamy, and magnificent story . . . Twists, turns, titillating and explosive sexual chemistry."
—*The Road to Romance*

"Perfect for readers who enjoy their romance with a hint of suspense."
—*Curled Up with a Good Book*

"Blew me away . . . a great read."
—*Fallen Angel Reviews*

Bound and Determined
(writing as Shelley Bradley)

"Much sexy fun is had by all."
—Angela Knight, *New York Times* bestselling author

"Steamier than a Florida night, with characters who will keep you laughing and have you panting for more!"
—Susan Johnson, *New York Times* bestselling author

"A searing, frolicking adventure of suspense, love, and passion!"
—Lora Leigh, #1 *New York Times* bestselling author

Ours to Love

SHAYLA BLACK

HEAT
NEW YORK

THE BERKLEY PUBLISHING GROUP
Published by the Penguin Group
Penguin Group (USA) Inc.
375 Hudson Street, New York, New York 10014, USA

USA | Canada | UK | Ireland | Australia | New Zealand | India | South Africa | China

Penguin Books Ltd., Registered Offices: 80 Strand, London WC2R 0RL, England
For more information about the Penguin Group, visit penguin.com.

OURS TO LOVE

This book is an original publication of The Berkley Publishing Group.

Copyright © 2013 by Shelley Bradley, LLC.
All rights reserved. No part of this book may be reproduced, scanned, or distributed in any printed or
electronic form without permission. Please do not participate in or encourage piracy of copyrighted
materials in violation of the author's rights. Purchase only authorized editions.

HEAT and the HEAT design are trademarks of Penguin Group (USA) Inc.

Heat trade paperback ISBN: 978-0-425-25339-7

An application to register this book for cataloging has been submitted to the Library of Congress.

PUBLISHING HISTORY
Heat trade paperback edition / May 2013

PRINTED IN THE UNITED STATES OF AMERICA

10   9   8   7   6   5   4   3

Cover photograph © Hasan Basri Yontar/iStockphoto.
Cover design by Marc Cohen.
Text design by Kristin del Rosario.

This is a work of fiction. Names, characters, places, and incidents either are the product
of the author's imagination or are used fictitiously, and any resemblance to actual persons,
living or dead, business establishments, events, or locales is entirely coincidental.
The publisher does not have any control over and does not assume any responsibility for
author or third-party websites or their content.

To the warm and beautiful Liz Berry,
who championed this story from the beginning
and opened her heart to prove that some feelings are just universal.
You are stunning in every way.
Thank you for your kindness and friendship.
Thanks especially for just being you.

Chapter One

Club Dominion—Dallas, Texas, late June

AFTER warming up the submissive's curvy, feminine ass with his hand, Xander Santiago cast her a discerning eye. Nice rosy shade. Graceful, compliant, docile, the woman remained bent and restrained over the spanking bench, her swollen, exposed pussy juicy as a ripe peach.

As the heavy beats of Nine Inch Nails throbbed through the dungeon, he walked a circle around her, smiling faintly at her flushed cheeks and eyes fluttering closed in ecstasy. Whitney had been the right choice for this evening's session, experienced but so sweet. She trembled with the desire to please. And to fuck.

She was exactly what his brother, Javier, needed.

"See the way she's trying to lift her ass to you? The way her pussy weeps? It's slick and swollen, but she wants more. A session with the flogger will send her to subspace," Xander coached, handing him the implement by the thick handle, the long, braided tails gleaming under the stark lights. "Your turn. Deep breath. You know what to do."

Javier nodded, but his brows drew together. Sweat trickled from his temple. He didn't grab the flogger, but plowed a jerky, bronzed hand through the waves of his dark hair, which looked as if he hadn't bothered to trim it in months. That fit, since his brother seemingly hadn't given a shit about anything except anger and vodka in far too long.

Damn it, Javier needed to look deep and find some self-control. Xander hoped that teaching him to embrace the inner Dominant so clearly buried under layers of stress, pain, and guilt would stop his full-blown slide into self-destruction. Since neither grief counseling nor time had done a damn bit of good, it was the only way Xander knew to keep his brother together.

If it didn't work, he'd almost certainly be putting Javier in an early grave.

Xander grabbed his brother's wrist and shoved the flogger in his hand. Javier gripped it in a white-knuckled fist, his gaze bouncing around the room.

"Breathe." Xander snapped his fingers. "Focus, man. She's right there, waiting for you. Get a grip and take control."

Javier gave a rough nod, then drew in a jagged breath. He swung his arm back in a jerky arc, but his position looked sloppy. He would likely hit the back of Whitney's thighs, not her luscious ass, and cause her the wrong sort of pain.

"Goddamn it," Javier cursed softly, shaking his head and blinking rapidly.

Xander clapped his brother on the shoulder. "Focus on Whitney." He leaned into his brother's face, forcing Javier's gaze to his. "Your thoughts should only be on her now. Take in her demeanor, posture, and other nonverbal cues, then decide what's most likely to give her the sensations she needs."

Javier lifted his head, staring blankly, his breathing alarmingly rapid.

"Are you seeing her? Are you listening for her safe word?" Xander demanded.

Squeezing his eyes shut, Javier gripped the flogger tighter, the veins of his wrist standing out. His arm shook as he dragged in an uneven breath, nervous energy pinging off his body.

Alarm bells went off in Xander's head. "Javier?"

"What?" he barked.

Xander got in his face, whispering tersely. "Snap out of it! Tell me her safe word."

Javier's nostrils flared. He pinched his eyes shut again, then flashed them wide open with a shake of his head. Fuck, his brother was trying to force himself back to the here and now—and it wasn't working. Xander scrubbed a hand over his face, frustration eating at him.

"You can do this," he cajoled. "I've given you the knowledge. You have the instinct. You're totally in control when you're on your game. Find that now. Use the power she's giving you, Javier. Feel her trust and get into your Dom space."

Javier sucked in a sharp breath and squared his shoulders, his whole body taut and hyperfocused. Then he nodded. Xander frowned, watchful, as he leaned away to let his brother wield the flogger on Whitney's ass. But Javier just stared sightlessly at the firm red globes of her flesh and swallowed. He swayed on his feet. His breathing turned choppier again.

Fuck. He felt his brother slipping through his fingers, little by little. Day by day. One step forward, three steps back. Xander cursed Francesca all over again. She'd taken the strong, commanding older brother he'd worshipped as a kid and turned him inside out with lies and guilt. The last year had eaten away his indomitable will, leaving behind an empty shell. Even from the grave, the beautiful, terrible bitch had her teeth in him.

"Javier!"

His brother's blue eyes cut over to him, dilated, not quite focused. Damn it, he was shaking again. Xander bit back a frustrated scream.

"Focus. Either tell me her safe word or give me the flogger," he growled.

"I-I . . ." Javier's fingers curled into a fist, and he hung his head. "Fuck. I have to get out of here."

"Get your shit together and tell me what's going on," he growled in low tones, hoping no one around them would hear.

Javier jerked his gaze back to Whitney's ass. The pleasure Xander had given her during the warm-up had begun to dissipate. She tensed, coming back to her body, back to reality. Xander leaned around the spanking bench to peer into the sub's pretty face. Her heavy green eyes surveyed the bits of the room she could see, her platinum hair moving as she now swung her head from side to side.

With a curse, he made his way over to her and laid a firm hand on her back. "Easy, Whitney."

"Permission to speak, Sir?"

Well, hell. Xander didn't want to hear it, but she'd earned it. "Yes, little sub."

"Have I done something wrong?" She sounded anxious.

"It's not you," he assured quickly, petting her soft skin.

Xander hesitated. What else could he say? Certainly not that his workaholic brother's wife had cheated on him with another man who'd murdered her, and a year later Javier was still guilt-ridden and broken. He continued to experience episodes of mental vacancy and uncontrollable rage. Sometimes—like now—he'd turn into a full-blown train wreck almost without warning.

"He's had some difficulties lately." Thank God no one in Dallas paid attention to the Who's Who of Los Angeles' wealthy unless they were movie stars. If they did, Whitney would know all about Javier's fucking tragic crap. "He just needs some time to get himself back in the right frame of mind. I'll keep you safe. Are you doing all right? Do you need water or anything?"

Sympathy crossed Whitney's soft face. "I'm sorry to hear that. No, Sir. I'm fine. I'll be patient if it pleases you both."

Xander kissed the girl's cheek. "Brave little sub. I'll reward you later."

That made her grin, and he let his lips curl up in a reassuring smile.

Until the flogger slammed into his chest. He caught it reflexively, then turned to see Javier storming toward the exit.

Shit! He couldn't leave his brother to his own devices, not when he seemed to be in the middle of another meltdown. Twice in the last year, Xander had rushed him to the emergency room to have his stomach pumped before he died of alcohol poisoning. But Xander also couldn't leave Whitney restrained without protection in the middle of a kink club on a Saturday night. There were predators everywhere, and even though the club owner, Mitchell Thorpe, inspected every member with a magnifying glass, no system was perfect.

He looked around the dungeon and spotted a familiar figure. Grabbing the woman's slender arm, he pulled her close. Her blue eyes flared, then danced with mischief when she recognized him.

She grinned as she flipped her black hair over the pale skin of her shoulder. "Last I heard, you still have to have my consent to manhandle me. Not that I'm objecting."

That was Callie. A sub with a brattier mouth he'd never met.

"Emergency," he growled. "Free Whitney for me and take care of her."

Her face turned immediately serious. "Of course. Go. Call me if you need anything else."

Bratty . . . but deeply loyal and reliable. Callie would do exactly as she promised.

"Thanks," Xander murmured, then ran after Javier, catching his brother by the arm as he pushed his way into the cramped dressing room. It was empty now, as most people were actively playing this time of the evening, like he and his brother would have been if Javier could get his head screwed on straight.

"What is your problem?" Xander demanded as he spun Javier around. Silence. "Talk to me."

"Back the fuck off." Javier jerked his arm away with a snarl.

God, more anger. Javier had oceans of it, an infinite mass of seething, burning rage that he didn't really understand. His brother had never explained his abrupt change in behavior over the last year. Was his guilt for being unable to save Francesca from a terrible death? Was it the anger step of his grieving process? Maybe they needed to get all this shit out in the open.

"Listen to me." He gripped Javier's shoulders. "I'm sorry you lost Francesca. But she was a vapid, cheating parasite. You didn't love her. I'd bet both my balls that you wanted to divorce her but didn't seek one because it would have cost a fucking fortune. Instead, you worked ridiculous hours to avoid her, didn't you? And rather than facing the problem head-on, she *chose* to run off with her lover, and *he* killed her. Not you. That wasn't your fault."

"Not entirely." Javier pinned him with seething blue eyes, wrenching free and slamming his fist into the locker. "It was yours, too."

Xander cursed under his breath. *This again?* "I couldn't have saved her, Javi."

"You could have at least tried!" He shoved his way into Xander's face, grinding his teeth so hard, the tendons in his neck stood out. An angry flush colored his cheeks. "For over three decades, I handled our parents, was the model student, and assumed the reins of the family businesses—all so you could continue to do what you excel at: play. I asked you for one favor in return. *One.* And you refused."

Javier hadn't done all of that exclusively for him. He'd done it mostly because he couldn't stand not being best at everything, and because that billion dollar conglomerate of companies had been his birthright. Javier had been the heir. Xander knew well that his parents had designated him the spare. Educated and pampered, but not really valued for any contribution he might make. After all, with a brother so capable, his contribution hadn't been necessary.

"You asked for something impossible," Xander insisted.

"Nearly every damn night you find a woman or two to bend to your will. Francesca needed your guidance and discipline. I was up to my eyeballs in the acquisition of Reptor, working eighteen hours a day. All you had to do was give her your firm hand."

Just like the day Javier had asked him to be Francesca's Dom, Xander thought his brother was out of his mind. He silently counted to ten, trying to hold on to his temper. "There were so many problems with your request, I don't even know where to start! First, I've never collared a sub of my own, and I wasn't about to take twenty-four/seven responsibility for *your* pampered wife. The absolute cornerstone of the lifestyle is safe, sane, and consensual. I didn't see how that arrangement would have been safe when I wanted to throttle her every waking moment. I don't think she was remotely sane. Even if none of that had been a problem, she wasn't submissive. She would have never consented to give me her power. If I'd taken it, I would have been nothing more than an abusive bully, because I know damn well that ass would have required beating daily. Hell, probably every hour on the hour."

Javier's eyes narrowed. "She might have been submissive for you, but you wouldn't even try. And I know why. You wanted to fuck her. You only refused my request because I excluded sex in the proposed contract."

"I also want to ride a wild bull someday for the rush of it, but that doesn't mean I'm stupid enough to do it." Xander scowled at his brother. "Yeah, I wanted to fuck her once upon a time. I admit it. She was beautiful. But she was a viper who damn near sucked the life out of you, brother. I told you she would before you married her. But you haven't listened to a fucking word I've said since we were kids. *You* wanted her. Instead of banging her once, you convinced yourself that, being an executive's daughter, she would make a model executive's wife, so you put a ring on her finger."

"It was one of the terms of a delicate merger. It made sense at the time."

"It was a bad deal."

"And you love to say 'I told you so.'"

"Francesca's father dangled her out there like a carrot when she was really the stick. You were dumb enough to take the bait. She beat you down mentally for years. Hell, she's still doing it!"

His brother bristled. "The potential for revenue growth as a result of that merger was exponential."

"At the cost of your sanity?"

Javier looked away with a curse, and Xander knew his brother was about to walk out on him again, probably to find another bottle and finish himself for good. He'd intentionally removed every gun from the Dallas house they'd been staying in for the last few weeks, and the L.A. mansion before that. No sense tempting fate.

Knowing this tactic wasn't working, Xander tried another. "The business is suffering, Javier. Going downhill fast. You're unfocused and floundering. Your episodes are more common than you've let on, aren't they? The sharks are circling. Goddamn it, let me help."

"No." Javier's refusal rolled around the quiet room like a shout.

"Why? I've got a fucking MBA I've never used because you've never needed or wanted me."

"So . . . would you squeeze in research and development somewhere between your daily dose of spanking and fucking? I can't have you demanding that your executive assistant strip the minute she walks in the door. It's called sexual harassment. We'd be sued blind."

Javier's sarcasm cut him like an ax to the chest. "You have no idea what I'm capable of, but you're never going to find out because you refuse to share our family business. And despite the guilt you're trying to shove down my throat, you would *never* have shared your wife in any way, either."

He'd lived in his big brother's shadow for nearly thirty years, wishing he could please his parents. Finally, he'd realized that was impossible and gave up, pursuing pleasure instead. He'd decided very early in life that he didn't want Javier's grudging seconds, either.

"Bullshit. I asked for your help. I fucking *begged* you," his brother snapped.

"When Francesca got beyond your desire or ability to handle her, you looked to me like some BDSM Band-Aid. You've been training in the lifestyle for months now. You know why passing her off to me would have never worked, even if the issue of fucking her never came up. She wasn't going to recognize you as her husband, me as her Master, and suddenly be happy."

"Maybe not happy, but at least she wouldn't have been in Aruba being murdered by her lover."

Xander shook his head, wondering if Javier could even see reality at this point. "If it hadn't been that guy, it would have been someone else. And in the meantime, all she would have done was play us against one another to get her way. She would have torn us apart."

"Well, then she won because she's still doing it." Javier stalked off, turning back only long enough to growl at him. "Fuck off, Xander. For good."

* * *

WITH Javier sacked out on the impeccable leather of the passenger seat of his new Audi sedan, Xander drove through the black night and headed east. He hit the steering wheel to the beat of the heavy alternative song. The angry music suited him.

He didn't see any fucking end to this mess in sight and he didn't know what else to do. Tonight's move would put him on Javier's shit list for the rest of his life . . . but at least his brother would be alive to hate him.

When his phone rang, Xander glanced at the Bluetooth display and answered with a smile. "Cherry!"

"Logan is going to kill you if he hears you've been calling me that," said his best friend's wife.

"I think it's sweet, all that red hair and innocence."

She snorted. "Being married to Logan . . . not so innocent anymore. You on the road?"

"Yeah. We'll be arriving in the wee hours of the morning, maybe threeish. Sorry about that . . ."

"No worries. My new boss is very understanding."

"So I'll finally get to meet the infamous Jack Cole?"

"Probably. He's twice as cantankerous now that he's got a baby who doesn't sleep as much as he'd like, but the upside is that he's rarely in the office early these days." Tara sounded cheerful about that fact, and Xander had to smile.

"Thanks for letting us crash at your place until we can find some digs of our own."

"No problem. Just remember the ground rules: Always put the lid to the toilet seat down, you must at least wear underwear around the house, and no flirting with Kata unless you want Hunter to kill you. He's, um . . . intensely protective."

"And Logan's not?" Xander quipped.

"Okay, there's a point. But you get my drift."

"Yes, Katalina the lovely Latina is off limits. I'll manage somehow."

"I saw how popular you were the last time you were in Lafayette. I think you'll more than manage. What about Javier?"

Xander heard the shift in her voice, the concern. His mood had been scratched raw after their ugly fight. He'd spent the next few hours duping Javier. It pained him to have to deceive his own brother, and Xander couldn't handle Tara's tenderness right now. "No need to worry about my brother hitting on Kata. After the healthy dose of hydromorphone I gave him back in Dallas, the only thing he'll be hitting for a while is the sheets."

"How did you get—" She sighed. "Oh my God, are you sleeping with a doctor?"

Xander grinned. "She's got some really fabulous qualities."

"Do you mean her prescription pad or her breasts?"

"I have to choose?" he teased to lighten the mood.

"I swear, your dick gets so much usage, I'm stunned it hasn't fallen off from exhaustion or you haven't contracted some exotic disease no one's ever heard of."

Xander winced at the familiar jibe, but played along. "I think you missed me, Tara. You know, there are lots of advantages to hooking up with a playboy rather than a SEAL."

"I don't think so. Instead of the occasional dangerous terrorist, I'd have to worry about all those jealous husbands or angry fathers shooting you. Pass."

Xander laughed. He absolutely adored this verbal sparring with Logan's wife. She always assumed he was joking. Since he had no reason to take himself seriously, it worked.

"All kidding aside, what about Javier. Is he okay?" she asked.

Fuck no, and Tara must know that or he wouldn't be drugging his brother and hauling him across state lines in the middle of the night. He rubbed a hand across gritty, exhausted eyes. "I hope he will be. Eventually. But like I said, babysitting a grown man is a bigger job than I can manage alone. I'm sorry to bring my trouble to you."

"If Logan wasn't out on a mission, he would want you to. I do, too. Kata is on board. Jack, Deke, and Tyler are all ready to pitch in. And Deke's wife, Kimber, is a nurse. She can help us if we run into something medical. Luc and Alyssa Traverson have promised you some really excellent food from Bonheur."

"Wonderful. Just make sure you hold the wine," Xander quipped, though it wasn't exactly funny. He was damn tired of seeing Javier losing himself in a bottle.

"Will do. I found a house I think you'll love. The offices you asked about should be easy, as well. I've got a few leads. You can check those out tomorrow while one of the big boys babysits."

"Javier will love that . . ." Sarcasm dripped from his voice.

"The offices or the babysitter?"

"Both probably. But that's his problem. If he'd bothered to get his head out of his ass in the last year, none of this would be happening."

Tara made a sympathetic sound. "I got an e-mail today from Logan. He's expecting to be home in a week or so and should have some leave. Hunter is settling into his new post-navy job with Jack and Deke at Oracle, but I'm sure he can spare a few hours here and there. Between the two of them, they'll get Javier's mind focused on PT and off of whatever is eating him up."

"The physical therapy will do him good. Thanks, Tara. I really don't know what I would have done without you. Javier bought a first-class ticket to self-destruction. I can't think of another way to prevent him from finishing that trip."

"We'll find something to get him back on track so you can go back to being your charming, absolutely incorrigible self."

* * *

LONDON McLane knocked on the little bungalow's door promptly at eight the next morning. She was a little winded and a lot tense, but she'd walked the half mile here by herself. Technically, she wasn't supposed to do anything alone until the blackouts stopped, but that could be years, if ever. She was tired of being a burden to everyone around her. Her first priority was to show herself—and her family—that she could finally be self-sufficient.

At twenty-five, she had done nothing that the average adult did every day, like drive, hold a job, or spend a quiet evening alone. She didn't want a safe existence; she wanted an extraordinary life, one where she could climb mountains, fall in love, help others, push past her every fear, and be completely at peace with herself.

After nearly ten years, London was determined that the time for being a prisoner in her own body was over. The rest of her life started today . . . even if she wasn't exactly sure how to begin it.

Kata Edgington opened the door, her bright smile welcoming. The lovely brunette hugged her. "Come on in, honey. How are you? Trip back to Cali good? Have you moved to Lafayette for good?"

She stepped in the cheery bungalow, tucking a pale strand of hair behind her ear. "Yes. I shipped the rest of my clothes out here, over my mother's objection. But she was going to smother me back home. I've visited enough to know that Lafayette will be a good change for me. It's completely different than Orange County, for sure. I'm cleared to walk as much as I'm able and I'm going to take advantage of every opportunity. I can even try jogging, so I'm definitely going to train for my goal of finishing that 5K this fall. I have some new meds that should help." She made a face at the thought of the horse pills she had to take daily. "But I won't need more surgery unless the condition worsens."

The other woman's eyes softened with compassion. "I'm so sorry. It must seem like you've been going through this forever."

Before she could stop it, London flashed back to wet roads, the loud roar of Evanescence blasting over the sports car's speakers, Amber and her boyfriend arguing about his something-something on the side with another girl just before . . .

London shuddered and tried to focus on Kata. "Yeah, but I'm putting it behind me. Time to really start living."

Kata wrapped an arm around her in a quick hug, then looked out the door before shutting it. "You didn't come with Alyssa or Luc?"

Her cousin, Alyssa, and the woman's husband had done more than enough already, letting her visit off and on for months, and now letting her move in. She helped when she could, cooked, did laundry—anything she could think of. It wasn't enough, and London knew it. Soon, she hoped she'd be able to help more.

"No. They have such busy lives. I have to start taking care of myself. I can't be trapped by my limitations anymore."

"Honey, if you fall and hit your head—"

"At least then I'd feel something." She'd take pain over the decades of emptiness and regret she'd have if she stayed the course. "I will never be independent unless I push myself."

Kata pursed her lips as if she didn't like it and was about to say so.

"You ready to walk with me?" London changed the subject.

She grimaced, her eyes flashing an apology. "I should have called, but everything happened so fast. I'm sorry; I can't leave. I'm babysitting . . . sort of."

"Are you watching little Caleb?"

Shaking her head, Kata's dark hair spilled around her shoulders. "No. He's with Deke and Kimber. I think his mommy and daddy have plans for him later."

Kata's husband, Hunter, seemed awfully fond of his sister's energetic rug rat, so the assumption had been a natural one. The toddler ran and jumped, making truck noises and pretending to soar like an airplane. She was sure it wouldn't be long before Hunter wanted rug rats of his own, and they'd make great parents. She wasn't jealous of any of them . . . exactly. Envious, yes. She loved children, but was nowhere near able to be a fit mother. Not that she even had a man in her life or her bed, so children were hardly an issue.

She pasted on a smile. "Well, if you're watching Tyler's little demon spawns, it's awfully quiet."

"You'd have heard them a mile away. Seth is a terror in his terrible twos. And for a baby, Chase has a damn healthy set of lungs." Kata giggled. "I'm actually watching a grown man. It's a favor to Logan's best friend. Remember me telling you about Xander?"

"The billionaire playboy?" London liked whenever Alyssa's friends dished about the fast-driving, hard-loving enigma. From their stories, she knew that Xander must be handsome, charming, and of course, the love-'em-and-leave-'em type. But as far as she was concerned, all those women in Xander's life were lucky. At least they'd been loved at some point.

"That one. OMG, I don't think that man goes a day without picking up at least one random girl, and from what I hear, showing her a really good time." Kata smiled, then sobered. "Anyway, he brought his brother to me. Javier is falling apart."

That sounded awful. "Can I help?"

Compassion softened Kata's eyes. "It's sweet of you to offer, honey, but I'm not sure how much any of us can do but try to help him move on. His wife was murdered about a year ago."

Sympathy hit London hard. "Oh my gosh, that's terrible! Did they find her killer?"

"No."

How terrible. "Do the police have any idea why she was killed?"

Kata started to reply, but her answer was interrupted by a pained moan, a rustle, then a crash. She ran down the hall and into the first room on the left. London followed, concern for a man she'd never met twisting her up. Javier's heart must be utterly shattered to need this much help a year after his wife's death. He must have loved her very much.

As she ran into the room behind Kata, a man lurched from the bed and stumbled into the nightstand, wearing only a pair of dark gray boxer briefs that hugged his lean hips and thighs, and clung to his gorgeous backside. Bronze skin covered a muscled back and wide shoulders. Even stooped over, he stood tall. Big and powerful. Shaggy dark hair brushed the strong column of his neck, slightly askew and wavy.

Kata grabbed his arm, holding him back from taking another step and likely falling on his face. "Throw back the covers and help me get him into the bed again."

London jolted into action and ran to shove the sheet and blanket down. When she looked up, Kata had eased behind Javier, grabbed both bulging biceps, and was trying to turn him back toward the bed, but he'd wedged her between his solid body and the nightstand, leaving her no room for leverage. London stepped in front of the poor widower to help and looked up at him. Sympathy was the last thing on her mind.

Even with pale eyes half-open and dazed, Javier was the most beautiful man she'd ever seen. His nearness washed through her veins in an icy-hot rush. Her stomach plummeted to her knees. And a little bit lower, between her legs . . . she didn't want to think about that sudden ache. Damn, he smelled manly. It wasn't cologne. Older than her by probably a decade, he wore his experience on his face in the faint lines around his mouth, and the notch between his brows. The strong slashes of his cheekbones told her that he'd look like all kinds of warrior avenger when he was angry. Everything about him made her want to press herself against him, wrap her arms around him, promise him that somehow she would make his pain go away.

"A little help, please?"

Kata's question jolted London into action. She grabbed Javier's waist. God, he radiated heat. It seared down her palms, staggering her. If this man tumbled her to a bed and covered her body with his, he'd burn her up with his heat alone, not to mention that sinful streak of a mouth, wide and somehow commanding. The thought of him slanting those lips over hers . . . She almost couldn't breathe.

"London? You okay?"

The concern in Kata's voice ripped her attention away from Javier, and she looked around the bronzed muscles of his shoulder to find the woman's dark gaze questioning her.

"Fine. Sorry. Sometimes, I'm a bit slow." *Like when I see gorgeous, mostly naked hunks.*

Kata sent her an encouraging smile. "You're fine, sweetie."

Between them, Javier's knees gave out. He slumped forward, and London caught him, staggering to bear his weight. She wrapped her arms around his middle. His hot chest seared her through her thin mesh T-shirt. Despite the heat, her nipples tightened, bunched.

If this was sexual attraction, now she knew why so many people read and sang songs about it. As it threatened to knock London back, she sucked in a breath, trying to find her balance as she staggered to the bed with Javier leaning all over her. He was mostly unconscious. He wouldn't remember this or her. At best, he'd think she was a nice person for helping when he needed it. At worst, he would think of her as a pudgy blonde, starstruck because of her abysmal lack of experience with men. Either way, she was insignificant to him. Time to pull her head out of the clouds and her girl parts away from fantasy land. She tried to console herself with the thought that maybe he was a horrible human being. Or bad in bed—not that she'd know the difference. But another glance at him had her changing her mind. This man would never be bad at anything.

Together, she and Kata wrangled him back into bed. Even his legs were heavy, and she had to wrap her arms around his lean middle to straighten him across the mattress. With her face all but buried in the hard ridges of his abdominal muscles and the healthy bulge a few inches lower, it was little wonder the view sharpened the ache right between her legs.

Being closer to him than Kata was, London reached across Javier to flip the blankets back over his body. He moaned, cursed faintly. She glanced his way to find his hazy stare on her breasts, now dangling less than a foot from his face. He peered up at her with a smile.

"Beauty," he whispered.

Me? Impossible. The guy was lost in his own world, maybe even hallucinating about his late wife.

Then he closed his eyes again, and it didn't matter anymore.

To a man like him, she would never be important. While she . . . well, she had a bad feeling he'd haunt her dreams for many nights to come.

Chapter Two

JAVIER woke slowly, aware of a baseball bat slamming repeatedly into his forehead. At least that's what the painful throbbing in his head felt like. With a groan, he ventured to open one eye just a slit. Sunlight streamed through the window, stabbing him with a pickax. He fell back with a curse.

What had he done last night?

Mentally sifting through his memories, Javier remembered Dominion and Whitney's red ass. Anxiety had hit him then, freezing him up. Xander had tried to coach him through it, but Javier remembered anger gripping him. He'd walked out on his brother. And God, he'd abandoned a restrained sub who'd been all warmed up and needing play. He'd left her in a public place, where she was vulnerable to any abusive troll. He hadn't assured her that she'd been lovely and pleasing. He'd simply thrown the flogger and fled. But it wasn't the first time he'd failed to protect and nurture someone in his care. He could captain a multibillion-dollar company, but damn it if his personal relationships weren't a fucking wreck.

What had he done after that? Who else had he hurt with his thoughtless actions? Most everything between the club and this moment stretched out like a big black void.

Except his fight with Xander.

With crystal clarity, he remembered spilling out every dreadful accusation he'd allowed to fester inside of him for the past year. He'd laid the blame for Francesca's death at his brother's feet. Javier squeezed his eyes shut. It wasn't totally Xander's fault; his late wife had made her choices, which apparently included some lethal lothario who'd paid more attention to her than he had. But if Xander had taken Francesca in hand, she wouldn't have been in Aruba with her killer. That fact was inescapable. And thinking this much right now made his head hurt even worse.

He rolled to his side with a pained moan. His stomach turned. God, was he going to be sick? How much had he had to drink last night?

"Good morning, sleeping beauty," drawled a feminine voice nearby.

Since he hadn't awakened with a woman in over a year, that brought Javier's eyes open wide. Feet away, he saw a beautiful Latina wearing a thin black tank with a built-in but wholly inadequate bra, sitting in the corner of an unfamiliar room. Her coffee-colored hair hung in waves, the ends curling around her ample breasts. Her plump nipples pressed hard against the thin cotton. She'd drawn up one of her knees against her chest and curled an arm around it. Her black yoga pants stretched tightly across lush hips and thighs.

"Good morning." He propped himself up on his elbows and stared. Shit, he had no memory of this gorgeous woman. If he'd finally decided to get back on the proverbial bike and start riding again, he'd chosen well, but he wished to fuck he could remember it. When would he have found her? Where? His head throbbed. Nothing made sense.

A small smile played at the corners of her mouth. She reached to the little table beside the chair, picked up a steaming mug, and sipped. "Coffee?"

"Please," he croaked. It would help to clear his head, and maybe while she fetched the brew he might get some spark of recollection. "Black."

But no. He watched her curvy backside retreat until she disappeared down the hall and around a corner. Nothing. Why couldn't he remember getting her supine and under him?

She came back a few moments later with another piping-hot mug and set it with a saucer on the little bedside table, along with two familiar orange tablets. "There you go. With a little ibuprofen, as well."

Bless her. Javier eased up, surprised to realize he was wearing his boxers and nothing else. He didn't bother covering himself with the sheet because the gorgeous brunette had presumably seen and touched it all. Hadn't she?

"So . . ." he started as he grabbed his coffee and gulped it, using it to wash down the pills.

"So." She took a sip from her own mug and raised a brow.

Hell, she wasn't giving him anything to work with. He was just going to have to be indelicate. "I'm sorry, but I have to confess . . . I don't remember your name."

She looked even more amused, which confused him. Why wasn't she pissed off? "I'm Kata."

Still not ringing any bells. "I'm Javier."

"I know." Now she looked like she was suppressing a laugh as she sipped more of her coffee.

"Listen, you're probably going to think I'm an ass, but I don't remember anything about last night. Did we, um . . ." The word "fuck" sounded too raunchy to say to her clean-scrubbed face. "Make love" was too personal. He didn't make love to anyone. "Have sex?"

"You don't remember?" She batted her lashes, looking just a little bit crushed.

Immediately, he felt like a heel and took her hand, giving it a squeeze. "Damn it! I must have had too much to drink and . . ." Shit, that sounded bad. He needed to shut up and focus on what had happened last night. It would be so much easier if pain wasn't still thundering in his head. But he owed it to Kata to try.

After leaving Dominion, Xander had dragged his ass back to the Dallas mansion they'd rented. A member of the staff had brought him a dinner plate. He'd halfheartedly picked at it before prowling the house like a caged beast desperate for freedom. When he stalked back to his room, a convenient glass of Cîroc had been sitting on his nightstand, luring him wordlessly to oblivion. He'd downed it gratefully.

Only now was he questioning where it had come from. Xander had done his level best to remove all the booze from the house. So why had that glass been there? And why did he feel as if he had more than the usual hangover? Unless . . . Xander had put the vodka there and laced it with something stronger. How the hell else could he be here, wherever here was, with a complete stranger?

"Where am I?" he asked.

"You're in Lafayette, Louisiana."

What? Wasn't Lafayette basically at the crossroads between Nowhere Town and Hicksville? Yes, it was the ass crack of the world. He'd never been here, never wanted to even visit. There was no way he could have driven himself the six hours to Lafayette last night and not remembered it. This had to be his brother's doing. *That son of a bitch!* Apparently, Xander didn't understand the meaning of "fuck off," but Javier swore he'd pound it through his brother's skull.

But that also meant he'd never touched Kata, and she'd been in on this scheme all along.

"This is the first time we've met, isn't it?"

A genuine smile flashed across her face. "You figured that out pretty quickly. Yeah."

"You might have told me that instead of letting me squirm." He sent her a chastising glance.

Her smiled widened. "I might have . . . but where's the fun in that? Your brother brought you here in the middle of the night and dumped you in bed. I was asleep, so this is the first time we're meeting."

Well, hell. If Kata was acquainted with his brother, it was a good bet that Xander knew Kata in the biblical sense. He eased back in the bed with a sigh and used the sheet to cover himself. She laughed and stood, reaching her hands up high, stretching. In this position, there was no way he could miss the wink of her diamond naval ring and the twin circles pushing against the fabric around her pierced nipples. *Gorgeous.* Xander might be a complete douche . . . but he had great taste in women.

"Where is my brother?"

"According to the note I found, Xander is out with Tara, my sister-in-law. We share this place. No idea when they'll be back."

Javier ground his teeth together. "Thank you. I'll be leaving now. My brother might have brought me here, but I won't impose on you anymore. Lovely meeting you. Thanks for the coffee and ibuprofen."

Javier staggered to his feet. The blood rushed out of his head, and he damn near fell back to the bed. Steadying himself on the nearby lamp, he almost knocked it over, then barely righted the modern, brushed nickel contraption . . . just as his stomach turned over. That only made his head throb more. He sagged back to the mattress. So much for his grand exit.

Later, when he felt better, he'd leave. After he'd seen Xander. Yeah, he wanted to kick baby brother's ass first. If he left now, it would only look as if he was tucking tail and running. Xander didn't scare him at all, but Javier had to admit that his brother was far sneakier than he'd given the asshole credit for.

So who exactly was Kata and why would she help his brother? Hadn't Kata mentioned that Xander had sneaked away with another woman? Maybe that meant Kata wasn't fucking his younger brother. Maybe . . . but unlikely. Xander nailed every pretty female who moved and breathed. But Kata had said earlier that Tara was her sister-in-law? Fuck, the whole morning had been one confusion after another.

"Are you married?"

"Yep. So is Tara. We're the wives of the Edgington brothers, in case Xander ever mentioned them."

Logan and Hunter, the Navy SEALs. Yes, Javier had a vague recollection of Xander talking them up. For ogling Kata, her husband could kill him in twenty ways in under a minute with his bare hands without breaking a sweat, while Javier was too sick to defend himself. How fucking comforting that wasn't.

"Is your husband here?"

She laughed. "No, and no turning green on me. I don't expect him home for a while."

He sagged back to the pillow with relief. Good. So he wasn't going to have his balls forcibly detached from his body and shoved down his throat. That was the only good news he'd had all morning.

"I suppose you know why Xander brought me here?"

Kata pursed her full lips and hesitated, as if searching for the right words. "He said something about removing your distractions."

"You don't have a drop of liquor in this house, do you?"

"Not as of this morning." She sent him a sympathetic smile.

It raised his hackles. His motherfucking brother was babying him. Xander was definitely a dead man. The second he walked in the door, Javier planned to skewer him. Why the hell hadn't his brother just confronted him?

Last night's argument filtered back through his brain. That had been one hell of a confrontation. Xander had tried to reason with him . . . in his way. Javier had to admit that he hadn't exactly been listening. Or been reasonable. *Shit*. But no denying that it had felt good to unleash his anger and tell Xander exactly what he thought.

Javier ground his teeth together. "Did my brother say how long he intends this little visit to last?"

"Sorry." She shrugged noncommittally. "Um . . . not to overstep, but I'm a probation officer for Lafayette Parish, which means I'm part cop. But I'm also part therapist. I'd be happy to listen and talk things through with you."

The notion of spilling all his secrets, his anger, especially to a beauty he'd just met, horrified him. "You don't even know me."

"Sometimes an impartial stranger can give the best advice."

Her kindness took him aback, and he felt the anger clawing up inside him again. "What is there to say, Kata? My wife ran off with her lover, who killed her brutally. I'm a little bitter."

"You have every right to be. Grief is a long, difficult process. I can't imagine how difficult it is to lose a spouse, especially so violently."

"I don't want to talk about it."

"Okay. The offer is there. I won't be offended if you don't pick me, but you need someone to talk to who will listen and be an objective ear. And I think you need to stop looking for answers or absolution in the bottom of a bottle and find yourself again."

Her words stung almost as much as the burning embarrassment coursing through his blood. Damn, the woman thought he was a broken alcoholic.

Are you? He heard the whisper in his head.

"I'm fine," he barked at her.

Disappointment settled across her delicate features. "Right. So is Xander, according to him. You like booze. He likes girls. Neither of you is remotely screwed up. Got it. I'm making eggs and bacon. Want any?"

Her sarcasm didn't quite hide her hurt. Javier held in a wince. He didn't owe her any explanations, especially ones that would be like ripping out his entrails and handing them over to her on a platter, but shame that he'd upset her stung. He might not owe her his life story, but he owed her some damn courtesy. She'd only been trying to help.

"I'm sorry, Kata. My head hurts. I'm mad at my brother." *I don't know where I'm going, what I'm doing, or if I even give a damn anymore.* "But I'd love some breakfast."

Not really, but for her, he'd choke it down. He'd already given her enough grief.

"You're a terrible liar, but I'll do my best to make it worth eating."

"I'll help," he called to her retreating back, then looked around the room.

He spotted last night's trousers folded up on the dresser. They'd be a wrinkled mess, but that was the least of his worries now. Slowly, he stood, steadying himself with a death grip on the headboard. His headache had eased from a full-throttle, heavy-metal pounding to an annoying, repetitive gong. Finally, he made his way across the room, grabbed his pants, and found the bathroom across the hall. Kata had laid out a new toothbrush and comb for him. He took the time to use both before donning his pants, somewhat ready to face the world.

After retrieving his coffee cup, he ambled down the hall to find Kata humming around the kitchen with the song on the radio, bacon sizzling in a pan. It smelled surprisingly good.

"Can I help?"

She sent him an amused smile over her shoulder. "Do billionaires cook?"

"No," he admitted sheepishly. "I set a mean table."

Kata laughed, then nodded to the little iron bistro breakfast set in the corner. She'd already done everything, including set out fresh flowers.

"Well, then. I'll go . . . admire your hard work."

"You do that." She winked. "There's fresh coffee in the pot. I won't be much longer here."

Sure enough, they were scarfing down hot eggs and crisp bacon within minutes. Javier cleaned his plate, more hungry than he'd imagined. Just as he set down his coffee cup and put a hand over his full belly, someone knocked on the door.

Kata didn't seem surprised at all, merely jumped up and pulled the door open with a smile. "Tyler!"

The big blond man behind her walked in, dangling a plastic grocery sack from one meaty fist, and held out his arms. She walked into them, and he hugged her tight, smiling at Javier over her delicate shoulder. Tyler wore a wholly satisfied look. No, it was more than that. He wore the air of a sublimely happy man, his face a billboard advertising that his entire world was settled to his satisfaction. Javier nearly choked on envy.

Tyler wrapped a large hair-roughened hand around Kata's ribs and tickled her. She shoved him away, but as Tyler walked past, she swatted his ass. "Menace."

"Twihard." He grinned.

She sighed. "I'm never going to live that down. And neither are you. Everyone's onto you, pal. I know you swiped my DVD of *Breaking Dawn, Part 1*."

"Maybe . . . But on me, fandom is cute."

Kata turned and rolled her eyes. "Whatever. Javier, this is Tyler Murphy, former LAPD vice detective, PI, and bad boy."

"I am *not* formerly a bad boy," Tyler objected.

"Oh, I'm so going to tell Delaney you said that." She shot him an evil grin.

Tyler grunted at her, then approached him, hand outstretched. "Good to meet you, Javier. I hope you're less of a pain in the ass than your brother. I get damn tired of him flirting with my wife."

Despite the affable smile, Tyler didn't look like a guy he wanted to cross, even when his head wasn't pounding. Bursting with muscle under a tight black T-shirt, the garment showed off hard biceps and rippling abs. Even black sweatpants and running shoes didn't lessen the appearance of power.

He shook Tyler's hand. "That's my little brother, douche bag extraordinaire." *Funny that he flirts with your wife when he wanted nothing to do with mine.*

Tyler smiled and glanced at his watch. "I see Kata fed you. Way to keep on schedule." He put out his fist toward her, and she bumped it with her own.

Javier frowned at their odd relationship. Not flirtatious, but not like siblings, either. They were . . . friends. He'd heard of men and woman connecting platonically. He hadn't really believed it. Every female friend Xander had ever had he'd fucked. Their father had been little better. In college, Javier had friends, too, but they'd all come with benefits. This friendship before him looked foreign yet somehow comfortable. He sat back to watch.

With a grin, Tyler tossed the plastic bag his way.

Javier caught it reflexively. "What's this?"

"Everything you'll need for the first part of your day. We'll want to get a move on before it gets too much hotter. A three-mile run when it's ninety degrees with ninety percent humidity is more than exercise. It's a really shitty test of endurance."

He heard Tyler's words, but they didn't compute until he opened the bag in his lap and found a white tank, gray running shorts, socks, and athletic shoes. They expected him to run three miles in the stifling heat, while hung over, with a stomach full of eggs?

"I've got bottles of water ready for both of you." Kata reached inside the refrigerator.

Shaking his head, Javier dropped the bag of clothes on the table and looked at the two of them as if they were insane. "No offense, but I'm not jogging. I don't care if Xander thinks I need it. I actually think I need to sleep a bit longer, then figure out how to leave this little town so I can get on with my life. Now if you'll excuse me . . ."

Tyler tsked and shook his head. "If we don't start that jog now, you'll be late to yoga with Morgan. Now, she looks little, but I know from experience that breast-feeding moms on a tight schedule

have absolutely no patience for male drama. Since she's married to
Jack Cole, odds are that he's taught her some really low-down, dirty
ways to separate a man from his balls. I wouldn't want to test her, so
let's get hopping."

Yoga? After jogging? What the hell did Xander have up his sleeve?
"No thanks. Like I said, not interested." He turned to Kata. "Do you
know where the rest of my clothes are? And my phone? I'll call for a
taxi."

Kata shook her head, and Tyler burst out laughing.

"What's so funny?" Javier demanded.

Before either one of them could answer, Kata's phone rang, and
she picked it up. "Hello?" She paused, her dark gaze zeroing in on
him. "Yes." Another pause. "Yes." A longer hesitation. "No." Another
one. "I think that would be a good idea. Thanks!"

She hung up with a sweet-as-pie smile. Javier didn't trust it for a
minute.

"What the hell is going on here?"

"Xander is on his way back. He'll be here in about an hour. He
says he'll explain then."

Tyler approached and gave him a hearty slap on the back. "Great.
That will give us enough time to get in those three miles. Let's go."

"I'd really rather not," Javier drawled.

With a shrug of his beefy shoulders, Tyler grinned. "Yeah,
well . . . I'll file that somewhere between *too fucking bad* and *it
sucks to be you.*"

Javier glared at Tyler. The big, blond muscle monkey was too
damn cheerful for his taste, and he really wanted to shove the guy's
balls up his throat right now just to show Tyler that he wasn't anyone's bitch. But the anger was starting to grab hold of him again. His
thoughts raced. His sense of balance flirted with shaky. Javier forced
himself to draw in a few deep breaths and grabbed the plastic bag.

"Fine. I'll get changed." Only because it suited him. If he didn't
have any liquor to drown out the fury starting to roll through him,

he'd try to outrun it instead. He doubted it would work, but his other options were to tear apart Kata's kitchen and scare the hell out of her or to get into a fight with Tyler, who looked more than capable of keeping up.

Javier hoped that the second his brother walked through the door, he'd feel a violent need to puke on Xander's designer shoes.

A few minutes and a change of clothes later, he and Tyler stretched, then hit the street at a slow jog. House after house rolled by, each little cottage looking much like the last, except the color of the trim. Some boasted long porches that shaded his-and-hers rocking chairs. Despite the early hour, the heat and humidity were already oppressive.

"I'd forgotten how much I hate coming to the South," he grumbled, already starting to sweat.

Tyler looked perfectly happy and flashed Javier a grin. "I'm from L.A., too. Here takes getting used to . . . but it grows on you."

He refused to stay here long enough for that.

"If you don't like Xander, why are you helping him?" Javier asked Tyler as they rounded a corner, off a quiet residential street and onto a busier main road. Cars buzzed past in the morning rush. A few bleary-eyed professionals walked by with their steaming caffeination. A few other people jogged in the opposite direction, happily sweating. Javier scowled and turned to Tyler, who still wore that goddamn smile.

"He did me a great favor I can never repay."

Money was easy for Xander since he didn't personally have to earn it. Javier snorted cynically. "I'm sure he didn't expect you to repay him. My brother likes to give money away. I think it makes him feel better about his poor-little-rich-boy life."

Now huffing and puffing as Tyler picked up the speed, Javier's own words rolled around in his head. Shit, he sounded bitter and cynical. Maybe because he was. He hated the fact that Francesca had come between them—and still did—but he couldn't seem to get past the fact that she would be alive today if Xander had just said yes when Javier had needed him.

"It wasn't money." Tyler's grin finally fell. "He saved my wife's life and helped me put a completely evil fucker behind bars. He could have sat on his charming ass and used his time to pick up women. I know he does that."

"Since he was thirteen." Javier smiled tightly.

Tyler frowned. "I get the feeling you don't like your brother much."

Since the big guy was already in Xander's court, Javier didn't feel the need to explain. "Do you love your siblings all the time?"

"Don't have any, but I know if I had a brother I trusted to have my back, I'd be pretty damn happy about it."

"I'd like one of those too, but I don't have one." When Tyler opened his mouth, Javier shook his head, wishing like hell he could return to Kata's house and crawl back in bed. This three-mile jog made his lungs feel as if they were about to burst. "I'm glad he helped you and your wife. Xander can be a great guy." *When it suits him.*

"He's on your side, dude. He's worried about you."

Javier kept his more skeptical thoughts to himself. "Touching, isn't it?"

Tyler scowled but kept thankfully silent for the rest of the torturous run. Javier focused on the pounding of the pavement beneath his feet, the heavy pull of oxygen into his lungs, the mad beating of his heart. He was not enjoying this . . . but for the first time in a long time, his thoughts felt sharp and focused, his head clear. Fresh air filled him. By the time they arrived back at Kata's house, he didn't have the energy to feel angry, but he did feel oddly calm.

Until he and Tyler stepped into the kitchen, and Xander sat there with a gorgeous redhead, both nursing cups of coffee and sharing a joke. The unruffled bastard looked like he didn't have a care in the world. How nice to shed all sense of responsibility like a cheap coat.

"You son of a bitch!" He charged across the kitchen.

Tyler jerked him back by grabbing a handful of his sweaty tank and holding tight.

His brother nodded at him, then turned to the redhead. "Morning, Javier. This is Tara Edgington."

Logan's wife? Seemed like a safe bet.

"Hi," he barked, then winced at his own rudeness. His anger was for Xander, not this lovely woman deluded enough to help him. Stiffly, he held out his hand to Tara.

She smiled kindly and shook his outstretched hand. "Hope you're feeling okay this morning and that Tyler didn't break you." She sent the big blond guy a mock glare.

"I'll save that for weight lifting tomorrow." He winked.

"No more torture with Tyler." Javier shook his head. "This morning was enough. I appreciate your hospitality, but I need to be getting back to Dallas now. If I could impose upon you for a shower, then I'll get out of your way."

Tara didn't answer, just sent Xander a look that told him the ball was in his brother's court. Kata eased back into the room, wearing a pair of black capri pants and a floral halter top that hugged her generous tits. She propped one hip against the cabinet and sent him an apologetic smile.

"It's been fun." Tyler slapped him on the back. "See you tomorrow at six a.m. We'll beat some of this heat and get in a bit of lifting, too."

"Don't bother. I won't—" Javier didn't get to finish his sentence before Tyler shut the door, cutting him off.

Fuck, little brother had brought him deep into his territory, and everyone here would take his side every single time. As soon as he had a shower, he'd find this town's little airport or rent a damn car to drive himself back to Dallas.

"Sit down," Xander demanded.

Javier raised an angry brow at his brother's high-handed tactics. He could feel a fresh rage brimming and tried like hell to hold it in check. "I told you to fuck off, so you decided to drug me and bring me here? You can't force me to stay, so I'm not sitting down. If you didn't want me for an enemy . . ." He shrugged. "You should have thought of that when I actually needed your help. Now I don't and I'm leaving."

He turned toward Kata, intending to slip through the door and head to the bathroom for a much-needed shower.

"I can't keep you here." Xander said to his back. "But I think once you're done listening to me that you'll want to stay."

"What part of 'fuck off' doesn't translate for you?" he scowled back at Xander.

If the words bothered him, his brother didn't show it. "I understand. I just don't care. So here's the deal: You've got a few choices to make. You either stay here for six weeks, follow my instructions, and get your shit together, or I go to the press with *all* your problems. The drinking, the 'episodes,' and the fact that, right now, you're incompetent to run the business."

Shock slammed Javier, and anger followed fast on its heels. "Are you out of your fucking mind? If you tell them everything . . . The business is already in a downward spiral. You said yourself the board of directors is nervous. If you air my laundry publicly, you'll kill what's left. You'll not only destroy me, but— Oh, is this some power play? You think you want to take the reins, little brother?"

Xander wouldn't last a week in the pressure cooker of the CEO's seat. The fifteen-hour days and lost weekends would really interfere with his party schedule. He'd never shown interest in responsibility of any kind. Why would he start now?

"I will if I have to," Xander vowed. "You step one foot out of Lafayette, you deviate one minute from the schedule I'm laying out for you for the next six weeks, and I will go to the press, the business be damned. I have enough money saved to last three lifetimes. But I only have one brother, and I'm not going to watch you kill yourself over that bitch."

The words stunned Javier. Xander would burn down everything just to try to save him? He wasn't sure if he should charge across the kitchen and strangle Xander where he sat . . . or give him a really big bear hug. His brother watched him with resolute hazel eyes that held a faint hint of regret. This was Xander's way of showing him that he cared. But Javier knew damn well that his brother had him by the balls. Xander bluffed often, but never with him. Of course, Javier could run to the press with stories of Xander's exploits, but they already knew. *Damn!*

"It's my life to end. I know you're trying to help me, and you can do that by getting the hell out of it," he snapped.

"Not gonna happen." Xander shook his head.

His temper surged. "What the hell? You can't force me to stay here."

"I think I am. Because what you're doing now, burying all your stress and grief and letting it eat you up inside, is destroying you."

Javier hated to admit that his brother was right. And if he risked getting the press involved in his personal struggles, S.I. Industries would crash fast. He owed more to the board of directors, the hardworking employees, and his parents, God rest them.

"Fine. I'll stay," he growled. "So . . . you think you're my life coach now? Or are you trying to be my Dom?"

Tara and Kata both snickered at that. Xander cut the redhead a stare of displeasure that didn't faze her in the least. With a sigh, he faced Javier.

"I'll be whatever you need, do whatever you need, until you're able to pick up and move on. But I draw the line at spanking you."

At his brother's teasing, more anger spread through him, but it was tempered by a grudging acceptance. Xander meant well, even if his methods thoroughly annoyed Javier. "Fuck off."

"You've said that before. Didn't work. I'm also giving you six weeks to start turning the business around. You've shown up every day, even the day of Francesca's funeral. I give you a lot of credit for that. But you're not focused. It's time to start making good decisions again. Want help? I'll work hand-in-hand with you to rebuild the business."

Though Xander was extending the olive branch, Javier couldn't make himself take it. He had to stand on his own two feet. If he fell, he couldn't take Xander with him. Besides, his pride rankled. He was already being forced to stay in this little town against his will. Javier liked things he could control, and the business was one of them. His father had entrusted him with his legacy. He'd gotten S.I. Industries into trouble. He would dig it out. After all, what did Xander know about running a high-tech conglomerate?

"I'll take care of S.I. Industries. I always have."

His little brother shrugged, then tossed a set of keys across the table. "These open your new offices. I'll take you over there in a bit. It's not much, but the best I could do on short notice. It's not furnished, but most of what you need will be delivered tomorrow. I called back to the offices in L.A. to have your assistant transfer your work here. She quit. Friday was her last day."

And he'd drunk his way through it. *Fuck.*

Javier sighed heavily, shoulders sagging. Janice had been his fourth executive assistant in the last ten months. "I'll call Henner and get him to send whatever we need."

"After all, what are VPs and right hands for?" Xander quipped.

No way he could miss the jibe there. Javier shook his head. For years, Xander had wanted nothing to do with the business except to cash the checks that came his way so he could buy new cars and pretty trinkets for his whores. Xander's sudden interest in the business wouldn't last.

"Exactly," he bit back.

Xander had dragged him to this pissant town, forced him to change his whole life for six weeks, then shoved him into this power struggle. And wanted him to . . . what? Be happy? Trust him as a business advisor? Not get angry?

He turned to Kata. "It looks like I'll be pressing on your hospitality a bit longer. Would you mind very much if I had a shower before I go to my new offices?"

Kata shook her head and led him to the bathroom, fetching him a clean towel. "He really does want what's best for you."

Javier smiled, but it was hollow and false. If his brother had wanted what was best for him, he would have said yes a year ago to helping him with Francesca. If this latest scheme of Xander's was his way of helping, Javier wanted nothing to do with it—or him.

Chapter Three

A week later

XANDER groaned as the light shafted through the window of his bedroom in the rented house. He grimaced and tried to open his eyes, peering through the slits at the dark, heavy beams crisscrossing the white ceiling. He'd been too busy last night to close the shutters or pull the thick drapes. And the reason for his haste curled up against his side, her long hair draped over his chest in mahogany tangles, her ass pressing into his hip.

Megan, he vaguely recalled, but who knew for sure? This wasn't the only time this week he'd picked women up and spent all night trying to lose himself inside them. Their names and faces were running together.

Something tugged on his rigid cock, and he frowned at the woman beside him. Both of Megan's hands were tucked under her face, so Xander lifted the sheet to see what the hell had him by the balls—literally. A pretty face with smeared mascara and swollen lips peeked up, her red hair mussed, her green eyes dancing with mischief as she lowered her tongue to the head of his stiff shaft. Shelby? Yeah, that sounded right.

The memories of last night rushed back to him. A smoky, loud nightclub. Three friends, one who'd just broken up with her boyfriend after two terrible years. Xander had been amused to pick up a blonde, a brunette, and a redhead all at once. They'd been a good way to not think about all the other shit in his life. But this morning . . . all the shit in his life was still there. Unfortunately, so were the women.

With a sigh, he shoved his fingers into Shelby's hair and pulled, lifting her mouth from his cock and sending her a disapproving glare. He had to pee, yes, but mostly he just wasn't feeling it. What had seemed so entertaining last night just annoyed him now. He was thirty fucking years old. How long was he going to behave as if life was an eternal party? Then again, it wasn't as if Javier was going to suddenly welcome him into the business with open arms and give his life purpose.

"Where's . . ." What the hell was her name, the blonde with the ex-boyfriend? "Alexis?"

Shelby frowned. "She had an early shift this morning. Don't you remember fucking her good-bye?"

Now that she mentioned it, his groggy brain served up the memory. In fact, everything was beginning to come back to him.

Last night when they'd first hit the bedroom, he'd stripped Alexis down and sunk directly into her pussy. Shelby had kindly undressed herself and shoved her doctor-given C-cups in his face. He'd sucked her nipples as he surged into Alexis again and again. For a girl with a boyfriend, she'd sure been sex starved.

Three noisy orgasms later, he'd finished with Alexis, and Shelby had been beyond ready. A few tugs on his cock and a fresh condom, and he'd been ready to go. Megan had been watching all the while, fingering herself. By the time he'd gotten to her, he'd let her suck him softly in the shower so he could glove up again, then given her a ride for a good, long hour. Shelby and Alexis had taken care of one another while they'd watched. Then he'd done round two with Alexis this morning before she dashed off at o' dark hundred.

Now that he remembered, Xander wished he could fucking forget.

Rolling out of the bed, he left a disgruntled Shelby and a slumbering Megan behind. With a glance back, he grimaced. He'd enjoyed the decadence last night. But now, with morning breath and sticky sheets? Not so much.

"I've got someplace to be shortly, ladies," he lied. "Help yourself to whatever is in the refrigerator. Thank you for spending the night with me. I'm sure you can find the way out."

After a long shower, he emerged, gratified to see that the girls had grabbed their things and departed—mostly. The little pair of green lace panties on his pillow made him sigh aloud. As he wandered over, Xander could see that Megan had helpfully safety pinned a note to them with her name and phone number.

Just what he didn't want. With a thumb and forefinger, he plucked the thong off his pillow and tossed it in the trash, then washed his hands. As he dressed for the day, he rang for the maid and asked her to change his sheets again. The older woman raised a brow, but wisely said nothing. He didn't need more regret. He already had plenty.

Grabbing his keys, he dashed out the door, climbing into his Audi and heading to the temporary offices he'd found for S.I. Industries. Javier wouldn't want him here, but that was too damn bad. If his brother had taken a single step to self-improvement in the last week, it had been a tiny one.

The sunlight blinded Xander as he climbed out of his car and emerged into the oppressive morning heat. He raced inside to the blessed air-conditioning, then spotted the frowning redhead at the reception desk, juggling a beautiful baby on her lap. The interior door to Javier's office was closed.

"Is he any better today?" Xander murmured quietly.

Morgan Cole had been kind enough to stop in for a few hours each morning, her infant son in tow, and help Javier with some administrative work. In return, his brother had already bought her a new top-of-the-line SUV.

"Javier?" She glanced up from the fussing baby in her lap and whispered, "Maybe a little. He didn't break out a bottle until eleven this morning. It's progress."

Was it really? Javier would still be sauced by the end of the lunch hour. Fuck. His brother slaved over his desk nearly every day until the wee hours of the morning. In fairness, he'd greeted Tyler every morning for a run and some weight lifting, then met with Morgan for yoga before coming here. Between nine and ten in the morning, everyone said that Javier looked really centered. Functional. By noon, he was stressed, wasted, and lashing out.

Xander clawed a hand through his hair, trying to smile. "Thanks. And your son?"

Morgan shook her head as the baby started to fuss. "I hate to do this, but I need to take Brice home. His fever has returned."

That wasn't good news. The baby needed care, but having no administrative support/babysitter, even for a few days, would put Javier further behind, send him deeper into stress—and a bottle. Xander wished like hell Javier would accept his help but . . . he knew he couldn't push his brother anymore or he'd snap.

"Yeah, absolutely," he assured Morgan. "Do what you need to do. Family first."

With an apologetic smile, she rose and gathered her things. "I'll call around and see if I can find someone who can be here for your brother. I'm not going to let him drown."

It wasn't Morgan's problem, and she didn't have to care, but Xander was grateful that she did. "Thank you."

At the door, she cradled the baby against her and paused. "I know you're worried and things between you two haven't been easy, but give Javier time. He's got some demons and he won't let them loose. He'll have to eventually. Maybe he's just not ready yet."

S.I. Industries didn't have months for Javier to "find himself" again. He'd been reading business blogs and the *Wall Street Journal*. Scuttlebutt was that unless its research and development teams started showing Uncle Sam something new and snazzy soon, the government would start doing all its business with other manufacturers, like current darling United Velocity. And if it didn't have the cash flow to prototype and build cool new military gadgets, S.I. Industries would be history.

Xander chomped at the bit to jump in, his brother's wishes be damned, and help out. But it would only drive a bigger wedge between them. Javier was more important to him than the business. But if Javier lost his birthright, it would devastate him and probably put the final nail in his coffin. Even as a kid, his brother hadn't taken failure well. Javier was a born leader, and his desire and aptitude to engage in teamwork had never been stellar. As an adult, nothing had changed.

"I've been trying to find the crash method to get him back into his head and caring about his life. We're running out of time."

"You've done a lot of the right things, even if it's tough love." She cocked her head as she gently bounced the whimpering baby. "Jack thinks he needs something to focus on or something to care about besides business."

"That bottle of Cîroc isn't going to do it," he snapped.

"But the bottle doesn't have expectations or judge him. He doesn't have to feel guilt or anger or whatever's eating him up with vodka. Did he grieve for his wife?"

Xander didn't have the answer to that question. Francesca's body had been found while he'd been ass deep in the sting that he'd helped Tyler orchestrate to bring down Los Angeles' crooked assistant district attorney. The press had been swarming. Xander had done his best to leave his brother alone and draw the pesky reporters, along with the limelight, away from Javier. The brother he'd known before Francesca's death had always been serious, focused, short-tempered, and driven. But he hadn't been an angry drunk.

"Maybe. I don't know." It shamed him to admit that. "But it's been a year."

"There's no limit to the amount of time it takes to grieve. Jack's *grandpère* passed away two days after Brice's birth, almost nine months ago. I still see the sadness on Jack's face from time to time. He didn't forget the man he loved, but he's slowly laying him to rest. Maybe Javier just isn't there with Francesca's memory yet. He must have loved her very much."

"Not at all, actually."

Morgan winced, then softened as she glimpsed the baby sleeping listlessly in her arms. "Has he ever been in love? Really in love?"

"I don't know. Until he married Francesca, I'd never seen him prefer one woman over another. And even then . . ." Xander frowned, ashamed to realize that he actually knew very little about his brother's personal life. Five years' difference in age hadn't always made them miles apart, but lately, it certainly hadn't helped. "I don't know if he's capable of the devotion you're talking about."

"Were your parents affectionate?"

Xander snorted. "Sure. Dad loved bending his assistants over his desk, and Mom loved Nordstrom."

Morgan's face was full of pity, and Xander wished to hell he'd kept his mouth shut. "So his experiences with love haven't been great, it sounds like. I hate to sound like Dr. Phil, but maybe Jack is right and Javier needs something to care about. Or someone."

As much as Xander hated it, the theory had validity. Javier needed something to fight for. He carried on as if he had no outlet in life except business and a bottle. Neither could make him feel truly valued. He couldn't invest his heart in either one. But if he had a reason to care, a reason to live, how much would that improve his outlook? At the very least, Javier's mood might improve with a good fuck. As far as Xander knew, his brother hadn't taken anyone to bed in over a year. No wonder his mood sucked.

Mentally he flipped through all the women he knew. Francesca had been tall, thin, exotic, and dark. Xander knew more than a few of that type. Problem was, they would look at Javier with dollar signs in their eyes, not as a man who needed a little TLC to start healing.

"Any ideas where I could find this someone to care about him? I need her quick."

Morgan raised a fiery brow. "If you're going to be in a hurry, maybe he's better off with a dog. I didn't say Javier needs just anyone. He needs someone special."

Yeah. Did that exist? Xander had been sampling females for years. Other than his buddies' wives, all great women he admired for more than their beauty, he'd never met one he'd want to keep forever, much less one who could be his brother's savior.

Javier opened the door to his interior office, holding the bottle of vodka by its neck. He glanced at Morgan with concern, ignoring Xander altogether. "The baby still feverish?"

She nodded, regret molding her expression. "Yes. I'll see if I can find someone else to help you out. I'll call and let you know."

Though Javier desperately needed things typed, organized, and read, and Morgan had volunteered while her cable TV show was on a brief hiatus, he showed no displeasure for the disruption of her duties or the change in his own workload.

"Take care of that pretty baby." Javier smiled benignly.

The bottle wasn't quite half gone. Maybe his brother was still capable of a reasonable conversation. Maybe they could discuss what was lacking in Javier's life and he could help fix it. Fuck, he was allergic to emotion. His trying to fix his brother was a joke, but someone had to.

"Thank you." Morgan gathered the rest of her things and headed out to her car, kissing the baby's little head, dusted with dark hair like his daddy.

Xander wondered what it would be like to love someone enough to want to put a ring on her finger and plant a seed in her womb. He shrugged. Not that it mattered. He didn't see that happening, ever.

Javier watched Morgan, too. His expression held a gravity, a sadness . . . longing. Not for Morgan herself, but what she represented. Home, hearth, love, devotion. Forever.

And maybe, Xander mused, he needed to get laid again. Or fuck someone more interesting. That wouldn't make his problems go away, but it damn sure would help him forget for a while.

As soon as Morgan drove off, Javier turned to him. With a narrow-eyed glare that dared him to object, he took a long draw from the bottle of Cîroc.

"Eat anything before you started drinking?" Xander asked.

"Fuck off."

"I can tell that vodka is helping you make great decisions."

Javier glared. "Fuck off."

"Has your vocabulary been reduced to two words now?"

"No. Please fuck off."

They were getting nowhere, and Javier was hating him more every day. Xander would put up with his brother's enmity for the rest of their lives and be the fucking scapegoat, but only if Javier came back. Xander was taking a huge gamble with the last of his family, and he hoped the plan didn't blow up in his face.

It was on the tip of his tongue to ask Javier yet again if he could help S.I. Industries recover, but he already knew the answer. Being so rejected by his brother at every turn shouldn't hurt so much, but hell . . . he was only human, too.

The more he tried to help Javier, the more his brother pushed him away. He was damn tired of it, mostly because he didn't know what else to do.

"You want me to fuck off and throw in the towel? Leave you to drown in work and good vodka and pretend that I don't give a damn? What kind of brother would I be?"

Javier sent him a cold glare. "The kind who abandoned me when I needed him most and allowed Francesca to die. I asked for your help then. I don't need it now."

Javier was so shut down. He would rather crash and burn than feel or change. Xander suppressed a curse. He'd thought a few weeks away from the distractions of the big city and the introduction into a caring circle of friends, a focus back on work, would all help him. But Javier was just sinking deeper.

"I'm not to blame. I didn't wrap a rope around Fran's throat and squeeze. Instead of playing the blame game with me, why don't you try to find your wife's killer, put the mess to rest that way. I'll help you."

"Like you 'helped' before? No thanks. I've got that covered. I've hired a P.I. who's in Aruba now. Nick is the best. He'll learn the bastard's identity. Then I'll hunt him to the ends of the Earth to put him down myself if I have to."

Xander was glad to hear it. Closure might bring Javier peace. "You can't go vigilante on me. Think. Let the police—"

"Goddamn it, get your nose out of my business and fuck off."

With a sigh, Xander stared at his brother. He didn't want to give up or admit defeat. But Javier . . . well, he couldn't force his brother to let go of his guilt or see reason. "I've done everything I can think of to help you, and you still insist on pushing me away. You know what? Fine. If you want me to fuck off, you've got it." He turned and made for the door, pausing as he pushed it open. "I'll leave you the hell alone until your six weeks are up. You can have the house to yourself. I'll crash elsewhere. If you keep up your end of the bargain, I'll keep my mouth shut and stay out of your hair."

"Good. I didn't ask for your shit anyway. And take your whores with you. They were loud last night while I was trying to sleep."

Gritting his teeth, he repressed the urge to plow his fist into the wall of glass beside him. "You got it. And one more thing, Javier."

"What?"

"Fuck off. For good."

He charged out the door, slamming it behind him and prowling to his Audi. He needed a good drink and an even better fuck. And he knew exactly where to go.

* * *

AFTER walking to Sexy Sirens alone, London let herself in with her cousin Alyssa's key and disabled the alarm. She didn't reset it behind her or lock the door, since the other woman should be only minutes behind her and the club's sign still indicated the place was closed.

The interior looked dormant, but a sense of anticipation hung in the air. The lights were dark, the bar dry, the speakers silent, but within hours all of that would change. Men would file in, and raucous music would fill the air with its raunchy, insistent beat. The booze would flow. The whistles and catcalls would start. Women would strut out wearing next to nothing and entice every man in the place.

Not that she wanted to be an exotic dancer, exactly. But she'd love to tempt any man at this point. Hell, she was beyond grateful to just be moving without wheelchairs or walkers. She was making friends beyond her nurses and physical therapists. She'd even been on a few dates with a nice guy, and he'd kissed her once or twice . . . but Brian had been on the hospital staff. Of course once he'd seen the terrible roadmap of red scars on her lower back, he'd been repulsed and mumbled an excuse about being too busy to date anymore. Embarrassed and deflated, she'd let him go without fuss. Letting anyone see her back wasn't a mistake she planned on making again. But here she could pretend that none of that existed.

After nearly ten years of recovery and rehab, she'd fled her mother's nest and flown halfway across the country to visit her cousin for a while. Alyssa and Luc had been so kind and offered to take her in. She wished she could pay rent or babysit their beautiful little girl in return—something. But that was impossible, at least for now. Someday . . .

Squelching the guilt and sadness, she made her way through the empty club, her sensible sandals clicking as she meandered up on the stage, fingers grazing the shining metal pole in the middle. What would it be like to have the confidence and the body to strip in front of a roomful of men? To hear their appreciative whistles and suggestive comments? To know they felt lust when they looked at her, not pity?

She'd never know, but she could pretend here and now.

With a grin, she clambered off the stage and darted to the dressing room, finding a pair of her cousin's sexiest stilettos. Tottering in on them, she flipped on the lights and the music, as Alyssa had shown her the first time she'd come to Sexy Sirens. It might be a place where men could escape a bad work or home life, hang and relax, but right now it would be her place to fantasize that she was sexy, that she knew exactly how to make a man's tongue hang from his mouth and beg for her. She chose a sexy tune with a grinding beat by Rihanna. Her sensual voice flowed over her confession that it felt so good being bad.

London closed her eyes and let her hips sway as she made her way back to the stage. The heat from the intense overhead lights sizzled across her skin. She bobbed her head from side to side with the beat of the music, then speared a hand through her pale hair, winding the long strands between her ample breasts. She turned slowly, balanced on the sexy shoes, gripping her hips, arching her back, and sticking out her ass, just like Alyssa had taught her.

The lessons in strip aerobics her cousin had been giving her had become the highlight of her time in Lafayette. Her sexy-as-sin cousin used to take off her clothes for a living until she'd turned her hand to owning this club and a nearby gourmet restaurant with her famous chef husband. To Alyssa, exotic dancing had once been necessary to keep food in her belly and a roof over her head. But she'd proposed it to London so that she could work on her strength, flexibility, weight loss, and self-confidence. On the first two, she'd made a great deal of progress with every sort of doctor and therapist known to man. The third she'd been trying on her own and had taken off thirty pounds . . . but still had thirty to go. But none of that made her feel like the cheerleader and straight-A student she'd once been, just like a recovering invalid.

Shoving the morose thought aside, she prowled toward the pole and rolled her body against it, starting with the valley between her breasts, down her abdomen, then between her legs, where she lingered for a moment, pressing, before she tossed back her head with a shiver.

Curling one calf around the pole, London clutched it with one hand and arched her back. She lifted one of her hands to her neck, gripping lightly before she caressed her way down her collarbones, over the swells of her breasts. Then she turned her fingers toward the stage and palmed her way down her abdomen before pressing into the top of her mons. In her mind, gorgeous men cheered for her, pounded the stage, demanded more. And she gave it to them, fingering the buttons on her delicate floral blouse.

She toyed with the little plastic discs, imagining the chants for her to show her breasts, the lust swirling in the room. Opening her eyes, London took a quick peek around Sexy Sirens. Still as empty as the moment she walked in. No one would see her scars. No one would know except maybe Alyssa, and she wouldn't care or judge.

Biting her lip, she let the first button free from its hole, exposing a hint of the white lace of her bra. Heat flushed all through her body.

More.

She loosened the second button and tugged the edges of the loose blouse under her breasts. Grabbing the pole with one hand, she bent back, head falling as if to look at the audience upside down. She imagined dozens of stares on her, intent, wanting her. Wriggling one shoulder, she let the blouse slide off one shoulder.

Slowly, she arched up, rolling her body flush against the pole in an undulating wave. Mouth falling open, she swung her hips as she tore through the rest of the buttons on her shirt until it hung open. With a roll of her other shoulder, the flimsy material slid off and down her arms, then fluttered to the stage. Now only the band of her lacy underwire bra and her long hair covered her back. She felt a slight chill—and more than a bit self-conscious—being so exposed. But she also felt damn free for once in her life.

Thank God no one was here.

She smiled, indulging the daydream a bit longer. Yes, she might black out. She might even fall off the stage and hurt herself. But she was enjoying her precious moments of independence and fantasy too much to stop now.

Biting her lip and sending her imaginary audience a come-hither glance, she closed her eyes in not altogether feigned ecstasy, then reached for the snap of her capri pants. It came undone with a quick flick of her fingers. London rubbed her flushed cheek against the pole, the metal cool against her feverish face. Then she opened her eyes, imagining someone dark and handsome in one of the empty seats in the front row. He'd stare at her with scorching lust and reach out for her, knowing he could only look, but never touch. The ache between her legs grew hotter, and she squirmed, rocking her hips to ease the ache. It only made her throbbing pick up tempo.

The music paused. She inserted her own heavy breathing, her breasts lifting and falling to the silent beat. When the loud, sexy music crashed in again, she grabbed the waistband of her pants and wriggled them lower. But that man in the front row . . . he needed to be teased more.

With a grin, she spun around and made sure that her hair tossed down her back. She gripped her thighs and stuck out her ass in a slow circle. Then, finally, she swung her hips from side to side, easing her cargo capris down, over her backside, down her thighs at a teasing pace, exposing the new white lace thong she'd recently bought with her bra because she'd been desperate to feel sexy, like a female who could capture attention from a sigh-worthy guy—like her imaginary hottie in the front row.

When the pants pooled around her ankles, she stepped out of

them, wearing only her delicate bra, barely there underwear, and strappy fuck-me stilettos in sinful red designed to win a man's attention and have his tongue hanging down to his knees.

London strutted away from the pole toward the front of the stage, swaying her hips as she pressed her palms up her hips, over her heavy breasts, then filtered them through her loose hair as she tossed her head back as if wracked by desire. The long strands caressed the small of her back, the curls she'd fought half her life flowing freely over her skin in a tease that made her gasp.

The song geared up for its big ending, and a heavy drumbeat pounded over the speakers. She undulated her hips in tight circles, then bent at the waist, over her leg, feeling her way up her thigh, fingers grazing her moistening folds and pressing in for a hot, secret moment before she turned again and sashayed for the pole, flipping her hair over her hated back. London grabbed the shiny pole, swung herself around it, wrapped her calf along the bottom, then dipped back to regard her imaginary audience as the music came to a breathless halt.

In the sudden silence, she smiled, feeling both a bit silly, but totally, wonderfully free.

Until she heard clapping . . . and an unmistakably male wolf whistle.

Panic spiked through her bloodstream, and she gasped, eyes wide with horror. She slapped one arm across her breasts. As they spilled over her arm, she shoved the other over her hips to shield her sex, barely concealed by the stupid little thong that had made her feel so sexy minutes ago. Now, she wondered if it would make her a rape victim. For more than one reason, she didn't dare turn her back on whomever lurked just beyond the circle of light so she could find her clothes. Instead, she backed away slowly, watching as the man emerged from the shadows.

As he stepped into the bright light, London stared in shock. It was as if this man had been plucked from her imagination. Dark hair, olive complexion, square jaw and strong chin, eyes glittering with mischief that reflected in his faint grin. Tall, well-dressed, beautiful—and not taking his gaze off of her for an instant.

Her heart thumped even harder. "W-we're closed."

He shrugged and stepped closer to the stage. "The door was open."

"Well, Sirens won't be open until four. Come back then."

The guy wasn't deterred in the least. He sauntered closer. "I'm sorry if I startled you. Your dance was so sweetly seductive, I couldn't pass up the opportunity to express my appreciation. In fact, I'd like to appreciate you even more. What's your name, *belleza*?"

In case he was a rapist, she didn't feel the need to be polite. "You need to leave."

He held up both hands in a gesture meant to convey that he was harmless—not that she believed it. She scrambled back.

"Stop. Breathe. Listen." His voice dropped an octave as he stepped forward again.

Instantly, she found herself following instructions, then wondered why. Something in his voice maybe? It carried a stern note of a command, but his expression read gentle. Whatever it was, London responded. She dropped her gaze to the scratched-up stage, frantically trying to gather her thoughts.

"Good girl, *belleza*. I'm not going to hurt you. Relax."

Again, she found herself doing as he bid and being oddly happy that he'd praised her. Almost proud. God, was she so thirsty for something good in her life that she'd fall for kind words from a potential ax murderer?

"Nothing to worry about," he promised. "I'm a friend of Alyssa Traverson, the owner."

That raised her hackles. He should have stuck to the truth and said he was simply a customer. "I know most of her friends. I don't know you. What's your name?"

"I'm Xander."

The Xander? Logan's billionaire playboy pal? He was dressed expensively. Though Xander's eyes appeared hazel, rather than blue like his brother's, he looked enough like Javier otherwise—ungodly handsome—to convince her she'd guessed right.

The good news was, if he was a friend of Logan's, he wasn't an ax murderer or a rapist. In fact, she'd heard the stories about the ways in which Xander had helped both Logan and Tyler save their wives from some really dangerous situations. From everything she could tell, both of those men had great creep radars, so Xander wasn't a psycho.

But he was unnerving. She'd read about men who could make a woman's heart skip a bit, but London had believed it was all crap until recently. Xander and Javier were both lip-bitingly hot.

"What's your name?" Xander asked.

"L-London."

"Like the city?" he smiled.

She nodded. Hell, his gaze was so fixed on her that her brain shut down. When he looked at her like that, she couldn't think of anything to say.

"Have you ever been there?"

"No." She tried to smile. "Someday."

"You should see it." He smiled. "It's unique. And beautiful, just like you, *belleza*."

"What does that mean?"

"Beauty."

Exactly what his brother had murmured to her in his stupor.

"Don't frown at me. You looked gorgeous onstage. Do you dance here?"

Was he kidding? In the thong she was still wearing—with little else to cover her—she scrambled back to find her clothes, grabbing her blouse first and holding it up over her torso. She'd been so startled, then blinded by his gorgeousness, she'd forgotten that she was damn-near naked.

He laughed. "Hmm, covered or not, you're still sexy. You have the most tempting sugary pink nipples."

London spread her shirt across her breasts even as she felt heat crawl up her cheeks. "You can't see that. I'm wearing a bra."

"Made of peekaboo lace."

A quick glace down proved him right, and since her thong was made out of the same fabric, the chances were that he could see pretty much everything down there, too. Mortification swept over her in a hot wave. It shouldn't bother her, really. So many doctors and medical professionals over the years had seen her mostly naked, but those people had looked at her like a specimen. Xander stared at her like a predator sizing up a meal. Hungry. Intense. His gaze heated. Desire simmered. And she couldn't help but respond. Yes, she was flattered, but more, she felt an answering flutter between her legs.

"Could you . . ." She bit her lip, then forced her words out. "Could you be a gentleman and turn around so I can get dressed?"

He shrugged, but quirked a smile in her direction that said he'd be working to get her out of all those garments again soon. "Sure."

"Thank you," she said stiffly as he turned away.

She struggled into her clothes, tugging up her cargo capri pants, shrugging into her floral blouse with shaking fingers. This was the prudent thing, walking away from a womanizer already eyeing her. She had no experience with that kind of man—or any kind, for that matter.

But wasn't that why she'd left her mom's house and moved here, to break away from the shadow of her illness and go to a place where no one knew or remembered the tragedy of her adolescence? So she could finally experience life. So she could truly *live*.

Absolutely.

So Xander wasn't going to win any husband-of-the-year awards. London wasn't looking to get married. Sure, she'd like to have a boyfriend someday. Right now, all she wanted to do was meet people, date, and okay, maybe have a little sex. Or a lot. She had as much libido as the next girl, maybe more since she didn't exactly know what she was missing. But books and movies provided tantalizing glimpses. Even if it wasn't like all the glorified fictional accounts, well . . . then she'd know, right? She could finally say she'd experienced something—with a man who knew what the hell he was doing. If Xander had slept with that many women, why would he mind one more? She doubted that her virginity or her past would even matter to him.

Decision made, London loosened her top button and pulled aside the edges of her blouse so he'd get a good glimpse at her cleavage. "You can turn around now."

He did, appreciation lighting his eyes instantly. "Lovely. I didn't mean to scare you or peek uninvited. The door was open, I walked in, and you looked so beautiful that I simply couldn't stop you. So glad I didn't."

Xander reached out slowly, seeming to give her plenty of opportunity to back away. Heat rushed up her body. Her heart chugged and pulsed violently, but she refused to give in to the urge to scamper away.

With a reassuring smile, he helped her off the stage, then curled his fingers around her elbow with a proprietary grip, using it to draw her closer. "Come with me. Sit and talk." The words were half-request, half-command. He gestured to the club's dark bar. London didn't see the harm.

"All right."

"Excellent. I can't promise that I won't try to proposition you, but you're always free to say no." He sent her a disarming grin. "I'd like to get to know you. For now, I'll keep my hands to myself," he promised. "Mostly. Until you tell me otherwise."

London hesitated, trying to think things through, but it was damn difficult with him so near. "You don't give up, do you?"

"Not when I want something."

With a very charming and no doubt well-practiced smile, he led her to the bar and eased her into a booth in the corner. It didn't escape her notice that he situated himself squarely between her and the exit.

Staring at him from under her lashes, London settled herself into the seat he'd indicated, peeking at his chiseled face, lingering on the sensual curve of his lips, then trailing down to his bulging shoulders and broad chest. When she realized she was flat-out staring, she jerked her gaze back up to his face. He flashed her a *gotcha* smile with lots of white teeth and cockiness. He'd seen her mostly naked and was still flirting. That was a good sign.

"How long had you been, um . . . watching me?" she asked.

"I was going to call out to you as you fired up the music, but once you started dancing, I couldn't stop someone that sexy. Besides, you looked like you were having fun."

Her mother called men like him incorrigible. He was definitely the sort to ask forgiveness, not permission. "I was, but no one was supposed to see that. Any chance you'll forget about it?"

"Not even a remote one." Xander's grin widened as he leaned over the table and stared intently. "Tell me something about you, sexy London."

"I'm twenty-five and I just moved here. And . . ." She had nothing else interesting to say. "What about you?"

"I'm thirty, I'm here for a few weeks, and . . ." He grabbed her hand and folded it between both of his, surrounding her with strong fingers. "I'm wondering why you go a little tense every time I say you're sexy."

He'd noticed? "It's a great pickup line, but . . ."

"You don't believe that I'm going to put your striptease in my spank bank?" He winked. "We'll chat for a bit. In, say, ten minutes, I'll tell you that you're sexy again and hope it will feel better to you. Deal?"

That sounded great, but she was hardly a size four. "Are you teasing me?"

"Why would you think that, *belleza*?"

His subtle challenge made her doubt it, but insecurity didn't go away that simply. "I'm sure I looked about as coordinated as an elephant on roller skates out there. And almost as big as one, too."

He narrowed his eyes. "Who told you that you're less than beautiful?"

"No one, but I'm not blind." She shook her head, flustered. "Look, I appreciate your kind words, but—"

"No buts. I find you attractive, and I see no reason to lie about it. You aren't beautiful in the way I typically see." When she stiffened, he went on. "That's a good thing, *belleza*. You're not wearing five pounds of makeup, haven't slathered on false eyelashes, or had your teeth bleached. Your nails aren't covered by acrylic talons and your toenails aren't dotted with daisies or glitter . . . or whatever the trend of the moment is. You're not wearing a skirt so short that I can see whether you're waxed or shaved. Your gorgeous breasts aren't silicone, and you haven't been on some stupid starvation diet that makes you look as if you've barely survived Auschwitz. You look good in your own skin. Natural. Do you know how long it's been since I've seen a woman like that?"

She frowned. "Since when do men like women less than perfect?"

"I can't speak for all men. There are a ton of douche bags out there who don't care how fake a girl is as long as she looks hot. I know because I used to be one of them." He shrugged. "But I've gotten to a point in life where I prefer what's real."

London blinked at him, head cocked, and peered at him intently. "I don't know how to take you."

"Are you always this suspicious?"

With a little flush, she sat back, casting her gaze slightly down and wincing. She should stop annoying Xander and let him do his worst, which would undoubtedly be the best thing that had ever happened in her admittedly dull life. "It's just that . . . I don't have a lot of experience. I'm guessing you do."

"A great deal. I won't lie about that. But that also means I know what I like."

"So you're not kidding?"

Xander dragged her to her feet, captured her waist, and brought her back to his chest. "*Belleza*, does this feel like I'm kidding?" He rolled his hips against her ass and pressed his hard cock into her. "Like I thought you didn't look incredible and I wasn't desperate to touch you?"

London froze, and Xander pressed a lingering kiss to her neck that made her shiver, her breath catch.

"You don't have to flatter me. I know how I look."

"You have no idea how you look to *me*." His voice dropped, going both husky and hard. "You're sweet." He dragged his lips across her neck again. His tongue slipped out and he tasted her skin. "Soft." He caressed his way across the slight bulge of her abdomen, over the curve of her hip, then down her slightly parted thighs.

London gasped at the tingles spreading across her skin as Xander skimmed across her thigh, planted his palm on the extra-soft skin just inside . . . then began to work his way back up. "So supple."

When his thumb crept just inches shy of her moistening secrets, she began to tremble all over. "I want to touch you, *belleza*. Tear your clothes off and feel just how wet I can make you. I want to show you how much pleasure I can give you."

And wouldn't she like that, too?

"Don't." Her voice trembled.

He removed his hands and took a half-step back. "Don't what, touch you? Compliment you? Want you?"

"No." London drew in a shaking breath. "Don't stop."

Chapter Four

SHOCK pinged through Xander's system. The girl who wanted him to turn around so she could dress in privacy now wanted him to seduce her? That would absolutely be his pleasure. And, very shortly, hers, too. Mentally, he calculated how long it would take him to get her naked and under him. Ten minutes, tops. He'd shoot for five since he was so fucking eager to brush his lips over every inch of her skin, drag his tongue across her nipples, then slide his cock slowly and deeply inside that undoubtedly sweet pussy.

Dropping his face back to the fragrant curve between her neck and shoulder, he swept kisses across her skin. So fucking soft— everywhere, every inch. Jesus, he could touch her all damn day and not be bored. And she smelled so luscious, a bit citrusy in the first breath, but then jasmine and vanilla came along and flirted with his sense of smell, luring him even closer.

More. He definitely needed more of her. Granted, it never took his cock long to stand up and salute beauty, but this one might have set a record, even for him. Lovely, pale, and so naturally submissive. And real. She was everything he prized. Everything he craved. Everything he'd been missing in life.

He glanced down to see her lush ass covered in ugly beige cargo pants. If he got his hands on her, he'd rip those off. He'd love to dress her in little skirts that would give him easy access to every one of her soft secrets. When they were alone, panties would definitely be forbidden, along with anything that obstructed him from all the slick softness he desperately wanted to see, touch . . . taste. He was going to have to ask Alyssa where and why she'd been hiding this delicious indulgence.

With an expectant grin, he braced his hands on London's waist and turned her to face him. An even row of little white teeth emerged to chew on that plump lower lip uncertainly. Her body shook with obvious nerves.

Frowning, Xander braced a finger under her chin and lifted gently. "Look at me."

Her thick lashes fluttered open over eyes so blue they punched him in the gut. It wasn't just with their beautiful color; it was everything about her. He'd fucked some of the most physically beautiful women in the world, on every continent except Antarctica. He'd skipped that one; nothing to see there, and he hated cold. But he'd joined the mile-high club at seventeen, so that evened things out. But all those memories faded as he looked at London.

What jabbed him now was her expressiveness. Every thought in her head was all over her face. Fear. Anxiety. Curiosity. And the shyest desire. She looked at him like a penniless kid peeking in a candy store's window. But she didn't make a single move toward him.

He'd come here to find a convenient girl to spend the afternoon with and work out some of his tension. Xander couldn't escape the feeling that he'd found much more. They'd barely exchanged more than a handful of words, but she already presented him so many intriguing contradictions. A beauty whose striptease had him needing to adjust himself in his way-too-tight pants so unsure of her own appeal. She never had answered his question about whether she danced here, and now he was inclined to think that she not only didn't work for Alyssa, she'd never taken her clothes off in public. Which begged the question . . . why was London onstage stripping when she hadn't expected an audience?

Her chest rose enticingly with a deep breath, and Xander couldn't fail to notice that the top button popped open above her luscious breasts and gave him a sinful shot of her cleavage. Before the sight short-circuited his brain altogether and he abandoned his finessed seduction, he met her stare.

London's eyes were definitely the windows to her soul. Inside, he saw a woman so kind and gentle. But he sensed a wildness, an impatience. Need.

"You want me to kiss you?" he murmured against her mouth.

She drew in a little breath, lips parted. "Yes."

London breathed the word, and it went straight to his cock. "You want me to take off your clothes, taste your body, then fuck you deep and swallow your cries of pleasure with my lips?"

Parting her glossy lips, she blinked at him again, hesitating. She swayed on her feet, digging her fingers into his shoulders to steady herself. "Yes."

Fuck, yes. Right here. Right now. They were alone. But something about this girl . . . He wouldn't be satisfied with a quickie on the rickety little table, bracing her back against the wall as he shoved his cock into her. She needed more care. Why else would he call her a beauty in his ancestors' language when "babe" worked for nearly every other conquest? Xander deeply suspected that unleashing all his desire burning for London by spreading her legs right here would scare her. This one was a project. He had hours to kill. Hell, days and weeks. He could devote time to this beauty's seduction.

"That's what I want, too, *belleza*. But not here."

And now that he'd promised to leave the rental house to Javier, he couldn't take London there. He also wasn't keen on bringing her to the scene of his debauched antics with Megan, Shelby and . . . what was her name? Alexis. Yeah, London didn't belong there.

"Is your place nearby?"

She looked slightly panicked. "No. I mean, yes, I live nearby, but we can't go there. I'm staying with family. My cousin . . ."

"Might walk in on us?"

"Exactly."

He remembered seeing a hotel not far from here. It wasn't a five-star establishment, but it would have to do. Xander took her hand. "I've got an idea, if you'll come with me."

At that moment, the phone in her pants pocket dinged with a text message. She took it out, read, frowned, then tapped out a reply before pocketing her phone again and drawing in a deep breath. "I think I've got a better idea. Come with me?"

He smiled, anticipation exploding through his body, flooding his eager cock even more painfully. "Lead the way, *belleza*."

London squeezed past him, and he palmed her ass as she did. At her indrawn breath, he flashed her a grin. Then she made her way to the front door and locked it. The decisive metallic *clink* resounded through the empty space. Now they were totally alone. Oh, yeah. This was going to be good.

Once they cleared the bar, Xander snagged her hand, clasping it tightly in his, then followed her across the concrete floor, up the stairs at the back of the club. She opened the door at the top. Once inside, a four-posted bed filled the space. Man, what he couldn't do here with London and a nice, long length of nylon restraints. The thought had him shoving back a groan.

Inside, sharp, artsy black-and-white photographs, mostly landscapes, hung on the walls. The white comforter looked downy and inviting as sunlight streamed in across the bed.

Xander closed the door behind them. "Excellent. No one will disturb us?"

She licked her lips nervously. "Not for a few hours."

"Oh, *belleza* . . . You are in so much trouble. God, you don't even know how thoroughly I'm going to fuck you."

She swallowed, then blinked up at him with those blue eyes. "Then . . . you'll have to show me."

Her sweet little voice sounded breathless, and he saw the pulse pounding at the base of her neck. London was more than a little nervous. He'd calm her down and jack her up on pleasure, then she'd stop overthinking it.

"That's my plan." He drew her closer, flush against him. "Don't worry. I've got you."

She tried to nod, but he tangled his hands in her hair so she couldn't move. He didn't quite have her where he wanted her, but soon.

Nudging her back, he laid her across the bed, following her down into the cloud of soft white bedding. She looked gorgeous with her pale hair spread all around and her soft face just beneath him, her heavy-lidded eyes more than a bit aroused. This one would be responsive, and despite last night's depravity, Xander couldn't wait. Something about her was new and fresh. Different. Almost pure.

Covering her body with his own, he hissed at the feel of her curves melding against him. Then he cupped her cheek in his hand. Beautiful. She blinked up at him, her fair skin glowing rosy. Already, he felt like one lucky son of a bitch.

"Y-you're staring."

"I'm contemplating all the ways I'm going to make you come for me." Her breath caught and her cheeks flushed. Xander simply smiled. "Shy, *belleza*?"

"A little."

Clearly more than a little, but he let the white lie slide for now. Rather than using his lips to berate her, he'd ten times rather kiss her.

Xander leaned in, giving her time to object. But she didn't. He brushed his lips over hers softly, seeking and testing. She opened beneath him like a butterfly, tentatively at first before her lips finally parted. She let him in, gasping as he entered her mouth, his tongue sliding against hers in a slow, sexy tango.

London gripped his shoulders, almost frozen beneath him. She panted hard. He could feel her heart racing against his chest.

"Relax. It's okay. I'll make you feel good."

At his whisper, London nodded. She was doing her best to trust him, and for now it would have to be enough. He'd prove his point soon. Until he could, Xander slipped a hand behind her nape, slanted his mouth over hers, and feasted.

The sweetness he'd tasted on her tongue the first time now exploded across his senses. She surrendered to the kiss, her body turning soft beneath him as she grabbed him like she'd never let go.

With a groan, he thrust deeper between her lips. She arched up under him, opening wider to admit every thrust of his tongue. The kiss turned hungrier, and Xander ate at her ruthlessly, losing himself inside her mouth. Fuck, he could drown here, forget all his problems. He didn't need one of Alyssa's strippers; he needed this girl. Later—much later—he'd figure out why she'd been taking her clothes off on Sexy Sirens' stage without an audience.

Right now, he just wanted to get inside her in every way he could.

He seized her lips again, sinking down and easing to her side. She turned to him, slinging her thigh over his hip in silent protest. Very soon, he'd take advantage of that. For now, he gently pushed her back to the bed, then turned his attention to the buttons of her blouse. One after the other, he slipped them through their moorings like a hot knife through butter.

In moments, he was prying the fabric apart and tapering off the hot kiss to look down at her. Holy fucking jackpot. Those breasts spilled above the white lace of her bra. They were works of art, round and pale and soft. And so real. Xander couldn't wait to get his hands on them, his lips. To cup them, graze her nipples with his fingers, and listen to her gasp, then see her eyes flutter closed. He'd tear off that damn bra and suck her nipples until they swelled red.

Through the lace now, he could see they were sweet pink nubs, standing up straight, begging for attention.

"I need that bra gone. And the shirt. Strip them off for me."

London didn't move. "Um . . . can we close the blinds first?"

And ruin what he was sure would be one of the best views he'd had in a very long while? "No, *belleza*. I'm going to be an indulgent lover. I'm going to make sure you come well and often. But no one can see in this window, and I'm not going to let you hide from me."

She flushed again, pausing to process his words. A bit of panic tightened her face, but she forged on. "I'd be more relaxed if the room was dark."

He shook his head. "You'd stay buried in your comfort zone and not really surrender everything to me. That's not how I roll. Blinds open. Take off your blouse, *belleza*." He'd work the bra off himself. In fact, that would be fun.

London hesitated. She sat up, watching him with wide eyes, then looked down at herself, frowning. Displeasure crossed her face. Quickly, she laid flat again and wriggled out of the blouse. Xander didn't like the suspicions careening through his head. London didn't like her body? Because she was a woman and not a twig? Because she was curvaceous, rather than built like a boy?

Before he could get angry on her behalf, she tossed the blouse aside, then tucked her arms awkwardly behind her, clearly reaching for her bra strap. "This, too?"

He raised a brow at her. Everything about her expression told him that she was fighting her self-consciousness, and he gave her credit for trying. But she was trying to be in control of this situation, and that wouldn't do.

"On second thought, *belleza*, that will be my pleasure. I want to unwrap you slowly, at my leisure. For my pleasure."

London gnawed at her lip, as if that answer bothered her for some reason, then she sighed. "Look, I'm more than a little self-conscious. I'm sure you've been with prettier women, and you probably won't like—"

"You finishing that sentence, so don't. Stop worrying about what you think I'll like and give me what I ask for. We'll get along fine."

"You're bossy."

If she only knew . . . Xander smiled. "It's not the first time someone's said that. I doubt very much it will be the last."

Before she could comment on that and stall again, he laid across her body, edging her legs apart with his own and pressing his throbbing cock against her soft, sweltering pussy. He grabbed her hips and, fully clothed, he pushed up against her with a long groan. Yeah, they'd get naked and busy. He was going to have to exercise patience first and figure out her odd reticence.

Xander captured her mouth again. He'd never get tired of kissing her. She didn't do it expertly. In fact, he'd guess that she hadn't been kissed a lot or had endured a string of boyfriends who didn't worship this lush mouth properly. Either way, he'd rectify that.

As she melted beneath him, opening to him with more enthusiasm than finesse, he rolled to his back, draping her across his body. He wrapped his arms around her, fingers zeroing in on her bra. She barely had time to gasp before all four hooks across the middle of her back slid open. For such a lacy garment, it was quite supportive. Xander approved. With breasts like hers, she needed it. And he loved working his way down to her skin, feeling those hooks come undone one at a time under his fingers.

He peeled the delicate straps down her arms, then tossed her bra to the floor. "You won't need that for a while."

London flushed. "You're awfully good at removing bras. Clearly, you've done that many, many times. You're a terrible man, aren't you?"

Xander curled a grin at her. He couldn't remember the last time a woman had made him laugh while she aroused the hell out of him. "The worst. You'll probably regret this tomorrow."

That made her pause, then she shook her head. "Not if you make me feel good. Not if you give me something to remember. That's all I want."

She was saying good-bye before they'd even fucked? That bothered him, but he let it go for now. They were done when he said they were done. What he really needed to do was give her so much ecstasy that she couldn't bear to let him go.

Happy with his game plan, he rolled her to her back again, then rose to his knees and proceeded to work his way out of his gray dress shirt. He sent it sailing across the room, and it landed somewhere near her bra. And when he glanced back at London, she was gaping at his chest, her gaze sliding from his pectorals, down his abdominals, down to his—

"Oh. Wow. You're . . . I think I've swallowed my tongue."

Xander laughed. She was so artless, so unpracticed. Every response was like the first thought off the top of her head, all spoken without a filter. No fake purring or cheesy lines or centerfold poses with porn star faces. London was totally herself. He adored that.

"Don't do that, *belleza*. I'll need that tongue later." He winked.

She flushed even deeper. "You're making me dizzy."

"I haven't given you a good reason for that yet. Soon . . ."

And thinking about all the ways he could truly make her dizzy, he jumped off the bed and took advantage of her supine body. "Stay right there. Don't move a muscle. Can you do that for me?"

"What are you going to do?"

"Make you feel fantastic. I just need you to promise me that you'll lie here like a good girl for me."

A shadow of indecision passed across her face. "It's not going to hurt?"

"If it does, I'm doing something wrong." He grinned reassuringly.

She nodded, fidgeting a bit nervously before she settled down. "All right."

No games, no "I'm going to be your best ever, baby" comments. Anticipation lighting him up like a fireworks show, Xander attacked the buttons on her cargo capris. She barely had time to gasp before he had her zipper down, the garment around her ankles, and falling to the floor.

Wow. Just wow. He couldn't think much else as he looked down at her body clad only in a really tiny white lacy thong. He'd seen her wear it onstage, but taking it all in now that he was much closer and more personal, Xander liked it even better. Her thighs were smooth and pale and just a bit plump. They'd cushion his head when he ate at her pussy. He couldn't wait to wrap his fingers around those legs and pry them far apart as he crawled in between. Little tufts of fair hair protected her mons. He'd love to have her bare. She'd be pink and pretty and perfect, and his mouth watered just thinking about her.

"You're staring . . . down there." She sounded almost embarrassed about her own body. That wouldn't do.

"At your pussy, *belleza*? Yes. You're beautiful."

"That's not pretty, it's functional."

"I think it's both. You don't want to argue with me, do you?" He edged his voice with a bit of sharpness to let her know he'd find that unacceptable.

She hesitated, going somewhere up in her head. Xander cleared his throat and raised a brow, letting her know he expected an answer. Obviously, she had no idea that he was a Dom. Hell, she probably didn't even know that she was a natural sub. If she did, she'd certainly never explored this side of her sexuality. But he'd guide London and let her instincts lead her closer to him for now. Soon, he'd tie her down, take her through the dynamic. And God, he couldn't wait to feel that lush ass under his hand, reddening for his gaze and his pleasure.

Yeah, he was a pervert. Sue him.

"N-no," she answered finally, a bit uncertainly. He let it slide.

"Good girl. Give me the panties."

Her pretty blue eyes flared wide with shock. "Give them to you? Like . . . take them off and just hand them over to—" She shook her head, then stopped herself, sighing. "Really?"

"I want to get at your pussy. Show me that you want me there. Now, *belleza*."

She sucked in a deep breath, clearly gathering her courage. "One promise?"

The note of apprehension that crept into her voice gave him pause. Something was really hanging her up. Her lack of experience? Xander had been with thousands of women. He knew one relatively untried when he touched her. This one was too old to be virginal, but she'd clearly been handled in the past by the inept and clueless. It made him want to give her a totally different experience, so he was prepared to be indulgent—to a point.

"What's is it, *belleza*?"

"Don't look at my back. Promise me, and I'll do whatever else you want."

He frowned. *Her back?* With any new sub, he always negotiated. Safe, sane, and consensual, after all. For now, he'd consider that a soft limit—which meant he'd push it soon. "Sure."

London released a pent-up breath, seemingly relieved at his agreement. "Thank you."

Then she shimmied out of her little thong, wriggling it down her hips, past her thighs. Xander didn't look any lower. Her feet were probably petite, and she likely had little red toe nails or something equally cute. But he fixed his stare on her pussy and didn't let up. Yep, sweet pink flesh, just like he suspected. Her folds were slick and a little swollen. But he knew how to make her even more ready.

"That grin scares me." She watched him with a little smile.

He dove between her legs, licking his lips. "It should, *belleza*."

Without a word, he shoved her thighs wide and pried her folds apart with his thumbs. Then he raked her pussy with the flat of his tongue, lapping at the juices already spilling for him. She gasped, fisted the sheets—and he nearly fucking died. More than sweet, London was utterly addicting, and he drank her up like he couldn't get enough. Suddenly, he wondered if he ever would. Everything about her—the way she arched, the little noises in the back of her throat, how quickly her clit hardened against his tongue—it all excited the hell out of him.

"That's it," he encouraged her. "You're hot and slick and scrumptious." He nudged her with his nose, and the scent of her exploded all through his senses again. "Hmm, I'm going to keep you on my skin all day long. I'm going to remember this every second. And it's going to make me pull you back into bed so I can taste you again and again. Come on my tongue, *belleza*."

She reached down and thrust her fingers into his hair, bucking up against his mouth. She swelled once more. London was going to come for him in seconds. Her body tensed, gathering up like a storm. He could feel it brewing inside her. She was unraveling for him. When she did, he'd watch the show, marvel at how beautiful she was, then fuck her blind.

And if he stretched this out for a few hours, he wouldn't have to think about how useless he was otherwise and how much Javier—Never mind. Not going down that mental path. Why bother when London was way more engrossing than his moronic pity party?

Using his tongue, he swiped at her small opening, licking up and all the way over her sweet candy clit. God, he could imagine her waxed. In fact, he already knew he was going to want to fuck her after today. He'd talk her into getting bare in every way for him.

The idea made his dick harder. He hadn't known that was even possible.

"Xander!" she cried out, panting and half-afraid.

He simply moaned against her in acknowledgement, but nothing was going to make him give up this tasty treat before he blew her mind and she came apart.

But she stiffened, trying to clamp down on his head with her plush thighs. She shoved and pushed at him. What the hell? Had he hurt her somehow.

"What's wrong, *belleza*?"

She shook her head. "It was too much, too big. Too fast."

Seriously? That only reinforced his certainty that whomever she'd been sleeping with was a complete clusterfuck in bed.

"Then it's perfect. Big and fast will roll right over you and feel so good." He lowered his head to her pussy again, thumbing her clit along the way.

"And mow me down." London tensed. "I-I'm not very good at orgasm."

Not good at it? Who'd sold her that shitty bridge? "I'm sure you're more than good at it. Whoever's been trying to give them to you isn't worthy. I'll change that, *belleza*. With me, you'll be an expert. I promise."

With her still sputtering and drawing in shuddering breaths, Xander kissed his way over her flesh with an open-mouthed passion, eating her without restraint or pause. In seconds, he'd pushed her up against the passionate cliff again. She might be fighting what was unfamiliar to her, but he'd make sure she didn't do it for long.

"Let it go." No way she could miss the demand in his tone. She was far too sweet, too submissive not to comply. "Spread wider for me."

Sure enough, she did as he'd asked. As soon as she had no defenses against his probing tongue, he added a finger. She followed his orders. Damn, she was tight, and his finger felt like it might strangle under the clamping vise of her walls. Shit, just how tight was she? How long had it been? Or had her past boyfriends all had pencil dicks?

The questions swirled in his brain until she screamed in high-pitched ecstasy, her pussy pulsing on his finger. He tried to add a second to rub her G-spot and enhance the orgasm, but damn if he could wedge it in. So he rubbed it with one digit, reveling in the sight and feel of her body writhing with pleasure she couldn't contain. Her fair face flushed, and every lush curve of her body undulated with the force of the bursting climax.

Finally, her body released its death grip on his finger, and he lifted his head as she exhaled a shuddering sigh. God, she looked beautiful, flushed and tousled, slightly sweaty and dazed. Utterly sated. His heart thudded out of control—something that hadn't happened to him in years. Xander realized just how jaded he'd become, but with London, it was like he was experiencing everything for the first time again.

How fucking much did he love that?

"How do you feel, *belleza*?" he purred.

"Am I alive?" she barely got the words out before her eyes slid shut and she went limp beneath him.

He laughed as he slowly withdrew his finger and licked it clean. Damn, he was going to have to go down on her again before he was through. He kissed his way up her body. "Oh, yeah. But you might not think you are by the time I'm done with you."

Xander saw the smile float across her face as he dug for a condom from his pocket, then reached for his zipper. London's eyes went wider with every inch of skin he exposed. When he shucked everything and stood completely naked before her, she clapped a hand over her mouth like a virginal maiden of days gone by.

Everything inside him froze. *Virginal maiden.* Was it even possible?

His brain gyrated around in his head as he mulled that over and over. *Fuck.* Was that why she was so unused to kissing or a man eating her pussy? Was that why she didn't shave or wax? Why she seemed so nervous? Why she'd felt so tight around his finger?

The pieces snapped into place, and he rolled to his back, staring unblinkingly at the industrial ceiling. The more he thought about it, the more he knew he'd guessed right. *Oh, fuck!* He didn't have many rules in life—no poaching a buddy's wife or girlfriend, always leave a woman sexually happier than he found her, don't stay longer than a night or two—but the most important one was no virgins. They wanted more than he could give. No, they expected it. A messy responsibility all the way around—one he didn't want.

But London . . . he wanted her *so* bad. How truly important was that rule?

Torn between his logical thoughts and his throbbing cock, he rolled to his side and fastened his gaze on her. "You're a virgin, aren't you?"

Okay, so the delivery of that question wasn't as smooth as he'd planned, but he'd gotten his point across. He also had his answer as soon as she started blushing.

"I-It doesn't matter."

"That's a yes." *Oh, hell. Now what?*

Xander sat up and heaved a great big sigh. Stay or go? Get up or glove up? He felt London's gaze on his back, then she sat up beside him, clutching the comforter against her bare breasts. They still spilled out. And he wasn't going to forget—or stop wanting—her anytime soon.

"It's not like I was hanging on to it for someone or something important. I . . . just couldn't get around to it sooner. I really want to . . . you know. Um, have sex." She wrapped a soft hand around his biceps, and he felt her touch jolt him all the way down to his cock. It still throbbed in protest. *Son of a bitch.*

He shook his head. If she couldn't bring herself to say the word "fuck," she wasn't ready to do it. He disentangled himself and stood, jumping quickly into his boxer briefs and trousers.

When he looked back at her, all rumpled and soft, her lips swollen, her cheeks still flushed, he cursed himself seven ways from Sunday. He wasn't ready to leave her alone. The thought of never taking that mouth, of never tasting her pink folds again, of never sinking deep inside her bugged the hell out of him. But this girl deserved more than a hit and run. She deserved devotion. Xander knew himself too well; he wasn't the man to give her more than a good time.

"You're saying no?" She looked betrayed. "Why does my virginity matter to you? It's no big deal."

"So you're just looking to get rid of it, and I'll do?" He raised a brow at her.

It should relieve him that she just needed a cock and he happened to be convenient. Maybe a girl like that wouldn't get attached after all. But it wasn't relief he felt. Aggravation would be a better description. Absolute fucking fury, actually. So strong it took him by surprise. On some level he didn't want to examine, he couldn't stand the thought of her wanting a penis. He wanted her to want *him*.

Xander raked a hand through his hair. He wasn't making any sense. Fabulous. She'd robbed him of rational thought. Maybe he'd let all the shit with Javier derail his logic. Maybe he was feeling just useless enough that he wanted to mean something to fucking someone.

And maybe he was just losing his mind.

"Yes," she admitted. "Well, at first. But you're obviously really knowledgeable at everything. I mean sex and all." She flushed. "You're fun and nice and sexy. I like you. Why not?"

Why not? Good question. She didn't seem clingy. It wasn't like she knew enough about him to be interested in him for his money. He could totally understand how someone in their twenties would be missing out if they hadn't experienced sex. Hell, he got cranky after a couple of days.

But somehow being merely suitable frustrated him. He wasn't good enough to help Javier, and Xander was so fucking tired of not mattering to the people who mattered to him. And now he was just okay for London. Granted, he didn't know her well enough for her to be as important to him as his brother, but somehow, he couldn't blow off her unintended slight. Nor could he simply let her go.

Didn't that put him between the proverbial rock and a hard place?

"Look, I know I'm not the most beautiful woman ever. It's all right if you're not—"

He silenced her with a scorching stare. Really? She was going to play that card? He'd all but swallowed her whole when he should have realized long ago that something was off with her. But he'd kept plowing ahead, wanting it. No, wanting it from her. Fuck, he still did.

"Not interested?" he asked sharply. "Because being hard enough to pound nails says that I'm indifferent to you?"

She sighed. "I don't know. I've already admitted that I've never done this. Look, I get it. For whatever reason, you don't want to. It's not me, it's you—or what's that stupid cliché? Actually, never mind. We'll just . . . part here. I liked you, and you made me feel really good, so thanks for that."

She backed off the bed, wrapping the big, downy comforter around her, anchoring it with one hand and searching for her clothes with the other. When she'd managed to gather everything, she inched back toward an adjoining door, and her gaze melded with his until she ass-ended her way into the little bathroom.

What the hell was up that she didn't want him to see her back? Why was she still a virgin? Why did he want her way beyond reason?

"Could you do me a favor and be gone before I come out? This is already awkward enough. I can't take more."

Before he could answer, she shut the door.

Okay, now that really pissed him off. Granted, he'd put a stop to the sex, but now that they weren't having it, she was just done? Like she was only interested if he was putting out?

Buttoning his trousers, he charged for the bathroom door and opened it. Time to stop acting like a pussy and start acting like a Dom.

As he walked in, she shrieked and scrambled to cover herself with the comforter again. "What the hell are you doing in here? Don't you knock?"

Her bra dangled from her hand, and Xander was tempted to take it from her and tuck it in his pocket. And he still might, depending on what she said next.

"Tell me something and be honest, *belleza*. If I let you leave here with your virginity intact, will you be looking for someone else to give it to?"

London frowned at him. "You said no. I respect that. I'm not going to bother you anymore."

"Answer the fucking question." God, what was it about this woman that had him coming apart at the seams?

"I-I don't know. Not actively, but . . . You can't think that I want to be a virgin for the rest of my life."

Yeah, good point there. He didn't blame her. He also felt like he'd go postal if he knew that someone else had touched her. Well, wasn't that just perfect?

Xander scrubbed a hand across his face. "You surprised me. I wasn't expecting a virgin. I'm sorry if I didn't handle it well. I think . . ." His brain raced. Was he really about to suggest this? Yeah. Dumbass. "I think we should have lunch tomorrow and discuss what's next for us. I'm not saying no. I like you, probably more than I should. I . . ." He shrugged. "I don't know much about virgins. I've never been with one. I just need a bit of time to think about it."

She sighed, and her shoulders drooped. "You either want me or you don't. And I don't mean physically. I saw that you wanted me that way." She flushed. "What I mean is something different. I don't want your pity, and I'm not expecting you to fake anything."

"I'm not."

And that was the problem. Xander realized that he'd been faking everything for years. Hell, maybe a decade or more. He hadn't fucked anyone who truly excited him in forever. Why London? Why now? He didn't have those answers. Maybe he'd figure that out before he saw her again.

She cocked a head at him. "I don't understand."

"I could be an asshole and fuck you, then never call again. I could take what you're offering without caring how it affected you.

Normally, I could. With you . . ." He shook his head. "For some damn reason, that's not possible."

She shoved him out of the bathroom, which took him by surprise. As he stumbled back, she slammed the door in his face and locked it. What the fuck? "What are you doing?"

London didn't answer him for a long minute, then she wrenched the door open and strutted past him, fully dressed again. She tossed the comforter back on the bed and reached for her shoes, hopping into them. Xander watched her, agape. She wasn't angry exactly, but he had no idea what to make of her mood.

"*Belleza?*"

Looking over her shoulder, she tossed him one last glance. The hurt in her eyes spoke volumes. Then she yanked the bedroom door open and left, her steps echoing down the wooden staircase. Seriously, she thought she was leaving? He usually did the leaving. What the hell was going on?

"London!" he shouted, jogging after her. He caught up to her halfway down the stairs and grabbed her arm. "Talk to me."

"I think I've humiliated myself enough for one day. It was stupid to think that a man as gorgeous as you would actually want anything to do with . . ." She refused to meet his gaze, instead shaking her head. "Look, it's fine. No harm, no foul. We can just forget this happened. W-will you just let go?"

Xander couldn't explain it because fuck if he understood a damn thing that was going on, but everything inside him told him not to let her out the door, to carry her back up the stairs, strip her down, and open her body to him right now. Be her first.

"No." He stood firm. "I won't let you go. And I won't forget. Give me your number. Promise you'll have lunch with me. We'll work it out, because whether you believe it or not, I *do* want you. Very much."

She hesitated a long time, then rattled off a number. Xander whipped his phone out of his pocket and programmed in the number. He recognized the area code as one from the Los Angeles area and froze. Did she know who he was? Know his reputation? Just another mystery to pile on top of the enigma she'd become.

When he looked up again, it was to see her at the bottom of the stairs. *Goddamn it!*

He shoved his phone back in his pocket and took off after her again, meeting her as she tried to unlock the front door. He trapped her body against the door with his own. Her shoulders heaved, and she drew in a shuddering breath. Fuck, he'd made her cry.

Gently, he tried to turn her into his embrace, but she resisted. Xander wasn't about to be deterred. He took hold of her chin and turned her face to him. Oh, she resisted, but he was more determined. Finally, he forced her watery gaze his way. Tears made silvery paths down both cheeks. His heart sank, and he felt like a fucking heel.

"*Belleza* . . . Don't cry."

"Don't worry. It's all me."

"Because I hurt you." He cradled her face in his hand. "I think you're so sexy. I'm already thinking about the next time I can hold you. It will all be different. I'm sorry I fucked this up."

Her chin trembled as she resisted the urge to cry more. Instead, she merely shrugged. "It's all right."

She was done. Absolutely fucking finished for the day, and if he wanted to touch her again, he was going to have to be patient and get his head out of his ass. He'd have to go in with a plan and not hesitate an instant.

"It will be. I'm going to call you tonight, *belleza*. We'll have lunch tomorrow and talk. And everything else, if you still want to. All right?"

With a sad nod, she raised a hand. "Bye, Xander."

Then she was out the front door, striding through the parking lot, and gone.

Chapter Five

LONDON'S head was still reeling as she walked back to her cousin's house. Thoughts of Xander and every wicked, wonderful thing he'd done to her replayed in slow motion through her head. She'd had a real orgasm, given to her by a *gorgeous* man. Sophisticated, charming, experienced, clearly smart. Too tempting to resist.

But she'd been a stupid little virgin. Overweight. Scarred. Skittish. She shouldn't have been surprised or felt as if he'd ripped her heart open when he'd refused to have sex with her. Oh well. Eventually, she'd go out and meet a guy named Bill. Or Alan. Ben might work. Or Tom. Yes, they all sounded staid and responsible and not at all wild. None of them would have seduced her in a strip club and made her go up in flames with that hungry mouth against her sex. None of them would have been experienced enough to have guessed that she was a virgin. None of them would have affected her enough to make her cry.

And odds were, none of them could have made her blood pump or given her coma-inducing orgasms like Xander.

London sighed. She probably shouldn't have started anything at all with him, but if she wanted to break out of her shell and start living, she was going to have to take chances. Still, she supposed she needed to start with someone who wasn't quite so beautiful and so obviously one of the foremost experts on pleasuring a woman. Lesson learned. She was moving on.

It wasn't like Xander would call her or anything.

The afternoon air mugged her with humidity as she put one foot in front of the other toward Alyssa and Luc's place. Her little strappy sandals wore a sore spot along one of her toes, and perspiration started to trickle under the long fall of her hair. The moisture from her orgasm seeped down her thighs. She shoved the thought to the back of her mind.

Suddenly, her phone rang. She pulled it from her pocket and checked the caller ID, happily surprised to see a familiar number. "Hi, Kata. Up for a walk? I'm all for training more for the 5K. I just need to change shoes."

"Are you kidding me? Too damn hot now." Hunter's wife groaned, and London could picture the sassy brunette now, fanning herself. "Actually, I was wondering if you'd found a job."

How would she? She couldn't drive and had no work experience. She was good with computers and had aced accounting. She liked working with people. But apparently none of that counted for much unless she would be content making minimum wage flipping burgers. That was before she divulged her medical issues.

"No," she admitted quietly.

"I might have one, if you have some time for a quick interview."

"Now?"

"The sooner the better."

London pulled her shirt from her sticky skin and grimaced. "I need to shower and change clothes and—" Putting on makeup might be a nice idea. Maybe taming her hair into something that looked remotely professional. Trying not to look like a woman who'd had her first orgasm today. "Can you pick me up at Alyssa and Luc's house in forty-five minutes?"

"Sure. I think this will be a good fit for you, hon." Kata hung up.

And it occurred to London that she hadn't asked the other woman what sort of job she'd be interviewing for. If it was something like shoveling gator poop in the swamps, that wasn't what she had in mind.

She stepped into the house. The stillness told her that she was alone, which fit, given the text Alyssa had sent her earlier about taking her daughter to the doctor. Then she sent Luc a quick message asking him to lock up Sirens since she'd "forgotten." The truth was, she'd been too frazzled by Xander.

Rolling her eyes at her own stupidity, she marched up the stairs, got clean, and dolled up as much as she could in the time remaining. And still, even as her body tingled, she tried not to think about Xander. In the end, he'd be happy not to have to deal with her.

A horn honked outside the house, and London jolted. Time to stop woolgathering.

Racing to her closet, she hopped into a sedate gray skirt and a soft pink blouse with a scalloped neckline and gentle gathers at the waist. It flattered her, she supposed, as she looked in the mirror. But it looked a bit like something her grandmother would have worn.

The horn sounded impatiently again, and London slipped into a pair of supple black leather peep-toes—one of her few indulgences—grabbed the big claw clip from the dresser and rolled her hair into a French twist before jogging down the stairs.

Locking the door behind her quickly, she dashed to Kata's car and climbed into the roaring Mustang with sleek leather seats and a blast of air-conditioning that made her sigh gratefully. "Thanks for doing this. I know it's the middle of your workday."

"I've put in some killer hours lately. They owe me a little comp time." The beautiful Latina smiled.

London fidgeted nervously. "What should I know about this job?"

Kata hesitated, then shook her head. "Go into this as a blank slate with an open mind. You might be a bit surprised, but don't show it. We'll talk afterward, okay?"

"Surprised? What kind of work is this?"

"Secretarial. He's an executive who desperately needs an assistant. You can do this. Forget your preconceived notions. Your boss might be a bit grouchy . . . but you're sweet as pie. It should balance out."

She frowned. Kata wasn't telling her something. A big something. But before London could protest, the other woman turned off the road, into a parking lot, and whipped the car into an empty space up front.

"Take the elevator to suite four twenty."

"Who—?"

"Go!" Kata all but shoved her out of the car. "He's expecting you now."

With a sigh, London pushed the car door open and made her way into the comfortably cooled building. Muzak hummed softly in the lobby. Lush plants dotted two sleek planters made of some shiny black stone with a water feature between them. A granite bench lined the front. The elevator dinged just beyond.

As it opened and a family poured out, London wiped damp palms on her skirt and wandered inside, her stomach a ball of nerves. She could do this. *Smile. Be nice. Focus on your education. Stay calm. Show that you can be helpful.*

When she reached the door to suite four-twenty, she stood in front of it. Barge in? Or knock? It was a public place . . . sort of.

As she stood there nibbling on her lip, the door tore open so quickly, she was surprised it didn't come off its hinges. A scowling man towered over her, focusing in on her with narrowed blue eyes in a swarthy face. Dark hair stuck up at every angle, looking like he'd run his hands through it all day long. The pungent smell of alcohol wafted off of him.

"Who are you?" he barked.

She pressed her lips together to smother a gasp. She was going to kill Kata. This was the hunk who'd been sleeping off his hangover in Kata's guest room. The one reeling with grief over his late wife. The one who had made her instantly weak-kneed. Xander's brother, Javier.

"London McLane, sir. I was told you were expecting me."

* * *

JAVIER clutched the last of the vodka in his hand, the bottle hidden by the door, and stared at the curvaceous blonde. Sir? Yes, he liked that coming from her pretty mouth. His first instinct was to shove her against the wall, bury her lips under his, and kiss her until she begged for more.

She blinked up at him with big blue eyes, looking as if she smothered the shock of surprise. Yeah, he supposed no one expected their prospective boss to be well sauced by early afternoon.

He stared back at the woman. Fuck, what fair skin. She'd turn rosy when she flushed with arousal, when he rubbed his stubble over her cheeks, down her neck, between her thighs as he ate her sweet pussy.

For the first time in weeks, his cock filled and lengthened, as if rising to greet her. With a scowl, he turned away and took refuge in the interior office, behind his desk. He hoped to hell she followed. He couldn't turn back toward her without embarrassing himself.

As he plopped back in his chair and settled his crotch under the desk, Javier was gratified to see that . . . what was her name—Lauren? Lacey? He couldn't remember—had followed and perched herself in the sturdy chair on the other side of his rented desk that had seen better days.

"Résumé?"

She swallowed nervously, then reached inside her big purse to extract a manila folder. Opening it with delicate fingers, she withdrew it and handed it to him. Her scent came with it, something tart and sweet at once. It had a hint of something intriguing. In fact, that described everything about her, especially her eyes with their long lashes and gentle tilt. They had a secret language all their own.

Javier wanted to fuck her.

Instead, he cleared his throat, leaned back in his sprawling leather office chair, and skimmed her résumé. London, that was her name. He set the bottle of vodka on the floor and gazed down the details of her life, reduced to a single, neatly typed piece of paper.

"Why did you get your GED, instead of graduating from high school?"

She raised her chin slightly and squared her shoulders. "I was injured as a sophomore. It required extensive hospitalization and therapy. By the time I recovered, I'd missed too much school to graduate with the rest of my class."

Javier lifted his eyes from her résumé and studied her. So injured that she'd missed months of school? "It sounds serious."

"It was. I'm mostly recovered now."

Mostly. There was something she wasn't telling him. Javier had been in business with sharks too long to fall for her guppy tale.

"Any residual issues that will affect your work performance?" Technically, he wasn't allowed to ask that . . . and she probably had no idea.

"I have some new medication, so I'm hopeful there won't be any problems."

Not a precise answer, and he didn't like it. But he wasn't perfect, either. He should probably send her on her way now, but he'd had little luck keeping assistants. He needed one desperately. Morgan had recommended her.

"I don't see any work experience here." He glanced at the résumé again. It was either that or fuse his gaze to her large, pillowy breasts.

"I recently graduated from college. My schooling was delayed, due to my injuries."

He glanced at her. A bit older than twenty-two, he guessed, but not by much. Christ, that made him feel old. After the year he'd had, he felt downright ancient.

Drawing in a centering breath, he scanned the page in his hand. "I've never heard of this university."

She frowned, and he wished he would have kept his mouth shut. He didn't have a lot of candidates, and none he'd liked so far. But his instinct told him she was different, maybe just what he needed—someone who would work hard, someone he could mold into the perfect assistant. Putting her on the spot was doing nothing but making her uncomfortable. He had to stop prodding her, demanding personal information. He hadn't even asked about her typing abilities, computer skills, and salary requirements. He'd jumped straight to *her*.

"Due to my injuries, I attended a university online."

Javier watched as she crossed her legs primly at the ankles and tucked them under her chair, then folded her hands in her lap. Under that annoying blouse, he saw a hint of her lace bra. She radiated innocence—something he hadn't seen in more years than he could count. Everything about her fascinated him.

Yes, he definitely wanted to fuck her.

And the minute he hired her, that option would go out the window. The last thing a tanking, multibillion-dollar business with cutthroat competitors needed was a sexual harassment suit with its CEO at the center. Even if it annoyed him, he needed an assistant more than he needed a soft woman in his bed.

Forcing himself back to business, he dug through the mountain of papers on his desk that needed filing, then found a notepad. Flipping through the pages, he came to one that outlined the strategy for the prototype of a lighter tactical vehicle that had recently come from their research and development folks. The updated Humvee-style vehicle had ambulance capabilities, was lighter, and was able to travel more than 100 miles per hour, so it was much faster. If they played this right, S.I. Industries would reach the marketplace with this quickly. It wasn't as exciting as the advanced tactical laser technology that Chad Brenner had once created for the company, which had made a fortune, but this new development would still make millions.

If S.I. Industries could get its shit together and release the vehicle before competitors like United Velocity flooded the market.

Javier grabbed the vodka and stood once more, tossing the notepad in her direction. "Everything I've worked on this week has been associated with what I call Project Recovery. Here's how I'd like to organize all the information."

She glanced at it, read mutely, then looked up at him with an efficient nod—and big eyes that made him hard all over again. What would it be like if she knelt for him? Would she look at him like that as she took his cock in her mouth?

Swallowing back his lust, he turned and headed for the door, more to hide his stiff dick than to leave her. "Do you have any questions about what's on the page?"

"No, sir."

Her reply jolted his bloodstream with even more lust. She probably thought of him as a boss or someone's father, and spoke to him that way out of deference to his age. Sweet little London could have no idea that he itched to pull up her skirt, tear down her panties, and spank her pretty ass so he could see it turn red and to test whether that would make her wet.

"Good. I have an empty filing cabinet and a box of folders. Organize the papers on this desk according to what's on this page. You have thirty minutes. When you're done, the memo on the following two pages needs to be typed and e-mailed to the contact name on the bottom of the page. You'll have an additional fifteen minutes for that. Then we'll discuss your performance, and if it's warranted, your salary requirements. Is anything I've said unclear?"

She glanced at the other pages in question, skimming quickly. Then she shook her head. "No, sir."

"Excellent. I'll leave you to it."

In the next forty-five minutes, he could call the nearby liquor store and pay a ridiculous upcharge for another bottle of Cîroc. And on any other day, he would. Today . . . he didn't want to miss a moment of watching her. Sure, he could lie to himself and say that he wanted to see if she was competent and completed both tasks on time—and he did. But mostly he just wanted to look at her. Something about her grace, her big blue eyes, those fucking luscious breasts, her sweetness . . .

As he let himself out the door to his office, he plopped his ass in the vacant assistant's chair in the reception area and watched through the little vertical window with sightlines to the interior office he'd claimed. He hadn't had sex with a woman since before Francesca's death. Free time had been at a minimum for the past year, yes, but so had the drive. London had jump-started that.

It would be better for her if he let the urge die.

Still, he didn't peel his gaze from her as she bustled around his desk, organizing everything. She quickly made folders corresponding to the subjects he'd indicated on the tablet and placed them in the filing cabinet. Efficiently, she grabbed all the papers and began sorting them into stacks, checking his notes for reference now and again. He didn't think she'd actually finish on time; he'd left far too much shit for any one person to classify and file away that quickly.

To his shock, London stood and looked around the room with a satisfied sigh in just twenty-eight minutes. She typed like a fiend on crack and finished the memo in just under seven minutes. He watched as she reread it, fixed his tragic grammar, spell-checked it, then sent it off with four minutes to spare.

Hot damn. A smart one who cared about the work more than her fingernails. Who hadn't tried to slough off because she thought he was too busy or too drunk to notice. This one might be just the ticket.

London made her way to the office door and opened it. Javier met her there. He knew he should take a step back and not crowd her, but the sight of her—even though he'd been watching her for far too long—flattened him like a bulldozer. *Holy fuck.* She really was pretty. Not a model. Not very concerned about her appearance at all, in fact. He'd love to see her in something younger. No sexier. Might as well not bullshit himself.

Stifling his fantasy of the big bad boss bending his secretary over the desk and fucking her brains out, he raised a brow at her. "Did you finish?"

She dropped her gaze. "Yes, sir."

Javier sucked in a breath. Did she have any idea that she put off such a sweetly submissive vibe? Did she have any idea that every-thing about her made him want to rip out the zipper of his pants, climb on top of her, and not come up for air until next week? Xander had been pushing this Dom/sub shit down his throat for months. Hell, his brother had even tried to give him some pointers when Francesca's behavior had first started to spin out of control. But none of it had really, truly sunk in. Javier was Neanderthal enough to admit that he enjoyed the sight of a submissive woman lowering her gaze. It was the surrender of her will, the implicit permission to touch her in just about any way he wanted. What man didn't want that? But when London did it, the gesture short-circuited his brain, and all the blood up there zoomed down fast, filling up his cock until it was really clear which head was truly running the show.

"Very good," he praised, then cleared his throat to rid his voice of the husky tone. "Tell me what you've done."

Nodding, she met his gaze again. "There are eleven file folders in the filing cabinet, each folder with the heading you recommended, in alphabetical order. The appropriate documents are in each folder. I created a twelfth for accounts payable related to the project. If I worked for you, I probably would have made a copy of the invoices and filed the originals with the usual AP stuff, but put the copies with this project so you could keep track of costs associated exclusively with this endeavor."

Exactly what he would have asked for if she'd truly been working for him. "Excellent. And the e-mail?"

"Sent precisely as you requested. I took the liberty of fixing some commas and rearranging a few phrases for clarity. I copied you on the message."

Javier pulled out his cell phone and opened his e-mail. The message in question popped up, and he quickly scanned it. "Perfect."

London gave him a smile, one that spoke eloquently without words that she was genuinely happy to please him. Fuck, if she kept doing that, she was going to wind up bent over his desk, and he'd be ass deep in a sexual harassment suit that would bury S.I. Industries for good.

He should pat her on her head and send her on her way. He definitely shouldn't hire her.

Dragging in a deep breath, he edged past her and sat, shoving his bottle to a corner of the desk, out of her way. Then he gestured to the guest chair across the desk, silently asking her to take it. Primly, she sat, back straight, knees together. What he'd really like to see was her sitting there in a short skirt, sans panties, with her legs spread wide.

He suppressed a smile. He didn't have to ask if his thoughts would shock innocent little London. Hell, they shocked him.

"Tell me your medical limitations."

She swallowed, then sent him a shaky nod. "I may occasionally lose my balance and fall. In the past, I've experienced a few blackouts, but since my new medication, I've been significantly better. I'm only out for a few minutes, at most. I don't anticipate that any other part of my condition will cause you issues, sir."

Damn, he wanted to ask her about this injury and what the hell had happened. It had deeply affected her, he could tell. For such a smart, gorgeous girl, her confidence wasn't what it should be. She completed tasks easily and with aplomb, but her interaction with him was a bit tentative, just shy of jumpy. When he asked her about the injury, she turned stiff. Definitely something there.

"Aren't you going to ask me about my vodka?"

London hesitated. Clearly, she hadn't been expecting the question. "No, sir."

"Do you disapprove?" he challenged.

"It's not my place." She dropped her gaze to the clasped hands in her lap.

"It's not," he agreed. "Glad to hear we won't be having a conversation about it."

"You wouldn't be drinking it if you were happy, but that's none of my business. I would, however, be forced to call a taxi for you if you intended to drive inebriated."

"Because . . . ?"

"I wouldn't want you to go to jail. Or for you to be a danger to others."

Ah, a soft little heart. He liked that. "This job may only last five weeks. If I decide to keep you, it may require relocation."

She swallowed, looking a bit nervous. "I'll work hard to make you want to keep me on."

He believed she would.

"Is this a fair salary to you?" Javier quoted a number that made her eyes widen, and he suppressed a smile.

"Yes, sir."

"Excellent. You'll also receive health-care benefits without any restrictions on preexisting conditions, a healthy 401(k) plan, and three weeks' paid vacation after the first six months."

"Y-you're hiring me?"

It was a stupid decision, given how badly he wanted to fuck her. And he would probably regret it some afternoon when he'd had too much vodka to care about the lawsuit coming his way. But she gave him hope that he could function in this office and make good progress on the projects at hand. The fact that she also gave him an eternal erection was something he'd have to try his best to overlook or overcome.

"HR will insist that you have a drug test first. Give me your e-mail address, and I will have someone contact you with instructions on getting tested tomorrow. Once that unpleasantness is behind us, if you can start Monday, then you have a job, little one."

The smile he expected never came. In fact, she looked downright worried. "Sir . . ."

"Tell me the problem."

"My injuries still cause me some pain, and my doctor has prescribed meds. I try not to take them, but I sometimes have trouble sleeping."

Him, too. But Javier was willing to bet that if they tossed aside the strictures of the boss-assistant relationship, they could work themselves to sweaty exhaustion and get a great night's sleep afterward.

He pushed aside visions of damp, tangled sheets and entwined bodies. "We'll make sure HR and the drug testers know about your situation. Don't worry. Unless I say otherwise, be here Monday at 8:30 a.m. Understood?"

She blinked up at him. Javier didn't think he'd ever get over those lovely blue eyes and their innocence. "Yes, sir. Anything else?"

The demand that she burn that blouse sat on the tip of his tongue, but he bit it back. Since he couldn't quite stop himself from wanting her, even in that sexless get-up, he'd best let her wear whatever old-fashioned attire she had.

"Don't be late."

* * *

LONDON was still trembling when Alyssa picked her up from her job interview a few minutes later. Her cousin opened the car door from the inside and stuck her head out the window. "Kata called me, and I drove like a maniac to get here. I had to hear the news. What happened?"

"He hired me!" London was still pinching herself as she climbed into the car.

According to the paperwork she'd seen and the auto-signature line on his e-mail, he was Javier Santiago, CEO of S.I. Industries. Imagine, someone of his stature wanted to hire *her* as his assistant—and for that salary. It was double what she would have expected. He would be exacting, and she'd earn every penny of it, but for now she was just enjoying the feeling of being employed for the first time ever. She was finally on the road to having a real life.

Having a sex life would have to come later. Xander kept tugging at her thoughts—and other parts of her—but he'd said no. She had to respect that. Besides, slipping between the sheets with her boss' brother probably wasn't smart. Someone would come along. It wasn't the right time, place, or man yet. Yeah, she'd love to have someone as knowledgeable as Xander, but it wasn't meant to be. She'd deal with it. One Mount Everest at a time.

"Oh, sweetie, that's great!" Alyssa practically bounced in her seat. "When do you start?"

"Monday!"

"You'll need new clothes." Alyssa eyed her dusty pink blouse.

London refused to lean on her cousin's hospitality any more than necessary. "I'll buy some things after I've gotten a few paychecks."

"We'll take you this weekend." When London opened her mouth to object, Alyssa shook her head. "You can pay me back later."

London mumbled her thanks, then settled back into the passenger's seat and watched the afternoon scenery go by.

"Sorry about skipping out on you earlier today. Things just got crazy at Bonheur, and after that, Chloe had a doctor's appointment." The little girl, strapped to her car seat in the back, giggled at the sound of her name. Alyssa looked at her in the rearview mirror and smiled. "There's mommy's pretty girl who did so good. Thankfully, she doesn't have a cold, just a bit of allergies."

"It's fine," London assured. "We'll have the next aerobics class later."

"Right after dinner, I hope. I need the exercise!" Alyssa grumbled.

London had no idea why her cousin would imagine that. Her body looked just as slender and sexy as ever. Given how often she heard gasps and groans coming from Luc and Alyssa's bedroom in the middle of the night, she supposed they got a lot of their own exercise.

"That's sounds good."

"Did you lock up Sirens behind you?"

"I asked Luc to. I had to, um . . . leave suddenly." London gazed at her cousin's profile, watching as Lys stared intently at the traffic. "I met someone while I was there."

Alyssa turned a sharp gaze to her. "How? The club should have been closed."

"I'd unlocked the door, using your keys. I didn't lock it behind me, thinking you'd just be a few minutes away." She skipped the part where she'd stupidly stripped on the stage to fulfill a fantasy that would never come true. "As I was getting ready to leave, this guy came in. We talked for a bit." She looked out the passenger window, hoping Alyssa couldn't see how flushed her face had become. "He said that you know him. Xander?"

Lys froze, then slowly eased the water bottle in her hand away from her mouth. "You met Xander?"

She nodded. "He asked me out, but—"

"He asked you out?" Alyssa looked as if she was about to choke.

"Yes." London peered at her cousin. "Is that bad?"

"Wait. A little over six feet tall, wicked hazel eyes, voice as smooth as melted butter? *That* Xander?"

She'd described him perfectly. "Logan's friend, right? Yeah, that's him. But I said no."

Well, that wasn't exactly how it had happened, but she didn't want to discuss the details.

"You turned Xander down?" When she nodded, Alyssa looked downright stunned, then she laughed. "You've got to be the first woman ever in recorded history to do that. I'm dying to know. How did he take it?"

London shrugged. What did she say now? She didn't really want to admit that she'd thrown herself at him and he'd turned her down first. The whole episode had been a bit humiliating. But it wasn't as if she was going to see him anymore. "He seemed surprised, but he was pretty nice about it. No big deal."

"You turned him down." Alyssa shook her head as if she still couldn't believe it.

"Yeah, well . . . I didn't stay after that. In fact, I didn't tell him that we're cousins. If you see him, I'd appreciate if you wouldn't mention knowing me. Things were a little awkward and—"

"Awkward?" Alyssa shot her a suspicious glare. "Okay, what happened? The *whole* story."

He stripped me naked and put his mouth on my pink parts and made me scream with incredible pleasure. Best not to say that. "We had a misunderstanding. Nothing major. I just think it would be less embarrassing if we didn't run into one another again."

This time, her cousin hesitated even longer. "That's probably for the best. He's . . . way too much for you."

Her cousin's words echoed her own suspicions, but it irked London. "What do you mean?"

"Well, if you were going to learn to fly a plane, I wouldn't recommend that you start with an F-22."

"Meaning?" London probed.

"He goes fast, baby girl. To call him a playboy would be a huge understatement, like saying Luc can boil water."

In other words, Xander was really talented. Yeah, she already knew that firsthand. And if he was brilliant orally, it stood to reason that he'd be great with other horizontal activities. Heck, he could probably wow her standing or sitting or . . . The thought made her squirm in her seat. "I see."

"No, you probably don't." Alyssa surged into traffic as the light turned green. "Xander isn't just a rich, very charming playboy, he's a Dom."

"A what?"

Alyssa blinked, looking as if she'd rather not be having this conversation, as if she was having to explain the birds and the bees to a child. London bristled. She was naïve, not stupid.

"A sexual Dominant."

She had only the vaguest idea what that meant from a few books she'd read and some of the conversations she'd listened in on among Luc's friends. But given the deep timbre, the snap in Xander's voice when he commanded her to do something, Lys' words shouldn't surprise her. "He likes to tie women up and hurt them?"

"I don't know his particular kink. I'm sure he ties them up. I've never heard that he's a sadist, just that he likes females in abundant supply and under his control. Probably best that you didn't go out with him."

Probably so, but still she wanted to understand her cousin's insistence. "He just suggested lunch. What could he really do to me in a public place?"

"He's clever. I wouldn't put much past him. If you're looking for someone to date, I'd pick someone a bit younger and less likely to seduce you in the first ten minutes."

London frowned. Hadn't she thought the same thing herself? Besides, following Alyssa's advice would be the cautious thing to do. But she'd been cautious for as long as she could remember, staying in her wheelchair until every specialist had given her the green light to progress, not walking unassisted until her physical therapist had browbeat her into grabbing some independence. She had skipped celebrating her twenty-first birthday in favor of studying for finals and not having to go to a bar where she'd be pitied for her lack of mobility. It had taken her father's sudden death from a heart attack two years ago to realize that life was short and she was wasting hers away by bowing to fear.

"Maybe I want to be seduced," she admitted softly.

Alyssa whipped her gaze around and blinked at her in stunned silence.

"I'm twenty-five. Most people my age have experienced *some* romantic milestones in their lives by now." Before today, the highlight of her romantic past had been a sloppy kiss from Justin Chambers at the homecoming dance in the tenth grade.

"I know, sweetie. I'm not saying that you shouldn't date and experience men, just that . . . with Xander it would be over about an hour after it began."

She was probably stupid to believe that she could handle such a man for even that long. No doubt, ending their brief association had been the right move. "But at least I'd have some experience."

"Oh, you would." Alyssa nodded. "But could you live with a hit-and-run?"

Would it be? Probably. When she'd been the one to insist on leaving, she'd probably thrown him for a loop. But really, out of sight would be out of mind for him. He'd probably never call her. And even if he did . . . Well, that was that.

The only other man she'd like to date was his brother. But besides being her new boss, he seemed like a grieving widower leaning on alcohol to make it through the day. Javier had problems. And she was insane to assume that he would ever think of her as a potential date. Starting Monday, they'd have a strictly working relationship.

"It's a moot point. I said no. Xander has no idea who I am. I don't see why our paths would cross again." She winced. "Except that I'll be working for his brother."

Alyssa's face softened. "I feel so bad for Javier. I don't know all the details, but that man's life has fallen apart in the last year. If Xander has forced him to spend six weeks here to sober up and re-focus on his responsibilities, Javier must be one bottle away from total collapse."

London believed that. The man who had interviewed her today had been hanging onto his self-possession by a thread. London had the feeling that as soon as she left the office, he'd disappear into his bottle for the night. Something about the desperate yearning on his face made her want to save him. God, that didn't sound smart. After her own difficulties, she always wanted to help others climb their personal mountains. But getting too wrapped up in Javier . . . she could already see that he was too proud to want her help. If she tried, she'd only crash and burn.

"Well, starting Monday, my job will be to make his work life easier. Hopefully, that will ease his load some." She was going to be his assistant, *not* his savior. While avoiding his brother.

Not for one moment did she think that would be easy.

Chapter Six

MONDAY morning, Alyssa dropped London off at S.I. Industries' office shortly before eight thirty a.m. She paced the abandoned hallway until Javier arrived a few minutes later, looking completely put together and so insanely hot that he made her weak-kneed. He'd gotten a haircut over the weekend. The shorter style accentuated the slashes of his cheekbones. He'd paired his sharp charcoal suit with a burgundy shirt. Everything fit like it had been made for his body. Given the quality of the fabric and the stitching, it probably had.

He approached her silently on Italian leather loafers, his gait relaxed, just like his smile. She smiled in return. It was a reflex, both because it was polite and because she couldn't not turn her lips up at the gorgeous man. She couldn't read his enigmatic expression precisely, but the fact that he looked almost happy lightened her heart. Maybe they'd have smooth sailing today.

"Good morning." His deep voice pinged inside her.

London hoped Javier didn't notice the little tremor of excitement that went through her. He was her boss. She had to remember that. "Good morning, sir."

Javier handed her a ring with two keys and pressed it into her palm. She blinked up at him in question as he turned to the office door and unlocked it. "The first opens the office door. If you're ever here before I am, let yourself in."

"Oh, that's great. Thank you." The little show of his trust made her determined to truly earn it and be an important asset to him. Granted, he was only going to be here for a few weeks, and she would have to earn the right to keep her job longer than that, but London was determined to do it. If she needed to relocate, she'd figure it out, but at least she'd be employed.

"You won't, however, be staying later than me. I won't have you risk your safety by working in a deserted office or walking in an empty parking lot alone. Are we clear?"

London nodded. Under his drinking and his problems, he was a caring person. She liked that about him. "Of course."

"Excellent. The second key is to my rental house."

She started, peering at him in confusion. She couldn't have heard that right. "Your house, sir?"

His gaze slid away, and he focused on opening the door. "Clearly, you know that I'm fond of vodka. And now that my playboy brother and I are no longer sharing a house . . . well, let's just say that if I ever fail to appear at the office by noon, please come find me. I'll be asking for your phone number and texting you the address in the next few minutes. You don't have any problems with that, I trust?"

London tried to process all that as Javier opened the door and gestured her into the office. Shadows clung, and he flipped on all the lights, chasing them away. She hoped shock didn't show all over her face.

"N-no, but I . . . I'm afraid I don't understand. If you failed to appear by noon, wouldn't you want me to get in touch with your brother? He's family, after all. You barely know me, sir."

"Xander and I are currently not speaking. I don't anticipate that changing anytime soon. I forbid you to call him on my behalf for any reason." And his tone told her that was the end of that conversation. Prying now would be a bad idea. But that didn't stop the vicious curiosity.

"All right."

"You're keeping the thousand questions assaulting your brain to yourself. Good." Javier closed the door behind him and strode across the floor to her desk, just outside the inner office he occupied. "Discretion is a very important part of this job. We're often dealing in government secrets. As such, I've got some NDAs for you to fill out." He grabbed them out of a drawer and set them on her desk in the front part of the office, along with a pen, then he looked at her expectantly.

She followed him, then set down her purse on the corner of the desk. Frowning, she looked between him and the forms in question. "NDAs?"

"Nondisclosure agreements. You are not at liberty to say who you work for, what you do, divulge any information you come across, or photocopy, photograph, or otherwise record in any way the information you see while working here, blah, blah, blah. It's all in black-and-white. Read it and come to me with any questions."

London nodded. "Um, m-my cousin and her husband already know that I'm working for you."

He raised a displeased brow. "Your cousin *and* her husband?"

"Alyssa and Luc? I live with them, and they—"

"Ah, I'd wondered how you knew Morgan. It was too much to hope that she'd worked with you previously or was one of your neighbors." He sighed. "Everyone here is some friend of my brother's. I suppose you know the annoying shitbag, too?"

London couldn't help it. A hot rush of blood flushed its way up her face. "He seemed charming."

Javier cursed under his breath. "I don't want the details. I'll pretend I don't know far too much about my brother's . . . proclivities and we'll leave it at that."

Somehow, London feared that she'd upset him. "I-I don't know him well. We just—"

"I already know. While you work for me, I don't want to hear a word about Xander. Understood?"

She didn't understand it and had the distinct impression that the possibility that she'd slept with Xander upset him. But she didn't say anything more. "Yes, sir."

"Tell no one else who you work for, especially not Xander. I don't need him to babysit me, and I won't let him use you to do it for him. If I find out that you've breathed a word about anything that happens in this office to him, you're fired."

Wow. Okay, then. His words alone communicated the gravity of his command, but the stern expression on his face really underscored it. *Bad blood much?* London didn't understand, and she was just here to do a job. But she had to admit that their intense sibling rivalry bothered her.

"That won't be a problem, sir."

"Very good." He extracted another key and opened the door to his interior office, then turned back to her. "I tried to stock your desk with everything you might need, but take a look around and let me know what you're missing. When you've signed the NDAs, give them to me. Your e-mail should be set up. Please send me a quick message with your cell number and any upcoming doctor appointments you might have."

London jotted down a few notes so she didn't forget anything. "I will."

"For my edification, do you take any medication for your condition during the day?"

She shook her head, trying not to let that feeling of defeat creep in. She'd refused to continue feeling broken or letting her limitations stop her from performing the duties of her first-ever job. "I take most before bed or with breakfast."

He nodded once. "I expect if that changes you'll inform me."

"Sir, even if it changes, I won't let the meds interfere with my performance."

His gaze softened. "I believe you. I simply wanted to watch after you. This job is demanding, and I won't have you sacrificing your health for it."

Inside, she melted. Under all that stern control and intimidating mien, he'd twice shown that he cared about people. It was kind of sweet . . . and he'd probably drop her with one of those razor-sharp glances if she suggested that aloud. "Thank you."

With a nod, he disappeared into his office, shutting the door behind him. She quickly completed all the items on her checklist, stunned by the shiny new laptop and all the first-rate supplies in her desk. He'd thought of everything and then some. The matching desk set looked both feminine and expensive. The desk phone was light and state-of-the-art. Her three-hole punch wasn't mere plastic. With its sturdy metal base, it appeared strong enough to transform a tome into a binder-ready document in a snap.

After sending the e-mail with her phone number, she picked up her signed forms, along with a pad of paper and a pencil, then knocked on his door.

"Yes." From the little vertical window along the wall separating them, she could see that he hadn't even looked up.

Hesitant, she opened the door and walked to the far side of his desk. "Here are the forms all signed. I understand completely."

She set them on the desk between them, and he reached for the papers, scanning each for her signature. "Thank you." Just then, his e-mail dinged, and he looked at his computer screen, a little smile hovering over his lips. "And your cell number. Excellent." He input it into his own phone, then looked at her expectantly. "Anything else?"

"I have plenty of supplies. Thank you, sir. I'm settled and ready for work." She sat gingerly in the chair opposite him and lifted her pad and pencil. "What can I do for you today?"

Javier sighed, then paused, clearly sorting through a mental list a mile long. "The first thing I need in order to successfully work remotely from the rest of the company is a better communication method with some of my head R & D researchers. Find me a secure video-conferencing service that isn't terrible and won't cost me half my fortune, if you can."

She jotted the note. "Any service you've tried and ruled out?"

He rattled off a few names, and she noted those as well. "I'll get right on that."

"Work on this, too." He tossed a file folder across the desk at her. "The head of security is having a conniption about this list of spare system log-ins, but the VP of R & D says they need all these. I haven't had time to sort it all out. Why they're coming to the CEO with their squabbles, I have no idea. Would you also read through last year's statement to our board of directors. Our next one will be due in a month or so. The previous one was a hot mess. Last June wasn't good for me." He cleared his throat, clearly dismissing the topic. "This year, I'm determined to make the report spectacular."

Hadn't Kata said that Javier lost his wife about a year ago? If he'd been grieving, of course the report hadn't been his best work. Why hadn't someone taken that off his plate? "Do you have reports from previous years that you'd like me to emulate?"

"Not really. Put your own stamp on it. I'll give you the name of a contact in our public affairs department who can help you compile the numbers and facts you'll need. She'll work with you to format something. But if it looks or reads anything like last year's, please change everything. I'd like to see a draft in two weeks."

London gave him a shaky nod. "Understood. Anything else?"

"Not at the moment." He returned to looking at the stacks of papers on his desk.

She frowned. "Didn't I file those during my interview?"

"Most of them, yes. I keep referring back to them." He peered closer, dropping his massive shoulders, then pulling back to bring the pages into focus. "But they're damn hard to read."

Hmm. She hadn't had that problem. "Maybe I should scan them for you so you can view them on your monitor and make them as big as you'd like. Squinting at them is bound to give you a headache."

"Good idea." He scooped all the papers up and handed them to her. "When you're done, you can file them again."

"I'd planned on it." She stood and hovered awkwardly. "When was the last time you had your eyes checked, sir? I could make you an appointment."

"I may be older than you, but I assure you, I'm not ancient." His expression warned her not to speak another word in that direction.

"I wasn't—"

Javier cut her off by holding up a single finger. "That will be all, thank you."

She closed her mouth, feeling somewhere between chastised and frustrated. But she couldn't get into an argument with her boss on the first day. Normally, she didn't have much of a temper . . . but at the moment, she resisted the urge to stamp a foot and at least demand that he let her finish a sentence. It was for his own good.

London pivoted on one heel and stalked toward her desk. "Bossiness runs in the family."

"I heard that." He sounded like he was laughing.

Turning back, she leaned into the doorway. "It's true."

Something passed over his face. "You have no idea, little one."

That comment made her shiver. Xander had said something very similar. What the hell did it mean? She had the feeling he'd hidden a wealth of meaning there and that if she dug for it, she could open a proverbial Pandora's box. "Before I work on the items you gave me, should I bring you coffee?"

He gave her a longing look, then shook his head. "Tyler—have you met him?"

She nodded. "A couple of times."

"Yeah, he's been appointed as my personal trainer while I'm in Lafayette. He's . . . an aerobic sadist who's got me on so much organic and natural food, I think my body's gone into shock. If I drank coffee, he'd only have me run an extra few miles."

London tried to hold it back, but it was no use. She laughed. "You poor man. I'm sure it's better for you or something. I'll think of you while I imbibe my caffeinated battery acid."

"If I smell it, you'll regret it."

He tossed the words back playfully, but somehow she rather thought he meant them.

Shaking her head ruefully, she shut the door between them and made her way back to her desk to begin work. The video-conferencing problem wouldn't be solved in ten minutes, but it didn't take her long to find a few viable options. She gathered information from all of the possible vendors, then compiled it, planning to present it to Javier at the end of the day. The folder of security's beefs was a bit harder to understand. Why on earth were they bothering a CEO about extra log-ins to the company's major database that hadn't been deactivated? Someone very zealous in the security department had looked at each account and flagged a few with what he called "suspicious" activity.

Frowning, she called the man, Doug Maynard. He explained the situation. London tried to grasp everything he said.

"Mr. Maynard—"

"Doug," he corrected.

"Thank you. I'm at a bit of a loss here. If R & D is using these log-ins, and they say having the extras is necessary, why are you lobbying so hard to have them taken down?"

"How long have you worked here?" Doug asked sharply.

Well, hell. "Today is my first day."

"So you're not yet familiar with how seriously we have to take security here. We're dealing with government secrets and top-secret military equipment. Many of our projects are for weapons and their systems that won't be seen by others for three to five years, sometimes more. Not only do we have to worry about possible espionage from hostile countries, there's also a genuine issue with corporate espionage. We're a top-tier company in a cutthroat business. We've been the target of many a corporate spy wanting to sell our secrets to competitors. It's not like we're just worried about the KGB or Interpol these days. We've had attempted breaches from everyone from the Taliban to General Dynamics. So our systems being accessed from outside our firewall by untraceable IPs is troubling, don't you think? We have to run a tight ship or we will get our asses handed to us and soldiers lose their lives. The sooner you learn that, the sooner you'll be an asset to this company. Until then, don't question me again."

London sat back in her chair, blinking rapidly. Doug had a point—many of them. But really, she'd had no idea. Her innocent question had sparked a tirade. It wasn't her fault she'd just started today. Even so, shame crawled through her.

"I'm sorry. I didn't know. Mr. Santiago asked me to look into it, and I'm trying to understand—"

"Stop wasting my time," he shouted, and she was pretty sure people in Siberia could hear the conversation. "We need Santiago's authority to pull the plug on these log-ins because R & D has thrown such a hissy. So be a good little girl and tell him that we're doing this to keep the company safe. I already suspect that we've had a few secrets about Project Recovery make it out the door. Tell Santiago that. We've invested millions in that, and I don't care if you have to give him the blow job of a lifetime to make him pull his head out of the past and focus on this company."

She opened her mouth to reply—no idea what she'd planned to say—when she saw Javier standing in the door, looking thunderously angry. No doubt, he'd heard every word of Doug's diatribe.

"Give me that." Javier strode toward her, hand outstretched impatiently for the desk phone currently pressed to her ear.

She muted the call. "I can handle this. I'll take care of it."

"Not this time. Close your ears, little one." He grabbed the phone out of her hand. "Don't be a stupid motherfucker, Doug. And don't ever talk to my assistant like that again. She's been here two hours, and she was following my directive. If you've got commentary above yes or no, you take it up with me. If you suggest one more inappropriate activity between London and me, I'll take your head off personally."

He hung up on Doug, then speared her with a stern glance. She had the oddest urge to apologize, but she hadn't done anything wrong. She met Javier's gaze. "He's really upset that, in his eyes, you're jeopardizing the company by leaving us open to attack—"

"I know exactly what he's upset about, and I'll deal with him." Suddenly, he sent her a considering stare. "This is a high-testosterone environment. There are a lot of loudmouths around here. You can't let them eat you up or you won't last."

A little prickle of fear stabbed at her. "I told him that I hadn't been here long and that I didn't know."

Javier was shaking his head before she even finished her sentence. "With that, all you said was, 'I don't know anything so tell me what to do.' Never give anyone that much ammunition to project themselves as the voice of authority over you. What you should have said was that you simply had a directive and you expected him to respond properly and responsibly. Put any further commentary in writing to you and copy me. Don't get in a dialogue with most of these windbags. They are convinced they're right and nothing you say otherwise will make them change their minds. If you hadn't guessed, I run everything with a bit of an iron fist."

She blinked up at him. That shouldn't be sexy. But everything about him was. The way he protected and watched out for her. The way he tried to teach her how best to survive in this company.

London cocked her head and regarded him with more curiosity than she should. "Do you always help your assistants this much or are you just giving me all this advice because you think I'm helpless?"

Javier stared at her with blue eyes, so dark and focused. His stare drew on, and she had to ignore her pounding heart. Finally, he inhaled sharply, as if he'd reached a decision. "The HR-appropriate response is that, while it's your job to assist me in performing my work functions, I feel it's my duty to make sure that you're given a work environment that's professional and tolerable, so I apologize for my profanity earlier. And I'll just apologize now for any and all of my lapses in sobriety."

Yeah, that was a fairly appropriate response that HR would mostly approve of, minus the alcohol, but she had a feeling that didn't have a lot to do with it.

"And the truth?" she whispered.

He leaned closer, and God his closeness made her downright dizzy. The heady, musky scent of his skin wafted toward her, and she had to hold in an audible sigh.

"The truth." He regarded her with another of those unreadable stares. "Your confidence is lacking, little one. If you work for me more than five minutes, you'll need more spine. I'm troubled by the thought that you don't quite realize your value yet, and I'd like you to see that, first of all, no one has the right to treat you so rudely in the workplace. And second, that you're every bit as smart as Doug. You just haven't had the opportunity yet to learn everything you need to do the job well. That will come in time. I'm hoping your confidence will, too. You're far too smart, efficient, and . . . pleasant not to hold your head high. Next time you encounter Doug or another jerk like him, I expect you to politely put him in his place."

London sat back in her seat, amazed. He seemed to actually care about her. About her self-esteem, her growth, her happiness—at least to a degree. Because he wanted her to succeed? His intent stare made her wonder if it might be something more personal. She felt ridiculously lucky to work for such a kind, experienced executive. The fact that he was incredibly hot was just another perk of the job.

"Thank you, sir. I'll learn and do better next time."

"I know you will. I have faith in you." He stood and glanced at his watch. "Normally, I would take a new assistant out for lunch on her first day, but I have an urgent, somewhat personal meeting that can't wait. He's due here at noon. Please be gone before he arrives. Don't return before one."

As Javier turned his back to her, she reared back and watched him close the door and return to his desk, breezing through his e-mails as if he hadn't just built her up with one sentence, then shut her out with the next. She looked at the time in the lower right corner of her laptop. Ten minutes until Javier's appointment showed up. She should probably get ready to go and try to talk herself out of feeling hurt by his sudden dismissal. It wasn't like they had a relationship beyond boss-assistant. He owed her nothing but a paycheck.

As she put her computer to sleep and gathered up her things, a thirtyish man entered the office, dressed in jeans and a T-shirt that read WELCOME TO SHIT CREEK. SORRY, WE'RE OUT OF PADDLES rippling across his considerable chest. Muscles bunched with every casual swing of his arms as he crossed the floor. Was Lafayette just populated with hot men? The first time she'd come here, she'd imagined it would be all swamp people and lots of crawfish stew. She liked this reality much better.

London gathered up her purse. "You are . . . ?"

"Nick Navarro, private investigator. Javier is expecting me."

"Mr. Santiago is in his office. I'll let him know you're here."

He reached across the space separating them and cupped her elbow. "Wait. Is he sober?"

She sat back in her chair, her thoughts racing. How long had her new boss been drinking? "Completely. I'll be back at one."

"You're his assistant, right?" At her nod, he sighed. "You're new, aren't you? Look, don't go too far for lunch. After I'm done here, he's going to need all the assisting you can give."

The thought of eating her sack lunch at her desk drifted through her mind, and she'd nearly decided to do just that when Javier stepped out of his office. "Hi, Nick. Thanks for coming. London, you may go now. Good-bye."

He stepped back and admitted Nick into the inner office. The door shut behind them again. They shouldn't, but Javier's words stung. After all, his private business was none of hers, but it bothered her that he'd disregarded her completely. She could help him if he'd let her, listen and offer a sympathetic ear. She'd been through tough times, too.

But why would he confide in a girl he barely knew? He'd probably been blowing smoke up her ass earlier with all the talk about her self-esteem. Most likely, he saw her as being barely competent enough to walk across the street without someone holding her hand. She was a warm body he'd hired to answer his phones for five weeks, nothing more.

She would prove him wrong.

Shaking her head, London stood and made her way out the door. There was a drugstore down the street. Javier would likely need a few items this afternoon. She could shop there and eat her sandwich while she did, maybe call Alyssa and check in.

The problem was, all of that only took her twenty-five minutes. Then she found herself facing another thirty minutes or more of hundred-degree heat with ninety-five percent humidity. She even walked back to the office slowly, but made it to the door with half her lunch hour to spare. Javier wouldn't be happy, and she was sorry for it, but she stepped into the air-conditioned comfort of the professional suite with a relieved sigh.

"Say that again," she heard Javier snap.

"You heard me, man." The other man hesitated. "All right. Go on torturing yourself . . . I've identified your late wife's killer as a paid assassin. The images captured on the hotel's security camera match this criminal. His actual name isn't known in law enforcement circles, just his face."

"An assassin? You're absolutely sure?"

"Yep. A French national. He struggles to step foot on European or American soil without being arrested. Disguises don't help much with facial recognition software these days. So he's taken to living most of the year in Cuba. He spends summers in Laos, except when he's working, of course."

"Two huge shitholes. How would this man have met Fran? And when?"

"As far as I can piece together, they met in a bar a few weeks before he killed her. He took a rental house in Aruba that May and probably orchestrated the meeting because she'd already been marked. They became lovers the night they met. She returned home for a bit, and they started corresponding through Facebook. Then e-mails and Skype. She used her next trip to Aruba, ostensibly to hunt for a vacation home and hang out with her girlfriends, as an excuse to see him again."

London watched through the little window as Javier sucked in a breath, reeling back as if Nick had physically hit him. She held a death grip on her purse. Javier's late wife had been unfaithful? Had he known that before today? Why would she cheat on him? He had to be one of the most gorgeous men on the planet. Kind yet commanding. Rich, educated . . . What the hell else had the woman been searching for in a husband?

"The assassin used the alias Jacques Valjean," Nick said.

"Like the last name of that character from *Les Misérables*?"

Nick smiled wryly. "Yeah, that one. Clever, huh?"

She peeked again through the interior window of the office to see Javier pacing. He looked agitated, furious. He grabbed a bottle of Cîroc. It was already over a third empty.

"What else?" he demanded.

"We've narrowed the time of death to somewhere between two and three the morning of June fourth last year. The cause of death was strangulation with a rope, as you know. As best we can piece together, her killer carried her body in a large suitcase down the back stairs, made his way to her rental car, then drove it and her into the ocean."

"And how did he disappear afterward?"

The other man shrugged. "It wouldn't have been too hard. And he was long gone, his lease on his rental house expired, before he became a suspect. Aruban investigators . . . not known for their prompt, quality work."

Javier clenched his jaw, and London's heart ached for him. He'd loved this woman, and while he'd believed she was searching for a vacation paradise they could share, she'd been unfaithful? Strangled and dumped like garbage by a professional assassin? The shock of her infidelity would be enough, but to know she'd been murdered by her lover who'd marked her for death all along. . . What agony Javier must be enduring.

"None of this answers my real question: why? Why was an assassin paid to target Fran in the first place? She was the daughter and wife of an executive. She knew nothing important. If her murder is related to corporate espionage, why not hit the direct target, me? I doubt whoever hired her killer wanted her Versace handbags. So what could he have wanted?"

"I'm still digging for a logical explanation. All I know is that this assassin is expensive as fuck and works in secrecy. He's been hired in the past by some unsavory governments to off high-profile dictators and military officials. But I have no idea who might have hired him to take out your wife. I'm wading through all the correspondence with his Aruban landlord to see if we can determine a real name or permanent address—quietly. I don't want to alert him or give him any reason to trace this back to you through me."

Absolutely not. Fear lumped in London's stomach at the thought of Javier dealing with this cold-blooded killer. She barely knew her boss, but already she was attached—probably more than she should be. The idea of him in danger made her faint and anxious. A part of her wished they would stop this investigation altogether. If Nick dug into this assassin's life to find out who'd hired him, the killer might figure it out. What if he came after Javier?

"I've got another new piece of information." Nick said, his voice thick with tension. "Sit."

"I can face bad news standing, thank you." He took another swig of vodka.

"I think it's a mistake."

"If I wanted your advice, I'd ask for it." Javier raised a brow at him. "Tell me now."

"The Aruban coroner was paid to hide the fact that your wife was pregnant, about four weeks."

London bit her lip to hold in a gasp. He hadn't just lost a wife, but a child, as well? God, no wonder that man was broken. Everything inside her wanted to soothe her boss, tell him that she would help however she could, stand by his side, do anything to help him heal.

Of course he wouldn't care. She was his assistant, not his girlfriend or his lover. Still, she made the silent pledge to herself to try to put him back together personally somehow, just as he was guiding her professionally.

She doubled her pledge to herself when she saw Javier retreat behind his desk and gulp down nearly half of what was left in his bottle.

"Anything else?" he asked Nick. The voice was dispassionate, but she saw the strain in his profile evident in his pinched mouth and clenched jaw.

"Not now. If I make any progress in finding the identity of the assassin or the person who hired him, you'll be the first to know."

"You're keeping this very quiet, I trust?"

"A mouse is louder, man. I promise."

Javier nodded. "Thank you. London will show you out."

As Nick turned in her direction, she scrambled to roll her chair back under her desk. She opened the folder Javier had given her earlier this morning with the complaints about the excess log-ins and pretended to study them.

"You can stop eavesdropping now," Nick said wryly, stepping out of Javier's office and closing the door behind him.

She looked up, grimacing guiltily. "His secrets are safe with me."

"I hope so," the private investigator murmured. "He needs someone in his corner."

London studied the man. Shaggy dark hair, a faded tee, slightly disreputable jeans . . . He didn't look like prime private investigator material, but he was making painful progress with the case. And he cared about Javier on some level. She had to respect that.

"How long have you known him?" she asked.

"About five years. He only calls me when the cases are tough. He'd been cutting through red tape and bureaucratic bullshit about Francesca's murder for the last eleven months. I stepped in a few weeks ago."

"Has he always been a drinker?"

"Never."

London wasn't sure if that was a good sign or a bad one. She let out a shuddering breath.

"He needs someone to care about him, and I'm only answering your questions because I'm hoping you're that person. You double-cross him, and I'll cut you up into tiny pieces and bury you around the four corners of the Earth. No one will ever guess what happened to you."

Nick didn't crack a smile, so she didn't take it as a joke.

"No worries about that. He took a chance on me when he hired me. I already owe him a debt I can't repay." She clenched and unclenched her fist nervously, then decided to go for broke. "Why don't he and his brother talk?"

Shrugging, Nick shook his head. "I don't know much about his relationship with Xander. I know Javier doesn't suffer laziness and excess easily. As far as I can tell, Xander has devoted his life to wine, women, and song . . . and not necessarily in that order."

Maybe that had caused their rift, but she sensed it was something deeper. "Thank you."

Nick thumbed toward Javier's office behind him. "Watch out for him. I have a feeling this case is going to get uglier before I solve it, and he's unexpectedly heavy on the vodka."

She couldn't drive him home since she didn't have a driver's license, but she'd figure it out. "I will."

With that, Nick left. And London sat glued to her seat in indecision. Stay here and pretend that she'd heard nothing or knock on his door and see if she could lend an ear?

In the end, Javier took the decision from her hands. He left his desk, opened the door with one hand. The other held an empty bottle. He swayed on his feet, and he stared at her with accusing eyes.

"You came back early."

"I-I had nowhere else to go. I didn't realize . . ."

"I give you directives for a reason." He pounded his fist on her desk, his face contorted with anger. But she saw the pain beneath.

She flinched, then her temper flared. "I'm your assistant. You picked me. Let me assist you, damn it."

"No cursing, little one. You're my professional right hand. I don't need you in my personal life."

Though he was right, it hurt a little. Still, London hesitated, debating the wisdom of the words on the tip of her tongue. If she wanted to save her own ass, she should definitely shut up now. If she wanted to save his, she had to get brave.

"Are you sure? You need something. Otherwise, you wouldn't have polished off a whole bottle of vodka by barely one o'clock in the afternoon. Would you like me to apologize to you? Fine. I'm sorry I overheard. I'm sorry if you lost a beloved wife and a child on the way. I'm sorry if you're sad or embarrassed or feel like the situation is totally out of your control. I'm sorry you've isolated yourself so seriously that you're relying on your brand-new assistant to help you out of your binge, rather than your brother or friends. I'm sorry if I'm upsetting you even more. But I'm never going to apologize for trying to help you." She reached into her purse and pulled out her baggie of items, slamming it on the desk. "Here's some ibuprofen and reading glasses."

Javier cursed, then tossed the empty bottle in the trash can. "Where the hell did you come from? You're the first person on my payroll in at least ten years who's given a shit *and* had the balls to stand up to me. And you're barely more than a baby." He shook his head. "Everything you heard is confidential."

The intimation that she'd tell anyone deeply affronted her. "Of course."

He swayed on his feet, and she jumped up to guide him into her office chair. He plopped down, the bulky piece of furniture rolling across her plastic mat. He anchored himself by wrapping his hands around her hips.

London went hot all over. Javier Santiago was touching her. Her breath caught . . . just like it did when she remembered the sinful way his brother had put his mouth on her and given her a scream-worthy orgasm. And somehow, she couldn't escape the notion that if Javier knew what she and Xander had done mere days ago, he wouldn't be pleased.

"Sir?"

"Fuck, yes," he practically groaned. "That word on your lips is so sweet."

Something started pounding between her legs, and she feared it was desire. She understood why he'd want the professional deference of her calling him "sir," but his voice suggested that the pleasure he derived was almost sexual. She didn't understand. But she wanted to.

"You should probably let go of me." That was the last thing London wanted, but she would hate to add to his pile of regrets. He didn't need more of those.

He struggled to his feet, feeling his way up by steadying himself on her waist. God, he was everywhere on her, and it took everything she had not to press herself against him. What kind of girl was she that she took pleasure from one brother while also desiring the other? London didn't have the answer. Then one of his hands brushed her breast on the way to her shoulder. The thought dissipated under the heat of his touch.

Javier held her close and stared down into her eyes. "You're right. I should." He slurred his words now. "You're so beautiful, London. Do you know that I spent most of our interview thinking about how badly I want to fuck you?"

Heat blasted her. Her jaw dropped. She blinked, trying to process what he'd said. He wanted to . . . *Whoa!* She really should be insulted or worried or afraid—something appropriate in this situation. But all she could feel was a tingling behind her throbbing clit that spelled trouble.

"Sir, I—"

"You'll call me that someday and mean it when you kneel for me, little one."

Kneel? Like she was praying? "I don't understand."

He sent her a wobbly smile and brushed his body against hers. He tucked his face in her neck and inhaled sharply. The scent of booze wafted from him, but that wasn't enough to suppress her desire. She also smelled his strength, his musk, and his need. Desiring him when he was so nearly unhinged wasn't smart. Wanting to "fix" him now probably put her in the utterly stupid category . . . but she couldn't really help how she felt.

"I know. But if I had my way, you would."

Javier swayed toward her, eyes closing, head cocking, mouth drawing closer to her own. He intended to kiss her? The man she'd encountered this morning would be horrified if he could see him-self now. And as much as she wanted to know if she could soothe him with her kiss, she had a feeling it would only make him lament everything more tomorrow.

"You can't—" She pushed at him, only meaning to put a bit of distance between them.

Instead, he fell back into her chair limply, passed out before his ass ever hit the cushion.

His snoring started moments later, and she stared at him, shak-ing her head. Well, that probably ended the workday. And she couldn't just leave him here.

With a sigh, she found her cell phone in her purse and dialed Alyssa. "Hi. Um, I need help. Or rather, Javier does. Can you come get us? I don't think he should be alone tonight."

Chapter Seven

XANDER prowled his hotel suite. It wasn't the Ritz, and everything smelled faintly like mildew, but that wasn't what agitated him. He gripped his phone, nearly crushing it between his fingers. It was the only way he could manage to resist throwing it against the wall.

London. He hadn't stopped thinking about her over the last few days. The cloud of her pale hair. Her responsiveness. Her plump, perfect breasts. The shy flirtation of her gaze between thick lashes contrasted so sharply with her sexy as hell striptease. The way she'd offered him her virginity so easily, but then given him an invalid phone number—all while looking so guileless.

He'd been trying to both reach her for the last forty-eight hours and find someone who would take his mind off of her. Neither tactic had done a damn bit of good. And he'd had enough.

For whatever reason, he was hung up on this girl. It was a momentary thing. Probably. Like every other woman, once he'd had her a time or two, he'd be over her, right? He didn't want to be the one to take her virginity. He didn't want to hurt her and he didn't want the responsibility. Well, at least logically. Deep down, on some visceral level he'd never felt, he wanted to put his stamp on her, leave some permanent mark on her, and know in that moment she was *his*.

What the fuck was wrong with him?

No idea, but whatever it was urged him to grab his keys and leave his suite, drive across town in the light afternoon traffic. After a phone call to Tara, he verified Luc and Alyssa's address and found himself ringing the doorbell ten minutes later.

Luc opened the door, juggling his little daughter, Chloe. "Xander! Hey, man. Come on in."

As Luc stepped back to admit him, Xander stepped in. He heard Alyssa bustling around the kitchen. "Thank you. I wondered if I could talk to your wife for a moment. I have a question I think only she can answer. It's about someone I met at Sirens."

Understanding dawned on Luc's dark face, and he winked. "She makes it a point to treat her girls at the club as much like family as they'll let her, so she probably knows something about every one of them. But don't be surprised if she gives you the 'mommy hen' speech. I don't think she's recovered yet from Tyler plowing his way through her staff. Thank God for Delaney."

Luc laughed, and Xander tried to follow suit as the other man led him to the kitchen. Alyssa was seasoning meat and searching for a pan in the cabinet under the stove when she popped her head up and smiled.

"Hi! I was going to call you and tell you that your brother is here."

Of all the subjects he didn't want to discuss now. Javier was a buzzkill, one who had made himself quite plain with his litany of "fuck offs." Javier didn't want or need him as a business partner or a brother, so . . . "Then I won't stay long. The other day, I was at Sirens and I met a girl named London. Does she work for you?"

Alyssa paused, frowning, then flicked a glance over at Luc. Then she sighed. "London doesn't work for me. She's my cousin."

Her . . . He sighed. *Oh, fuck.* "I didn't know that."

Alyssa slanted him a stare. "She told me that you met her. You asked her to lunch?"

Among other things. He hoped to hell they didn't notice him turning red, but he felt heat crawl up his face. "I want to talk to her."

The first thing he really wanted to do was make her look at him and explain her rationale for running out and leaving him a phone number for a video store going out of business. The second thing he wanted to do was strip away whatever ugly pants she had on today, toss her over his lap, and spank her ass red. Then he wanted to arouse her to the brink of her sanity, until she begged him to fuck her. Then? Oh, yeah. He'd give her everything she wanted and more.

"We should talk about your brother first. He's beyond drunk. A private eye came to see him, and told him that—"

"Javier isn't my problem. He wants me out of his life, so I'm butting out. I'll hire someone to get him out of your hair and take him home. I'm just here for London."

Exasperation filled Alyssa's sigh, but she shrugged. "All right. Follow me."

He fell in behind the woman, her stilettos clicking across the tile floor as she exited the kitchen and made her way down the hall to a cozy little den off the left. A big chocolate brown sofa in rich leather lined one wall. Javier lay sprawled across its length, eyes closed, looking halfway to passed out. And perched on the edge of the sofa next to him, holding his hand, was London.

The sight of her was a blow to his chest, as if he couldn't find air for a long moment. Sun slanted through the window, creating a halo around her pale hair, which fell softly down her back. She wore a sundress, something brightly colored and beach-worthy, topped with a little sweater. Concern tightened her profile. When the hell had she met Javier, much less gotten to know him enough to be worried about him?

She spoke softly to his brother, whispers he couldn't altogether hear. His first instinct was to rip her away from Javier and kiss her breathless. Another part of him was damn glad Javier was allowing someone to give a shit about him.

"Honey," Alyssa called. "You have a guest."

London lifted her head and looked his way. He sent her a stare with just a hint of displeasure. Her gasp was gratifying.

"Xander."

He smiled, but it wasn't polite. "I tried to call you."

London winced as she unlaced her fingers from Javier's, rose, and approached. "How are you?"

"Honestly? A little pissed off. Why did you do it?"

She dropped her gaze and shrugged one shoulder. "I didn't think it would matter."

"Because you didn't think I would call." Xander didn't ask; he knew.

That pissed him off even more, even as he acknowledged that with just about every other woman and every other phone number, he would have dumped both. Why was London different?

"I didn't think I'd be calling a video store, getting their going-out-of-business spiel."

"I'm sorry." At his raised brow, she rushed on. "Really. I guess I should have had the guts to just tell you that I didn't think seeing you again was a good idea."

"I was just suggesting lunch."

London hesitated, then looked over her shoulder to Javier, who watched them with bleary, half-closed eyes. His brother was drunk off his ass. Again. How fucking perfect.

Alyssa looked between them in the uncomfortable pause, then smiled. "I'll just . . . finish what I was doing in the kitchen."

When the woman slipped out, Xander edged closer to London. "The other day, you wanted more than lunch. I'm willing to give it to you. In fact, I'm dying to."

The words slipped out of his mouth. He still wasn't sure that he should take responsibility for her first experience. But who better? He had very little purpose in life, but he knew how to make a woman feel damn good in bed. Leaving her in inept hands . . . No, he couldn't do that. She'd waited all this time for reasons he still couldn't fathom. He wanted her to enjoy her first experience. And he was determined to have a part of her no other man ever would.

London opened her mouth, then looked back to Javier again. Xander leaned so that he could see her face. Her expression drop-kicked him. She looked at Javier with concern, the softness there so full of kindness. But she also looked at him like he was a god, like she wanted to curl up against his brother, lose her clothes, and give him every bit of herself.

Goddamn it.

Yeah, he could just turn and go. There were plenty of other women in the world, even in this pissant town. He could get laid anywhere, anytime, by virtually anyone he wanted. But he wanted her.

Xander raked a hand through his hair, at a loss to explain why he'd fixated on this little virgin. What was it about her that kept tugging him back?

She was real. She'd said no. And for the first time in a long time he wanted to know a woman beyond her appearance and her preferences in bed.

"You don't have to tell me what you think I want to hear, Xander," she said, turning back to him. "You made yourself clear. I accept that you're not really interested—"

"No, that's what *you* decided. That's not what I said." He cut her off, anger and surprising jealousy brewing. "You surprised me. I wanted to talk to you more, make sure you really wanted sex before I took something from you that I can't give back. London, I went down on you until you came on my tongue. What more would you like me to do to prove that I'm interested?"

She blushed, then cast a nervous glance back to Javier again, who looked on with sleepy eyes. He couldn't be hearing much, and that was just fine with Xander.

"Do you have to bring that up?" London flushed sweetly.

"If you're going to act like I don't exist, then yes. I'm not giving you an easy opportunity to walk away from me again. I want you, London."

"You want a lot of girls, prettier ones. Wouldn't you rather have one more experienced? I think maybe I need someone who's more my speed."

"What? A 'nice' guy you meet at a library or church group?"

"Yeah. Maybe."

Hell if that visual didn't crawl up his back and gnaw at his brain. "Bullshit. Is a guy like that going to make your blood race, *belleza*?"

"That may be what you want, but I'm looking for something more . . . meaningful."

"Meaningful? You offered me your virginity on your cousin's bed like you couldn't wait to get rid of it." He cocked his head. Predictably, she didn't answer. "You're afraid."

"A little." She bit her lip as if that was a hard admission.

He softened. She'd been protecting herself. Clearly, she knew his reputation. And really, he didn't blame her. In her shoes, he would be reluctant, too. That didn't make him less annoyed.

"I understand. Just go to lunch with me. We'll talk." When she looked ready to refuse, he rushed on. "Just talk. I'll set your mind at ease. If you're still not sure or not ready, I'll walk away. No harm. No foul."

He wasn't sure he could keep his word on that, so he'd just have to do his best to convince her. Because the thought of never seeing her again made him surprisingly crazy. He wasn't sure if it was the thrill of the chase he'd never had to give, or because with her he saw the world through fresh eyes. Sex, which had long ago ceased being different or interesting, had been novel with her. Because it had been novel *to* her.

Xander wasn't giving up.

"Take a chance." He stepped even closer and wrapped an arm around her waist, bringing her closer. "If you're worried that you're somehow too inexperienced to be woman enough or some such shit, don't. I haven't stopped thinking about you for days."

Beneath him, her sweet pink lips parted. She blinked, and longing filled those lovely blue eyes. No way he could resist that. He didn't even try.

Lowering his head, he layered his mouth over London's. God, she was everything he remembered and more. That citrusy-floral scent swamped him as her lips dissolved against his like the most sugary cotton candy. He sank into her silken mouth, wrapping his hands in her hair and dragging her closer. A kiss alone rarely got him hard anymore, but his cock was standing up full and stretched tall to greet her.

Jesus, he wanted to inhale London. Her sweetness . . . that's what had lingered in his memory. She'd rolled around in his mind, and he'd half-wondered if he'd imagined her honeyed taste and the cloud-soft feel of her body against his. For years, he'd been fucking females who felt more like tree branches. Girls, not women. London had reformed him. From now on, boobs and hips were an absolute must.

Beneath him, she opened her lips wider, and he greedily drank in every new bit of herself she yielded to him. He thrust his way into her mouth with a hungry groan, prowling, staking a claim. Would he ever grow tired of the way she melted into him? Her submission to the kiss, no matter how hungry it turned, was absolute. With her, he felt ten feet tall. She was so damn perfect. And she made him so fucking hard.

This vertical shit wasn't working, but Javier took up the only sofa in the room. Xander settled for a wall, backing London up against it and taking complete control of the kiss. Then he nipped his way over her neck, his mouth resting at her ear. "You make me so hot, *belleza*. I was an idiot last week to hesitate. I haven't forgotten you. I haven't wanted anyone else—"

London pushed away from him. "Enough."

She panted, wedging a hand between them to rest on the swells of her breasts, as if she was trying to catch her breath. Even that looked sexy as hell, and he'd give anything to have his palm right where she had hers. Which gave him all kinds of great ideas.

He cupped the indentation of her waist and leaned into the plush flesh of her abdomen, letting her feel how much he wanted her. "It's not enough at all. I don't know if I can get enough. I'm dying to touch you. Give me a second chance, and I'll make this so good for you."

He didn't give her a chance to reply before he let his palm drift up. He cupped her breast and thumbed her nipple. She swayed a bit on her feet and moaned softly. Her eyes fluttered closed. Her body turned so pliant against him.

"Xander . . ." She half-opened her blue eyes to him, both vulnerable and damn sexy.

He sucked in a breath as he teased her nipple again with a slow caress. Passion softened her face, shaped by a bit of surprise. She hadn't expected to be this aroused by his touch. She was so new to desire, and Xander wanted to fan that flame until she burned so hot she never thought of leaving his bed.

"*Belleza*, I'll give you so much pleasure." He kept thumbing the hard bud of her nipple slowly, back and forth, marveling as her cheeks flushed rosy. Her lips parted in silent invitation, his for the taking.

Fuck, he didn't think he could wait much longer. Here wasn't the place to take her virginity. Now wasn't the time. But he had to have more of her. He had to see those gorgeous breasts again. Suck them. Taste them. Remind her how good he could make her feel.

One after the other, he tore through the buttons on her dress and shoved the edges of the garment wide. With one hand, he reached behind her to unsnap her bra. It fell slightly away from her body, and her breasts hung free in his hand. The bra still covered her nipples, and the wall, coupled with his closeness, impeded him. Damn. He wanted to see her bare. He wanted that sunlight to slant through the window over her fair skin and light up those pink nipples before he put them in his mouth. He wanted to rip all her clothes away, guide her to her knees, and feed his cock past those pretty little lips.

"Xander," she panted, her voice breathy and slurred.

It was the sweetest sound he'd ever heard. He breathed his appreciation across her skin, a little groan in the sound of her name as he kissed her neck, then brushed his lips down her collarbones, to the swells of her breasts. He eased the bra aside and latched onto her nipple. Hard against his tongue. Oh so sweet. She threaded her fingers in his hair and brought him closer. Yes, perfect. Almost exactly where he wanted her. Supine on a bed would be better, with him between her spread legs. Soon, he promised himself. Very soon.

He pushed the bra down a bit farther, but the sleeves of her dress made removing it impossible. Fine, he'd work around it.

"*Belleza*, whatever you want, I want to give to you. Open to me. I promise I'll do whatever it takes to make this an experience you never forget."

Leather creaked, and Xander heard a roar from the other side of the room. "Get your fucking hands off my assistant!"

Javier. Xander recognized his brother's voice.

London was Javier's assistant? When had *that* happened?

Javi reached between him and London to grab him by the neck of his T-shirt, then shove him against the wall face-first. Xander fought, but his brother was surprisingly strong and agile for a drunk man.

"Let me the fuck go." Xander elbowed Javier, who grunted and loosened his grip.

He turned to find Javier in his face, his breath reeking of vodka . . . and his hot stare all over London's mostly exposed breasts. His brother looked rapt. Javier held his breath, as if he was afraid that moving or speaking would break the spell. London met his brother's gaze, trembling, as if she was both fascinated and terrified. She stood frozen, her heartbeat throbbing in her neck. Xander had no doubt that in seconds, his brother would have his hands all over the breasts only he'd ever touched.

Fuck that. Xander wasn't letting Javier horn in. Besides, the boss shouldn't even be thinking about sex and his employee in the same sentence.

But Javier was definitely thinking it. He raised his hand toward her, heading straight for her plump breast rising and falling with each ragged breath, toward that hard nipple still wet from his mouth.

"Don't," Xander snarled.

His command broke the spell. With a gasp, London scrambled back into her bra, trying to reach behind her to fasten it again. Tears welled in her eyes. And that pissed Xander off.

"You embarrassed her," he accused Javier, reaching over to help her with her bra.

His brother growled and stepped between them, shoving his hand away. "You don't ever touch her again."

It was on the tip of his tongue to tell his brother that London had offered him her virginity, but that would only upset her more, besides being disrespectful to her. "We were talking, and you weren't invited to our conversation."

"That wasn't talking; it was mauling. I know way too much about who and what you are to believe that you'll be good for her." Thunder rolled across Javier's dark face. "You'll fuck London, then leave her for some skanky whore willing to blow you in a bathroom stall. Tell me I'm wrong. Tell me you've never come down a girl's throat while you're cruising at twice the speed limit down the Santa Monica freeway at two in the morning."

Xander couldn't say that he hadn't done either of those things. Seeing red, he clenched his jaw and surged forward, right in Javier's face. "Shut up. This is between London and me. You're her boss. Not her boyfriend. Not her lover. Not her Master. I know you want to control everything and everyone around you. Guess the fuck what? That doesn't work with me. You're the *Titanic*, Javier. You're going down and you won't let anyone help you. I'm not letting you take London with you."

Javier opened his mouth, a snarl already on his lips. A little sob broke the tense moment. Xander looked past his brother, who whipped his head around toward London. Her blue eyes were filled with tears, her nose red, her chin trembling. She wouldn't be a pretty crier. She'd gone splotchy across her chest, her eyes were reddening. His heart dropped.

"Stop it, both of you." She barely managed to choke out the words.

While he and Javier had been at one another's throats, she'd struggled back into her bra and nearly finished buttoning her dress. As the last hint of cleavage disappeared behind the modest cotton, he felt some of the tension leave his brother. Javier wanted her—more than a little. And London wasn't immune. That was a wrinkle he hadn't seen coming. *Fuck*.

"I'm sorry." He reached around his brother to pull her close and comfort her.

Javier remained a wall between them, totally unwilling to move his tall frame. "Are you all right, little one?"

She flushed, looking down. Her body softened. Xander didn't miss her submissive posture. No way Javier would, either. A glance told Xander that, without a doubt, Javier knew that she could—and would—probably enjoy submitting.

"I'm fine," she whispered. "I'm . . ."

London looked as if she wanted to apologize to Javier, but found it too awkward to apologize to her boss for being wrapped in the embrace of the brother he despised. Javier gave an abrupt nod, ending that conversation.

"I'd like to go home. Can you take me?" Javier asked London, never once casting a glance in Xander's direction.

Xander didn't want that to hurt, but it was just another affirmation that his own brother didn't need or want him in any area of his life. London couldn't have been his assistant for more than a day or two. Why was he willing to rely on her and not his own flesh and blood? That mystery aside, there was no way in hell he was leaving London alone with Javier when he was this drunk. And horny.

"I'll drive." He phrased it like an offer, but it was a demand, pure and simple.

Javier whipped his gaze around. "Have you still not learned the meaning of 'fuck off'?"

"I don't trust you in this state with her."

"Bastard." His brother's face twisted with anger. "I would never hurt her. You know that."

"Yeah?" Xander challenged. "What about Whitney?"

Javi flushed an angry red. "I was . . . having an episode that day."

"And you could have one in the next ten minutes. If you want London to go with you, I'm driving."

As Javier opened his mouth to argue, London stepped between them and put a hand on both of their chests. Xander felt her light touch reverberate through his entire body. Lust flooded his veins. Even one small moment with her made him completely hot to touch her, kiss her. Anymore, he had to work up enthusiasm to fuck a girl he'd usually consider pretty. But London changed the game completely.

"It's for the best, sir. You're in no shape to drive, and I can't. Let Xander."

"What do you mean you can't?" Javier frowned.

Embarrassment crossed her face as she dropped her arms away from them both and looked down again. "I'm not medically cleared or able to drive."

Javier's face softened, and he cupped her shoulder. "Is that the reason for your prescriptions, little one?"

Xander's gaze fell to his brother's caress. He frowned. How the hell had Javier known that she took any meds? He hadn't known anything about it himself. Then again, he hadn't asked.

"Yes," she whispered.

"Are you sick?" Xander didn't mean to grill her, but his demanding tone made him wince.

"N-no. Not the way you mean." But she wouldn't meet his gaze.

He pressed a finger under her chin and lifted her face to him. "Does that have anything to do with why you didn't want me to see your back when I had you naked?"

London flushed an even deeper shade of red, then risked a glance at Javier, whose eyes bulged. He looked twenty kinds of furious.

"You dirty motherfucker!" Javi charged at him. "What did you do to her?"

"Stop it!" London screamed. "Both of you. Sir." She turned to Javier. "I met Xander just before you interviewed me. Our connection is personal and will in no way affect my job performance. You've asked me not to bring my work home; I won't bring my home life to work." Before Xander could silently cheer that she hadn't bowed to his brother's pressure and severed their connection, she turned to him, her blue eyes hurt and admonishing. "I don't know why you're trying to convince me that you've, um, changed your mind. Or are trying to stake some claim on me when we both know that your brother is strictly my boss and that you'll move on before the sheets are even cold. Please leave me out of your arguments. I won't be another something to come between you two. I'm going to tell Luc where I'm going. I'll meet you both by the front door."

London exited the room, and Xander couldn't miss that both he and Javier watched her leave. Silent tension thickened the air in the room. They'd both fucked up. Xander had suspected when he met her that, under her sweet nature, she had hidden depths. Now she was showing that she had limits she'd enforce, that she possessed more than a bit of spine. He liked it.

Beside him, Javier raked a hand through his hair and muttered a curse, staring at the empty space she'd just occupied. "I don't want you anywhere near her."

Xander stiffened. "I don't want you anywhere near her, either. But I'm not going to get my way on that. Neither are you."

Knowing they'd just argue again, and that making sure London was all right was more important than whatever had crawled up Javier's ass, Xander left the room in search of her. Behind him, he heard Javier cross the hall into the powder bath and shut the door. *Good.* Maybe he'd have a few minutes alone with London.

Instead, he ran into Luc, who glared at him with a raised brow. "Let's make this quick. London is gathering a few things in her bedroom, and I don't know how long your brother needs to pee, but I doubt it's more than a minute. Quickly, what is going on with you three, and why is my wife's cousin crying?"

While Xander would really like to tell Luc that it was none of his business, that wasn't going to fly. The man would tell Alyssa, who would blow her stack and come between him and London. Time to be blisteringly honest.

"Javier has had too much to drink to be driving, and if London can't drive—can you explain that?"

"No. That's her secret. If she wants you to know, she'll tell you."

Xander's mind flew with a million possibilities, most of them terrible. What the hell had happened? Who would hurt someone so sweet? Frustration wracked him, but a glance at the chef's stubborn expression told Xander that he wasn't going to budge.

"All right," he conceded. "If she doesn't drive, someone's got to. I volunteered. I don't trust my brother alone with London."

"Why should I trust her alone with *you*? We all know you're the king of one-night stands." Luc crossed his arms over his chest.

"London is a grown woman."

"She isn't completely a woman, and you're too smart not to know it."

Of course he knew. "Give her some credit. She may not be the most experienced, but she's smart enough to make her own decisions."

"Maybe, but just so we're clear, I have a huge collection of knives, some very sharp. Others . . . not so much." Luc shrugged like it didn't matter, but tension tightened his shoulders. "With those, it takes a while to slice things."

Xander rolled his eyes and tried not to groan. "Luc, come on, man . . ."

"Seriously? Do I sound like I'm kidding to you?"

Not at all. *Fuck.* "I'm trying to protect London here. Javi is a natural Dom who's been burying his instinct and need under work, guilt, and booze. He's not centered. Before we came here, I paired him with a sub at Thorpe's club in Dallas. He walked off. Just flat left. If I hadn't been there, he would have abandoned that girl while restrained to a spanking bench in the middle of the dungeon. If you're not aware, Logan, Hunter, or Jack will tell you that's *bad*."

"I don't need them to explain, but it's not like London is going to let your older brother tie her down and take a paddle to her tonight."

Something burned his chest, searing, clutching. *Jealousy.* Spec-fucking-tacular. "The way Javi looks at her, he might try to persuade her. Or at least attempt to get her on her back so he can slide between her legs."

Luc raised a brow at him. "She'd have to let him first. London is a really sweet girl."

Yes, she was, but she wanted to be rid of her virginity. And Xander had seen the way she'd looked at his brother. She would welcome him. "I don't want to give him that chance. As far as I'm concerned, she's mine. No way am I giving Javier the chance to steal her out from under me before I've even had a damn date with her." Before he had the opportunity to make her his own.

"London being alone with Javier would only bother you if you thought she was interested in your brother, too."

On the other side of the wall, the toilet flushed. Javier would be coming out soon. He and Luc needed to settle this quickly.

"It doesn't matter." Xander shook his head. "I saw her first."

"That's mature," Luc pointed out.

"I'm not ready to let her go, especially to Javi. He's a mess!"

"Maybe, but I don't think you're ready to be a one-woman man. It would be better for her if you left her alone."

As the tap water in the sink in the bathroom on the other side of the wall began to run, everything inside Xander rebelled. "I can be good for her."

"She doesn't have enough experience to deal with you," Luc argued.

"I'll handle her carefully."

"But you'll still leave her someday, probably soon."

Normally, he'd agree, but now? "You don't know that. Either way, I'm not relinquishing her. I can give her an experience to remember."

Luc cocked his head to one side, considering. "And who's going to be there for her when the orgasm fades?"

"Why are you acting like you're a father and she's your teenage daughter? I've sworn that I'll be good to her. I've said that I'm interested in her. I can't commit to more than that. I only met her about three days ago."

With a bob of his head, Luc seemed to ponder that point, then he changed tactics completely. "You know, I think your brother really needs you."

Xander bristled. "Not to hear him tell it."

"As you pointed out, he's weighted down by anger, guilt, and booze. What the hell does he know? He needs a stable force in his life. If you're not even willing to commit to your own brother, what makes you think you can do any better with London?"

"*Not willing?* I brought Javi here to try to stabilize him. *He* threw me out. Now he's latched onto Alyssa's cousin like a life preserver. But I won't give her up."

"I doubt Javier will, either," Luc pointed out. "You know the answer to this, don't you?"

The tap water in the hall bath turned off. Javier would be out here in seconds.

"What?" Xander asked.

"Share her."

Xander's jaw fucking dropped. He'd heard Logan's drunken rant about Deke and Luc sharing his sister, Kimber, once upon a time. A virgin taken by two men . . . until she'd finally chosen Deke and married him.

"Two minutes ago, you didn't want me touching her."

"I still don't. But you're not going to give up. I saw the way your brother has been watching her all afternoon. He's not giving up, either. London doesn't need to be in the middle of your argument. She's got enough problems of her own. Share her, and when you're ready to move on, she'll probably still have Javier." He shrugged. "No one gets hurt."

Sucking in a breath, Xander's thoughts raced. Did he want to fight to keep London until death do them part? Probably not. Hell, he barely kept a woman longer than a few hours. From now until the day he died should be a long damn time. He could enjoy her for now . . . But sharing her? Leaving her to Javier?

The lock on the bathroom door rattled. He snapped his fingers impatiently, trying to untangle his thoughts as Javier swung the door open.

"You're insane," Xander muttered to Luc, then headed for the front door, determined to beat his brother to it—and the girl.

Chapter Eight

XANDER used the key to open the door of his brother's darkened house. London wrapped her arm around Javier's muscled torso as he leaned on her for balance, secretly reveling in his closeness. Despite what he'd said under the influence of vodka, Javier was too refined to start any sort of torrid affair with his assistant. A man of his stature in the business world would want someone sharp, witty, at the top of her game. His equal. That wasn't her, and she had to get the foolish idea that she could help him—and that he might want her in return—out of her head.

Once inside, Xander flipped on lights. The foyer looked into the living room. Both sumptuously decorated and spotless. White marble floors and expensive throw rugs all added elegance, as well as accented the huge picture windows along the back of the house. They looked out over the pool glimmering in the backyard. A chandelier glittered overhead. The space was every bit as sophisticated as Javier himself.

"This way." Xander directed her through the living room, then down a little hallway. He opened another door, turned on a light inside the room, and stepped back.

London gasped. The bedroom was enormous. A contemporary

version of a four-poster bed dominated the space with clean lines and dark woods. An off-white comforter in a downy, textured fabric covered it. Throw pillows in greens, golds, and rusts decorated the pristine surface. French doors, flanked by two sizeable windows, led out to the patio, lit by the last rays of dusk. Along one wall rested a fireplace. Right beside it, a sitting area with built-in bookshelves gave one a cozy place to curl up with a book or a loved one and enjoy a relaxing evening. On the far side of the room, double doors stood open, leading to a shadowy bathroom. She had an impression of size and luxury. The standing glass shower seemed to glow in the near dark.

"I'll take him. Pull back the bed. He needs to lie down," Xander ordered.

When he came to support his brother, however, Javier balked. "I don't need to fucking lie down. Piss off," he told Xander. "You're welcome to stay, little one."

London gnawed her lip. As tempting as that sounded, it would be a bad idea. She had no idea why Xander had insisted on coming along, but she was both glad he had and worried he could make more waves.

"If you want to go, I'll be fine."

Xander frowned at her as if she'd lost her mind. "I'm not leaving you. I've handled him like this before. I know what to do."

And she had no clue. Sad but true.

"Thanks." She turned to Javier. "Lie down for me, please."

"He's going to be a bastard to deal with until he's had a shower and a meal. I'll get him in the shower if you'll whip him up some soup in the kitchen."

She nodded and turned away. Javier would probably feel more human—and be more like himself—once he'd washed away the drunk and put something better in his stomach.

London made her way back through the house, then groped her way through the darkened kitchen until she found a light switch. As she illuminated the space again, she gasped at the beauty of the modern dark wood cabinets, stainless steel everything, and lovely Carrara marble counters. Everything in the house looked like it belonged in a magazine spread.

It didn't take her long to make Javier something. There wasn't much to choose from. She microwaved some soup, made a grilled cheese sandwich, then poured a tall glass of water to combat his dehydration. Once she'd gathered everything, London rummaged through the cabinets until she found a tray on which to put it all.

Loading it up, she balanced her way to the bedroom at the back of the house and found Xander waiting. The shower still ran in the background.

He took the tray from her and set it on the dresser, then gathered her up in his arms. As he pressed her against that commanding, muscled body, she peered up at him. Her knees went weak. He really was gorgeous and smelled insanely good, too. A bit muskier than his brother. Intense. He kissed that way as well. No doubt he'd make love with that same relentless focus.

Xander controlled himself, holding back the dark side she could feel straining against its internal leash. Even across a room, she was painfully aware of him, but when he touched her like this, she completely melted.

She shouldn't want Xander. He wasn't going to stay with her. He'd probably never fall in love. But that was all right. He'd bring her pleasure and help her see possibilities. That was the most she could hope for.

"I'm sorry about earlier, at Luc's place. I didn't mean to embarrass or upset you," he murmured in her ear, kissing her temple, her cheek, angling toward her mouth.

London reared back in surprise. She'd never expected an apology. Logan's other friends had always depicted him as a playboy who jetted from one bed to another, and often bailed out his buddies from their scrapes with danger because he liked the edge. But the man in front of her didn't seem shallow and adrenaline-seeking. He brushed his lips across hers, the kiss lingering for a heartbeat, opening up something in her chest, before he pulled away with a regretful sigh.

"I know." London couldn't resist filtering her fingers through his soft, inky hair. "It's . . . complicated. I just started working for your brother today. He'd probably fire me for even telling you that. He was adamant about keeping you out of the loop about the business."

Xander clenched his jaw. Something painful tightened his face. "He won't fire you. He might say that, but . . . he's just mixed up right now."

London nodded. "Do you have any interest in the business?"

"Absolutely. I didn't have to get an MBA, but I did, thinking that I could be useful to my brother and the board of directors."

Xander didn't say more, but she could guess that Javier had shut his younger brother out long before now. While she'd like to believe that wasn't the boss she knew, the first thing she'd realized about Javier, after she stopped staring at his beauty, was that he sought total and complete control of everything in the office. In the bedroom, too? Alyssa had already mentioned that Xander was a Dom, and London had done a few Google searches to get an idea of what that meant. But Javier seemed to fit the bill, too. The thought of being at either man's mercy made her absolutely weak-kneed.

It's not relevant. Focus!

London gnawed on her lip and got back to the subject at hand, trying to decide how much to say. Javier didn't want Xander involved. But Javier might *need* his brother. Family, along with their love and support, could save a person. She knew that firsthand. Her parents had been there for her every step of the way after her accident. She might never have pulled through if not for them and the unflagging strength they'd lent her day after day, year after year.

Since the brothers weren't really communicating now . . . maybe she could help.

"Javier might also fire me for divulging what I'm about to tell you. But he needs you more than I need this job. I want him to get better."

Xander cupped her face in his hands and stared down into her eyes, into her soul. "Tell me. Help me to help him. I dragged him here to Lafayette against his will, hoping to find something or someone to make him want to live again without burying himself in work and vodka. I'm out of answers, *belleza*."

Seeing Xander's concern, his heart, London nodded, then explained Nick Navarro's visit earlier and the resulting binge. Xander listened in absolute silence, but she sensed the shock rolling through his body. He tensed, shifted, his face gathering into a scowl.

"Jesus Christ! An assassin? And Navarro didn't even have a theory about why anyone would hire this bastard to kill Francesca?"

"If he did, I didn't hear that part, but did you know that she was pregnant?"

Xander clenched his jaw again, his face stony with pain. "No."

"Your brother lost a beloved wife and their child all at once. And after all that, he learned that she'd been unfaithful and—"

"Is that the story Javier told you?" Xander scowled. "Because that's an utter load of bullshit. They had a corporate marriage. It was a condition of a merger. Francesca was beautiful, but an annoying pain in the ass. Unless Javier wanted to talk to her about Prada or Tiffany, she had no interest in him. They were married six years, but they were more like strangers."

"I never loved her. She knew that, and she didn't care." Javier stepped out of the bathroom with a towel wrapped around his waist and his short hair finger-combed in inky waves against his scalp.

London felt her mouth go completely dry. Wide shoulders bulged with muscle. The hard swells of his pectorals were dusted with dark hair that joined just at the top of his abdomen, bisected the ridges, then disappeared into the snowy white towel. She was dying to know what lay underneath.

The moment she had the thought, London ripped her gaze away. Her boss was telling her something important, and here she was ogling him like an idiot. She jerked her gaze up to meet his. His deep blue eyes held a hint of mirth, but his stern expression made her wonder if she'd imagined it.

Then his words sank in. He'd never loved his wife. *Wow.*

"I-I didn't know." She shook her head. "I just assumed because you're so . . . upset that you must have been madly—"

"No." Javier raised a brow as he stepped back into the bathroom and turned the shower off. "I thought it wise to listen to you two gossip about me so I'd know exactly what you were saying behind my back."

His words made her feel two inches tall. "I'm sorry, sir."

She dropped her gaze in shame. He'd explicitly asked her never to discuss anything with Xander, and she'd violated his trust on day one. She worked for Javier. He'd asked her merely to follow directions, not exercise her own judgment. "If you'd like my resignation, I understand."

"Why did you tell him, little one?"

"Because she's worried about you, jackass," Xander butted in.

"I'd like to hear her say it, if you don't mind," Javier said stiffly, then turned to her. "Is that the truth?"

She still couldn't quite meet his gaze. "Yes. You were so upset after Mr. Navarro left. I genuinely believe that family always helps during difficult times. I don't know you well, but I'm gathering that asking for help doesn't come easily for you. I believe Xander will always be here for you, if you'd let him."

"You don't know him at all, little one. Watch yourself."

"Don't you *dare* go down that road. I couldn't have saved Francesca," Xander snarled. "You know it."

London watched, stunned and blinking, as Javier growled and charged his younger brother, all but bumping chests. How was Xander supposed to have saved the woman? Why were they both so angry? London didn't understand at all, but she sensed they were getting to the heart of the matter.

Javier bared his teeth. "You could have fucking tried."

"You're being irrational about this because it's easier than dealing with your own guilt. You didn't love her and you didn't want to deal with her. Instead of divorcing Fran, you tried to foist her off on me. I might be a hell of a Dom, but she didn't need a Master; she needed a heart."

London opened her mouth in a silent gasp. Javier had *given* his wife to his brother? For what? Sex?

She glanced at her boss, who wasn't denying it. He merely clenched his fists and sent his brother an inferno-hot glare.

"Don't look at me like that," Xander growled. "Fran self-destructed. That's not your fault. That's not my fault. She knew what kind of marriage this was and she still agreed. She made bad choices all by herself and paid for it. You can't take the blame for her shit, brother. And I won't, either."

"Get the fuck out," Javier snapped.

"Fine." Xander gnashed his teeth together. "Do whatever the fuck you want with your life. I tried to save you. I tried to help you. I volunteered to work with you, to listen, to be your rock. You threw it all back in my face. You want to kill yourself with booze? You've made it clear that I can't stop you, so I'm going to stop trying."

Xander pivoted around and stormed toward the bedroom door. London knew, just knew, if she let the brothers separate like this, they stood a good chance of being estranged forever—and that presumed that Javier didn't recklessly manage to end his life first. Her money was on him doing just that.

"Stop it, both of you! You're acting like children!"

They turned identical expressions of gaping surprise on her. It would have been easy to buckle under the weight of those stares, but London stood firm. They'd both unwittingly given her so much just in the span of a few days. If she could help them find their way back to one another, then she'd consider the debt repaid.

"I don't have any siblings," she said, forcing a calm note into her voice. "I've always wanted some. And if I had them, I would love my brothers or sisters no matter what. You're one another's flesh and blood. How much family do you have left?"

Neither answered. The silence was telling.

"Exactly. Is your pride so important, Javier, that you're willing to alienate your only brother? You need to learn to think with your heart a little. I didn't know Francesca, but I know women. If you didn't love her and tried to give her away to another man for . . . whatever, I'd be hurt and do terrible things, too."

"It isn't what you think. It had nothing to do with sex."

She raised a brow. "If you tried to make Xander her Dom . . . doesn't that mean you were giving your brother command of her body?"

The two brothers glanced at one another before Xander sighed. "It's not unheard of in the BDSM community for Doms to have subs they never have sex with. Some subs want and need boundaries. Francesca could certainly have used them."

Obviously. London wasn't going to argue that.

"When she was getting really out of control a few months before her murder, Javier suggested that I become Fran's Dom. He had a contract drawn up, stipulating what I could and couldn't do with her. Sex wasn't included. I would have done nothing more than try to modify her behavior with a series of rewards and punishments, whatever the situation called for."

That sounded a bit like parenting a child. "Were you going to ground her if she misbehaved? Take away her credit cards?"

"I would have curtailed her outings for sure. I definitely would have taken away her credit cards when she acted out. Anytime she mouthed off, I would have spanked her ass red."

London started, her eyes going wide. "Spanked her, as in your hand on her butt?"

"For starters. But that kind of behavior modification only works when the person the Dom intends to top is actually submissive. It's a power exchange. The submissive *agrees* to give the Dominant all her trust and free will. She can stop anything too difficult or painful with a safe word, but other than that, she's handing all authority over her body and will to her Dom. Don't frown. Submissives crave the feeling of being treasured, even owned. A good Master will move heaven and earth to keep his submissive safe, as well as nurture her body and soul."

She didn't understand exactly how it worked. But Xander's words hit her on a visceral level. Yes, she'd fought hard to break out of her battered body, leave her mother's nest, and start a new life. Her mother loved her . . . but she'd known that the woman had carried a terrible burden for her for ten years. It had been time for both of them to move on. What Xander described sounded different.

"The Dom *wants* this responsibility?"

"Absolutely. If he's doing everything right, he gets to watch her learn, blossom, and grow. He comes to know her inside and out, help her overcome whatever fears or blocks are preventing her from truly being happy. In turn, she gives back to him by submitting even more of herself. Bonds between Masters and their subs can get exceptionally deep."

"And you've had this experience?" London almost didn't want to know. It would hurt to hear that he'd taken someone under his wing and cared for her so deeply. But curiosity won out.

"No. I've seen it in action, but my knowledge of a total power exchange, the sort that Javier proposed, is theoretical. I don't have any firsthand experience with a twenty-four/seven relationship. But even that wasn't my biggest concern. Fran simply wasn't submissive. If she didn't give her power to me freely, then I'd just be taking it.

And that would make me all kinds of asshole." He looked at his brother. "Javi, there was just no way I could have saved her."

Javier didn't say a word, just glared at his younger brother.

Though her head was spinning with the intriguing possibilities Xander discussed, London stepped in again. "Maybe you couldn't have saved Fran, Xander, but if she'd believed that someone cared about her, even as just a friend, it might have made a difference."

"Exactly!" Javier added.

"She was *your* wife," Xander pointed out. "You should have cared first."

London couldn't argue with Xander's logic, but Javier's stricken face made her desperate to move on. "Maybe so, but that's water under the bridge now. She's gone. You two are left and you have only one another. I'm not going to watch you tear yourselves apart. Javier, by now you should understand the destruction that happens when you wash your hands of someone who's meant to be in your life. So either start trying to get along with your brother—because you know I'm right—or I'll call Luc to come get me."

Dead silence followed. They both stared at her in stunned silence. Yes, she had a reputation for being sweet as pie, but she had a stubborn streak and temper. She wasn't afraid to use either when necessary.

"Am I staying or going?" She crossed her arms over her chest.

The brothers looked at one another. They seemed to have some silent communication for a long stretch of seconds.

Finally, Javier nodded. "Stay."

It sounded mostly like a command, but London heard a bit of a plea in there. She fought down a smile.

"Please, *belleza*." Xander didn't even try to disguise his imploring tone. "We both want you here."

"Last chance, then," she warned them. "Behave, you two."

They both nodded, but silence ensued. The enmity had drained from the room, but it appeared that neither man knew how to break the ice. It was a miracle they hadn't already thrown down.

"Were you shocked to learn that Francesca was pregnant?" she asked Javier.

Xander jumped in. "You two didn't always get along, but losing your son or daughter must have been a tough pill to swallow. Why didn't you tell me? I know you wanted kids."

Javier sighed, then scrubbed a tired hand across his face. "Today was the first I'd heard of it. I did want kids, but I couldn't bring myself to get Francesca pregnant intentionally. I wasn't convinced she was capable of loving someone more than herself. So I was always careful. Nick said the coroner thought she was about four weeks pregnant." He drew in a deep breath. "I hadn't touched Fran in at least three months."

London gasped. The baby hadn't been his? She stared at him, openmouthed, trying to decide how to respond. With some expression of sympathy? Or outrage on his behalf? He probably didn't want to talk about it at all.

"That's terrible." The words slipped out, but they didn't feel bad. They definitely weren't insincere. "And you had no idea that she was pregnant?"

Javier shook his head. "I doubt she did, either."

"Francesca always acted hormonal and difficult," Xander added. "Nothing in her behavior would have been a tip-off."

"You never liked her." Javier didn't ask; it was a statement.

"Did you?" Xander countered.

Javier shrugged. "Like London said, it doesn't matter anymore." He regarded her. "Whatever you made smells excellent."

Between his naked chest and his information bombshells, she'd completely forgotten about the food. "Just canned soup and grilled cheese. Do you want it in bed?"

As soon as the words were out, London flushed. That sounded far more sexual then she intended. A little smile toyed at Javier's full lips.

Xander gave an annoyed huff. "Put some clothes on, Javi. I'll go out to the car and retrieve London's bag and the stuff she grabbed from your office on the way over."

That was a relief. It would save her a trip. And it would give her a few moments alone with her boss.

She turned to find him disappearing back into the bathroom. The light to the closet flipped on, and he returned a minute later wearing a dark charcoal gray pair of sweatpants—and nothing else. The pants fit too well to not see the outline of his firm, narrow hips and lean backside without any trace of underwear.

Both brothers were put together so well, and each made her feel something different. To her, Javier represented security, protection. Reassurance. But he taught her, too. In a fraction of a day, he'd contributed to her professional growth. Her family had merely wanted to coddle her to the point of smothering, but Javier wanted her to blossom and succeed. And Xander . . . he made her hot, reckless. When she was with him, she wanted the clothes to come off and for him to leap on and show her all the joys of being female. London remembered having boyfriends before the accident, and several had made her fifteen-year-old heart swoon. None had made her long to press every inch of her body against his and plead for his touch. The idea of turning her body and her will over to either one of them made her tingle and ache in some really interesting places.

Javier made his way to the bed, and London followed, grabbing the tray from the dresser and bringing it to him. "If it's gotten cold, I'll make you something else."

He shook his head with a vague smile. She put the tray on his lap and straightened. They were too close, and she almost couldn't breathe. But when she tried to step back, Javier grabbed her wrist and held just tight enough to prevent escape.

"Why my brother?"

"Excuse me?" What exactly did he want to know?

"Out of all the men in this world—hell, in this town—why choose my brother?"

She opened her mouth, but nothing came out. "I-I . . . well, initially he chose me."

"I'll bet he did." Javier sounded bitter about that.

"Why are you so angry? We haven't, um . . . slept together."

"Yet."

"You're my boss." But they had chemistry. She might be innocent, but she wasn't stupid. Javier had given her more than one indication that he wanted her, too.

The possibility poured over her like a landslide of lava. She tried to shove her heated reaction aside. Even if he desired her, was it because he wanted *her* . . . or merely because his brother did?

"Answer my question," Javier demanded. "Why Xander?"

"He's charming. He makes me feel good about me, and I haven't had that in a really long time. When I'm with him, I feel pretty and not like I'm in someone's way or like I should be better."

"That isn't strictly for your benefit, you know. It's a tactic. Make you feel good and special, part you from your clothes. He wants to fuck you."

His words were like a slap. "Thank you for making me feel stupid. Because, of course, no man could possibly like or want me as I am."

She tried to tug his wrist from his grasp, but Javier wasn't letting go.

"I'm sorry. That's not at all what I'm saying, little one. Please . . . I think you're wonderful and beautiful and special. I mean that. With Xander, it's a line. He's not known for his depth or sincerity."

London frowned. "You act like your brother is a sexual predator. He had the opportunity to . . . you know, the day we met. We were in a bed, and I was naked. I asked him to. He didn't."

She could tell that surprised Javier, but he eventually shrugged.

"Probably another tactic. You're talking about a man who's slept with probably five thousand women. You don't seduce that many females without playing a lot of head games."

Five thousand? London felt sick to her stomach and for the first time, she wondered if Javier was right. "Oh my . . . Then why *me*?"

He reared back. "Are you kidding? You're the kind of woman a man looks at and thinks of nothing but losing himself in the soft depths of her body again and again until she never looks at another man."

More shock pinged through her system. "You . . . you haven't thought that."

Javier tugged on her wrist and brought her closer. "Oh yes, I have. From the moment I saw you. I tried to tell myself to stay away. You don't need a broken man. I don't need a sexual harassment lawsuit. What you say or do now has no bearing on whether you stay employed. I want to be clear about that. If you turn me down, you'll have a job."

"Thank you," she said automatically. London had no idea how else to reply. Everything was happening so quickly.

"I want you to think about something. You know how many women Xander has taken to bed. Know how many I've slept with in the last seven years? One."

Another stunner. Javier lobbed them at her, one after the other. "So . . . even though you didn't love Francesca—"

"I was faithful to her until the day she died." He gave a bitter laugh. "Hell, even since she died."

"Why?"

He took a bite of the sandwich, and to London it seemed as if he was looking for something to do, a way to stall, until he could get his head together. "Our father was a terrible skirt-chaser. About the time I turned ten, I realized that he was putting far more energy into fucking his secretary than into caring for his wife, kids, or S.I. Industries. It left a dirty taste in my mouth. I couldn't give Francesca everything I should have. But I could give her fidelity."

London really couldn't breathe now. Javier took a bite of soup. The action was so simple—a direct contrast to the complex man sitting in front of her.

"Why be faithful to a dead woman you didn't love? Penance?"

"Probably." He shrugged. "At first, I was too shocked that she was dead and that she'd been unfaithful. After a few weeks, I got angry, both at her and myself. I was too mired in fury and vodka to care about sex. Then . . . one day turned into the next. Lately, I've been spending all my time warring between being CEO and turning this company around, and drowning my inner demons with booze. They're mutually exclusive, and I've felt torn in two."

She sank to the edge of the bed beside him and moved the tray so she could wrap her arms around him. He might not want her comfort, but he needed it. "I'm here to help however I can. I'll listen and assist with the business. I can talk to you when the need for booze settles in. I'll do whatever."

"Kiss me."

The command came out of nowhere, and the longing to do exactly what he said assaulted her. She couldn't deny that she wanted to feel him, heal him, melt into him. He was broken, and yet she admired so many of his qualities. Stalwart. Some would call him stubborn, but when he believed in something, he gave himself to the cause. And he was faithful.

She doubted Xander would ever be. After having that much sexual freedom, he would always want it, right? London knew she wasn't a raving beauty, but Xander had qualities she admired as well. Persistent, funny, intuitive, willing to stick his neck out for the people who mattered. Maybe . . . he'd never met a woman he could really care about.

God, that line of thought was *so* dangerous to her heart.

The reality was, she admired and wanted them both. She'd developed feelings for both. And she had no idea what to do.

Torn, her thoughts racing, she bent to him, leaned in . . . and kissed his cheek. She'd started something with Xander purely to lose her virginity with a hot guy who would give her pleasure. She'd begun working for Javier with the idea of growing into someone professional and productive that she could be proud of. But she'd never intended to desire them both. Worse, in the span of one day, that desire had taken root and flourished like a weed, tenacious and unwanted. How would she ever choose, especially when either of them could steal her heart—then break it without ever meaning to?

"London . . ." he whispered gruffly in her ear, then took hold of her shoulders and forced her to meet his gaze.

"You're having problems. I think Xander is, too. He's had five thousand lovers. You've had a handful." She drew in a shaky breath and bucked up her courage. "I've never had one. I'm overwhelmed."

Javier sat up straighter in the bed, shock transforming his face. "You're a . . . virgin?"

"Yes. Long story. A lot of reasons. I'm ready to change, but at my speed."

He nodded. "I'd be good to you. I can be damn patient."

"You're trying to steal me away from your own brother?"

Wincing, Javier took another bite of his sandwich, washing it down with the water. "Women are like rest stops to Xander. When he finds one, he hops in, relieves himself, then heads back down the road to find another. You deserve better."

Interesting analogy. "I wasn't looking for a commitment, just sex. But you're still my boss. Mixing business and pleasure . . . not such a good idea."

"It's a cliché. Everyone is different. I know you met Xander first and that he's—" Javier swallowed as if digesting a painful thought— "touched you. He'll find a new girl tomorrow. Me? You're the first thing I've given a damn about in years."

Chapter Nine

LONDON left Javier's bedroom, shutting the door behind her, looking pale and tense. Xander dropped her suitcase and his brother's briefcase right where he stood and charged over to her.

"What happened?" He grabbed her by the shoulders. "What's wrong?"

She shook her head, but wouldn't meet his gaze. "Nothing."

The Dom in him wanted to punish her for lying, but she hadn't agreed to submit to him, or sleep with him, or even go on a date with him. That rankled. Still, he couldn't let her distress slide. "I can handle the truth."

"I'm fine."

Brushing past him, she plucked up her suitcase, then rolled it through the kitchen and the den, then down the hallway to the other two bedrooms. Naturally, she chose the most feminine one, decorated in cream, blush, and plum with lots of mirrors and crystals, hinting at a graceful sophistication. Xander followed.

"I can help you," he insisted. "Let me take what's troubling you off your shoulders."

She stopped, her shoulders losing their starch. "It's just something I have to work out in my head. Thanks, though. The good news is, Javier is finally asleep."

Clearly, she wasn't going to share. Xander tried not to take her lack of trust in him personally, but since he was the only other person in the room, he failed miserably. But pushing her wasn't going to accomplish anything.

"Are you hungry, *belleza*? Can I take you out for something to eat?" Maybe they could talk there. She could relax with a nice glass of wine, and they could clear the air. "There's a lovely French place—"

"We can't leave your brother. How about calling for pizza? I need to look at all the stuff Javier had scattered across his desk and see what's critical or has an immediate deadline."

Not exactly the seduction he had in mind. Xander had gone to Luc and Alyssa's house full of plans. London needed to hear how beautiful she was. She needed to feel wanted. But everything had turned to shit the second he'd seen her clutching Javier's hand.

From what he could tell, London had done all the right things to help his brother. After Navarro's visit and the ensuing Cîroc, her decision to get Javier out of the office had been a godsend. If not for London, what would have happened? Would his brother have found another bottle and finally drank himself to death?

London was right; Javier shouldn't be left alone. Once upon a time, Xander would have happily left his older brother to take care of himself—and everything else. He usually did it so well. But Javi had suffered a huge blow today. Guilt was eating him alive, and Xander knew his brother would take on even more for the life forming in Fran's womb that had been suddenly snuffed out.

But the timing just frustrated the hell out of Xander. He'd finally found London after days of searching. He was beginning to get closer to her and slowly winning her over. Javier now stood squarely in his way. How long before his brother pulled his head out of his ass and came after her, too? His guess was not long at all. Javier felt protective of London—at the very least. After all, she was his employee, but Xander didn't think that was the basis for his brother's care.

The whole situation had thrown him a curveball. Xander had to think fast or he'd lose London before he even had her. Luc's advice suddenly echoed in his head.

Share her.

"Let me help." He nodded to the briefcase.

London looked like she wanted to say yes, but she shook her head as she picked it up, brushed past him, and headed to the kitchen. "He'd kill me."

Xander followed. "No offense, but you've worked there a few hours. I've been around this company my whole life. I own half of it, so your NDA can't actually apply to me. Contrary to what Javier thinks, I'm not useless."

"I never meant to imply that you were." She looked horrified he might think that. Still, she hesitated, clearly weighing the pros and cons in her head. Finally, she dragged the briefcase to the table and set it in the middle. "I know who makes a great pizza in this town. If you call them, I'll spread this out, and we'll get started."

Xander wanted to celebrate with a fist pump. He was getting to spend time with London *and* dig into the family business. Being excited about the first made sense. His *belleza* was gorgeous, and his first taste of her had merely whetted his appetite. He couldn't wait to get his mouth on her again. If she gave him half the chance, he'd spread her across the kitchen table, take off that fetching little innocent-miss dress, and make a banquet of her body faster than she could blink.

But he was also thrilled to finally get a shot to participate in the business his family had spent two generations building. He hated feeling distant and useless. Resenting Javier just wore on him. If the booze had taken his brother under, then Xander was more than happy to step in until Javier was well.

London rattled off the name of a local Italian place that delivered, and he looked it up on his phone, dialing as they discussed their favorite toppings. As he ordered, he watched her spread papers out into neat piles all over the table, occasionally gnawing her lip or making clucking sounds until she'd been through everything in the briefcase.

"The last thing I did before lunch today was talk to Doug Maynard—"

Xander snorted. "He's a douche bag."

"I gathered that right away," she said. "But he had some valid points."

"About the most effective ways to be a pain in the ass?"

London slanted him a chastising stare. "Be serious."

He kind of was, but figured that repeating himself wouldn't win any points. "What valid points did he give you?"

"The log-ins that R & D says they need for external testers and contractors . . . They're being used all over the world. People we don't really know are accessing S.I.'s databases, including the top-secret files that house upcoming projects. Is that normal? I mean, why do testers need to read about stuff that's still in the prototype phase?"

"Yes, and they don't." A bolt of worry jolted Xander. "Let me see." He held out his hand, and London immediately placed a folder in his palm.

"Inside is a list of three log-ins in particular. One has been accessed multiple times from India, the UK, and Dubai. Would the U.S. government approve people in far-flung regions knowing their future secrets?"

"It depends on what they're accessing and the situation." But probably not.

London dug through another pile of papers until she found the list she sought. Quickly, she scanned it, and Xander had to admit that he was impressed. Within a few hours, she'd developed a sense of their business, using nothing more than whatever Javier had managed to squeeze in before Navarro showed up and her own common sense.

"From this list," she began, "I'd say what they accessed most had to do with Project Recovery. Javier mentioned it once. I did some filing for him about it. Sadly, I wasn't able to glean a lot about it yet."

And Xander had heard nothing more than bits and pieces before Javier saw him and fell silent. He knew it was meant to save the company from its current death spiral. He knew it was some sort of Humvee vehicle on steroids, but that's all he'd gleaned.

"Were you able to scrape together anything so we could read about it?"

She shook her head. "I think he keeps that kind of stuff locked up. And rightly so."

Agreed. Xander scanned the list of log-ins and the names of the files accessed, their dates, and the associated IP addresses. "Did you bring Javier's laptop?"

As if she'd already guessed his idea, London sent him an excited nod and pulled the computer from the briefcase. It booted up quickly, and on the second try, Xander guessed the password.

"How did you do that?" London looked amazed. He liked impressing her.

"We may not talk a lot now, but deep down, I know my brother." Grinning, he leaned closer and winked. "I've got other skills, too. Want to see?"

London rolled her eyes. "I'm sure you do. Let's stick to business, shall we? I'm thinking we might be dealing with something important."

Xander groaned in protest, and he only half meant it.

"I think we should start here." London pointed to the paper from security she'd set on the table, which listed all of the log-ins in question and their passwords.

With Javier's computer humming between them, he accessed one of the log-ins and looked through its browsing history through the databases. He saved the last ten files that the previous user had looked at and began to open them one by one.

As he launched the third file, Xander got a tingling on the back of his neck that he didn't like.

"We're in deep shit. Unless I'm way off base, someone is spying on us."

London leaned his way and looked at the screen. Schematics,

exact dimensions, and materials for Project Recovery used so far. The results of a past computer-simulated test and the projections of the vehicle's capabilities, right down to all the latest calculations and innovations, all displayed on the screen. According to the next document he opened, the prototype wouldn't be available for testing until September. Why would testers or other contractors need to know this stuff months in advance?

"As annoying as Doug Maynard is, I think he's right." London looked at him expectantly.

"We need to move on this pronto." The more he thought of someone stealing all of S.I. Industries' hard work and the money they'd already put into the project, which probably already totaled over ten million, the more furious he got.

"Maynard isn't going to take that directive from me," London pointed out.

"And I don't think we should wait until Javier is awake and sober again. That could take hours." Xander looked at his watch. "It's not quite five on the West Coast. I still might be able to catch him in the office."

The truth was, Doug probably wasn't going to listen to him either, but since Xander technically signed half his paycheck, the stupid fucker better strap on his ears real quick.

Dragging in a deep breath, he accessed the company's online directory and found Doug's office number. The man's assistant answered and indicated that he was in a meeting. She'd be happy to take a message.

Xander lacked the time and patience for that line. He didn't care if Maynard was talking to the president or jacking off in the men's room. Whatever it was could be interrupted—if he wanted to keep his job.

"This is Mr. Santiago. It's urgent. Put him on. Now."

The assistant, who sounded all of twelve, gasped. "Yes, sir. Right away, sir. I'll track him down for you, sir."

With a smirk, Xander shook his head. He liked that kind of respect in the dungeon with a beauty kneeling for him. From a woman over the phone clearly about to piss her panties because she feared him? Not his bag.

"She thinks you're your brother," London mouthed.

He muted the phone. "That's the idea. I would have had to leave the proverbial message that might have been picked up on the twelfth of never if I hadn't let her think I was Javier." He shrugged. "Hey, I'm getting the job done."

London hesitated. "I can't argue with that. But Javier might."

"He needs less stress and bullshit. I can make that happen, if he'll just let me."

A moment later, a familiar male voice came on the line. "Santiago?"

Xander unmuted the phone. "Hi, Doug. This is Xander."

An angry huff filled Xander's ear. "I thought you were my boss. I left a meeting to answer the phone for *you*. What for? Need someone on my security team to get a background on a stripper or two you'd like to fuck?"

Anger clawed up his gut, seizing his throat. Xander wanted to reach through the phone and throttle the son of a bitch. "Are you done trying to be a comedian, Doug? Do you want to keep earning a paycheck?"

"You're actually calling me in an official capacity?" Doug gave a hearty laugh, gasped for breath, then started again. "Seriously? Did your brother finally drink himself to death?"

"One more rude comment, one more breath that offends me, and you're fired. Am I clear?"

Doug stopped laughing. "You don't have that authority."

"You want to test me?"

There was a long pause, and Xander figured that Doug finally realized this wasn't a joke. "No."

"Right answer. Those log-ins that your department flagged with suspicious activity? Listen—"

"You've got to let us shut them down."

"That's why I'm calling. This is damn fishy. Whoever is accessing our files through these log-ins is probably selling us down the river. Who authorized the creation of these log-ins?"

"I think Sheppard in R & D. He calls them 'spares' for contractors or temp workers. It's bullshit."

"Absolutely. These log-ins have full clearance. When would Sheppard have authorized this?"

"I'm guessing about fifteen months ago, but the authorization trail is gone. We had a massive virus get behind our firewall a little over a year ago. The paperwork pertaining to these log-ins had been scanned and stored, then the paper destroyed. That's policy. But the virus ate all the files, along with everything on our backup storage system. We've been slowly validating the log-ins in every department, but Sheppard keeps saying that he and his guys don't have time for our pointless exercises."

Sheppard could kiss his ass, too. "So we have no idea exactly who has been accessing our information or why? And if we shut the log-ins down now, we may never know."

"That's not untrue," Maynard admitted slowly. "Damn it."

Xander pondered that reality. He wanted to stop the thieves' access to the internal systems and proprietary information . . . but he also wanted to catch them and nail their asses to a wall. "Can you misdirect them a bit? Maybe take everything regarding Project Recovery off our shared databases for a few weeks?" He looked down the list of dates and times the network had been accessed. Lately, the assholes had been hacking in all the time. "Maybe get someone you absolutely trust in R & D to help you work up some bogus information and insert it, call it the answer to our prayers or whatever? And put some tracking on the files. Let's see if we can catch ourselves a mole."

Doug didn't hesitate. "Sneaky. I like it. Your brother wouldn't approve."

Probably not. Javier tended to shoot very straight. But Xander firmly believed that when dealing with crooks, you had to be every bit as crooked.

"I'm assuming responsibility of this project." He glanced over at London. She looked both proud of him in a way he hadn't seen anyone look at him in . . . well, ever. But she also looked a bit regretful.

"Hang on a second, Doug."

Xander didn't wait for the other man's assent. He simply muted the phone and, with his free hand, grabbed London's. "This is the first project Javier gave you, isn't it?"

"Yes." She started shaking her head, her tone deferring. "It's not a problem. You understand what's going on. You're getting the job done, and that's more important."

"But you're important, too. If Javier hired you, it's because you're smart."

She winced. "That's not exactly what he said."

He stared at her in shock. "Javier admitted that he wants to sleep with you?"

London flushed a sweet pink and nodded. "So I doubt he'll be upset if I don't complete the project."

"He might be, but it's not him I'm worried about, *belleza*. Do you want to be involved? Do you want to learn?"

Her expression told him that she was really reluctant to answer. He mentally counted to five, then intentionally squared his shoulders at her and dropped his voice. "I asked you a question, London."

"Yes, sir."

Well, fuck. He'd never understood all those descriptions of people swooning over the objects of their lust/love/obsession. But he was getting it now. Smart, honest—and so beautifully submissive, London got to him in so many ways. A quick mental review of the last twenty girls he'd taken to bed made him realize that they all had a few things in common: They talked about almost nothing but themselves. They liked his prowess and his money. They had a plastic surgeon on speed dial. They fucked to get ahead or get off, not because it meant anything.

In that moment, he realized he'd never taken a woman to bed because she mattered to him. Sex had been recreation. No, escape. Buried balls-deep in one woman after the other, he didn't have to think about the fact that no one in his life who was supposed to value him did. Not his parents nor his brother . . . Hell, he'd taken two of his teachers to bed as a junior in high school. Even they'd cared mostly about how he looked and what he could make them feel, not who he was as a person or a student.

London would be totally different. She might say she just wanted someone to take her virginity, but she wouldn't touch a man who wouldn't be her lover in every sense of the word.

"Then let's work this project together, *belleza*," he suggested. "How's that?"

She sent him a shy glance, those blue eyes shining with hope. Goddamn, he'd do anything to keep that hope in her expression.

"I'd like that," she murmured.

"All you had to do was say the word."

Her smile beamed with growing confidence. It thrilled him like hell. It also aroused him, and his cock stood up, prodding his zipper, begging for her attention. How he'd love to grab some stolen moments with her, lay her out on the rug in front of the fireplace. It didn't matter that it was June and the temperature was flirting with one hundred during the day. The firelight would make her skin glow as he peeled off one garment at a time, loving each inch he revealed along the way. He'd worship her lips, her nipples, her pussy. He'd caress her waist, palm her hips, and ease his cock inside her deep, deeper, until she stretched to accommodate all of him. Until she knew that some part of her belonged to him and always would.

"Are you all right?" she asked suddenly.

Shit. Business. Doug Maynard on the other end of the phone. Get your blood flowing to the head up north.

Unmuting the phone, he sucked in a breath. "Okay, Doug. Let's implement this plan. Who can we trust to help you swap some of the info on the secret drives for bogus data?"

"My son-in-law. He's solid."

"All right. I'm trusting your judgment, so don't fuck me here. Try to get some really good IP trackers on those IDs. See what else you can dig up internally, have your son-in-law do a little recon on his coworkers, and see if anyone is having financial problems or is disgruntled—anything that might point a finger to someone willing to sell us out."

"You got it. I think that's the right move."

"Keep everything associated with Project Recovery safe. That's your new number one priority, got it?"

"Absolutely."

They hung up, and the pizza arrived.

"Any wine in the house?" London asked as she searched the kitchen and found plates, forks, and even a few veggies for salad.

Xander opened the lid, and heaven smelled a lot like basil and garlic to him in that moment. "No. Just vodka, which I poured down the drain earlier. Javier is going to love me for that."

With a rueful nod, London agreed. Together, they sat back at the kitchen table and ate enthusiastically, still studying the documents from Javier's briefcase. She moaned when she tasted a particularly cheesy bite, and that didn't help Xander's libido. If Javier stayed sacked out all night, how the hell was he going to restrain himself from sneaking into her room and doing his level best to seduce her? Maybe he shouldn't.

She blinked up at him as she swallowed a sip of water, hesitation stamped all over her face. "Can I ask you something?"

"Sure. Anything." Especially if it got him closer to her.

Still, she paused, looking like she was gathering her courage more than her words. "Your brother asked me this question, and I didn't have an answer. I think . . . because there isn't one." She shook her head, as if realizing that she was getting ahead of herself. "Why me? I'm not allergic to Google. I've seen pictures of you with gorgeous models, socialites, even porn stars. Javier seemed to think that you've slept with about five thousand women. Is he exaggerating?"

Normally, Xander would deliver a great line, something slick that flattered her and didn't really answer the question. It would make her feel special in that moment without admitting anything. But with London, he didn't want to do what he normally did. Because, to him, she wasn't like any other woman.

"Probably," he forced himself to admit. "I stopped counting years ago, but . . ." He did some quick mental math. Six girls a week for the last nearly sixteen years multiplied up really quickly. And he knew that some weeks he'd far exceeded six when he'd been doing them in duos or trios, like he had the night before he'd moved out of this house. "He's close."

London gasped softly. Xander forced himself not to flinch.

She withdrew from his personal space completely. "Then I can't possibly have anything you need. I think I'm in way over my head with you. You'll just laugh at me and think I'm a silly, overweight virgin who—"

"If you finish that sentence, I'm going to smack your ass so red, you won't sit for a week."

She gaped wordlessly for a moment, a bit like an earthbound fish seeking water. "I haven't agreed to give you my power."

True, but . . . He turned his best Dom stare on her, nailing her to her chair with one glance. Her breath caught. But he persisted, leaning in, raising a brow, until she finally lowered her gaze to her lap.

"Now you have. Such a naturally sweet sub." He hooked a finger under her chin and raised her gaze again. He caressed her rosy cheeks with his stare. "You're not in over your head. I will never think of you as silly. I adore you at exactly the size you are, *belleza*. You're curvy, womanly, *real*. As for being a virgin, it would be my honor to take that from you and give you pleasure in return. Actually, I'm dying for it." He flashed her a grin. "But that is totally up to you. Originally, you might have picked me to help you lose your V-card. But you're really helping me." He shook his head, trying to explain. "Something's changed for me, and I think it's you."

"Don't waste your lines on me, please."

That irked him, though he probably deserved it. "I'm absolutely serious. If you knew me better, you'd know this isn't seduction mode. It's me talking to you and trying to tell you something I've never wanted or needed to say to another woman. Ever."

London looked away, flustered. "It isn't about me. It's your brother and—"

"I've lived with him my entire life. No."

"I mean, it's the situation with Javier."

Xander turned that over in his head. "No. That's different, I admit. And I owe you for reaching out to him and doing your best to help. But that's not it. I've been trying to do the right thing for him all along, but mostly so I could get back to 'normal,' which I see now is completely fucked up. You've made me think, just by being you." He paused and dragged in a breath, realizing how heavy the conversation had become. And strangely, he was okay with it. "You've made me want to be a better man so I could be worthy of you."

She reared back . . . but her breathing turned ragged and shallow. "That's crazy. You barely know me."

"The little stuff, the idiosyncrasies and quirks, the way you like eggs, whether you prefer baths or showers, no. You're right. But I think I've got a pretty good idea about what's in here." He nudged his hand between the swells of her breasts, easing right over her heart. It was beating a bit faster than normal, and when he leaned in, it picked up speed again.

He smiled.

"You're making resisting you really challenging. You probably know that."

"It would be easy to tell you not to try. But I want you to be sure and ready. As much as I wanted you at your cousin's club, I'm glad I stopped. You deserve your first time to be special."

London studied him for long moments, her blue eyes torn. She finally dropped her gaze to eat another bite of pizza. "I want to believe you."

He'd played this game before. He told lies, and the women lied to themselves about believing his sincerity. It made them feel better about fucking him, and they could cast him in the role of asshole after the sheets had gone cold. But this wasn't a game to London. She really was struggling to believe that she had something different or more special than the thousands of women he'd taken to bed. Xander wished to hell he could put it into words. Or show her. Yeah, he'd like that most of all.

"I don't have the perfect words to make you understand how sincere I am. But I'm willing to talk as much as you need. I'm willing to wait as long as it takes. Everything else aside, we'll work together to keep the business afloat and fix Javier. Even if nothing ever happens between us, I'll be forever grateful that you made me question everything in my life."

London pressed her lips together, her body tense, leaning in his direction. Suddenly, she launched herself at him and closed her mouth over his. Lips so soft, molding perfectly to his. Xander seized the opportunity and dragged her against his body, his cock harder than ever. She whimpered and melted into him, surging into his mouth desperately. London thrilled him in every way. He absorbed her against him, exploring and learning her taste. She might be new in his life . . . but she felt so familiar. Almost like coming home.

His married buddies all talked like that, describing their wives as their anchor, their something to come back to, their someone to live for. Instead of scaring the crap out of him, it revved his blood up even more, and he pulled her closer, wondering if he could get that dress off in thirty seconds or less and claim her.

The phone's shrill ring clanged between them. Xander was all for ignoring it, but London started at the sound and began to pull back.

"I'm so embarrassed." She turned away.

Xander grabbed her elbow with one hand and the phone with the other. "Don't be. Let me handle this, then we'll talk more."

At her nod, he answered the call. It was Maynard calling back to discuss exactly how he'd had his son-in-law doctor the information on the database and how he personally planned to track the IP addresses associated with the log-ins. Forty long minutes later, he hung up and looked around to find London with her own laptop, her long, pale hair in a sleek little ponytail, wearing a pair of shapeless gray sweatpants with a breast-hugging pink tank top. That cinched it; his dick was totally in love.

"You're staring." That obviously made her nervous.

"I'll tell you what I'm thinking." He grinned.

"I can guess, and it won't help me get the draft of this annual report finished anytime soon."

"Last year's was terrible."

"Javier said as much. Why didn't he let you help him if he'd just learned of his wife's death?"

A simple question. The logical one. "I don't know, really. We both fell into our roles long ago. Honestly, I think I was mostly content with mine. Or I told myself I was. I guess . . . I finally realized that you can only have so many parties and so many flings before it's all just pointless. I'm thirty years old. I have nothing to show for it. In fact, I'm probably lucky that I don't have any children or diseases."

Her expression held more pity than he wanted.

Xander scowled. "I'm not looking for sympathy. Being a poor little rich boy, I know. Boohoo."

"So you had all the money you could want, all the material things it could buy." She shrugged. "Who loved you?"

Painful fucking question. The answer blazed across his brain like a flash fire, sizzling him all the way down to his soul. "I'm fine."

"I don't think you are. I know Javier isn't. It makes me want to grab you both and hug you so tight."

Anger rolled through him. Xander hated this defensive feeling, but there was no fighting it. "I don't need your pity."

She reared back in her seat and shook her head at him. "That's not it at all. I don't feel sorry for you. I just want you both to see how much joy loving and being loved can bring. My parents loved me unconditionally. We didn't have a lot, but they would have done anything for me. I had great friends. I even had a cat who followed me everywhere, a male Siamese named Merlin. I didn't need designer clothes or a bunch of diamonds to feel rich. I really wish you guys could know that feeling of belonging somewhere because you're treasured by the people around you."

God, she just kept digging that knife deeper. He'd never had that, and the longer she talked about the warmth and sense of belonging that love provided, the more he wanted it. Desperately. Like an addict craving a fix.

And suddenly everything snapped into place. He was falling in love with this girl he'd known for a handful of days, whom he hadn't slept with, one who was both innocent and wise, because she centered him. He looked at her and suddenly understood exactly what he'd been missing. What he could no longer live without.

Xander stared, wondering how the hell his whole world had tilted on its axis in the span of seventy-two hours. Fuck it. That didn't matter. What did matter was figuring out how to get closer to her, make her want him, depend on him, never want to leave him. She was tenderness and sunshine, and for the first time in his life, he was dying to feel it fill him up.

"I'd like that, too," he whispered.

Chapter Ten

SOMEWHERE around three a.m., Xander told London to close up the laptop and go to bed. He would have liked to slide in beside her and have her warm curves pressed against him, but she looked exhausted. After helping her as she worked so diligently and intuitively on the annual report for the last six hours so the board and employees would have a perfect grasp of where the company stood—and proving just how damn smart she was—London deserved her rest. Sure, he'd answered questions, and they had debated exactly what to say and how to say it, but she'd carefully crafted just the right words and created just the right visuals. He was damn impressed with her and he'd said so.

Xander stayed up another hour scanning the results and the few numbers she'd received from the public affairs department. Things were dismal. Orders were down more than twenty percent for most of their existing military hardware. Their competitors had made a lot of strides in the last year, while Javier had been drowning his grief and guilt. Thankfully, sales for their advanced tactical laser technology had been holding steady and keeping them afloat. But after tonight, a few things had become crystal clear, and he'd be talking to his older brother soon.

With a turn in at four in the morning, he wasn't thrilled to hear someone pounding on the door just before seven, then ringing the doorbell in quick succession when no one answered immediately. What the fuck?

Xander stumbled from bed, into the hallway, and to the front door. He hoped the asshole didn't mind if he answered the door in his boxer-briefs, but at this point, he didn't really give a shit.

He unlocked the door, then wrenched it open with a scowl. Xander wasn't exactly sure who he expected on the other side—a nosy neighbor, the paperboy, a corporate spy—but he was wrong on all counts.

"Logan!" His frown turned up into a smile. "Man, it's good to see you."

Logan Edgington stepped into the house, and the two friends shared a handshake and shoulder bump that quickly turned to a full-blown hug.

"When did you get in?" Xander asked, stepping back to let Logan in and shutting the door behind him.

"Last night. It's good to be home. I was thrilled when Tara told me you'd come to Lafayette."

"What brings you here? You just stop by to see little ol' me?"

"You wish." Logan rolled his eyes. "I told Tyler I'd relieve him of Javier's PT this morning since Del had to go into work early and left him with the kids. How is your brother?"

"About the same as the last e-mail I sent you." He shrugged. "One day at a time, you know?"

Logan nodded. "Absolutely. You don't look so hot yourself."

"I've had three hours of sleep, you sadistic bastard. Don't you know how to sleep in?"

His buddy laughed, and Xander rolled his eyes.

"If I was nice, I'd let you go back to bed and I'd return later. But nah. You get to deal with me now. Why don't you put some clothes on, dude? I'll make coffee."

Normally, Xander would give Logan shit about being a morning person and a pain in the ass, but he hadn't seen his friend in months. Putting up with a little fatigue to see his best friend was no hardship.

"On it." He hustled off to do exactly as Logan suggested, brushing his teeth before throwing on yesterday's pants. Then he headed back to the kitchen.

"Damn, it's good to see you. How long is your leave?" Xander asked, strolling into the kitchen.

"Technically, it's two weeks." Logan hesitated. "But I'm thinking of leaving the teams."

"*What?*" Xander blinked. Logan had been a SEAL for as long as they'd been friends. Until Logan married two years ago, he'd lived, eaten, breathed everything navy. He was a frogman through and through.

"Don't tell me you're getting soft," Xander joked. Hell, he wasn't sure what was running through Logan's head.

"Tara is pregnant."

Shock hit Xander quickly. He probably shouldn't be that surprised. Logan was completely smitten with his pretty redheaded wife and had been since he'd been her high school sweetheart. Tara was smart and funny—and perfect for Logan in every way. He'd known it was just a matter of time before they started having kids.

What surprised Xander most was that right after the surprise, jealousy blazed through his veins, quick and hot. Logan had everything a man could want: love, commitment, a caring family, good friends, and now a little one on the way. Logan might not have a ton of money, but Xander was living proof that millions couldn't buy the things that were most valuable in life.

"Congratulations, man!" He slapped Logan on the back. "You've got to be thrilled."

He nodded enthusiastically, but his expression was pensive. "Yeah. Tara didn't breathe a word about me leaving the teams, but I don't want her to raise our children alone. My mom did that, and she was miserable. I don't want to come home in a pine box, either. She needs me now. And I'm thirty, man. I'm getting old for this game."

Xander nodded, silently conceding Logan's point. "How do you feel about a career change? I thought you'd be career navy."

Logan dragged in a deep breath, obviously mentally grasping for words. "A bit sad, but I knew it had to end someday. I've loved serving my country. It's something I'll always be proud of. But maybe this is for the best. The timing is right. Just before I reconnected with Tara, they extended my last commission by an extra two years. Because who doesn't think Afghanistan is paradise, right?" He rolled his eyes. "So technically I could be free in a few weeks and take a civilian job."

But he didn't sound thrilled. "You're built for adrenaline."

His sigh spoke volumes. "I love what I do, but I love Tara more. I'm going to be a father come January." He grinned wryly. "I have a feeling that will be an adventure all its own."

"No doubt." Everyone seemed to be making their life an adventure these days, himself included.

"So where is your brother? I'd like to work his ass to a nub, then come back so we can hang out for a bit."

"In bed. Good luck working through the hangover."

Logan scowled. "So he's still drinking too much?"

"Yep," Xander said regretfully. "I've got no idea how to make him stop."

London emerged from the hallway and into the kitchen then, looking sweetly rumpled, her pale hair a cloud caressing her shoulders and hanging to the small of her back. That tight pink tank top made his morning wood rise all over again, and though she didn't have on a drop of makeup and wasn't wearing anything remotely sexy, Xander was still dying to touch her.

She caught sight of him and Logan sitting around the coffee cups and halted. "Morning. Hi, Logan."

Even that cute little blush crawling up her cheeks turned him on.

He'd love to give her something to blush about. He wondered what she'd say if she knew that he'd gone to bed last night and had to jack off to keep himself from sneaking into her bedroom and seducing her out of those clothes and under his body.

"Hi, yourself, London," Logan returned.

She sent him a faint smile of greeting. "It's good to see you."

"You, too. How are you, hon?"

"Good. Better, actually. How about you?"

"Great."

"Nice to have you home." Her soft voice wound gently through the room before she headed for the coffeepot.

Logan shot Xander a very sharp glare with a raised brow. It asked point-blank if he was sleeping with her.

Quickly, she poured a cup of coffee. Twisting her hair over one shoulder, she smiled shyly at them both. "I'm going to see if Javier is awake. He should know what happened last night."

And with that, she exited the kitchen. She hadn't even cleared the room yet before Logan sent him another questioning stare.

"What happened last night? Are you fucking kidding me?" Logan whispered furiously. "Alyssa's cousin? Dude, that's not cool. She's so innocent. She can't possibly play your games."

It would be easy to shut Logan up with the convenient part of the truth. "Relax. I haven't slept with her. Not for lack of trying."

"She's a virgin; I'd bet my life."

Xander nodded. "I'm giving her all the time and space she needs."

"You should just keep your distance. You know I love you like a brother, but she needs someone who will care about her, be there for her in the long run, and—"

"I think I'm in love with her."

"Are you fucking . . . whoa." Logan shifted on his stool. "Have you ever thought that in your life about any woman?"

"Nope." Xander swallowed, and realizing how much of his life he'd wasted felt like trying to choke down a big ball of regret. "She doesn't exactly trust me. Javier decided that she needed to know my 'number.'"

"Ouch!" Logan winced. "Do *you* even know your number?"

"Not exactly. A bunch." He shrugged. "But London is different. She's got a big heart. She cares about the people in her life. Everything about her is genuine. She likes me. But . . ." How the hell did he confess what came next? Who would believe that the man who'd rarely ever been told no would finally meet the woman he wasn't sure he could live without, only to find she was hung up on his own brother? "I think she has deeper feelings for Javier. It hurts like a bitch, and if I let her walk out the door, I'd survive, but I think it would hurt a shitload more than I even want to imagine."

"Wow, so this isn't just about her boobs?"

"No." He forced a grin. "But they are admittedly great."

"Horndog."

Xander shrugged. "I haven't slept with anyone else since I met her. Granted, that's only a few days."

"But for you, that's a feat."

"Exactly. That should tell you how serious I am."

Logan took a swig of coffee, clearly pondering the situation. "So . . . you're thinking that she's going to choose Javier?"

"There's a good chance."

He stared down into the black depths of his coffee. It smelled rich and tasted like ash on his tongue. He glanced toward the door to the master bedroom, but it was closed. And knowing that she went to his brother first, that she'd locked herself behind that door with him on purpose, hurt like a motherfucker.

"What are you going to do?"

Xander shrugged. "No clue. Luc thinks we should share her."

"Does Alyssa know her husband came up with *that* idea?"

He had to laugh. "No. I'm sure she would beat him with one of her stilettos if she did."

"Probably." Logan cocked his head and sent him a considering stare. "So what do you think? Could you share her with Javier? You sound awfully jealous."

In a way, he was. The idea of London loving only Javier killed him, like a blade stabbing into his heart and twisting. But she was good for his brother. Morgan had suggested that Javier needed someone to care about, and London could well be that person. Xander just didn't know if he could give her up to his brother exclusively. Then he inserted himself in that picture, watching Javier kiss her while he looked on . . . then palming her ass himself, kissing her neck, and whispering in her ear. In his fantasy, she turned to kiss him, too.

His cock just about exploded.

"You know, maybe it's possible. I might even like it." Then reality set in, and he sighed. "But asking a virgin for a ménage? It would be up to London, of course. Does she really want to take on two men, much less a playboy *and* an alcoholic? It might be more than she can handle."

"If she has feelings for you both, she'll try to make it work. The real question is, is she strong enough?"

"Yeah." Xander didn't hesitate. He didn't have any doubts about that. London might be naturally submissive, but she'd put them in their place when they'd needed it. She had spine.

They fell silent for a few minutes, and he could tell that Logan had a lot on his mind. Of course he did. The biggest blessing of his life coming early next year coupled with possibly the biggest career change of his life. Logan would carefully weigh everything before he did anything.

London walked back into the room and her gaze skittered up to his. Her blue eyes connecting with his jolted him like a lightning strike, sizzling across his skin. She passed him on her way to the coffeepot, sending a long glance over his bare torso before she looked away.

Xander grabbed her by the arm and swung her around to face him. She didn't have time to resist. He cupped her face in his hands. She tensed, but didn't fight. Instead, she let him stare down into her gorgeous blue eyes. "Did you sleep well, *belleza*?"

She relaxed. "Yes. I was so tired. I could have slept longer." She glared at Logan, then glanced back at Xander. "You?"

"Not so well, but I'll be fine."

Her face fell, and a concerned little frown made her pale brows draw together. She edged closer. "Are you worried about Javier?"

Among other things. "A bit. But he slept, right?"

She nodded. "I woke him with a cup of coffee. He should be joining us soon so we can talk about Maynard and stuff."

Xander wished she'd waited a bit, but understood her desire to be forthright with her boss and the man she was developing feelings for. "It's a good plan. We'll explain it together."

"He might not be happy, but I think we're doing the right thing. Thanks." She smiled.

He brushed a kiss to her forehead, then with a sigh of regret, let her go. For now. She didn't go far, thankfully, and he smelled her natural scent—that citrusy-floral—curl against his senses. The note of jasmine was stronger today, and it made him hard as hell. He leaned forward against the counter, pretending to study his coffee.

London pointed down the hall. "I'm going to grab a shower. If you're not here when I get back, send Tara my best."

"Absolutely." Logan gave her a kind smile.

She shuffled down the hall, grabbed a few things out of her bedroom, and disappeared into the bathroom across the hall. The second he heard the water running, Xander closed his eyes. He could imagine London naked and dripping, the water sliding over her pale skin as she dipped her head back and drenched herself, her hands caressing her flesh.

"You've got it bad," Logan observed.

Xander sighed. Why lie? "Yep. But so does Javier."

"Do you really think you could share London with him?"

"*I* could . . . probably, especially if that's what London needs. The question is, could he? He's never been good at sharing, especially S.I. Industries. It's our damn birthright, and I'm lucky if I get to attend the Christmas party every year."

"I know." Logan hesitated, then sent him a considering stare. "But I remember you telling me that when you and Javier were little kids, you shared a bedroom. You were close then. Remember that?"

He did. They'd often pretended to fall asleep then stayed up past their bedtime to drag out all their Hot Wheels and dump trucks to play into the wee hours. The nannies had been so surprised that both boys had been happy to nap well past kindergarten. Once their father discovered they'd been using their rest time to play, he'd separated them immediately. He'd chastised Javier severely about responsibility and proper behavior. His brother had already been a serious ten-year-old. After that, he'd become downright severe. Their relationship had never rebounded.

"Of course. What about it?"

"You once said that was the happiest time of your life."

Javier had cared about him then. They'd been on the same side, brothers united in sharing a passion and keeping a secret.

And Xander saw immediately where Logan was going with this logic.

"It was. I . . . have no idea how Javier feels. I mean, he wants her. He might even need her. It's possible that, in her, he's finally found a reason to give a shit again and keep living."

"I'm not seeing a downside to this."

Giving voice to his greatest fear scared the crap out of him, but he pressed on. Logan was a good sounding board, and Xander sensed that he was running out of time before things started happening with London and his brother. Whatever was brewing between the two of them would only simmer for so long. If he wanted to be a part of it all, he was going to have to forge his path. "The biggest one is, if London loves him and can't fall for me . . ."

"You'll be out in the cold, and it's going to hurt."

He frowned and studied his coffee. "Yeah."

"But if you do nothing, she'll probably choose Javier. He's got more baggage, sure. But in a lot of ways, he's safer. She's afraid of you."

"Afraid?" That bowled him over. "I'd never hurt her!"

"Not like that." Logan rolled his eyes. "Think, man. She looks at you like something beautiful she can't afford. She absolutely wants you, but I think your considerable experience scares her, especially since she doesn't have any herself. It's got to be daunting."

She'd said as much. Xander hadn't really listened. He'd never really considered it from that perspective. In truth, he was nervous, too. A virgin was new for him, and caring about her was even more unusual. Fucking to fuck . . . he could do that all night—and had. But finding some way to use his body and his touch to tell London that she was different to him? Without alienating his brother? Tall fucking order.

But it was his only shot.

"Good points. But I think I've got some ideas now. Would you forgive me if I asked you to be a good friend and fuck off for a while? Javier is going to skip PT this morning."

Logan laughed. "No sweat. Tara would thank you, too. She said she had her first bout of morning sickness yesterday, and she was sleeping when I left. I'm sure she'd be happy to have me back. I'll just . . . check on you later."

"Thanks. For everything. I needed this." Xander took the last swig of his coffee.

With a slap on his shoulder, Logan grabbed his empty mug and set it in the sink. "Good luck, man. Seriously. I like the way you are with her. Usually, most people think you're a douche before they get to know you, but she mellows you."

"Wow, don't hold back for me." He rolled his eyes as he walked Logan to the door.

"We're too close for that shit. I'll always give it to you straight. I expect you to do the same."

Xander nodded. "You're right. And you didn't ask for my advice, but I'm giving it to you anyway. Come home. Being a SEAL is great when you're young and unmarried. It's like wanting to be an astronaut or a race car driver when you're a kid. But when you grow up, you see the downside."

"Yeah. The world can be a dangerous place, and I sometimes hate how much Tara worries. She doesn't tell me. To my face, she smiles and hugs me tight and says that she can't wait until I get home. But once when I was leaving for a mission, I stood against the door after she'd closed it behind me and heard her sob her heart out. It killed me, and it will be twice as hard once our family has grown."

"Sounds like you've made up your mind."

"I think so. Like you, I'm concerned about my brother. Hunter recently reentered civilian life. He's doing pretty well with it. But I can tell he's still . . . adjusting." He sighed. "He'll be all right, but I think his transition—and mine—will be smoother if we do it together."

Xander related. He and Javier would be wrapped around a woman, not a patriotic duty. But he wouldn't turn his back on his brother again, no matter what.

He and Logan parted with a promise to get together for a beer soon. Xander shut the door and drew in a deep breath.

Time to change everything about his life.

When he left the foyer, he found London in the kitchen with damp hair, wearing a loose pink T-shirt and a pair of denim capri pants. The instant he entered the room, he smelled London in the air, so distinctly feminine. Her scent, the thought of sharing space with her, it all made him so fucking hard.

She fixed some toast and fruit, then placed it all on a tray, along with another cup of coffee and a tall glass of water. On the edge of the tray, she settled the file folder with all the information from Maynard. She frowned, quickly jogged back to the bedroom, then emerged with a bag from the drugstore. She rummaged inside and withdrew two ibuprofen from a new bottle and a pair of glasses.

Xander frowned. "Breakfast?"

"He's got to be hungry. He didn't eat much of his dinner. I figured I'd feed him and maybe he'd be less grumpy about the decision we made."

"And all the other stuff?"

She sighed. "Yesterday when Mr. Navarro arrived, Javier told me to leave the office. Something about the meeting seemed awfully tense to me and had disaster written all over it. There was nowhere to eat my sack lunch, so I went to the drugstore and bought him some ibuprofen for his inevitable hangover. He's also having trouble reading the documents in his office and he won't get his eyes checked, so I bought him a pair of readers to see if that will help."

A slow smile spread across Xander's face. She was totally smitten with his brother and was already thinking ahead for ways to make Javier's life easier. Little did she know he had some ideas of his own.

He still just had one hang-up.

Approaching her softly, he cupped her shoulders and brought her against his body. "You're so kind, *belleza*. Besides being beautiful, you're thoughtful. And wonderful. Are you trying to make us both fall in love with you?"

She gasped as if he'd accused her of something terrible or as if the idea shocked her. "No. Really, I just . . . He needs a friend."

"But you like him as more than a friend." Xander didn't ask. It wasn't a question.

"No." Her words lacked conviction. She flushed and looked away. "I don't know what to say."

"You're interested in Javier. I can see it." When she would have pulled away, he held tighter. "But you're not the kind of girl to have let me eat that sweet pussy if you didn't like me, too."

"Xander!" She swatted his shoulder, her face turning a deep rosy red.

He laughed deeply. "Am I wrong?"

"That's really . . . indelicate."

Probably so, and he didn't care at all. He took her by the shoulders again and trapped her against the counter, caging her in his arms. Leaning into her body, he let her feel exactly how hard she made him. Her body softened against him immediately. Her nipples beaded. But she looked torn.

Xander lifted a hand between them and cupped her breast, slowly thumbing her nipple until she closed her eyes and moaned. Triumph spiked. She wasn't in love with him yet, but he would work with desire.

"But true, *belleza*. You look beautiful in your desire. I'm thrilled that you want me."

She hunched her shoulders and turned her face away from him, clearly ashamed. "What is wrong with me?"

"Absolutely nothing. Go give my brother his breakfast in bed. I'll be in shortly."

London blinked at him in confusion. But as if she'd been given a reprieve, she snatched up the tray and scurried to the master bedroom.

Whistling, Xander made his way out to his car to grab a few essentials. Then he hopped in the shower and cleaned up, wrapping a towel around his waist and grabbing a couple of condoms from his wallet. Finally, he headed across the house to find the two most important people in his life.

* * *

LONDON balanced the tray in her shaking hands and eased the door to Javier's bedroom open with her hip. Her thoughts were still boomeranging in her head after her run-in with Xander in the kitchen. He knew she had feelings for them both. God, she'd barely been able to face that fact, much less try to decide what she should do. If she was smart, she'd step away from the situation. She needed the job, so she'd have to keep things strictly business with Javier. But she would have to stop seeing Xander altogether. She should probably drop off this tray, pack up her things, call Luc to come get her, and resume her normal life.

But her normal life wasn't making her happy. It wasn't actually living or growing. Nor could she just abandon the Santiago brothers. They were both hurting, both needing help that she could give. Without her to referee, it was possible their relationship would just disintegrate into more arguments. Their pride stood like a concrete wall between them. If she left, how would she make them see that they could be so positive in healing one another?

Spotting her, Javier sat up in bed with a smile. He'd showered, too, then lounged in bed, wearing a black T-shirt and gray sweats. "I would have come to the kitchen."

She set the tray over his lap, then eased down on the edge of the bed beside him. "I know. But I wanted to talk to you first. Eat."

Javier smiled as if it amused him to see her so bossy, but he dug into the fruit. It was good to see him smile and eat, look somewhat carefree after yesterday. It was good to see him doing something besides working himself into the ground and self-destructing.

"You look nervous. What have you done?"

Though he teased her, London couldn't help but wince. "Don't be angry, but—"

"When you start like that, I'm almost certain to be."

London sighed. God, she was flubbing this. "Xander helped me last night with the projects you gave me. I know that wasn't what you wanted—"

"And then he helped you out of your clothes and onto your back?"

Her jaw dropped. "No!"

She and Xander had remained on task last night . . . no matter how many times she'd looked across the little kitchen table and thought about how gorgeous he was, how desirable she felt around him, and how incredible it was to have his undivided charm directed at her. More than once, she wondered what would happen if they stopped working and started kissing . . .

"Really?"

"Really," she shot back. "Xander helped me with Maynard and assessing the situation with the log-ins. We've got a plan of attack, and I think he helped me make very smart choices. I'll tell you about them when you're feeling less sarcastic." She stood and glared down at him. "He was a perfect gentleman. Frankly, sir, my personal life is none of your concern. You're my boss, not my father."

She whirled toward the door. Sometimes Javier was so stubborn, she wanted to scream.

"Stop!" Javier snapped.

London halted entirely. She didn't mean to actually follow his orders, but that one syllable shot straight into her brain—then right down to her sex. She heard him set the tray on the nightstand and closed her eyes. Her clit began a slow throb.

What was it about these two men that just made everything inside her want to surrender to them both? Why couldn't she just pick one? Xander, maybe, so she didn't jeopardize her job. But then . . . how was she supposed to stop thinking about Javier? He needed someone to care about him, and she didn't seem to know how to do that without wanting him, too. She couldn't resist Xander, either. She liked his sense of play, his sexiness, the way he made her feel beautiful, special.

Her head was still racing when she pivoted to face her boss, chin jutting angrily. "What?"

Javier raised a brow at her tone. London swallowed. Clearly, he didn't like her anger. Well, too bad. Though his sharp gaze and his slow, graceful prowl from the bed made her nervous, she stood her ground. It didn't take him long to stand tall and tower over her. Her heart beat furiously. Her chest burned with anxiety. And that damn throbbing in her clit picked up speed.

"Careful, little one."

"I'm trying to tell you the truth. I'm sorry if you don't want to hear it. Xander helped me accomplish something last night I'm not sure I could have done myself. If you'd like to fire me for doing what I thought was best, then I'll accept that. But I think I've done everything I can to show you that I'm sincere in wanting what's best for you. And the business," she added hastily.

Javier studied her with his intent stare and didn't say anything for a long minute. London tried not to squirm. Finally, he looked at the tray, then picked up the readers with a frown. "What are these?"

If she told him, he'd only balk. "Just put them on."

He crossed his arms over his chest and regarded her with an expression that warned her that she was crossing the line. Javier wasn't going to budge unless she backed down. As much as it frustrated her, he somehow aroused her like crazy.

"Please put them on, sir." She softened her tone. "I'll show you."

"Much better." Javier still held the glasses as if they might bite him at any moment, but he slipped them on, then peered through the lenses and reared back with a frown.

Before he could yank them off, London grasped the folder with the lists from Maynard and put them under Javier's face. Immediately, he focused on the documents, coming a bit closer. He stared, his eyes moving across the page.

"I can see everything." He tore the glasses off and looked up at her. "The text is a bit big, but it's a marked improvement."

"These are readers, sir. They help magnify whatever's directly in front of you so you're able to see newspapers, phonebooks, faxes, etcetera. My mom has a pair in every room at home."

His face turned thunderous. "You think I'm old enough to be your parent?"

"No." London held in a sigh. "They're not just for people who are getting older, sir. I mean, the over-forty crowd uses them more, I know. But they're for anyone having trouble with their vision, and that's a lot of people. *I've* used them before," she pointed out. "If you'll just let me make you an appointment to see an optometrist, the doctor will find you the perfect prescription."

His slow nod and thoughtful expression didn't give her a warm fuzzy feeling. He tossed the folder with the papers aside and set the glasses on the nightstand. "Thank you."

"You're welcome."

Javier narrowed his eyes at her, and she could tell there was something running through his head. "You've worked for me for barely twenty-four hours, and yet you've gone out of your way to see me home safely, tuck me into bed, make sure I could see properly." He glanced at the tray. "You brought me something in case I have a headache. I even sense you're trying to nudge me to mend fences with my brother. Why?"

London blinked. Nothing like getting to the heart of the matter with a single question. "Because it's my nature, sir. I see a wrong and I want to right it. I see pain and I want to heal it."

"You have a soft heart. But it's going to take more than toast, a good pair of glasses, and a few pills to fix me, little one."

"I know, but if you'd let people into your life, they'll help you heal. You're self-destructing, sir. I don't want to see you keep tearing yourself apart over a woman who didn't deserve you. She's gone. It's tragic, yes. But you're still here. And you're not alone."

Javier reached out and gripped her arm, dragging her closer. She couldn't tell from his expression whether he was annoyed, amused, or touched. "Are you trying to be my savior?"

"If that's what it takes."

He leaned closer, and his body heat penetrated her skin. His scent saturated her. His stare drilled all the way down to her soul. "Because you're such a good employee and you care so very much about your job?"

Javier released her arm and walked a tight half-circle around her body, his shoulder brushing hers. Then he stood behind her. His hands gripped her hips, and he pulled her body against his. The first thing London felt was his erection pressing into the small of her back. Desire sliced through her defenses. She closed her eyes and tossed back her head on his shoulder with a ragged exhalation.

"Th-that's part of it."

He surrounded her now, blanketing her back, nuzzling her cheek with the bristles from his morning stubble. His hands covered her stomach and began inching upward toward her aching breasts. London was dying for him to touch her.

"But not all of it?"

What had they been talking about? God, she could barely think. London had a vague recollection and realized the point of his question. "No, that isn't all I care about."

His entire body tensed. His grip on her tightened. "So if I kissed you—"

"Please." The word slipped out, sounding more like a whimper.

She barely got it out before Javier jerked her around, tunneled his fingers through her hair, and pulled. He slanted his lips over hers and seized her mouth in a hungry kiss. London sank into his embrace, opening to him completely. She couldn't do it quickly enough to ease the ache growing inside her. Every inch of her mouth he dominated only made her want to give him more. Javier took greedily, then seized more, devastating and demanding. She whimpered and threw her arms around him, digging her fingertips into his shoulders to hold on as she felt sanity slipping.

But Javier broke the kiss for a moment, his lips hovering over hers. She blinked up at him. He stared into her eyes like he wanted to own her. Any resistance she had left melted.

Finally, he reached for the hem of her T-shirt and began easing it up. Fireworks burst inside her as she lifted her arms, ready to give him everything.

But as she leaned in to kiss his shoulder, she saw Xander standing in the doorway, dangling a black leather backpack from his hand, dressed in nothing but a towel, and watching them with a hunger that made her burn.

Chapter Eleven

LONDON gasped and stiffened in his arms. Javier eased back to see shock blanch her face stark white. *What the hell?*

He whirled around and found his brother watching them. Guilt smacked him, stinging through his entire body like a bitch. *Damn it.* He should have kept his distance. London worked for him and was involved with his brother. But those two very good reasons hadn't stopped his cock from taking over his brain and urging him to seduce her so he could devour all her sweetness for himself.

"Xander, I . . ." What the hell could he say that wasn't obvious? He wanted London. He was desperate for her warmth, for her caring. And those goddamn lush breasts taunted him beyond sanity.

"I'm sorry. Really. You must think the worst of me," she blurted out, shrinking back.

Xander shook his head and dropped the backpack in his grasp at his feet, leaning against the wall, his expression unreadable. "No, I think you look sexy. Carry on."

Javier frowned. He didn't want to let London go, but . . . "Don't you consider her yours? Weren't you warning me away from her just yesterday?"

"She's still mine. Kiss her again." Xander sent him a sly smile, wearing nothing but a towel tented by his stiff cock.

Little brother was turned on by watching them? It seemed so, but did that mean he wouldn't kill him with whatever weapon he had stashed in that backpack?

A glance at London's face told Javier that she was every bit as confused as he was. A little befuddlement wasn't going to stop him. He had his brother's blessing—for whatever reason—and he craved another taste of this woman. Just one more. Then maybe he could work through this hunger or sate it somehow. It would be so much easier if he didn't need her quite so much.

Cradling her face in his hands, Javier slanted his lips over hers once more. Falling into her mouth was like drowning in warm, sweet honey. Her flavor lured him deeper. She didn't kiss with a lot of expertise. It fit, given that she was a virgin. Except . . . why hadn't Xander rectified that yet? His brother wanted her far more than he wanted his average bimbo.

That question dissipated under the dazzling onslaught of London's natural sensuality. She swayed in his arms and curled her tongue shyly around his. Jesus, his cock hardened to a stiffness beyond painful, and he felt every one of the fifteen months since he'd last had sex. She flowed around him, her body soft and lovely, molding against him. He wanted her naked, on the bed, legs spread. Fuck, he'd love to tie her down and have her at his absolute mercy.

For now, Javier simply drew her closer, wrapping his arms around her and dragging every inch of her flush against him. She wasn't his to fuck, and he knew it, but maybe he could leave an impression on her. Brand her somehow. At least memorize her taste.

Suddenly, a shadow fell across his face. Javier opened his eyes to see Xander standing behind London, tugging one sleeve of her shirt down to expose a pale shoulder. His lips made a slow journey from the delicate cap up to her neck before he began to nibble on her ear.

"That's it, *belleza*," Xander whispered. "Kiss him. Yes, with all the passion I know you have. Show him how much you want him, how much you care. You look gorgeous taking your pleasure. You're driving us both insane with need."

Shock swirled through Javier—but not enough to make him lift his lips from London's. There probably wasn't a force on earth that would make him willing to do that right now. He wondered what the hell his brother was up to, then decided he didn't give a fuck. He was going to take as much from this girl as they would both let him. It was wretchedly selfish, and Javier knew it. But she was the first good thing that had happened to him in years. He was going to indulge his growing need for her until Xander yanked him away, beat the hell out of him, and tossed him out on his ass.

But what stunned him even more was the desire that sweltered hotter every time he watched Xander's lips trail over London's silky soft skin. The sight of her trembling between the two of them made his dick even harder, made some beast in him that wanted to ravage her roar with impatience. Had he ever been this aroused?

Never.

Javier eased back for a moment to watch his brother's lips move across London's soft skin again. His breathing turned so hard it lifted his chest and resounded in his ears.

"Don't stop what you're doing," Xander insisted, hazel eyes twinkling.

Suddenly, he got it. Xander was getting off watching him touch London as much as he liked seeing his brother touch her.

The realization detonated in his head like a bomb. Javier was slow to recover, as the aftermath left him reeling with possibilities. How much would Xander let him have of her? Could he get her nipples in his mouth? Could he persuade Xander to let the sweet girl suck his cock? Or could he actually pray for the Holy Grail and hope that he had the chance to fuck her?

As quickly as the desire tore through him, he looked at London, studied her face—her closed eyes, her flushed cheeks, her lips parted on a silent gasp. She was a stunning picture of passion he'd never forget.

"Do you like having both of us touch you, London?" Javier had to know, ached to hear her admit it. He'd never shared a woman with anyone. He had no doubt Xander had, but if London wanted this experience, there was no way he would let her leave this room before they thoroughly ravaged her.

"You see, that's London's little secret, brother. She wants us both. She confessed to me a few minutes ago in the kitchen."

Surprise rippled through Javier again. The morning had been full of them, but he wasn't going to let shock interfere. He resolved to keep rolling through every new revelation as long as it kept him near London and touching her.

But he had to hear that from her lush, swollen lips.

"Is Xander telling me the truth, little one? Do you want us both?" he murmured, his lips hovering just above hers.

"Yes." The word was a whimper, but she met his gaze squarely. He admired her honesty. Somehow, it made him want to fuck her more.

"Just like I said," Xander gloated. "You don't want to disappoint her, do you, brother?"

"Hell no. She deserves to get exactly what she wants."

Above her bare shoulder, Xander smiled. "Exactly. I believe when I walked in, you were about to take her shirt off. I'm waiting."

A hot wave of lust turned Javier's blood thick. He didn't hesitate, just grabbed London's thin T-shirt in hand and lifted it over her abdomen. When he reached her breasts, she grabbed the hem and held it down. She must know that once he saw them, touched them, there would be no stopping him. He would get inside her, stretch her little pussy to accommodate his throbbing cock, and take her as many times as Xander allowed.

For now, he loosened his grip on her shirt. "Are you afraid, little one?"

"No," she whispered. "But promise me you won't look at my back. Either of you."

He and Xander exchanged glances. His brother didn't seem surprised.

"All right, if that will make you feel better."

She nodded.

Javier hoped that was the extent of her hesitation, but he had to check. "If you're not ready for us, you can say no."

London lifted her heavy lids, her blue eyes looking slightly dazed. Her breaths came fast and heavy. When Xander reached around her, traced a finger over her erect nipple while grazing her neck with his lips again, she gasped. Then she grabbed her own T-shirt, backed away to face them both, and yanked it over her head, throwing it to the floor.

She lay back on the bed, propping herself up on her elbows. Her golden hair spread out across the soft-hued sheets. Fuck, she looked like a goddess. "I'm ready. I want this. I'm saying yes."

"Then we're not going to stop, *belleza*," Xander vowed, crawling on the bed after her and rolling against her side until he scooped her back against him. "We're both going to fuck you. Deep. Hard. Repeatedly."

A shudder tore through her body, and she looked at him with pleading eyes. Javier hoped Xander meant that. He couldn't resist her any more than he could resist the supple flesh spilling from the cups of her delicate lace bra. He crept onto the bed and half-covered her chest with his own.

The sight of her breasts at Luc and Alyssa's house, with Xander sucking her nipples, had aroused him so damn much. Now that he would get the opportunity to have his own mouth around those rosy crests, he wanted to taste the delicate flesh on his tongue . . . and watch his brother take her other nipple in his mouth so they could suckle her together and unravel her. So they could make her beg. Just the thought had him ready to beg, too.

London nodded as if words were too much effort for her reeling body. She melted into him, and Xander attacked the hooks of her bra, still nipping at her neck. The second his brother's fingers lifted from the garment, Javier dug under the heavy underwire cups and pulled the straps down her arms. He tossed it in the vague direction of her shirt, never taking his eyes off her.

Xander reached around her body and lifted her heavy breasts in his hands. "*Belleza*, arch your back. Offer Javier your nipples. Just like that. Now, be a good girl and let him suck them."

She nodded dreamily—and did exactly as Xander bid. He'd known all along that London was naturally submissive, but to see it in action . . . Fuck, he ached to be inside her, commanding her pleasure.

For now, he bent and kissed his way from her sweetly parted lips whispering a plea, then down her jaw, over the swells of her breasts. Clutching her hips in his hands, he curled his tongue around one of her nipples.

Her gasp shivered down Javier's spine. She lifted her hands and fisted them in his short hair, tugging him closer. He was dying to hear how he was making her feel, but he didn't want to leave the bounty of her sweet nipples to demand that she tell him. In the end, it didn't matter. Xander came to his rescue.

"Does that feel good, *belleza*? Does the tug of his mouth go straight to your pussy and make you ache? Are you wet for us?"

"Yes. I've never . . . felt like—" She panted. "I'm on fire. I need . . ."

"We know what you need," Javier murmured against her breasts.

He took her nipple in his mouth again, sucking at it, laving it with his tongue. He bit down gently to test his theory that she'd like a bit of pain with her pleasure. Her gasp echoed in the room and jolted a hot charge of desire through his body. Fuck, yes. Exactly as he suspected. Javier repeated the gesture with the other stiff bud, and she arched to him even more, shoving her breast deeper into his mouth. With a cry, she lifted her leg over his hip and rubbed her pussy against him.

"A little pain, *belleza*? Did Javier give that to you? Did you like it?"

London nodded frantically. "I ache everywhere."

"Good." Xander's voice dripped satisfaction. "She'll need clamps."

"She will." Javier rolled London flat on her back and suckled on the nearest nipple, moaning and palming the generous breast.

Xander thumbed and squeezed the other, but that wasn't enough.

"Suck that nipple, Xander. They're very sensitive. She wants it."

With a grin, Xander bent to her breast and breathed hotly on it, watching her every reaction like a predator about to pounce. His lips hovered just over the distended peak. To Javier's shock, its mate turned harder on his tongue. Goose pimples broke out all over her body. He groaned. This sweet, gorgeous woman just kept surprising him with her responsiveness over and over. How the hell would he ever let her go?

Now wasn't the time to worry about that. He had to savor the gift he'd been given.

London whimpered, a pleading sound that came straight from her chest. "Please . . . Oh, please. I can't—"

She blinked up at Xander, and the way she looked at his brother, then turned that same beseeching expression on him, as if they alone had the power to raise or destroy her, was all he needed to start tearing at the zipper of her pants.

Xander smiled wickedly, his tongue peeking out to toy with the side of her breast, but he didn't give her what she wanted yet. "Help him. Take off your pants, then I'll reward you. Are you wearing underwear?"

Damn, sometimes his brother was smart. London immediately began shoving at her denim capris and revealed a pair of simple gray cotton bikini panties. Keen disappointment swamped Javier. He wanted to see her pussy. Touch it. Smell it. Taste it. Study it before he pushed deep inside and let her tight flesh surround his aching cock.

"Oh, now that's a shame." Xander echoed his thoughts, fingering the waistband of her panties. "These aren't pretty."

"I-I wasn't expecting anyone to see . . ."

"Expect it from now on." The firm note in Xander's tone spelled out that it wasn't a suggestion. If London couldn't hear the command in his brother's tone, she'd learn quickly.

"A-all right." She blushed prettily, and Javier couldn't resist tweaking her nipple with his fingers.

London arched, gasped, and unconsciously spread her legs wider. That quickly, his patience ended.

Javier grabbed the little cotton panties in his hands, positioning a seam right between them. They were soft and looked like they'd been washed over and over. They were no match for his determination, and they quickly ripped apart. Xander laughed and repeated the action with the seam along her opposite hip. He tossed them away.

"I would have taken them off!" she protested. "Those are my favorite pair."

"Were," Xander corrected as he stroked his way down her abdomen, his fingers heading straight for her pussy.

"These are fit for the trash now." Javier smiled, turning a satisfied glance to his brother, then refocused on London. On her cunt.

It was sparsely covered with fine blond hair. A glance told him she was beyond wet, glistening with need. Xander pried her swollen lips apart with his fingers and pressed down on her clit, gently circling. Her breath caught, and a tremor went through her. But Xander lifted away, his fingers soaked. The musky scent of her filled the air as he put the digits in his mouth and sucked noisily. "Hmm. Just like I remember."

"Xander!" London blinked at him, embarrassed.

"What? You're so sweet, I couldn't resist. Can you, Javi?"

He and his brother had done very few things together since just before he'd started puberty. As children, he and Xander had been close and shared many of the same passions: Hot Wheels, ice cream, making forts out of pillows and blankets. He'd thought that rapport was lost forever. But now? It was surprising exactly how much he and Xander were on the same page with London.

"No," he ground out. "I want my mouth on her pussy."

"Soon," Xander promised. "First, London needs to learn a few rules. All of your underwear will be going in the trash, *belleza*. You don't wear them anymore. At all."

Her jaw dropped. "But I like them. You can't do that. I can't go commando. That's . . . that's unladylike. When I'm wearing skirts—"

"Oh, those will be great days. Instant access to your pussy." Xander flashed her a wolfish smile, then turned to him. "Anything sound better than that, Javier?"

"No. I would really look forward to coming to work."

Javier wasn't sure if Xander really intended to let his girl come to the office without undergarments, to work around him for eight-plus hours. Did Xander think that he wouldn't break down and fuck the girl? Hourly? Or did his brother intend to be there? He wasn't sure what the hell was going on, but he wasn't about to get off the ride.

London's eyes bulged wide. "At the office, too?"

"Absolutely." Xander nodded. "Tell her your fantasies, brother. I'll bet you've had them."

It was as if Xander had read his mind. And Javier didn't hate that. It was kind of uncanny the way they understood one another, at least when it came to London's seduction. "I want to bend you over my desk, little one, and flip up your skirt, caress that pretty bare ass, then ease my fingers into your pussy until you're sweetly wet and needy."

"Like now," Xander added, cupping her mound again, his fingers sliding through her folds.

She shuddered every time his brother came near her clit, and Javier couldn't wait to touch her, taste her, get inside her and lose himself.

"Exactly," he choked out, his voice rough. "I think constantly about teasing you until you're ready to come, then shoving my cock in that tight little cunt. I wouldn't give a shit if the phones were ringing or we were late for some appointment. If I was fucking you, your number one priority would be to let me. My cock should be the only thing you worry about in that moment."

"Imagine you fucking this pretty little girl, Javi, while I sat in your office chair and watched."

Javier's cock jerked in his sweat pants, and it took everything he had not to tear them off and sink into London's untried body. He didn't want to hurt her—would do anything to keep her safe—but this scene was quickly jacking up his arousal past his self-control.

"Or imagine that while you fucked her, she was sucking my cock."

That mental picture splashed across his brain, and Javier groaned. His restraint snapped. He wouldn't stop. Couldn't wait. He yanked off his T-shirt and devoured London's lips again with a ravaging passion that had her whimpering into his kiss. Then he shoved his pants down and off his hips. Her eyes widened, but Javier couldn't wait another second to touch Shangri-la. He slid his fingers down her body, straight into her pussy. His fingers tangled with Xander's, and his brother adjusted, moving lower to insert a finger inside her. Javier concentrated on her clit, rubbing her in slow, soft circles. London mewled.

"That would be spectacular." He swallowed past a thick ball of lust. "We'll have to do that. Have you seen her come?"

Xander nodded. "Flat fucking gorgeous. Her entire body flushes, and the scent of her pussy fills the air. She tastes *so* good."

Javier wanted firsthand knowledge of all that. He wanted to devour her, explore every untouched part of her body, wanted to hear her cry out his name as release wracked her.

"I don't think I can wait until we head to the office."

"Don't worry. We're going to fuck her now," Xander assured. "You want that, *belleza*?"

She arched her back to them, as if offering up her heavy breasts. Her nipples stood swollen and ready. Javier couldn't resist and dipped his head to take the delectable bead back in his mouth.

Xander groaned, and Javier glanced up to find him watching. "You like that? You saying yes? If so, I'll do the same to your other nipple."

"Yes!" she gasped out, wrapping one arm around Javier's head to bring him closer.

With a smile, Xander leaned down and finally drew the little red berry atop her breast into his mouth. He sucked strongly, cheeks hollowing. Javier did the same.

London panted and mewled. Under his fingers, her clit turned harder.

"Every time we suck her nipples she tightens around my finger, brother."

God, everything between them was dead fucking sexy. Javier found himself rubbing his burning cock against London's thigh, wondering how soon he could get inside her.

"So close . . ." she whimpered.

"You are," Xander agreed, his whisper hoarse. "But we didn't give you permission to come yet."

She blinked up at them looking somewhere between panicked and lost. "Permission?"

"Yeah, *belleza*. I have no doubt you'll lead us around by our cocks a lot, but you're talking to two Doms. If you don't know what that means, we'll be happy to teach you, but your orgasms are ours to control now. To build . . . then grant or withhold. Beg sweetly."

Javier froze. Xander was a Dom with years of experience. He'd mastered women from coast to coast, on multiple continents, sometimes two or three at a time. Javier winced. The last time he'd tried to top someone, it had been a disaster, even with Xander's help. Today, though, he didn't feel any of that disconnection between his head and body. He didn't feel any of that panic. But he'd be lying if he said he didn't have any concerns. Yes, he liked bondage and didn't mind giving a little pain if a woman enjoyed it, but the mental game of BDSM . . . The brain was the biggest erogenous zone, and he was so fucked up. He should probably sort out his own head before trying to play with anyone else's.

"Please . . ." London whispered, her back arching, her hips bucking.

She really did flush a pretty pink all over, Javier noticed almost absently. He watched Xander wedge another finger inside her tight opening. London winced a little, held her breath, then let out a long groan.

"Good morning, G-spot." He moved his arm, presumably wiggling his fingers inside her.

London clutched the sheets, her eyes widening. Javier took that as his cue and gathered moisture from her folds again before gently circling her clit once more.

"I can't stop it. I need . . ." London gasped. "Please let me. Anything. Whatever you want, I'll do it."

"You'll do it anyway," Xander growled. "Because everything we do is going to make you feel so good. You'll come to crave what we give you. You'll open your legs every time we tell you, anytime, anywhere, for any reason. Understood?"

Her breathing picked up speed. Her clit hardened under his finger.

"She's going to come," Javier told his brother.

Xander slanted him a glance. "You think we should let her?"

On one hand, he wanted to see her throw her head back and hear her scream. On the other hand, he loved her writhing and begging. Her orgasm later would be sweeter for the deprivation now.

"Not yet." Javier found himself smiling.

He hadn't had a hell of a lot to smile about in the last twelve months in particular, but this grin came from deep in his soul. Working with his brother to control London's pleasure clicked something into place for him. With Whitney, he'd been panicked and hazy. Now, he felt sharp and focused. A strange sense of anticipation parked inside his chest. Not just to have sex with London—though he was absolutely looking forward to that—but to do something that eased him deep inside besides lift a bottle. It felt weirdly like progress.

His brother nodded. "Good choice. Exactly what I was thinking. *Belleza*," he called to London.

"What? No! Please let me . . ." She worked her hips even harder, trying to get the right friction to send her over the edge.

Javier lifted his fingers from her clit immediately and was gratified to see Xander had removed his fingers from her pussy, too. The silent communication they had enjoyed as kids with their toys, the sort he'd thought was lost forever, sprung up between them again—as if it had always been. They were of like minds, both ready to see London wail, and beg, and suffer just a bit more.

Xander smacked the pad of her pussy with his hand. London gasped, her look pleading with his brother. Javier had no idea why watching Xander give his assistant a little discipline turned him inside out, but no denying it did.

"Take what we give you," he growled against her breast, pulling her nipple in his mouth again.

With his hot stare glued to London, Xander did the same. Together, they plucked and sucked, nipped and pinched her nipples. London sobbed now, one plea bleeding into the next, her words running together in a desperate cry. Javier couldn't keep his hands away from her drenched, swollen pussy, his fingers drifting down to pet her until her orgasm drew near. Then he'd retreat, focus on her nipples . . . and find his hands drifting between her spread thighs again. The cycle repeated itself so many times, he lost count. London turned incoherent, a beseeching supplicant squirming and mewling between them. Her skin flushed. Her eyes glazed over. She'd do anything for the pleasure they dangled just beyond her grasp.

"God, she's beautiful." Javier swallowed against his thick lust.

"She is. How badly do you want her?"

He frowned at Xander's question. "Fuck. More than anything."

"Explain how badly you want her. Describe it. Make sure she can hear you."

Javier drew in a shuddering breath. He didn't understand Xander's point, but he loved the idea that London would know how badly he wanted her. "I'm burning inside and out, little one. My skin sizzles. My cock is on fire. For you. I'm bursting to feel you all around me. I want to touch you everywhere. Inhale you. I'm dying to fuck you."

He wanted to be the last person she thought of when she drifted off to sleep tonight and the first person she thought of when she awoke tomorrow.

"Then do it," Xander drawled.

He blinked up at his brother. Everything about Xander's expression said that he was completely serious. "She's yours. I'd love to, but you—"

"I'm sharing."

"We can't share her virginity."

"Do you have feelings for her?"

London tried to rise from the bed. "Please don't ask that. I want you both. I'm eager to be with you, and the rest of it doesn't—"

"Matter?" Xander interrupted, then turned to Javier. "Yes, it does. Answer my question."

Jesus, his brother was cross-examining him when lust was fogging his logic so badly he wasn't sure he knew his own goddamn name. But if he wanted London . . . "Yes." He looked down at her spread across his rumpled bed, her innocent blue eyes giving way to a womanly knowledge, her rosy cheeks and swollen lips drawing him to her again and again. But it was her heart he yearned for most. "In you, I see the kind of person I'd like to be. I've spent too long in darkness, trying so hard to be in control, gathering all the bitter anger I could muster and shoving it into my heart so I wouldn't be weak. I've walked away from everything in life that matters, leaving myself only work and vodka. Then you came in, opened your sweetness to me, and . . ."

God, was he in love with her? Wasn't that impossible? He'd only known her for a few days. But during that time, he'd seen exactly who she was, and he knew that if she walked away for whatever reason, he would be devastated.

London reached up and pulled him to her, fusing their lips together for a tender moment. When he lifted his head to look at her, she wore her heart in her eyes, and Javier swore for sure that she could see through him, to all his emotions spilling out.

"You intrigued me when I met you . . . which was even before you met me. I saw you at Kata's house, the morning Xander brought you to Lafayette, before you woke. You stumbled from bed, and I helped you back in. You looked at me and called me beauty."

A pretty flush stained her cheeks again, and Javier caressed her soft skin in his palm. He didn't remember the incident, but it made him smile. "You cared about me even before you knew me."

She was simply that sort of person.

London nodded. "And I wanted you. It was my first thought when I saw you." Then she turned to Xander. "I was already daydreaming about someone just like you watching me before you appeared in the club. Then, when you stood there, it was as if I'd conjured you up. You were a fantasy come to life."

"That day in the club, what did you want me to do?"

She swallowed. "Watch me. Want me."

"I did. I still do. But you wanted me to fuck you, too. Now we will. Javier?"

His brother was suggesting that he be London's first lover. Need gripped him, strangling his good intentions. His balls were heavy, his cock felt ready to burst. But he had to think of London.

Gently, he lowered his lips to hers once more, hovering just over them. Her lips parted in breathless welcome beneath him.

"Come for me, little one."

She cocked her head in confusion . . . until he sifted his fingers through her saturated folds and gathered her moisture, spreading it over her clit again. Sucking in a shocked breath, she stiffened, legs parted wide, and moaned.

As soon as he circled her clit, all the sensations that he and Xander had been heaping on her for long minutes rushed over her. His brother helped, nuzzling her neck, her breasts, inhaling her scent, whispering naughty suggestions in her ear that Javier could barely hear. His heartbeat roared in his ears so loudly. The more London moaned, the more her clit hardened and her body writhed, the more she looked at him as if she was terrified he would shove her off the cliff and not be there to catch her. And the more he was determined to give her total pleasure.

Then her mouth opened in a silent scream. Javier felt the tremors jerk her body. She jolted, her body bowing. The musky scent of her pussy perfumed the air. Her pale skin flushed even rosier from head to toe. She let go completely and screamed until he thought the windows might shatter. It was one of the most beautiful sounds he'd ever heard.

"Fuck me," he heard Xander growl in her ear. "Such gorgeous surrender. I love the way you don't hold back."

Javier kissed his way across her jaw softly, up to her mouth. She panted, and he brushed his lips against hers lightly. "Thank you for trusting me. That was amazing."

He didn't speak those words lightly. The sight of her giving herself over, trusting him with her body so completely, humbled him. With a sob, London threw her arms around his neck and pulled him closer, burying her face in his shoulder. Her body shook, and almost instantly he felt tears wet his chest. They broke something inside him.

Gently, he set her away slightly so he could stare down into her eyes. "Little one? Did I upset you? Are you afraid?"

With a shake of her head, she seemed to struggle for words. "That blew me away. Until you two, I-I'd only ever had orgasms with my fingers and toys. I . . . wasn't prepared for how powerful you giving me the sensations would feel."

As if embarrassed, she buried her face against him once more, and Javier melted all over. Nothing about London was artificial. It didn't occur to her to hide or wear a mask. This wasn't a game to her. She simply opened herself up and gave.

Javier raised his gaze to meet Xander's, silently asking if they should wait for her. Maybe she wasn't ready for the two of them or for sex just now. His dick wanted to protest vociferously, but that wasn't what mattered.

"She's fine," his brother mouthed.

London needed to be held, he realized, so he cradled her body close. Xander snuggled in on her other side, and she curled an arm around his neck, too. Soon, his brother was kissing his way up, then setting his lips tenderly over hers. She responded to Xander's coaxing, opening for him and allowing him into the depths of her mouth—of her heart—with that kiss.

Then slowly, Xander pulled away. "He's going to be good to you, *belleza*. You know that, right?"

With a nod, London looked over to him with wide, trusting eyes. Xander passed a condom in his direction.

Javier shook his head, refusing to take the little foil package. "She's yours. You've already shared so much."

Xander grabbed his wrist and forced the little square into his hand. "You need her, and she wants you. Go on."

"You need her, too. Besides, I'm too close to the edge. This long without sex . . ." He kissed London's forehead. "The last thing in the world I want to do is hurt her because I can't restrain myself. You have far more experience. I'll just be a battering ram. You'll treat her right."

"You sure?" Xander frowned.

"I don't trust myself." Javier could just feel the regret oozing from his pores. "And I know you want her."

Xander nodded. *"Belleza?"*

Javier knew what Xander asked with that one endearment. Was she ready? Did she want him? Did she trust him? Did he matter to her? The questions were etched into his face. It occurred to him that he'd never seen his younger brother care this much about any one female. But something had changed in Xander when he'd been wrapped up in his own drama and too self-absorbed to realize that his playboy brother had finally mentally grown into a man.

London fingered a lock of Xander's hair away from his face. "I'd be honored. That is, if you still want me."

Xander ripped away the towel around his waist and tossed it to the ground, leaving himself completely naked. His cock stood tall and straight, weeping with a pearly drop at the tip.

With a last glance his way, Xander seemed to double-check that Javier was okay with this decision. Funny how they hadn't really been communicating for years, and suddenly, when it came to this girl, they were completely in sync. Javier nodded at him.

"Of course, I want you," Xander assured. "I've been trying every trick I know to get you to notice me so that I could get into your panties." He glanced down her naked body with a wink. "Oh, look. You don't have any panties."

She giggled through the remnants of her tears of release. The sweet, light sound warmed Javier's heart. Xander's driving desire to possess the girl was all over his face, in the tense set of his shoulders. God knew, his brother's cock had to be screaming for release almost as loudly as his own. But Xander took the time to try to make London feel at ease. He needed her relaxed so she could feel the pleasure.

Javier brushed strands of pale hair away from London's face, then kissed her forehead, her nose, then her lips for a soft moment. "You're in good hands." He looked his brother's way. "Would you like to be alone?"

Xander looked at him as if he'd lost his damn mind. "No. Stay. Talk to her. Help me keep her happy, surrounded, and aroused."

For whatever reason, Xander wanted him to be a part of the experience, to let him imprint himself in her memories at the same time. So she would relate pleasure with the both of them. Sometimes, his little brother had strokes of genius. He still wasn't sure why Xander would go so far out of his way to share his woman, and he supposed he should worry about the shit fit HR would have if they knew he'd just given his assistant an orgasm and hoped to fuck her soon. But for now, he shoved all those thoughts aside and simply savored her.

"Stay," London took his hand in her soft, capable one. "Please."

Chapter Twelve

LONDON shook. Excitement. Anticipation. A little anxiety. Everything about this moment stunned her. She watched the brothers, her head still reeling. This was like a fantasy, them both wanting her, compromising with one another and working together for their benefit—and hers. Individually, they touched her with a passion that made her sway, swoon. Ache. But together . . . what she felt became a devastating need, smashing all her preconceived notions of desire. The way they played her, each picking up where the other left off, taking cues from one another, boggled her mind. And delighted her body. Moisture flowed from her aching sex, coating her folds and swelling them. She was beyond ready to feel them deep inside her.

But this moment hovered between them. She held her breath. Would Javier stay? London felt sure that Xander would be a gentle lover—at first. Then he would unleash that nasty, wild side she saw beneath that wicked grin. But somehow, it would be less than perfect without Javier there, watching . . . preparing to take his turn next. Maybe because that was her fantasy, to have them both adoring her. Maybe because she had feelings for both and worried that if Javier walked away, it could only mean he didn't feel the same. Whatever it was, the moment tore at her composure.

Careful to keep her back concealed, London arched from the

bed enough to wrap her hand around his neck. She kissed him recklessly, with a desperation she couldn't contain. Javier didn't hesitate to respond. He grabbed her face in his hands, as if she were a precious treasure, and slanted his mouth over hers possessively, his tongue tangling with hers.

Desire became a drug that made her high and kept her reeling. She floated on pure pleasure. Her skin tingled. Her frantic heart pounded like a drum. After that orgasm, she should be sated. But no. She wanted more of every sexual, dominant act they could unleash on her. She trembled with the need to give herself over to them in every way.

Through her cloud of passion, she heard the sounds of ripping nearby. Javier jerked, and London turned. They both stared at Xander, watching as he tossed a condom wrapper on the nightstand and eased the latex down the fat head of his erection. She swallowed. His long, thick oh-my-God-will-it-fit cock made her eyes flare wide. Veins bulged and throbbed down his shaft. She reached out to touch him, lips parted, breath held.

Her fingers closed around the bare, bottom half of his shaft. His heat stunned her, as did his size once more. She couldn't get her fingers to meet around the thick column of flesh. But what amazed her most was his soft, soft skin.

Curious, with clit throbbing, she grazed her fingers up to the latex-covered tip, then down to the naked root, jutting out from a patch of black hair. Xander groaned and growled out a guttural curse, head thrown back.

"You're more sensitive without the condom?" she asked.

His body tightened, shoulders squaring. It was costing him self-control to let her touch him this way. But he was allowing it to put her at ease. Finally, he nodded.

Javier sidled closer, murmuring in her ear. "Skin-to-skin contact is always the most pleasurable. He will still enjoy every bit of your body, even with the condom. But he's protecting you, little one."

She'd known that, but still Xander's gesture touched her somehow. At first glance, he didn't seem like the type of man to sacrifice
his own comfort or happiness for anyone else. But he'd risked his
relationship with his brother to bring him to Lafayette so he could
save Javier. The way she'd heard it, he'd helped his friends from more
than one scrape, sometimes risking his own life. Xander clearly
wanted her, yet he'd offered her to his brother first because he loved
Javier. And now he stunted his own pleasure so he didn't put her at
risk. She realized that he had many material things—cars, houses,
fancy clothes, and flashy women—but did he have anything his heart
truly needed? London suspected that Xander had maneuvered this
situation with her and his brother because, deep down, he wanted
to be embraced, accepted. Not that Xander knew it consciously.
He didn't. But she wondered . . . when had anyone done anything
for him?

It wasn't much, but she could give him her virginity and her affection. He would probably take her heart, too. Just as his brother
would. But that was her problem. She knew that being young and
inexperienced meant that she was likely to get starry-eyed and think
she was in love. London promised herself that she would expect
nothing from them but pleasure.

She spread her legs for Xander, offering herself wholeheartedly.
And she clutched Javier's hand. He squeezed back as his brother
crawled over her body, breath rushing out in hot pants over her lips.
Then Xander slid the condom down fully and lowered himself onto
her, his erection nudging at her opening.

"It's going to be a bit painful at first. It's unavoidable," he said
with regret.

"It's okay."

"He'll be gentle, little one, or he'll answer to me," Javier promised, brushing a kiss across her cheek.

"Very gentle," Xander vowed. But he looked like the restraint might choke him. He was keeping himself on a tight leash, trying desperately to maintain his control.

"Breathe and focus," Javier told him.

Absently, Xander nodded. His entire body stiff with tension, he spread her thighs wider with his own and began probing lightly at her opening, inserting the head just a fraction, then withdrawing again.

The sensation merely teased her with the slick feel of him, there and gone again. But the sear of his skin covering hers, the taut need ripping across his face, the anticipation skittering through her veins made her heart skip beats. London drew in a deep breath to steady herself, then smiled up at Xander. "I'm not made of glass. Go ahead."

He swallowed, then looked at Javier, seeming to communicate something silently. His brother smiled. Reassuringly, yes. But also with a bit of mischief, like they'd become coconspirators.

Before London had time to wonder what they were plotting, Javier wrapped his fingers around her nape and turned her head toward him. His seeking lips found hers. She groaned as he claimed her mouth in a consuming kiss that curled up her toes.

At the same time Xander surged forward and broke through the thin barrier to her body. As she cried out into Javier's kiss, Xander sank down, down, deeper. The pain was a long, burning gash gouging her insides. She tore her lips from Javier's and sucked in a shocked breath, stiffening and fighting.

"Stop!" she sobbed.

Xander pinned her to the bed and held completely still for the span of a few breaths, crooning soothing sounds and whispered apologies to her. He feathered his lips over her cheek, her ear. Slowly, the pain subsided to a dull ache, then nothing at all.

As she exhaled raggedly, London relaxed. It was done. Losing her virginity wasn't the only key to finally living a whole, fulfilling life, but it was a start.

Suddenly, Xander wriggled his hips once more, working himself deeper still into her pussy, inch by aching inch. Javier seized her lips again.

"I'm sorry it hurt, *belleza*." His voice shuddered along with his body. "I don't know how long I can hold out. So tight. So . . . mine."

The gruff words zipped down her spine, lighting her body up. This time, when he withdrew and surged forward again, a brief blip of pain morphed in a tingling of nerve endings. The head of his shaft prodded a spot inside London that had her gasping. Her sex throbbed and burned. She tried to speak, but Javier's lips never left hers. Instead, he swallowed her cry.

Together, they piled on more sensations, Xander increasing the length of his strokes, still like molasses, zinging across every sensitive spot inside her. Javier now toying with her nipples, pinching one, then the other, gently twisting. London arched as every jolt of pleasure from her sensitive breasts shot down to her clit.

Finally, Javier lifted his head, already breathing hard, as he turned to watch his brother thrust into her body, then inch back. Xander's cock was glossy with her moisture, and a hint of blood stained the condom. London gave herself over to the rush of pleasure with a shuddering sigh.

"How does she feel?" Javier choked out the words to his brother.

"So fucking good. I'm fighting not to lose it. You're amazing, *belleza*. Move with me," Xander panted and grabbed her hips, coaching her silently to rock her body with his as he shoved inside even harder now, faster. "Help me, Javi," he panted. "I want her sky-high before she comes again."

"My pleasure." Javier smiled at her.

Xander balanced on his knees and grabbed her hips, lifting them off the mattress, then powered into her, one deep stroke after the next. Javier licked his fingers, then caressed his way down her abdomen to circle her clit again. Her stomach flipped. She was more sensitive than ever. Blood rushed through her body, swelled the folds of her sex. Every time Xander pushed into her, he bumped her clit. Javier rubbed it the rest of the time. Perspiration began to coat her skin until she couldn't find her next breath, until her whole body tightened.

"That's it, *belleza*. So beautiful. And you're so close . . ."

Javier nuzzled her breast. "Your skin is glowing. Open your eyes, little one. Look at me."

Slowly, she turned her head—and drowned in his blue gaze. It burned. He wanted her with a desperation that showed in every line of his body.

"Please, Javier . . ." London didn't even know what she was asking for exactly. Relief? Release? "Xander!"

But there was no relief in sight, just more endless pleasure that dragged her under like quicksand. Inescapable and thick, it would be her downfall.

With one hand, Javier continued to caress her clit. The other he wrapped around his thick cock, stroking it roughly up and down. The sight sent a sharp bolt of arousal between her legs. Her stare wouldn't leave that hand gripping his hard, needy flesh.

"He's going to fuck you next," Xander promised huskily. "The moment I roll away from you, he's going to blanket you and shove his way into this achingly tight little pussy. Can you take him?"

"Yes!" she screamed out the word, arching and thrashing.

"Good. I'm going to watch. And it won't be long before I'll want you again."

Release sat right there, taunting her, throbbing through her clit with promise. She held her breath, certain that at any moment, she would go tumbling over. Instead, the blood just continued to rush in, building and building the climax with every devastatingly slow stroke. The nerves between her thighs danced and scorched her. She mewled and scratched at the sheets, sent Javier pleading stares, doing her best to force Xander to push her over the edge.

"Faster!"

"That's not a polite way to ask for what you want," Xander chided.

London bit her lip until it hurt, then whimpered for more. "Please. I need more. Can't . . . take it."

"You can. Wait a little longer. I'm enjoying your pleading. Tell me you need it again." He surged deep inside her again, scraping his way up the sensitive walls of her channel.

"Yes." She could no longer string two words together. "Please. More. Now. Aching."

"So fucking sweet, but no coming yet." He turned to his brother. "Little London has never sucked a cock, I'll bet. Want to help her learn?"

Another boom of desire throbbed in her womb at Xander's growled words. And before she knew what was happening, Javier loomed over her as well, lifting her head in one hand and feeding her his hard shaft with the other. She welcomed him, openmouthed and curious. The experience was different—better—than expected. He cradled his hard length on her tongue, and she stretched her lips wide to accommodate his girth. The salty, fresh male taste of him made her moan. His scent produced a massive olfactory high, sending her head spinning. His musk pooled in the creases of his thighs and around his cock, potent and full of testosterone. London moaned as she sucked him gently deeper.

In response, Javier balanced himself over her and hissed in a breath, pressing far into her mouth, all the way to the opening of her throat. She met his gaze with a whimper.

"Fuck, that's hot." Xander's hoarse declaration scraped across her skin, making her shiver as he slid so, so deep inside her snug passage. "Breathe through your nose, *belleza*. Relax your throat. Javi's got more cock to give you. You want it all, don't you?"

London gave him a shaky nod. She did. She wanted everything they could both give her. She didn't know if this relationship would last beyond today. She didn't know if they'd forget her tomorrow. But right now, she wanted to know beyond any doubt that she'd given her all to please them as they pleased her.

She did as Xander instructed, dragging air through her nose and releasing the muscles in her throat. As he neared her lips again, she swirled her tongue around Javier's hot shaft.

"Shit!" he hissed, then grabbed her hair. Her scalp tingled with an odd pleasure/pain as he drove his cock in her mouth again, deeper than ever.

When he eased back, she sucked the head just past her lips, then swirled her tongue around the smooth-skinned glans like an ice cream, laving, relishing, worshipping.

Javier tossed his head back with a long groan. "Goddamn it!"

Deep breaths heaved in and out of his chest. London sucked even harder, toyed with him more. He stiffened on her tongue.

"Little one," Javier panted. "Baby . . ."

His gravelly voice thrilled her.

Xander lowered himself over her body once more and took her hips in hand, angling her so that he electrified that sensitive spot inside her. She gasped around Javier's cock, and he took advantage of it, thrusting completely into her mouth and prodding at her throat. She tried to relax and take him. He stared down at her, nostrils flaring, his expression a dark promise to ravage her completely the second he got inside her. Her clit throbbed furiously, and her womb tightened with need.

"You look incredible, *belleza*." Xander's voice slid over her like raw silk, raising goosebumps all over her body. You're pleasing him so much. Pleasing me so much. Focus here for a minute. Javier, let her go."

With a snarl, his brother withdrew from her mouth. London mewled in protest. She missed his flavor already, the intimacy of not just looking at him or touching him, but actually *tasting* his skin, measuring his desire for her on her tongue.

He continued to jerk his cock in his tight fist and glared at Xander. "Hurry."

With a smile, Xander pierced her with his stare, slid his hands around her hips to cup her ass and lift her right under him. Now he unleashed all the furious need he'd been withholding since he worked his way inside her. He pounded into her in long, rhythmic strokes that made her arch and want to beg. London had held her pleasure back for them, in part to stave off the inevitable moment when they turned their attention to another woman, in part to collect as many memories to savor as possible. But now the ravaging need unraveled her, dismantled her. Her pussy burned, clamping down on Xander as every surge of his erection hit deep and ignited her most sensitive spots.

She clawed at him. "Xander!"

"Now, *belleza*. Come!"

His words were somehow magical, bringing that slow, seemingly never-ending build inside her to a churning rise of sensations that finally peaked and rolled over her, heavy and mind-bending. Moments before it gave way to ecstasy, she knew this was going to stun her. Undo her. Change her.

And she wanted it more than anything.

The explosion sent her flying into a realm she'd never known. With an arch of her back and a scream that echoed off the walls, her pussy spasmed, pulsed. She utterly disintegrated in Xander's arms as his cock jerked inside her. He gritted his teeth, the tendons in his neck standing out, his face flushing, and groaned long and low with primal satisfaction.

His strokes slowed gradually. Her walls continued to pulse gently around him every few moments as they fought to catch their breath. Perspiration dampened every part of her skin now. Their heavy breathing mingled. London wasn't sure she could open her eyes, much less move a muscle. Two giant orgasms, the latest even more shattering than the first, turned her completely inside out. Lethargy dragged through her veins. She wanted to sleep for a week.

Xander pressed his forehead to hers and brushed the hair from her face, cuddling closer. "How do you feel, *belleza*?"

"Wow," she whispered. "That was . . . like nothing I imagined."

He lifted his head and smiled down at her. London's heart flipped in her chest. She felt it again when he feathered his thumb over her lower lip until it tingled. Then he kissed her softly.

"Usually, a woman's first time is too painful to be pleasurable, I'm told. You gave me something special, *belleza*. I wanted you to feel good about all of it."

She nodded. "I wouldn't change a moment."

"We're not done, are we?"

Javier's sharp tones startled her. She jerked around to find his body tighter than a bowstring. He'd clenched his jaw and stared at her through narrow eyes. His red cheekbones stood out like twin blades on either side of his face. His hand roughed up and down his cock in a tight, jerking grip.

Unbelievably, her pussy clenched again. One look at Javier . . . and she longed for him, too. To most it would seem odd, at least. Probably even wrong or sinful. But they both made her feel special in their own way. She didn't simply care for one or the other. If they each desired her, why not show them her want of them in return?

"Not at all, big brother." Xander slowly eased out of her tight passage and disposed of his condom. "Tag. You're it."

Her body tried to suck Xander back in, and once he was gone, she clenched around air, feeling oddly empty. She was sore in some interesting places. Her thighs felt as if they'd been spread wide for years. But that didn't stop her clit from aching once more, especially as Javier rolled on his condom and dove onto her body as if he couldn't wait another moment.

His hands trembled as he covered her. As he braced his weight on his elbows, he grazed her opening with the head of his shaft. Already, she could tell that he was a bit wider than Xander. Maybe not longer, but taking him was still going to be a stretch.

"Are you too sore?" he asked.

"Don't worry about me."

His mouth set into an angry line, and he glared sternly at her. "I refuse to hurt you if you're already in too much pain."

She might be a little tender, but it wasn't enough to want anything other than to take him deep inside her. London wanted him to know that she didn't desire or care less for him than his brother. Her feelings for Javier were every bit as strong as those for Xander.

"It's all right," she murmured. "I want you."

He seized her lips, pressing a series of urgent kisses over them that melted her all over again. Her desire resurged, and London tilted her head to allow him complete access to her mouth—just like she bent her knees and tilted her hips to take him inside her.

He resisted, inching his hips away. "You didn't exactly answer my question, little one."

"I'm fine. I promise."

"But sore, aren't you?"

"I'm not fragile. The human body is made for sex. It's already been worth whatever minor discomfort I might have."

Xander stuck a hand between them, skimming her clit with a devastating touch. As he rolled the deeply sensitive bud between his fingers, she cried out. He merely smiled with male satisfaction, making her ache all over again, and curled his fingers inside her wet opening.

"She's juicy," he told his brother.

"Is she still bleeding?" That prospect clearly worried Javier.

Xander withdrew his hand and held up his fingers. Glistening but clean.

Javier stared, still hesitating, though he looked as if he yearned desperately to pound her into oblivion.

"Tell him to fuck you, *belleza*," Xander whispered. "He acts as if he wants reassurance, but I guarantee that what he's really after is the chance to hear that you're eager for his cock to fill up that pretty, tight cunt and take everything he has to give."

"Really?" she murmured. He'd like her to ask *that*? Then again, it kind of made sense. Men watched porn. Now she was no expert, but she was fairly sure none of those actresses had made the faces or screamed the guttural sounds she had during orgasm. And most of the porn stars, besides moaning prettily, were brazen and appeared to love every form of sex. She wasn't dumb enough to believe it was all real. The actresses had looked somewhere between hilariously practiced and downright bored—at least from what she remembered as a teenager sneaking a peek at a neighbor's porn collection while dog sitting. It had been just before her accident, and she'd only watched for about five minutes. It had been four and a half minutes too many. A woman asking a man to fuck her was tame by comparison. Maybe Javier would like it.

"Damn it!" Javier clenched his jaw, looking somewhere between stunned and annoyed at his brother. "How did you read my fucking mind?"

"Been there, done that. Burned the T-shirt." Xander laughed.

They *were* serious. Both men were trying so hard to make her first experience both good and memorable, she didn't have any problem asking Javier to give her what she wanted. It was the truth.

"Will you fuck me?" she murmured shyly, feeling a flush stain her cheeks. "Please."

She'd rarely uttered that word in her life. At least not aloud. Her mother, an elementary school principal and a frequent Sunday school teacher at their church, would have had a conniption if she'd heard London say that. But now, sandwiched between two sexy-as-hell brothers, desperate to tell them how she felt, those words seemed lovely.

Xander groaned. "Hearing you say that is so fucking sexy."

"It is," Javier all but choked out. He must have known the confession was coming, but he still sucked in a breath and grabbed handfuls of her hair, then jerked back just enough to glide his lips over her throat and up to her ear. "You're sure, little one? It's been a long time for me. I don't think I can go easy on you."

His dark face was taut with a dominant snarl. His insistent words made her clit throb. She should probably be worried that he would ask for something she wasn't prepared to give. She should probably not spread her legs for her boss and allow him deep inside her since they had to work together, at least for the next few weeks. She knew it was stupid to hope that her attention and affection might prevent him from losing himself in a bottle again. But none of that stopped her. She wanted Javier so desperately. And he seemed to need her, at least a little.

"That's fine."

He raised a brow at her. "Fine? You'll just let me take whatever I want?"

London didn't hesitate. She probably should, but . . . "If I'm able, yes."

"Don't you want to know all the perverted shit that's running through my head before you agree?"

"If you want to tell me. But I trust you," she said honestly. "Whatever you need, I'm here."

Javier sucked in a stunned breath and reared back, dragging a hand through his short hair. "Amazing."

The whisper felt like praise, and London basked in it, glowed with it. She smiled at him.

He tightened a fist. His nostrils flared. Then he leaned over her once more, his stare drilling down into her. "How much do you trust me?"

How was she supposed to quantify that? "Well . . . You've gone out of your way to be careful with me since I came to work for you. You asked about my health, my medicine. You told Xander to be careful with me a bit ago. I have no reason to believe that you would hurt me. Take what you need."

"What do *you* need, little one?" He cupped her cheek, but the restraint was costing him.

In that moment, she only needed one thing. "To please you."

Javier swallowed, his whole body pinging with pent-up lust he seemed to be leashing with the tiniest of threads. "So sweetly submissive . . ."

"Isn't she? I picked up on it right away," Xander said.

London frowned. Was that true? If submissive meant wanting to do whatever it took to earn his praise and know that she'd made him happy, then yes. If it explained why she had the oddest urge to kneel or bow her head or something like it to indicate that she was placing herself totally in his hands, then she supposed she was submissive. The idea didn't bother her. She didn't know a lot about sex like this, but learning at their hands would be a joy.

Finally, Javier turned to his brother. "Did you take *everything* with you when you left? I need to test this."

Xander hesitated. "Are you sure? The last time, at Dominion—"

"Last time, I didn't have my head screwed on straight. I'm solid now. I'm not going to let anything happen to her. And you'll be here for both of us."

London wasn't exactly sure what they were talking about, but she watched and listened. Xander appeared as if he was debating the wisdom of helping Javier. Finally, he smirked. "I've got a few basics in the backpack."

She watched as Xander looked over at the leather bag he'd set on the floor. Javier's gaze followed before he smiled and kissed her with a demanding press of his lips, stealing inside to seize her mouth. She softened against him, clinging to his shoulders.

Under him, she seemed to sink into a cloud. Her head swam. Impatience gnawed at her. She wanted him to fill the terrible emptiness in her now.

Instead, he wrenched away from her. "Head on the pillow. Arms and legs outstretched."

London blinked at his commanding tone. A shudder ran through her, but she wouldn't disobey.

"Okay." She scooted her way toward the head of the bed, carefully concealing her back.

He raised a brow, communicating his displeasure without a word. "What did you call me at work, little one?"

"Sir?"

"Exactly. That's who I am in the bedroom, too. Do you understand?"

This was the Dominant in him; London knew that instinctively. And she welcomed it. Today, he would be exacting, and she would work hard to please him. But she was determined to do it.

"Do you understand?" he repeated into her silence, his voice deepening and turning a bit harder.

"Yes, Sir."

London scurried to put her head on the pillow. It smelled musky and mysterious, like Javier himself. Refusing to be distracted, she spread herself wide open across the king-size bed, feeling vulnerable, exposed. Suddenly uncertain, but so badly wanting his praise.

"Beautiful." He ran a finger up her thigh, his cock bobbing as he stepped closer so he could cup her breast, thumb her nipple.

She gasped, and Xander unzipped the backpack. In one hand he held a black leather backpack that contained who knew what. In the other, he carried a thin length of nylon rope. He stopped and stared at her. His cock rose again instantly. "Damn. I should have positioned you this way. You're gorgeous. Look at that pussy."

They both stared at her *there*, their gazes relentless. In that moment, she felt truly beautiful. Moisture gushed from her sex.

"What a beautiful sight. I could stare all night," Javier admitted, then spotted the rope in his hands. "Excellent. What else do you have in there?"

London stared at that length of rope as Javier took it from Xander's hands and prowled toward her. She swallowed, her heart taking off in her chest to rattle and thrum.

"Arms above your head, little one." Javier's hoarse demand was no less powerful.

Instantly, she obeyed. Gently, he grabbed her hands and crossed them, wrapping the rope around her wrists in a crisscross pattern. He looked over to his brother, who shook his head.

"Let me." Xander dropped the backpack and approached her with a rakish grin. "You make me want to fuck you all over again, *belleza*."

"My turn," Javier growled.

With a laugh, Xander turned his attention back to the rope. "I'm going to show you a Western-style binding. We'll have better control over the tension of the ropes. Avoiding excess pressure on the inside of the wrists protects the nerve endings just under the surface of the skin. And it's probably best if we keep the scene light for now. We don't know London's tolerance."

Javier listened attentively, his face a study of concentration. "Of course."

Somehow, she found the two of them collaborating for her domination and pleasure so sexy. It wasn't just the fact that they were both gorgeous and devoted to her in that moment. It was their harmony. They fed off one another's energy and knowledge. When she'd met them both a few days ago, they hadn't been speaking. That seemed a shame. They shared the same blood and so many of the same childhood memories. They should be sharing a brotherhood that would sustain and support them both throughout life. It was a silly fantasy that she could be the one to bring them together. Silly . . . but she couldn't help aching to make it come true.

"Now fold the rope in half and create a loop. Pass the rope around her wrists one time and feed the loose end through." Xander demonstrated, and London felt the rope wrap loosely around her wrists. "See how it looks a little like a slipknot? You finish the rest. Yep, like that. Now circle the two loose ends in opposite directions around her wrists, but keep space between her wrists or you'll put too much pressure where she's fragile." He brushed the fair skin just over her veins.

"Makes sense. Now what?" Javier asked.

"Wind the rope around her wrists a couple of times, then take the loose ends and feed them through the center loop. Right . . ." Xander pointed. "Like that. Perfect. Now watch me." He wound the rope to the inside, then split the ends in opposite directions. "Now take one end and feed it back through the horizontal loop in the opposite direction. Good. Tie it off, but use your index finger to check that there's enough space between the ropes wound between her wrists. If it's too tight, she'll feel a tingling sensation, which means you're compressing something you shouldn't. Touch her hands periodically. If her skin is too cool, it's a sure sign that her circulation has been hindered."

"Absolutely. That isn't the kind of pain I want to give little London."

Xander sent his brother a lopsided smile as he tied off the rope on the back side of her wrists. "Precisely. Now you finish."

Javier grabbed the two loose ends, and secured the nylon rope to the thick wood above her head with a sturdy knot. He looked at her with dark promise, letting her know it was just a matter of time before he unleashed all his pent-up lust on her.

Xander leaned in to inspect his brother's handiwork, and London gave her wrists an experimental tug. She wasn't going any place.

"You're good to go." He looked at Javier, his expression serious for a change. "I'm going to stay on top of your focus."

Javier gave his brother a sharp nod, then stepped back to study her. London felt his gaze all over her. Her nipples beaded, her belly knotted, and everything between her legs tightened. After so much pleasure, how could she feel anything but sated? She didn't know the answer, but there was no denying that she couldn't wait to feel Javier against her. Inside her.

"I won't let her down," he vowed.

"Please fuck me."

Xander raised a brow and smiled at her. "And manners, too. It doesn't get much better than that, brother."

Javier narrowed his eyes. "She's not restrained enough. Do you have more rope?"

"I've got even better stuff," Xander assured, then reached into his backpack.

When he sounded like he was really looking forward to something, London suspected that she should brace herself. But even knowing that whatever he had up his sleeve would test her hadn't prepared her for the sounds of rattling and the sight of thick metallic links of chain.

Wide-eyed, London gasped.

"Now you've got her attention." Xander smirked.

Javier's relentless stare on her sharpened. He gave her a predatory smile as he grabbed one length of chain out of his brother's hand. "That's perfect."

"You okay, *belleza*? Afraid?"

London blinked up at Xander. "Maybe a little."

Okay, maybe more than a little. But she wasn't going to confess that. She trusted Javier. Her fear was based solely on the unknown, but she couldn't say she'd lived if she didn't try new experiences. She let the beautiful, sexual anxiety fill her.

How long would it take him to finish binding her down? She soon had an answer.

Javier grabbed one ankle, wrapped a leather cuff around it that she hadn't noticed before, then secured it around the bedpost and hooked the end closed with some sort of fastening she couldn't see.

Then he stepped back to view his handiwork, sending her a long, low smile that made her shiver. Whatever he did next, he was going to be thorough. "Fasten the other."

Xander complied instantly, spreading her legs even farther apart in order to restrain her other ankle all the way across the big bed. Her muscles burned with the stretch, and her wet folds were now totally on display. They both zeroed in on her pussy and sent her nearly identical wicked smiles. Her womb clenched.

"Hurry!"

Javier crawled onto the bed and hovered above her, his stare penetrating deep. "You don't get to set the timetable or make the rules, little one. Dominant." He pointed to himself. "Lovely submissive." He put his hand over her chest, then cupped her breast.

"You do what we tell you," Xander added, running a hand up her thigh. "You take what we give you."

"And I have a feeling I'm going to enjoy hearing you beg often," Javier growled.

Every word they spoke only aroused her more. She whimpered and writhed, lifting her hips and staring at them with pleading eyes. "Yes, Sir. Just . . . please."

"God, that's music to my ears," Javier groaned, then pushed away from her.

He turned, searching around him in a circle—the chaise, the floor, the dresser—until he found what he was looking for. He grabbed the thick, round bolster pillow in chocolate satin and prowled toward her. "Arch for me."

Tossing her head back, she did as he asked. Javier slid the pillow under the middle of her back. She didn't have enough slack in the ropes binding her wrists to lift her upper body up. She could only stay in place, her breasts pointed to the ceiling in offering.

"She looks lovely," Xander praised. "Good call. You need a safe word, *belleza*."

"A what?"

Javier lifted the backpack and tore the zipper down, fishing around inside. "A word that tells us you've reached your mental or physical limits. A word not to be used lightly." He turned to his brother. "Clamps?"

For her nipples? Would they hurt? Would they just put pressure on her sensitive buds? Or would it be like their mouths, a sensation that tugged all the way down to her clit? She swallowed a lump of lust, wishing she could find out right now.

"Sorry. Next time," Xander said with regret to his brother, then focused on her. "Now think of a word. Something you wouldn't normally say during sex."

Since she didn't really know what words she might or might not use then, London drew a bit of a blank.

Xander smiled at her. "Something other than 'please' or 'yes' or 'harder.'"

Javier lifted something out of the backpack and tucked it into his palm with a chuckle. "I don't recommend 'hurry' or 'fuck me,' either. Whatever word you choose will make us stop immediately."

"And you shouldn't settle on anything like 'no' or 'stop,'" Xander advised.

"Because you won't listen?" She wasn't sure how she felt about that. Scared and excited and a little nervous, which didn't totally make sense. Everything was happening so fast, and she wasn't completely sure how she felt about it all. Except that she wanted these two men. London was crystal clear on that.

He shook his head. "If you want to pretend to protest and you want me to pretend that I'm not listening, I'm game."

"Me, too." Javier reached over to the nightstand, set something down out of her line of vision.

"And nothing smart-ass like 'pneumonoultramicroscopicsilico-volcanokoniosis.' I had a sub try that on me once." He smiled tightly.

"I gave her a really red butt and absolutely zero orgasms for that. Safe words are serious business, *belleza*. Pick one." Xander sounded emphatic.

"Now." Javier just sounded impatient.

He retrieved whatever he'd placed on the nightstand and slid it into his palm. She stared at his clenched fist and tried to imagine what he held. London's thoughts went wild, but she really had no idea.

"Um . . ." They both watched her, and it made her anxious. And, okay, it really turned her on. She blurted out the first word that came to mind. "Ford."

"Like the car?" Xander asked, seemingly confused.

God, she shouldn't have brought that up. She'd write it off to being rattled if they asked. But a ride inside a Ford was the reason that, at twenty-five, she was just now experiencing the absolute joy of sex. "Yes. Is that okay?"

He and his brother exchanged a glance before Javier snarled, "Ford. Got it. Don't forget it in case you need it."

As if she could. "Yes, Sir."

Javier looked Xander's way. "Are we done negotiating now?"

"We are."

The words had barely cleared Xander's mouth before Javier dove on the bed, between her spread legs. He knelt and opened the little bottle in his hand and put one drop of liquid directly on her clit. With a blistering stare, he spread it around in a slow circle. Any cool-off she'd managed while they'd talked? Gone.

Finishing with the bottle in his hand, Javier put the lid back on and threw it to Xander, who caught it and glanced at it with a wicked laugh.

"W-what is it?" She couldn't resist asking.

"A little sweet almond oil, a little cinnamon, rosemary extract, and some shit I can't pronounce . . ." Xander shrugged with a devilish grin.

"Wait one minute and you'll feel it, little one." Javier slammed his body over hers, his cock poised at her entrance. "Jesus, the waiting is killing me, but I'm determined that you'll come with me."

He slanted his lips over hers and plunged deep into her mouth, seizing her tongue with a growl. The kiss conveyed more than hunger or desperation. He grabbed hold of her like a lifeline, one he'd never let go. London clung with her body, skin to skin, writhing under him as much as the restraints allowed. He was poised above her, right there at her entrance, just waiting. But for what?

Suddenly, she felt a glimmer of something warm between her legs, centered under her clit. It didn't take long for the warmth to become a slow burn that made her gasp.

"She feels it now." Xander's voice was a hoarse purr very close to her ear. Somehow, it seared her everywhere, especially her pussy.

London whimpered, thrusting her hips up again at Javier. He inched back and took one of her nipples in his mouth, teeth nipping. He did the same with the other moments later. Arched up to him with a pillow at her back, she had no way to stop him—not that she wanted to. Her sensitive crests tingled and throbbed as he pulled on them with the suction of his mouth, making her womb pulse with need. The heat in her clit had gone from a kindling to an inferno, and with Javier all over her, kissing and touching her, pressing his thick erection against her thigh, she couldn't stand another moment of his teasing torment.

"Fuck me, damn it!"

Javier bared his teeth at her. "I'll punish you for demanding later."

Barely a moment passed before he surged forward and buried his cock completely inside her in one powerful thrust. As she stretched quickly to accommodate him, London moaned in a long, breathy sound. Her cries mingled with his low bellowing groan, seemingly ripped from his chest.

She wanted to wrap her arms around him, but unable to move

her arms or legs, she could only lay under him at his mercy. Even the firm bolster pillow at her back restricted the movement of her torso. She had only her hips free, and Javier took that movement away immediately when he grabbed them and lifted them into each one of his hard, desperate thrusts.

His every push inside her had him bumping her burning clit with his furious pace. Desire roared inside her, and even though she couldn't move, she felt as if she was floating, flying. Pleasure bent her mind, defied gravity. It built and ached and screamed as her fierce need for orgasm rose.

"Jesus, you're heaven, little one," he growled in her ear. "So tight. I won't last. Get ready to come."

Xander leaned in to whisper in her other ear, his lips brushing the sensitive spot beneath. "Does he fill you up, *belleza*? Does he make you need?"

"Yes!"

Her eyes slid shut at the sensory overload. These two beautiful men were unleashing all their carnal brilliance on her, and she was unraveling. With every one of Javier's powerful thrusts, they whittled away at her innocence, replacing an untried girl with a woman. Today was the first time she'd experienced ecstasy, and already she wondered how she would ever do without it.

Javier's breath sawed in his chest. His strokes inside her shortened, quickened, focusing on one spot that sent her eyes flaring wide. She sent a stunned look to Xander, who hovered above her. A smile spread across his face.

"Bingo," he told his brother. "You've got the right spot."

He'd abraded it half a dozen times with the head of his cock, and every nerve ending inside her sensitive channel came screaming awake again. The pressure and burning multiplied. How was it possible that she could climax yet again and with different sensations than before?

"You're tightening on me, little one. Fuck."

Incredibly, he swelled inside her. He slowed his strokes again, lengthened them, dragging the head of his cock over that spot on her inner wall, then igniting another at the top of her cervix. Over and over, he repeated the mind-boggling thrust until the burn magnified, the tingles all converged. And nothing like she'd ever imagined overwhelmed her, building, burning, bursting out with a force that had her shrieking at the top of her lungs as she clamped down on his cock, gripping as if she meant to keep him inside her forever. And she was still unable to process this much wracking pleasure . . .

"Fucking beautiful," Xander murmured. "That's it. Come undone. Give us everything."

"London!" Javier shouted, looking furiously possessive. As he shoved his way into her and completion froze his body, he stared down into her eyes—and marked her soul forever.

Chapter Thirteen

WHILE London showered, Xander joined Javier in the kitchen, unsure what to say. He could be confident in most every area of his life. But his brother's rejection had always blasted that down to the nub. Had something finally changed between them today?

As he entered the kitchen, Javier was burning toast—clearly not his first slices. The air smelled acrid. The coffee brewing in the pot looked like tar. Xander winced, but what could he do? He wasn't any more capable in the kitchen than Javier.

"Hey," Xander called.

Javier turned. He hesitated. The silence dripped awkwardness. "Hi."

Wow, the elephant had charged into the room as fast as a sprinter seeking an Olympic gold medal. Xander had hoped . . . Yeah, well, hopes were useless. They just needed to hash this out.

"I think London is happy with the way everything went down this morning."

Cutting his stare over, Javier nodded slowly. "I think so. You and I, we . . . made a good team."

He'd noticed that? Xander breathed a little sigh of relief. "We did. First time in a long time."

How did he say what he wanted to next? Just blurt that they could be good partners in a lot of things? Xander wondered if he should just vomit out that he'd never tried to abandon his brother in any way—not even with Fran. It would probably open up the whole can of worms again and end their current pseudo truce.

It didn't escape his notice that for once, Javier looked relaxed, almost happy. Now it was pushing noon, and his brother didn't look like he was in any hurry to find a bottle. If sharing London contributed to Javier's current Zen-like state, good. Watching her and his brother together had done something unusual to him. He'd been in ménages before, but always for fun. Everyone got off, and no one took anything seriously. Today had been entirely different. What they'd shared this morning had meant something to all of them. He'd expected that with London since it was her first time. Javier . . . being with her seemed to click his dominant gene into place. Xander had known his brother possessed it, but today it had finally roared to fire-breathing life.

Xander figured he'd been thrown for a loop most of all. Thousands of women in his Done column, and he'd really begun to believe that one was much like the next. Then he'd met London. Who knew that a virgin just coming out of her shell, possessing a huge heart, would blow him away the moment he took her under him? Everything had felt simply right. He being London's first lover; Javier being there to watch and help her achieve climax—the three of them completing some circle he didn't really comprehend.

But back to now. Xander swallowed nervously. If he didn't handle this conversation with his brother delicately, he'd jeopardize the possibility of continuing everything they'd shared this morning.

More toast popped up out of the toaster, smelling charred and looking every bit as black as the granite countertops.

"Damn it!" Javier grabbed and tossed the slices in the trash can he'd dragged over by his feet, now filled with half a loaf of burned bread. "This contraption is defective."

"Give up. The two of us together can't work a toaster." Xander shook his head.

"No shit." Javier sighed, then sipped his coffee with a grimace. "This is terrible, too."

"We should take London out to eat. Otherwise, we risk poisoning her."

There it was again, Javier's momentary hesitation. Something was running through his brother's head.

"We could do that." Javier tossed the coffee down the sink, slammed the mug down, and closed his eyes. When he turned back, he dragged in a deep breath. "What happened this morning, is all that over now?"

Xander didn't pretend to misunderstand. "I'm winging this, just like you. But I don't think so. We really did make a good team for her."

"Damn it, I'm not ready to let her go."

That wasn't a news flash to Xander. "It may surprise you, but I'm not ready to, either."

"I know. I watched you fuck her. I saw your face. You're invested."

Javier had always been a good judge of people, so the fact that he'd caught on so quickly shouldn't be a shock. "Yeah."

"Why did you share her with me? To atone for not helping with Fran?"

Xander reared back. Jesus, always back here . . . "No. You may not believe it, but I really couldn't have done anything to save Francesca." As Javier frowned, Xander's temper spiked, but he refused to let this line of communication close without a fight. "You started the day thinking of London as mine, right?"

"Yes." Javier gritted his teeth. Clearly, he hated to admit that.

"Imagine what would happen if she didn't like you and I'd ordered her to submit to you anyway."

Javier paced as he sorted through his thoughts. "It would have been ugly."

"Yep. Do you think that would have made her at all happy?"

"No." Javier squeezed his eyes shut.

"Even if I'd told her that she didn't have to have sex with you, just submit? Would she have liked it all right then?"

His pause was longer this time. Finally, Javier sighed. "It would have been emotional rape."

Inside, Xander wanted to cheer. But no way did he want to appear to be rubbing in the fact that he was right. "Exactly. Fran wasn't submissive *and* she loathed me. Don't ask me why I didn't explain this to you because I tried."

Javier thrust his hands over his face, grinding the heels of his palms into his eyes. He came up with an apology on his face. "Damn it, I'm sorry. I've been an ass. How are you not furious with me?" He frowned. "Why *did* you share London with me?"

The truth was, he needed his brother, his brother needed London, and she wanted them both. Not to mention that he was falling fast for her, too.

Xander opened his mouth, but London walked in, looking fresh-faced and glowing, hair in a sleek ponytail. "You two look awfully serious. What's going on?"

Javier looked at him. This conversation wasn't over, and it would be interesting to see what the rest of the day brought, especially when his brother put on his CEO hat. For now, Xander shrugged and grinned. "We were lamenting Javier's lack of cooking abilities."

London wrinkled her nose and stared at all the burned toast in the trash. "I see. Thank you for trying."

"Sorry I wasn't more successful. Hungry?" Javier asked.

She nodded. "Famished."

Xander felt pretty pleased about the morning's activities and figured that his expression was a smiling equivalent of his brother's. "So we helped you worked up an appetite, huh?"

Then she blushed and mock punched his shoulder. "Stop trying to embarrass me."

Even Javier cracked a smile at that. "There's a great place to grab some eggs on the way to the office. Can we take you there?"

She sent them both a sweet smile. "That would be nice."

Xander exhaled a sigh of relief. After all, she'd given him the wrong number once. He'd worried that maybe she really just wanted sex from him, and it was Javier she actually cared for. A glance at Javier told him that his brother had been worried that she wouldn't want him around, either. Fran aside, neither of them had ever worried about whether a woman wanted to stay or go. The moment was so fucking surreal.

It hit Xander that maybe he'd been invited along simply because he had the only car available. But whatever. He was going to work the situation to find the best outcome for them all.

First, he and his brother both needed showers if they were going to go anywhere and look halfway respectable. Thankfully, he and Javier could wear the same clothes for the most part. His brother might be an inch or so taller, but most things in his closet fit just fine. So he swiped a few garments, grabbed a shower in the hall bath, then hunted London down in the kitchen a few minutes later as she answered a text message with a frown.

Javier came into the kitchen from the other side of the house. "Everything all right?"

She lifted her head, and regret passed over her face. "It's Alyssa. I had my phone on vibrate, and I didn't let her know that I was staying here with you guys. She's been worried."

"Should we stop and see her after breakfast?" Javier asked.

"No. It's fine. I'm sure she'll have a million questions, but that's for another time. We have breakfast to eat and work to do, right?"

Javier nodded. "Absolutely."

Xander wondered again if that included him.

They made their way outside into the sweltering Louisiana summer, and Javier groaned. "I will never get used to this damn humidity. The whole town is long on laid-back and short on charm, and now I know why. How can anyone be happy when it's stifling?"

"Remind me to make fun of Logan for voluntarily choosing to live here. Stupid fuck."

Together, they climbed in the car and stopped at a twenty-four-hour diner. Technically, it was lunchtime, and the place was a bit crowded. Within a few minutes they had a booth in one corner. As they sat, Xander realized that he and his brother had unconsciously put London between them. No one seemed displeased with the arrangement.

They ordered, and as their drinks arrived, Javier looked too occupied with holding London's hand and kissing her fingers to notice that he wasn't drinking vodka. His brother whispered in her ear. She blushed, and Javier brushed his lips over her prettily glossed ones. Xander wanted some of that. He scooted closer to her, palmed her thigh, then crooked a finger under her chin to bring her face toward his for a kiss of his own. The press of lips lasted for a long heartbeat. He couldn't resist repeating it again. They hadn't been out of bed long, and already he wanted to drag her back.

Suddenly, London gasped into his mouth.

Xander lifted his head reluctantly. Right away, he realized that most of the diner's patrons were staring at the three of them.

"We need to lay off," Xander murmured. "This is the Bible Belt, and she lives here."

His brother scanned the room with a tremendous frown, but gave a jerky nod. He inched away, but Xander noticed that under the table, his brother still had his hand under her skirt. Why the fuck the sight turned him on so much, Xander had no idea, but damn . . .

"We have another problem," Javier murmured, his voice low. "She didn't take us seriously. Did you, little one?" His brother's arm moved, and Xander heard a snap of elastic. "She's wearing panties."

Xander turned a scowl to her. *"Belleza?"*

Her lashes fluttered down. Her breathing picked up. His cock throbbed for her.

"I thought it was just talk in the heat of the moment. They aren't hard to remove. I just have to—"

"Reach up under your skirt while staying hidden beneath the table and take them off without anyone knowing?" Xander challenged. "How do you propose doing that?"

London opened her mouth once, twice. Then she snapped it shut. "We're in public. I didn't imagine that—"

"We imagined it, and you're making it impossible."

"It's not like we can have sex here," she argued. "We'll get arrested."

"That's true, but your panties make us touching your pussy under the table very difficult. And that makes us unhappy."

"When we're unhappy, that means we'll make you having orgasms more challenging, little one," Javier cut in.

But his fingers were still under her skirt. London stiffened and bit her lip, then squirmed in her seat.

"Be still," Xander warned.

"But . . . he's—"

"Got his fingers on your clit?"

She blushed and looked around to see if anyone had heard them. "Yes."

"Because that's where he wants them. You have two choices, *belleza*. You can either use your safe word. If you do, we'll stop everything and have a long conversation about trust. Or you can be a good girl and open your pussy like you're asked."

He was pushing her hard, and he knew it. She was still more innocent than not, and they'd overwhelmed her. But she liked it. London was breathing fast, her nipples pressing against her shirt. She was simply having difficulty getting out of her own head and putting herself into their hands.

"We would never put you in a position to be in trouble with the law, little one. No one knows what's happening under the table besides the three of us. Right?"

London looked around the room. "R-right."

"Good. Now spread your legs wider." Xander helped the cause by grabbing her thigh and pulling it toward him.

Javier leaned over the table to nod at him. "Thank you."

"Your pleasure, I'm sure." He cracked a smile.

These easy moments he and his brother were sharing . . . they needed more. London wasn't just a girl they could both care about, Xander realized. She was someone who seemed to be slowly bridging nearly twenty-five years of divide between them. With her here, animosity and resentment weren't ruling their tempers. They united for the common purpose of giving her pleasure and keeping her happy. To some, it might not make sense. If they fought over everything else, why not fight over the girl, too? But London had a big enough heart for them both.

"Look at me," Xander demanded.

She turned glassy eyes his way. Maybe no one could see what Javier was doing to her under the table, but they could probably guess. London wore her pleasure all over her pink cheeks and in the breathless pants of her parted lips. The sight of her this way made the blood rush straight to his cock.

Suddenly, her eyes closed, and she gave him a soft little whimper.

"Javier's fingers in your pussy feel good?" he whispered.

London nodded.

"Are you going to be a sweet girl and come for him?"

Her eyes flew wide open with panic. "Not in public."

Xander raised a brow, then looked over to his brother. "Javier, your thoughts?"

"If she doesn't want it and she hasn't earned it . . ." He shrugged. "I think I'll just keep playing."

She released a shuddering breath. "But I ache."

"I'm sure you do," Javier said. "When you're ready to let go for me anytime and anywhere, I'll make it worth your while. Until then . . ."

The waitress arrived with their food, looking reluctant to approach the table, as if she realized that she was interrupting. Xander smiled benignly at her, and she set the steaming plates of eggs, bacon, and toast in front of them. She fetched Tabasco for him and Javier, then left them in blessed peace.

Except that Javier lifted his hand from London's pussy and licked his fingers. Xander could smell her soft, musky need, and his cock jerked. He gripped his plate. It was either that, or rip her clothes off and fuck her on the table for everyone to see. The second they hit that office— Xander cut off the thought. What if his brother showed him the exit again? If he allowed London to go alone with Javier, there was no way his brother wouldn't spend most of the afternoon with his cock in her sweet, tight cunt. And London had no reason to say no.

Xander wondered if that would leave him apart from the two people he cared about most.

Javier dug into his food, but it didn't take him long to wrap one hand around his fork and the other back up her skirt. London half-heartedly picked at her food, instead squirming in her seat, obviously biting her lip to hold in moans and fighting the urge to beg. Xander doused his eggs with Tabasco. Even so, they were tasteless to him.

He watched London and his brother with his cock hard and his anxiety high until she flushed a deep rosy shade. Perspiration dotted her upper lip. He'd given up trying to eat and merely watched, wondering if his brother would make her come in public.

London's breathing turned choppier. She gripped the table, eyes closed. A sensual expression of concentration passed over her face, brow furrowed, lips pursed. No doubt, she was seconds away from coming.

Suddenly, Javier withdrew his fingers and licked them again.

"Those panties are in my way too much to continue, little one. Next time you'll follow directions, yes?"

Her eyes fluttered open, and London looked ready to protest. Xander took her hand in his, tracing circles over the back of her palm lightly. "Don't argue. Just say yes and lose the panties once we get in the car. Then he'll be far more pleasant."

She snapped her gaze around to him, still looking as if she wanted to argue. "You're both pushy."

"That's not likely to change. Out of bed, we'll treat you like a princess," Javier promised. "We will spoil you, but we're going to get at your pussy without obstruction, without argument, and without waiting."

We. So . . . he and Javier were both in this odd relationship with London. He had no idea where it was going or how long it would last, but he couldn't deny that he was damn sure happier than he'd been in a long while.

Xander nodded. "Well said, brother."

He and his brother finished their breakfast. When he looked over, London had eaten half her food. Since she was still squirming in her seat, he figured she was preoccupied and let her lack of eating slide.

They paid the bill and left the restaurant. Javier climbed in the backseat of the car with London. Xander and his brother both turned to look at her expectantly, and his brother held out his hand, fingers gesturing with impatience.

She sighed. "You're serious?"

Javier merely raised a brow. He had the displeased Dom face down. Xander was almost proud.

"I don't understand."

"It's about trust," Xander said. "Will we hurt you? No. Will we touch you? Absolutely. Do you trust us to touch you?"

"Yes. But this seems so . . . unusual."

London had been so sheltered, and Xander knew they were asking for a lot very quickly. But having her here between him and his brother seemed to be working some magic on their rapport. Not to mention the fact that Xander was getting damn desperate to get inside her again.

With a huff, London rolled her eyes and tried to reach under her skirt as discreetly as possible. With a lot of grunting, wriggling, and tugging, she managed to lift her skirt enough and lower her panties. Pink silk trimmed in delicate white lace. In the rearview mirror, he watched as, with trembling fingers, she placed them in Javier's palm. His brother smiled wolfishly, brought her underwear to his nose, and sniffed deeply.

London gasped, looking somewhere between shocked and aroused.

The rest of the drive to the office was almost too short. Not only was he dying to know what Javier would have done with London in the backseat given more time, but dread had taken up residence in his gut again. Now that they'd arrived, would Javier lock him out?

As Xander parked, he shut the car off. In the sweltering Louisiana summer, he knew his brother wouldn't linger long in his black car without air-conditioning. Javier dove out, then held out his hand to London. Xander followed them out of the car, drawing in a bracing breath.

Before anyone could say a word, Javier's phone rang. He cursed and looked at the display. "Hi, Doug."

Maynard. Xander winced. He hadn't had a chance to tell Javier about all the decisions he and London had made last night. He presumed London hadn't either.

The other man kept talking in Javier's ear while they entered the office building. London dug out her keys, and they rode the elevator in silence.

Not surprisingly, the call dropped inside the little car.

Javier turned to Xander. "What the hell is Maynard talking about? What did you two decide about the log-ins?"

"The three of us," London volunteered. "I helped Xander and Doug, too."

His brother's expression didn't change. "Explain."

London opened the door as Javier's phone rang again.

"I'll call you back." Then Javier gestured them both into the office.

Xander swallowed and entered. This shouldn't mean so much. Even a week ago, he'd had no secret yen to get ass deep in S.I. Industries—or at least not one he was willing to admit aloud. But somehow, after spending more time with his brother, everything had changed. Now he knew just how deep Javier had fallen into guilt and booze. He realized the jeopardy their business was in. And for once, Xander felt how badly being without purpose chafed. London seemed to be the balm soothing all that.

They flipped on lights, and London went immediately to her workstation, turning on her computer. Javier opened his interior office door and stalked through, then turned back with an impatient glare. "Both of you, in here. Now."

Xander didn't love his older brother barking orders at him, but Javier could just as easily have thrown him out, so he shrugged and followed. It helped his mood to know that London wasn't wearing a damn thing under her skirt.

They sat at the little round conference table inside Javier's office. Xander figured at this point that the best defense was a good offense.

"I helped London with some of her work last night. I agreed with Maynard's assessment that it's likely someone outside the company has been accessing our most proprietary information regarding Project Recovery with these log-ins."

"So you kept them active?" Javier's tone suggested he was one hundred percent idiot.

Xander clenched his jaw. "If we take them down, we'll never know who's behind the spying. If we keep the log-ins up and provide the spy access to false information, then we might be able to track the culprit. I told Maynard to work with someone trusted in R & D to swap out the current project information visible to those IDs with something bogus and to call it the newest, most exciting shit ever." He shrugged. "See who bites."

Javier paused, considering. "I don't hate that idea."

From his brother, that was almost glowing praise.

"Maynard picked his son-in-law to doctor the data. We elected not to get Sheppard involved." He referenced the head of R & D. "If he was so gung ho to keep those log-ins up, I'm a little suspicious."

"That he's helping someone on the outside obtain our proprietary information?" When Xander nodded, Javier turned pensive. "It's possible. We should keep him in the dark for a bit. He's worked for me for the last eight years, and he's a smart bastard, but a mercenary one. It's possible he's selling the company out."

"The only thing that keeps bugging me is . . . Sheppard has had opportunities before, right? So why now?" Xander asked.

Javier cocked his head, silently agreeing. "Well, he got remarried. I'm told that wife number three has expensive taste."

"They're leaving for Fiji next week," London told Javier. "His assistant told me that when she sent me an e-mail asking to get on your calendar for a meeting."

"He's got to keep the new wife happy somehow," Xander pointed out.

Javier seemed to ponder their next move, then he turned to London. "I'm going to call Maynard back and get a quick status update. While I'm doing that, track down Sheppard and tell him I want to talk to him."

"Yes, sir." London excused herself and left the room.

Xander watched them both reach for phones, torn between keeping up with his brother and finding out exactly how wet London was without her panties. He didn't even have time to decide before she dashed back to Javier's office and tapped his brother's shoulder.

"Sir, Sheppard is on hold for you. He's very upset."

"Great," Javier rolled his eyes and muted the call, clutching the phone. "Maynard wants to discuss some suspicious activity that's occurred with those log-ins in the last few hours." His brother looked at London's expectant face, then the phone in his own hand. He sighed and shoved the phone into Xander's hand. "Talk to him. Listen to whatever the hell it is he's trying to say. I need to calm Sheppard before he goes ape shit and makes problems."

Xander grabbed the phone and watched with an odd sense of triumph as his brother stormed over to London's desk. He was in. Finally, he had some purpose—no matter how small—at S.I. Industries. By God, he would make the most of it and prove himself indispensable to Javier.

With a deep breath, he unmuted the call and greeted Maynard.

"Your brother is distracted. I tried to call him all fucking morning. I hope to hell you're prepared to listen," the head of security barked. "One of the log-ins has been accessed in the middle of the night from an Internet café in Cancun, Mexico. They downloaded all the new materials."

Someone from a vacation mecca working? "Do any of the contract employees or researchers live there?"

"No."

"Any of them on vacation?"

"No. I did some discreet probing before I called. No one."

As much as Xander hated to think of some ass-wipe stealing from them, if they were logging in and falling for the phony information they'd planted, so much the better. They would prosecute the thieves and roll out Project Recovery as scheduled.

"I've heard Sheppard shitting a brick from the third floor because, out of the blue, United Velocity is supposedly making a major announcement soon."

The company's biggest competitor for U.S. military dollars

having something press-worthy all of a sudden wasn't good . . . but it also wasn't proof positive that United Velocity had anything to do with the theft of S.I.'s research, even though they had scooped S.I. on its last few projects.

"Keep your ears to the ground and check in with me tomorrow so we can stay on top of this. And get your son-in-law working on more phony information, just in case." Xander had a plan. "We might need it later."

Maynard agreed, and they ended the call. A quick glance through the little vertical windows between this office and the outer reception revealed that Javier was still on the phone. In fact, he looked tense and red, like his blood pressure had just shot up a hundred points. London stood beside him with a supportive hand on his shoulder. The Javier he knew would have pushed her away. Xander was stunned when his brother paced the floor a few times, then grabbed London close and, with the phone pressed to his ear, buried his face in her neck.

Javier didn't need more stress; he needed results. And they all needed to figure out where this impromptu trio of theirs was headed.

Xander flipped through his list of contacts and found the one person he knew would get results in the most efficient, quiet way possible—an ex-military friend who happened to be his former bodyguard. Over the years, Decker McConnell had proven remarkably agile in digging through the refuse and rubble of humanity to uncover others' dirty little secrets. Now, he could do the digging that employees of S.I. Industries couldn't without raising brows. And if Decker managed a heaping plateful of catching the culprits and he wanted a side helping of blood . . . well, Xander wouldn't mind in the least.

Decker answered on the first ring. "What did you do to get in trouble now?"

With a smile, Xander sat in Javier's chair. "What makes you think I'm in trouble?"

The other man snorted. "Just every one of your phone calls for the last half-dozen years."

Yeah, Decker could extricate him from all kinds of trouble, which had come in handy more than occasionally.

"Besides that," Xander joked. "I have an issue, and I need your help."

"Please tell me this isn't another jealous husband threatening to kill you."

"Nope." Xander winced. Had his whole life been a fucking caricature? It seemed like everyone viewed his existence as the punch line to a dirty joke. On the other hand, what had he done except a whole lot of women?

He looked at London and wondered what it would be like if he could say he'd done the last woman he ever intended to do again. Surprisingly, the thought didn't give him hives. If he had to settle on one, he'd want one sweet, with a hint of spine and sass, who would try to understand him. He'd want one he could spoil and be himself with, who wasn't jaded. One who would always put their bond first. Funny, he'd never boiled down what he wanted in a woman to a simple checklist, but now that he had . . . was there any way that London didn't fit the bill?

Not that he could see.

Xander swallowed. "My problem has nothing to do with a woman. This is a corporate matter."

Decker listened as Xander described the situation, the compromised log-ins, the IP address of the latest access leading them to Cancun, the history of corporate espionage he couldn't prove but definitely suspected.

"Wow, this kind of issue is definitely off the beaten path for you," Decker quipped. "Any suspects in particular you want me to focus in on? And how are we for time frame?"

"We need this ASAP. Focus on employees of United Velocity." Xander tried to wrack his brain for anyone who might have a specific beef with S.I. Industries and only came up with one other name. "Also check into a guy named Chad Brenner. He used to be one of our scientists and invented a few really important technologies while he worked for us. Brenner didn't like the fact that, when he joined us, he signed away his intellectual property rights. Everything he built while employed by S.I. belonged to us because he created it on our dime. He sued and lost. It's been about two years, but maybe he's still bitter. I don't know. It's probably just simple corporate greed on United Velocity's part because they were in the toilet until the last year or so, and I think they're still on shaky ground. I really can't think of anyone else."

"I'll start there and check back in as soon as I've got something. I know a few guys who deal in what I like to call underground capitalism. I'll dig up something. If you don't hear from me for a few days, that means I'm finding something juicy."

They hung up, and Xander pocketed his phone. He probably ought to bring his brother up to speed, but a glance through the little window revealed that Javier's mood hadn't improved. Now he paced the floor, looking like he couldn't wait to rip someone a new asshole. Finally, he growled into the phone, then ended the call with an emphatic slam of the receiver.

"What's wrong?" Xander asked his brother, wandering out to the reception area. "Sheppard give you bad news?"

"United Velocity is having an unveiling of a new prototype of a light tactical vehicle *with* ambulance capabilities, just like ours. According to their press release a few minutes ago, they've just had a breakthrough and are eager to unveil it to the military community. Convenient, isn't it? We've only got twenty-six days to beat them to market."

"If they just read our bogus information last night, how would they already have translated it into a prototype they're ready to unveil?"

"I knew they'd been working on something similar. I'd heard

they were breathing down our necks and that it would be a race to see who got to market first."

"But we're almost ready?"

"Within three months, yes. But twenty-six days?" Javier raked a hand through his hair. Suddenly, he had that I-miss-vodka look on his face.

"If they've taken the bait, they're working with bogus information."

"If. But what if they using whatever they obtained from us before Maynard's son-in-law uploaded whatever crap he invented?"

Yeah, they really couldn't know what United Velocity had yet. Xander's stomach plummeted to his toes. Fuck. This was bad news all the way around—unless they did something quick.

"How long have they been working on that sort of vehicle?"

Javier shrugged. "That's anyone's guess. There are always whispers, but they've got their dirty little fingers in everyone's pie. I just don't know how they keep getting into ours. We can't let this go or we're sunk."

At the very least, getting trumped again would mean the end of S.I.'s reputation as forerunners in the defense contractor game. It would also mean the potential loss of up to a billion dollars in profit. The balance sheets couldn't afford that much red.

And he couldn't let his brother disappear back into a bottle of booze.

Xander sent an alarmed glance at London, and saw that she immediately grasped the problem. Concern tightened her face.

"So we'll ramp up everything and launch ours within twenty-five days," he told his brother. "We have a product that works. If they've looked at our bogus information, they don't. If they've looked at genuine research, we'll just beat them. We'll just have to show the world."

Javier's answer was an ugly curse.

Surreptitiously, he sent Decker a text and told him to hurry the fuck up because they were definitely on a tight schedule now, then he withdrew the car keys from his pants, passing London on his way out the door. "I've got to duck out. Distract him. Calm him. Seduce him if you need. But whatever you do, don't let him call for a bottle."

Her solemn nod told him that she totally understood. "I won't let either of you down."

Chapter Fourteen

LONDON watched Xander leave with no idea where he was going. But he'd be back. No way was he going to abandon his brother now. She cast a worried glance over at Javier. Every inch of his tall frame tightened as he paced the office, fists clenched. He was a powder keg waiting to explode.

Xander's words rolled through her head. *Distract him. Calm him. Seduce him if you need.* London had no idea if it would work, but Javier had been alone for too long. She had to try to show him that she stood by his side, ready to help, no matter what.

As he turned away and she watched the broad expanse of his back encased in a tailored charcoal coat retreat to the far side of the room, she quickly removed the clip from her hair and let it cascade over her shoulders, then released the top two buttons of her blouse. Her cleavage swelled above her white lace bra, and her pale tresses flirted with her curves, curling over one of her fair breasts. Would it be enough to entice him?

Javier punched the wall on the far side of the room. Startled, she jumped. Then she thanked God for the solid wood paneling along that wall, despite how ugly it was and how dark it made the room.

He pivoted back in her direction with angry precision. Immediately, his gaze lifted from the carpet to her, traveling up her body slowly until that stare fastened on her breasts. He stopped. Their gazes connected. His eyes turned from cold fury to a hot smolder. Sizzle spread through her.

"Your blouse is unbuttoned."

"I'm aware of that, Sir."

"If you don't fix it now, I'm going to fuck you."

This was exactly the reaction London had hoped for, but excitement still rushed through her body, converging between her legs. She blushed. "I'm looking forward to that, Sir."

He stalked in her direction. "You're trying to tempt me, little one."

Heat blasted off his body and enveloped her. In mere seconds, her clit began to throb. After a morning of sex, she shouldn't *need* him as much as she did. But with Javier, she couldn't seem to help herself.

"Is it working, Sir?" A glance down at the hard ridge of his cock beneath his pants proved that it was, but she wanted to hear him say it.

"It is. But like the first time I fucked you, you're topping me from the bottom. It's not only disrespectful of your boss, but it's disobedient toward your Dom."

London had no idea why, but the implied threat of punishment made her shiver. And it made her ache to play along. "I'm sorry, Sir, but my nipples are tight, and my breasts heavy. My, um . . . my body feels empty.

"Not your body; your pussy," he said with a low growl.

"Yes."

"Say it."

The flush crawled up her face, but she pressed on. "My pussy is so empty. I assumed you'd want me to advise you. But I can tell your brother or take care of myself in the bathroom, if you'd prefer."

His eyes narrowed, and London got the feeling she was in for one hell of a punishment. But at least Javier was no longer thinking about how stressed he was or how much he wanted to escape into vodka.

He stormed into his office and halted two feet from his desk, pointing to the ground. "Come here."

London did as he demanded, walking a bit more slowly than normal, swaying her hips. "Yes, Sir?"

"Bend over the desk. Lift your skirt. Show me your ass."

She froze, then exhaled, trying to relax. If she lifted her skirt the right way, he wouldn't see any of the scarring. She just had to keep her wits about her. Always hard with either of these men, but showing them . . . it was something she'd never voluntarily shown anyone who wasn't a medical professional. And probably never would.

London bit her lip, then turned to face the desk. She sent Javier a glance over her shoulder, fluttering her lashes at him. As she turned back, she saw Xander standing in the door again, that black leather backpack in his hand. Repressing a shiver, she leaned over the desk, then reached back to her pencil skirt, inching it up her thighs one fistful at a time, making them both wait. When she felt cool air caress the bottom of her cheeks, she stopped, then angled her head to send Xander a come-hither stare.

"Fuck!" Javier cursed, and she heard the raspy tug of his zipper a moment later. "That's not high enough, little one. Hike it up. Now."

Her womb clenched, and she could feel the blood running to her folds, flooding her clit. But she did as she was told, lifting the little black skirt to her hips and hoping they couldn't see any of the hated, jagged scars.

Xander marched over to her and grabbed her wrists, stretching her arms across the desk, startling her. He held a pair of handcuffs and quickly snapped one around her wrist, fed the other behind the chunky drawer pull in the middle of Javier's desk, then secured the other cuff around her free wrist. London pulled, and the metal clinked. She wasn't going anywhere.

"Spread your legs," Xander demanded. "Let him see that pussy he's going to fuck."

London swallowed. Her heart raced so quick and hard, it was almost a pain in her chest. Her thighs trembled, but she managed to spread them wide. She looked up in time to see Xander pluck something pink from the bag, along with a little tube. He set the pack on the floor, out of her sight, then joined Javier behind her.

"Damn, that's pretty," Xander said. "I brought condoms."

"She needs a goddamn spanking. The sassy girl is trying to tempt me."

"And it's working." Xander laughed. "When you're done with her punishment, I've got a surprise for her."

London wished she could see what was going on behind her, but suddenly Javier's voice took a much calmer tone. "Excellent. Good thinking."

Without warning, she felt a large palm strike the fleshiest part of her ass. She yelped. It stung. Hurt. And she knew there were more coming.

"Quiet," Javier barked. "Take your punishment with manners. When you tempt me like this, I'm going to turn your ass red. Tell me you understand."

She closed her eyes, letting the sensuality of the moment wash over her. "I understand, Sir."

She'd barely gotten the last word out when she felt his hand slap her other cheek. The initial pain made her gasp and her knees buckle. Then Javier grabbed her hips and rubbed her cheeks with his warm palm. The hurt instantly diffused to a tingling heat. Her skin felt alive.

And her pussy ached like never before.

"Oh!" The little exclamation slipped out.

Suddenly, she felt two fingers slip between her slick folds and sink deep inside her. She moaned and arched to take them deeper inside to ease her need.

"She's so wet, Javi," Xander reported. "She's ripe."

"So my bad girl is naughty, too?" He murmured in her ear.

London had no idea when he'd gotten so close, but when she tried to turn her gaze over her shoulder to him, Xander's free hand tangled in her hair, preventing all movement. "Stay still. Eyes forward. Take the rest of your punishment."

"Yes." Her voice shook, then she whimpered.

He withdrew his fingers from her needy channel.

Javier quickly took up where his brother left off. The next two blows hit lower on her ass, making the burn spread across her skin. After that, he inflicted two more back on the fleshy curve, then gave her another handful in the same spot for good measure. The pain always startled her. She braced and winced and dreaded . . . until he smoothed it all out with that magical touch of his, spreading the sweet heat everywhere and distributing the burn through her body.

London moaned as his lips traced over the hot flesh of her right cheek. His tongue peeked out to drag across one curve before he bit gently into her. An incomprehensible pleasure slid over her. She had no idea why she liked Javier's punishment. It hurt . . . but even the pain became something beautiful and wound through her body like the softest ribbon. It held her together when she really wanted to unravel.

Xander released her hair with a little warning tug, then backed up, standing somewhere behind her with his brother. He whistled. "That is one beautiful, rosy ass."

"It is," Javier agreed. "Any time you goad me into giving in, little one, expect me to retaliate."

"Would I be allowed to ask if you would please fuck me?" she panted.

"Do you ache?" he asked, sounding supremely satisfied by that prospect.

"Yes, Sir." She whimpered and squirmed.

"Do you need it?" he bellowed louder.

"I do." What she'd started to distract him had ended up consuming her. Her entire body was a living flame, and only he could douse it.

"Don't forget, Javi. I have something to add first. Wait patiently, *belleza*," Xander said.

Holy hell, was he going to spank her, too? The thought made her hot, dizzy, and weak with need.

Instead, she felt something cool slither over her back entrance. She gasped and tried to clench her cheeks together, but Xander pried them apart with his hands and slid one finger down slowly into the passage no one had ever touched.

"Xander?" Alarm made her voice a squeak.

"Shh. This won't hurt. But you have two men who want you, and we're going to want to fuck you at the same time. We have to stretch you to take us both."

Anal sex. She'd heard of it, of course. What they were saying made sense. But did women really let their men take them *there*?

Questions whizzed through her head as Xander withdrew his finger, then probed at her hole again, this time doubling the thickness of the intrusion.

"Damn, I want that," Javier groaned, then rushed beside her to growl in her ear. "I want to fuck you there and hear you whimper and yelp as I slowly feed you every inch of my cock. I want you to sit on it and squirm and cry, yet still take me because I want you to."

When he put it like that, London wanted it, too. It would probably hurt at least a bit at first, and still she wanted to do it because he wanted her with a primitive passion. And she desperately hoped that she meant something to him beyond sex. She hadn't started anything with either one of these men with the intent to fall in love . . . yet London suspected she was about to fall off the cliff.

"I want to take every perfect, pretty hole you have so deeply and thoroughly that you scream. Then I want to see Xander do the same before we take you together. Can you handle being between us as we both fuck you?"

London didn't know for sure, but she desperately wanted to try. With a mewl, she nodded at him. "Please . . ."

"Xander, be quick, damn it." Javier's deep growl told London that he was at the end of his rope.

"I can't rush this." Xander probed her, his two fingers thrusting deep and slow into her ass.

The sensations were foreign and primal. London arched to take more, and Xander petted her hip, then leaned in to whisper to her. "I can't wait until I'm feeding my cock into this tight little ass. I'll do it long and slow until you're screaming and clawing—then Javier will do the same, until you know exactly whose cocks belong here. It's the most submissive gift you can give us. Are you going to give it all to us?"

London didn't hesitate, just nodded frantically. "Yes. Whatever you want."

"Good girl, *belleza*," he crooned, then turned to his brother. "I think she's ready for the next step now. I'll bet her pussy is juicy and ripe."

Javier's fingers slid over her so-swollen folds, just barely touching her distended clit. London bit her lip to hold in a cry of need.

"Very juicy. And delicious. Do your thing."

She barely had time to question what either of them intended before Javier dropped between her legs, back propped against the desk, and fastened his mouth onto her pussy. She gasped at the rush of sensations to her clit . . . just as something hard and cold and foreign began to invade her ass and fill the empty space, burning and stretching. She tried to twist and slide away. It was a reflex, but Xander's hard slap to her ass and warning growl made her stand still so he could slowly feed the rest of the object into her untouched passage.

She wriggled and moaned, biting her lip as it widened and

stretched her even more, but Xander just kept pushing the soft plastic-like plug deep into her. Nerve endings she'd never known existed tingled to life. London tossed her head back with a cry at the pleasure-pain, urged higher by Javier's insistent tongue on her clit.

Pleasure roared through her blood, gathering to fill and heat and tighten everything between her legs.

"Come!" they both shouted.

Their insistence, their togetherness, the ecstasy they heaped on her made it impossible to resist. Javier's tongue rubbed her aching little bud as she exploded into a trembling heap of dazed pleasure so thick she felt drunk and weak. Xander stepped away and fumbled into the bag for something as Javier lapped at her once more, twice, then stood and jerked his pants down. His brother tossed him a little foil square. He ripped it open and scrambled to his feet behind her. Two seconds later, he prodded her pussy, sinking in so deep through her swollen tissues made tighter by the plug. The extra pressure awakened more nerve endings, and she howled for him.

Xander didn't wait long to jump into the action either, unzipping in front of her face. He took his hard cock in hand and caressed her lips with the silky velvet, hard head. She opened, and he slid deep onto her tongue, filling up her mouth and nostrils with everything that reminded her of Xander. Musky, manly, teasing—he rarely pounced, but slowly approached with something sly and irresistible, until succumbing was her only choice. She opened wider to take him in, laving him with her tongue as he held her chin with one hand and grabbed her hair with the other. Those sensations alone would put her on overload, but Javier behind her—inside her—filling her completely, stretching and scraping every sensitive nerve, compounded by his hand cupping her mound possessively, gently kindling her clit into a roaring burn. She couldn't take it. Couldn't stop it. Couldn't do anything but feel it.

She flipped her gaze up to Xander's face, pleading silently. He focused solely on her, staring at her, breathing with her, consuming her. She cried out around his cock, the sound beseeching, even as she felt herself tightening around Javier's thick, blunt cock. The bliss built again, the high of it starting to overwhelm her once more.

London held her breath as her every muscle tightened, filling until she was primed—and then she let go. The wave of ecstasy ripped through her body, over her head, making her jolt and scream and open herself all the way to her soul. Xander cursed. Javier groaned. Both picked up the pace, then released, cocks pounding and jerking as they poured into her.

Salty seed coated her tongue. Perspiration covered her skin. Repletion unfurled in her, a happy, hazy lethargy almost as addicting as the pleasure itself.

As Xander eased his cock from her mouth, she sank to the desk, blazing cheek resting on the cool wood, and closed her eyes in contentment.

"You all right?" he asked, bending to kiss her other overheated cheek.

Lazily, she smiled and nodded.

He laughed as he uncuffed her wrists with a few metallic clicks. "I think your assistant might be done for the day."

Gingerly, Javier withdrew. She heard the gentle whoosh of his condom hitting the trash can. "We may have worked her hard today, but I'd like to worship her just a bit more."

With a gentle hand around her middle, he assisted her to her feet. She swayed in his arms, loving how solid and comforting it felt to be in his embrace, especially when he called her beautiful and whispered kisses up her neck. She shivered. Xander approached, sandwiching her in between them and holding her close.

"I need to see you, little one," Javier murmured. "Undress for me."

"For us," Xander said. "I'm dying to see you, too."

Their request hit her like a splash of icy water into her eyes, shocking and painful. Something to be avoided at all costs. Brian, a man in the medical field, had seen her back and been too repulsed to continue dating her. But two beautiful billionaires catching sight of all her flaws?

London swallowed down bile as she wriggled out from between them and lowered her skirt. Hands shaking, she held back tears and fumbled with the buttons of her blouse. "No. I'll do most anything you ask of me, but don't ask me for that. Please."

They turned identical scowls her way, and she felt their confusion and disappointment like a palpable wave. Her stomach balled painfully, and she pressed a fist to it. It hurt her to upset them, probably more than it should. But it would hurt so much more to disgust them with all the scars she couldn't change. Even the thought of her horror and rejection was more than she could take.

Shoving the last button of her blouse into its mooring, she gave into her tears as she ran from the room, grabbed her purse, and emerged into the steamy Lafayette afternoon.

* * *

"WHAT the hell just happened?" Javier blinked. He didn't understand anything except that London's stricken, terrified expression made him feel sick to his stomach.

Xander scowled, and Javier understood. They had no idea what brick wall of a boundary they'd run into. He'd seen London naked this morning in his bed, her beautiful breasts rising above her soft stomach, tapering down into her plush thighs and the wet feminine flesh between that hugged his cock so snugly. She'd opened up and given more than he'd possibly hoped for—until this moment.

"No idea, but I'm going to find out. I'll be damned if London is going to walk home in this terrible heat in a business skirt and heels."

Xander nodded. "Good point."

Together, Javier and his brother ran for the door and scrambled down the stairs. He beat Xander by less than a second through the lobby, and saw London making her way across the parking lot, toward the street.

"London," he called out to her, every muscle in his gut tight with the need for her to turn and face him, return and explain—let him hold and reassure her.

She ignored them and kept walking away.

Suddenly, she paused and swayed on her feet, reaching out for something to grab and steady herself. There were no cars nearby, just air.

With a gasp, she stumbled. Her knees buckled, gave way. Javier sprinted after her with everything he had. Beside him, Xander did the same.

"London!"

They were too late to save her. They simply had to watch her crumble to the asphalt. Javier's heart stopped as her head hit the blacktop with a thud. Worry raced through his veins. The few feet between him and London seemed like an insurmountable divide. The more he ran toward her, the longer it seemed to take.

With a curse, he skidded to a halt beside her. Xander did the same, cradling her head in his hand. London was passed out cold.

The fear scratching through Javier's veins like a hundred needles bled all through his body and was mirrored on Xander's face.

"Call 911," Javier snapped.

Xander did that as Javier scooped her up in his arms. He debated the wisdom of moving her in this state. Was this one of the blackouts she'd mentioned the day he'd hired her?

"They'll be here in a minute." Xander pocketed his phone. "Do you know what might have caused this? She didn't eat a lot at breakfast."

"She told me she has occasional blackouts, but I don't know the cause. We've been strenuous with her today." And Javier wanted to kick himself for it. "Maybe . . ."

He couldn't choke out the rest of the words. Dread squeezed his heart as he carried her across the parking lot and into the lobby. A granite bench sat near the water feature, and he set her there. Her pale hair spilled over the edge as he knelt beside her. In the distance, he heard the wail of sirens. Cupping her cheek in his hand, he stared, willing her to open her pretty blue eyes and look at him.

On the other side of the bench, Xander crouched, clutching her hand. "*Belleza*, we're here, baby. Come back to us."

A small crowd had gathered around them, loitering near the elevators. A couple entering the building stopped in their tracks and stared. Javier ignored them. If they weren't able to help London, they were useless to him.

Turning his body to best block their view, Javier pressed his lips to London's ear. "Little one, I'm sorry . . ." For pushing her, for overusing her, for making her feel the urge to leave. For everything. Francesca had proven that he was bad with relationships. For London's sake, he should probably put a safe distance between them and leave her to Xander. Normally, he'd think his brother was far too much of a playboy to be serious about one woman, but everything about Xander's behavior with London was different. He would be better for her. Lighter. He could still be the Dom she needed, but he came with so much less baggage, so many fewer demands.

If she opened her eyes and recovered, he'd try to do the right thing by London and leave her alone.

Suddenly, a pair of EMTs jogged into the building, and the gawking couple moved out of the way to let them pass, rubbernecking on their way to the elevators.

Javier stood aside and let the two men in uniform near London. Xander stood by his side, watching with grim intent. The EMTs asked them questions about the incident, and it became clear that they were worried she might have a concussion after hitting her head. But neither he nor his brother had any idea what had caused her to pass out in the first place. Exhaustion? Low blood sugar? The mysterious health problems she'd mentioned?

Xander whipped out his phone and scrolled through his contacts for Alyssa. Before he could hit the button to dial her, the EMTs stuck a chunk of smelling salts beneath London's nose. She came awake with a sputtering cough, her lashes fluttering up and revealing dazed blue eyes. But she was all right. As she pushed upright, and the men assisted her, Javier exhaled in relief.

His brother hovered protectively, listening as they asked questions. She fished a bottle of medication from her purse, and she had a bit more conversation with the medical people. He couldn't hear because of the low murmur of her voice and the roar of his heart. Whatever she said, Xander's jaw tightened with anger, but he pocketed his phone and nodded.

As the EMTs packed up and headed for the door, Javier intercepted them. "Is she all right?"

One nodded. "She forgot to take her medicine, but this isn't the first time she's blacked out, according to her. I gave her an ice pack for that bump on her head, but otherwise, she's fine."

But it wasn't fine to him. He had too many unanswered questions. Yes, he probably should leave her in Xander's hands . . . but he couldn't stop caring.

As the EMTs left, he made his way over to London and Xander. It would hurt to watch them together. But he'd always have work. And vodka. It was probably all he deserved.

His brother took one arm to help her to her feet. Javier took the other. She wobbled, a bit unsteady at first. She blinked and shook her head, as if trying to reestablish her equilibrium. Then she stepped away from them.

"I'm fine. It happens. It's nothing. I need to go."

London looked around for the doors, then headed toward them. Xander flashed a stare at him that said he was letting her leave over his dead body. She might not be his, but he agreed with his brother.

"You need to come upstairs and explain," Javier found himself demanding.

"Right now," Xander added, blocking her path.

"Taking my virginity doesn't give you the right to strip me of all privacy and free will," she hissed.

About that, she was absolutely right, but that answer didn't set well with him. And Xander, always the lover, not the fighter, looked ready to punch something in frustration.

"It doesn't," Javier returned smoothly. "But as your boss, I deserve an explanation about why you intend to walk off the job in the middle of a crisis."

He was reaching with that argument. And he didn't care. If it got her to stay so he could understand and watch over her before he turned her back over to Xander, then he could relinquish her with a clear conscience.

London gnawed on her lower lip for a tense moment. "Fine. Ten minutes."

It was a small victory, and he didn't dare celebrate it now. "Put that ice on your head."

She did with a huff as they led her back into the elevator, ushering her into S.I. Industries' temporary offices again. Javier shut and locked the door behind them, then shepherded Xander to take her to his chair. His brother caught on and dropped her into the thick leather piece, pulling up one of the smaller chairs and getting right in her face. Javier paced around them.

"Are you really all right? You don't have to be brave," he said softly.

No matter what happened next, he cared for her and wanted her to know that her well-being meant a great deal to him.

She heaved a huge sigh, and tears started to gloss over her blue eyes. As they pooled then fell down her cheek, a bit of mascara stained just under her eyes. And still she looked so fucking beautiful that his heart wrenched. He had no idea how he'd ever manage to keep his distance once he bowed out and left her to his brother.

"I'm fine," she insisted. "Look, I didn't want to vomit out this whole sob story and make you feel sorry for me. I don't need more pity. I've had nothing else for years, and I wanted to see if someone actually could like me for me. Usually when I tell everyone this story, there's all kinds of sympathy, then people get distant. They hire and date 'normal' people. I won't be surprised when neither of you wants me again."

She shrugged like it didn't matter, but Javier could see on her face that it mattered very much. He didn't want to prove her sad theory right, but he wanted her safe and happy. Xander could give her that.

"Just after school let out for my sophomore year, I was with my friend Amber and her boyfriend, coming back from a day at the beach. While we were there, Amber found Josh under the pier with this other girl from school. They were making out, and Amber got furious. Josh tried to calm her down, but she insisted on leaving. We all got in the car, and she drove like a maniac. She was blasting music so I couldn't hear the whole argument. It started to rain, and Amber missed a red light. We got hit multiple times by oncoming traffic on the right, which spun the car around and into the path of a school bus that hit us head on after coming down a hill. Amber and Josh were killed instantly. I had what the doctors called a traumatic brain injury."

She swallowed, as if the rush of anger she'd used to get the story out had washed away, leaving her nothing but pain and a gritty determination to go on. Though stunned, Javier couldn't ever remember a time he'd wanted to touch her so badly.

"I'm so sorry, *belleza*," Xander murmured, gripping her hands. "Go on."

Her chin trembled as she fought the urge to speak without spilling more tears. "I had a skull fracture, hematoma, and some nerve damage. My jaw, elbow, and femur were all broken. I spent nearly two years in a coma. When I woke, everything had changed. There'd been a war. My parents had aged ten years. I'd missed prom. Graduation was around the corner, and I was going to be left behind. I couldn't walk or talk. The doctors told me I might not ever do either again. At that point, most of my 'friends' had bailed on me. But I kept fighting back. I've had three surgeries on my back to repair disk problems. As a result of the head trauma, I sometimes forget things. I can't drive and I may never be able to because I sometimes black out, like today. I'll probably never be able to be alone with my own child." Fresh tears spilled over, along with a whole bunch of anger. "But I *refuse* to be broken!"

"You're not, little one," Javier assured her, managing to speak past his own choked words.

His heart hurt. She'd suffered more than physically. The emotional scars ran deep. She felt defective and unwanted. Yet she'd gathered the courage to march into his office and interview for a job. Despite feeing imperfect, she'd given herself utterly to him and his brother. Her personal courage amazed him. After Francesca's death, he'd allowed guilt to stab him over and over until he'd nearly lain down and died willingly. London had latched onto her fighting spirit until she'd taught herself to talk and walk, to live and laugh and love again. He was humbled. God, he didn't deserve her.

"And now you're both staring at me like I'm a freak." She lurched to her feet, swiping angrily at her tears. "I've got to go. I'm sure you'll replace me in your office and your bed with someone better."

Xander stormed after her, but only Javier could reach the doorway in time to block her path. He didn't deserve her and he might be bad for her, but he'd be damned if he was going to prove her theory that no one could love her right. Because he already did. It was right there in his heart, on the tip of his tongue.

The fact that he loved her bowled him over. Holy fuck, when had that happened? Somewhere between her crisp sassiness during her job interview and seeing her angry tears at fate mingling with her strong will to carry on. But he now understood what he'd never felt for Francesca, this sweet feeling that seemed so potent and abiding. For London, he'd do anything—lie, kill, steal, die—if it made her happy and whole.

He crossed his arms over his chest and stared her down. It hurt him. He wanted to hold her desperately, but she would see it as pity and hate him for it. No matter what it cost him, he had to stay strong for her.

"You're not leaving. I'm not replacing you in my office or my bed, London. I want you to hear me very clearly. I want you in that chair." He pointed toward the assistant's chair in the reception area. "And I want you taking my cock every day and night, again and again. You're not broken. You're so beautiful that I sometimes can't believe my good fortune."

Over her shoulder, he glanced at Xander, who stalked toward her, then raised a shaking hand to her shoulder and turned her until he stared down into her eyes. His brother met her like a freight train, his body crashing into hers, his arms folding around her in a silent offer of his strength. For a terrible moment, she pushed at him, thrashing about to escape.

"I don't want your pity," she hurled at him.

"Good." Xander grabbed handfuls of her hair and yanked, forcing her head back. "Trust me, it's not pity I feel. You amaze me."

"For accomplishing nothing in life?" She screeched.

Her emotions were getting the better of her, and Javier couldn't stand it another moment. He blanketed her back, sandwiching her in between him and his brother. He braced heavy hands on her shoulders. "You've had to come further and fight harder than anyone I know. I could learn from you how to keep putting one foot in front of the other. In a handful of days, you've made me think that maybe vodka isn't the answer; persistence is. Just like you, I'll have good days and bad days. But I'll have full days. You refused to rot help-lessly in bed. You got up and learned to be productive, got yourself an education, and started on the path to a full life. Until you, I was throwing mine away slowly but surely, down the narrow neck of a bottle of Cîroc."

London began to turn toward him. Xander released her slowly. She blinked up at him, her wet eyes defiant, as if she dared him to leave her. Even if he wanted to, even if it would be good for her, Javier knew he wouldn't. Couldn't. More and more, he began to believe that they all belonged together. He'd never imagined sharing a woman with anyone, much less his brother. He certainly wouldn't have chosen it long-term.

But in that moment, that's exactly what he was choosing. His heart had chosen for him.

"I'm not leaving you. Neither is my brother. Trust us."

Confusion broke across her delicate face. A furrow marred her pale brows as she shook her head. "You can have anyone you want. He has." She pointed at Xander. "I'm—"

"Perfect for me and my brother. I'm done questioning it. How about you, Xander?"

He paused, this moment oddly introspective for him. Finally, he shrugged. "I've never felt this way, and I'm not ready to let what we have go. Somehow . . . this works."

London hung her head. "You could have better."

"There's no such thing, and if you keep up that self-deprecation, I'm going to paddle your ass black-and-blue."

She frowned and wrapped her arms around her middle, seeming to curl into herself as she stepped away. Javier watched her. If she got anywhere near that door, he would stop her. But if she needed a mo-ment's space, he would grant her that.

"I'll do my best to believe you. I'm sorry. It won't be overnight."

Frustrating, but understandable. She'd missed years of experiences, of maturing, of simply living. After that sort of trauma, it was understandable that she'd be cautious.

He nodded and tried to stay away, but he couldn't not touch her. Slowly, he approached and wrapped a hand around her arm, drawing her close and kissing the top of her head. "You scared me today."

"It's one of those things I can't help. With everything that's happened in the last twenty-four hours, I forgot my medication."

Xander flashed her a disapproving glare that Javier was sure was mirrored on his face. "Unacceptable. From now on, we'll help remind you."

"I'm not an invalid," she shot back to Xander.

"That doesn't mean we don't all need help now and then."

Xander was right, and Javier figured he could learn a lesson from that, too. Fuck, what an emotional, enlightening day it had been. And it was barely half over.

"Little one, tell me something." He caressed her cheek. "Why won't you undress for us?"

"I'm not going to give you the up close and visual of everything that's wrong with me. Consider that my . . . what did you call it? Hard limit. If that's a problem for you, then we should all move on." She picked up her purse again. "If you can deal with it, good. I'll be in here planning a launch party that will blow United Velocity's away."

Chapter Fifteen

XANDER watched London walk away and shut the door behind her. They hadn't hit a hard limit but a brick fucking wall. On any other woman, one not acting as his submissive, their private life and feelings were their own. It wasn't like he ever wanted to get deep with a woman, except in her pussy.

London changed everything.

"We can't let that go," Javier said.

"We can't," he agreed. "She's hiding from us."

"And herself. We have to help her accept who she is and that she's beautiful."

Javier was right, and that meant they had to get a bit more demanding. London would likely earn punishments before she let them behind her walls. Xander smiled. He was kind of looking forward to that.

"Yep."

Javier hesitated. "And we're in this together? I don't want you to start something that you won't finish."

He knew what his brother was asking. Xander paused, rechecking his thoughts. But they were unchanged. He wanted London at his side, between him and Javi. Somehow, she made their discord fade, made it possible for them to be brothers again. In turn, the budding woman and submissive needed him and his brother to guide, protect, and care for her. Every so often, it seemed that *he* actually shed light on her confusion and his brother's darkness. It was as if someone needed him for a change. He liked that feeling. A lot.

"Yep. We're in it together."

"You can't play with this girl, Xander. You can't fuck her a few times, then find your next slut du jour." Javier raked a hand through his hair. "If you're not *all* in, the time to get out is now."

Xander bristled. What the hell gave Javier the right to question him or tell him how to run his damn love life? He opened his mouth to tell his older brother to go to hell when he realized that Javier was protecting London. He wouldn't do that if he didn't care. Which meant that, his brother really did finally give a shit about something beyond guilt and booze.

And Javier was right. London didn't know anything about the fast lane, musical beds sort of life he'd been living for more than a decade. She had given herself totally to the two of them. They meant *something* to her. As fragile as her self-image was, he couldn't keep crawling in her pussy, then deal her the blow of choosing another, "perfect" girl over her later. It could crush her. And shockingly, that thought of never being with her again nearly dropped him to his knees.

Dragging in a ragged breath, Xander paced. No doubt, he cared more than a little. Maybe even more than a lot.

"I'm not getting out," he vowed.

Javier cocked his head. "Could you really live with her pussy being the last you ever fuck?"

Xander swallowed. Put like that, the situation sounded damn serious. London's had been the sweetest, yes. He hadn't had the pleasure of indulging since becoming her first, but the hunger to bind her to his bed and take her in every wicked way known to man gnawed at him. "I could. Other pussy . . . honestly, I've had it in all shapes, sizes, and colors. Every texture, every flavor, every day. I've sowed so many wild oats, the bucket's empty, man. I don't have to wonder what I might be missing out on. I already had it."

On the other hand, when he spent time with London and Javier, he felt this little mental *click*, like puzzle pieces had slid into place. They gave a shit about one another—and him. They actually seemed to like him as he was. Nothing had ever felt better. Hopeless romantics had talked about being "complete" for as long as he could remember. He finally got it.

In fact, Xander got everything. He'd been unconsciously seeking caring and acceptance in every bed he'd ever been in. He couldn't manufacture or pretend those feelings. He couldn't buy them, sell his soul for them—or fuck his way into them. They were more precious than diamonds and rarer than the clap at a convent. No way was he going to destroy what it had taken him a lifetime to find.

But he wasn't the only one who had to look in the mirror in order to make this work.

"I'm good. What about you?" Xander asked his brother.

"Me? Other women aren't going to be an issue."

"No, but vodka is. That's been your mistress for the last year. We don't have room for her in this relationship."

"That's not the same thing," Javier argued.

"Bullshit. You've let vodka console you a lot more than I have. London isn't going to put up with that shit. And she shouldn't have to. You can't shut her out or tell her to fuck off when she wants to talk to you about your bottle."

Javier's lips twitched into a snarl. "You handle your crap, and I'll deal with mine. Believe me, I know London is important. Maybe more important than anything else right now. I want the chance to make her deliriously happy."

Xander peered at his brother. "Are you thinking of marrying this girl?"

He shrugged. "Marriage didn't work well for me the first time, but I'm prepared to admit that I care about her more than I ever did Francesca. I don't know where that leaves us, but we'll figure it out."

"Yeah." Xander nodded. "I never thought I'd ever be monogamous, but . . . at this point I'm not saying never anymore. But she's bottled up, Javi, and wants to keep us on the other side of her defenses. I'm not sure she's looking at us as seriously as we're thinking about her."

Javier sighed like the weight of the world pressed on his shoulders. "I fucking had no idea she'd been through so much trauma."

"Me, either." And didn't he feel like an asshole for not finding out before now? He'd taken the most precious onetime gift she could give him, and he'd never asked many questions about how she'd come to be twenty-five and a virgin. Her explanation made so much sense, but the thought of her in that much darkness and pain twisted up his insides.

"We'll have to tread carefully," Javier said. "I know we can't force her trust, but we have to give her opportunities to see that she can count on us."

Absolutely. "Before she erects more walls between us."

"Fuck. How do we do that?"

Xander grinned. Yeah, this was when being more than a little cunning came in handy. "Take care of her. Use every opportunity to show her that we care. And on Friday, pack for an overnight stay. We'll pull out around three. I've got an idea."

* * *

THE days continued to slide by, Wednesday, Thursday . . . until Friday rolled around. Surprisingly, the rest of the week had been relatively drama-free, just intensely busy. London hadn't had much time for self-reflection. Her life had changed so much in less than a week, but she tossed analyzing that into the "later" category . . . just as she had calling her curious, concerned cousin.

For now, London quietly put into place all the necessary elements for a launch party for the Project Recovery prototype one day before United Velocity's. R & D was screaming that it would take every available hour to be ready, and Javier had begun to cut off Sheppard, the head of the department, with a terse "Get it done." Most of the invitees would attend over video conference, but for those who could come to the function in person in DC, she'd booked a secure office facility near the Capitol building. In light of the suspected information leaks, security would be tight, and Xander had assisted her with making sure those arrangements were in order. For someone who'd spent his entire adult life as a playboy, he had a way of buckling down and taking business very seriously.

Surprisingly, Javier had been far more focused—and sober—over the past few days. Maybe because they'd all been sharing the office space, and he hadn't wanted to endure his brother's well-meaning rebuke. Without the influence of vodka, he was nothing short of dynamic. He moved enormous amounts of work that had been sitting for months. The phones began ringing again, beginning with members of the board. By Friday, it was evident that Javier being "back" was making waves in the defense-contracting community. Everyone from the *Wall Street Journal* to *Defense Industry Daily* wanted the scoop. Even the *Los Angeles Times* tried to grab a few minutes of Javier's time. He accepted some calls, assuring people that he had something spectacular to unveil in a few short weeks and that he expected S.I. Industries to be at the top of the heap again by the New Year. Xander picked up the calls Javier couldn't, and London had overheard him attributing Javier's renewed dedication to both the end of his mourning and his new executive team, including his dynamo of an assistant. It probably shouldn't have, but that made her feel mushy and warm inside.

London sincerely hoped all that was true. Javier might backslide at some point. Not for one minute did she believe that he had fully dealt with Francesca's death. But for now, she liked her new, more productive boss.

He wasn't just her boss, though. Every day, he and Xander kissed her through coffee and muffins. Lunch they usually spent naked—sometimes in the office, sometimes in a nearby motel room. They stopped for a late dinner, often teasing her with whispers and not-so-innocent touches over multiple courses and a few glasses of wine, before heading to Javier's home. They'd hit the bed, and both men would devote hours to coaxing her submission and giving her pleasure until she finally curled up between them, sore, exhausted, and smiling. They repeated the cycle all over again the next day. When she stopped to think about the bubble of thrill her life had become, she couldn't stop grinning.

Still, London feared it was all temporary, and she told herself not to get too invested. Xander would soon want other women. Javier would soon want Cîroc. And she hadn't budged an inch about showing them the roadmap of scars crisscrossing her back. It had become like a "don't ask, don't tell" policy around the office and bedroom. But every time she insisted on simply unbuttoning her blouse, rather than taking it off, or wearing a tank top to bed, she knew they were disappointed. It wasn't as if she didn't want to trust them. Nor did she think they were shallow, but why run the risk of scaring them off? Hiding was so much safer.

"Shut down your computer, little one. We're leaving," Javier announced, briefcase in hand.

The door to his interior office was shut, the space inside dark. Beside him, Xander waited. He'd clearly cleaned off the project table they'd dragged into the empty room for him on the other side of the little reception area. Now, the two of them looked not only ready to leave, but eager. Xander's sly grin made her pause.

"It's only three o'clock."

"We didn't ask you for the time, *belleza*," Xander said. "We asked you to shut down and come with us."

And they weren't taking no for an answer. With a little shiver, she turned off her computer, grabbed her purse, and stood. "Where are we going?"

The two of them cast one another conspiratorial glances, then Xander crossed his arms over his chest. "It's a surprise."

It sounded both thrilling and ominous at once. She had no reason to balk. "Let me use the restroom and I'll be ready."

"When you're finished, open the door but stay inside."

Javier's demands would dampen her panties—if he'd let her wear any. Every time she tried, he simply tore them off.

Not certain what they were up to, she simply nodded and made her way to the little industrial bathroom. After taking care of business, she washed her hands, then opened the door. An instant later, Javier was practically on top of her. Xander awaited, too, holding a paper sack.

"Face the sink. Good. Bend over and brace your elbows on the counter."

London paused, and the sweet little ache they constantly kindled with nothing more than their voices flared to life between her legs again. Slowly, she complied, her mind racing. What were they up to?

The moment she was in place, they worked together to lift her skirt, rough hands brushing up her thighs, moving in tandem to reveal her ass and the pussy she'd taken to carefully shaving each morning. The long shirt she was wearing tucked in should cover her scars, but she still stiffened a bit.

In the mirror, she met their gazes. Neither could hide the excitement in their glittering eyes. Xander rustled in the bag, keeping it strategically placed behind her. He withdrew something, then handed it to Javier, who also removed an object from inside. Xander handed his mystery item to his brother, who smiled as he caressed her bare ass.

"God, this is one gorgeous backside," Javier praised, drawing his fingers down the crevice.

His fingers were slick and slightly cool. Lube. She shuddered. He lingered over her back entrance. Over the past few days, they'd both been working their fingers and progressively larger plugs inside her. After that, they usually couldn't wait to sheath up and fill her clenching, hungry pussy, riding her to one combustive orgasm after another. This time, Javier slid a new plug in her ass—definitely larger than the last, but he didn't reach for his zipper. Neither did Xander.

London sucked in a breath as Javier eased the plug in, then pulled it halfway free, only to thrust it deeper than before. He repeated the motion a few times, fucking her with it, and nerve endings she'd rarely felt roared to hot life. She gasped, clutching the edge of the counter. She stared at her dilating eyes in the mirror, stunned that they could turn her inside out so easily.

Behind her, they both moaned before Javier pressed it in completely, seating the base solidly against her cheeks. Xander reached around her and lazily stroked her clit, sending her libido into overdrive.

"She's so wet and ready." Xander took her by the elbow and helped her stand upright.

"Excellent. Take her out."

Reflexively, London clamped down on the plug and followed Xander. No doubt she was walking funny, but he said nothing. After washing his hands, Javier joined them, darting around her to lock the office door as they left.

The elevator ride was quiet, but London couldn't deny the silent hum of tension and arousal permeating the air. What the hell did they have in mind? And why wouldn't someone fuck her or touch her and make this terrible ache go away?

They drove out of Lafayette on I-49, which surprised her. Then they turned west at I-20, heading into east Texas. Even more shocking. What the heck were they up to? How long would they keep her needy and aware of her own body and near begging? On the road, they petted and touched. They kissed, praised, and toyed with her. But they didn't let her come. They just kept going, stopping only for gas, food, and quick bathroom breaks until the sun fell and the glittering lights of Dallas lay ahead.

Xander pulled into a sprawling, elegant mansion-looking hotel in an established, very posh neighborhood. With the plug still up her ass, she crawled ungracefully from the car with Javier's help and glanced wide-eyed at her surroundings. This place screamed old money.

As he exited the vehicle, Xander threw the keys at the valet as the bellman lugged suitcases from the trunk. Two of them. She didn't recognize the little bag she'd been keeping at Javier's among them.

"Where's my suitcase?" she whispered.

"I've got your toiletries, but you don't need anything else, little one." Javier grinned.

Did they plan to keep her naked all weekend? The idea alternately struck fear deep inside her. But she also couldn't deny arousal at their possessive caveman ways—and a pang of regret that she couldn't be nude or truly beautiful for them.

Soon, they made their way inside, to a palatial suite lavishly decorated in warm colors, antiques, polished dark woods. French doors opened onto a private walled patio with a table and several cozy chairs. Sumptuous linens covered the plump bed. The large marble bathroom had a double shower, plush towels, and fresh orchids. It was a luxurious dream. What the hell were they doing here?

Javier put his hands on her shoulders, his hot breath on her neck. "Would you like something to eat or drink?"

"N-no." What London really wanted were answers about why they'd come here and what they intended next, but if she demanded them, they would make her wait. And she really wanted an orgasm.

"Do you need a few minutes to nap?"

With her stomach in knots and her pussy on fire, did he think that was even possible? "No."

Out of the corner of her eye, she caught Xander prying into a suitcase. He extracted something black wrapped in plastic and disappeared into the bathroom. Javier caught her looking.

"Go with him."

She held in an impatient sigh. If she wanted to find out what these two were up to, she was going to have to play along.

London turned to make her way to the bathroom, but Javier caught her by the wrist and pulled her back against his body. His lips crashed down over hers, demanding and urgent. He anchored his fingers in her hair and pulled back gently until he had her under him precisely where he wanted her.

Just like every kiss he gave her, this one made her melt into him. The more she opened, the deeper he plunged until her head reeled, her heart chugged, and her pussy . . . When she was as wet as this, she missed panties.

A long, tingling moment later, he lifted his head and nuzzled her neck. "I'm crazy about you, little one."

Her heart skipped, tripped, then speeded up again. *I love you.* It sat on the tip of her tongue, but she kept it to herself. He enjoyed their time together, but while still dealing with his wife's tragic murder and whatever had driven him to drink in the first place, he wasn't going to fall in love again. Just like Xander wasn't going to give up his manwhore ways for her permanently. Hoping otherwise was for little girls who believe in fairy tales. "I feel the same, Sir."

The stark relief on his face puzzled her. Did he think she would be spending every day and night with him, opening herself in almost every way, if she didn't care?

Abruptly, he released her, then grabbed her shoulders and turned her toward the bathroom door. "Go on."

She walked gingerly into the bathroom. The bright lights rained a gentle heat on her face as Xander positioned her against the basin, lifted her skirt, and palmed her ass. Slowly, he slid the plug free. The removal of that insistent pressure made her sigh with relief. After washing the plug and his hands, he handed her the plastic-wrapped items in black.

"Put these on quickly. We don't want to be late." Xander brushed a kiss over her lips and was gone, shutting the door behind him.

It didn't take her long to figure out that the garments in the package revealed more than they concealed. A fishnet body stocking with sizeable round holes strategically arranged over her pussy and ass came first. After that, she pulled out a little leather . . . dress? She wasn't sure what else to call it. The bodice looked much like a bustier. Rather than lacing up the back, it zipped up the front and ended just below her breasts, which were completely exposed. They jutted out above the garment, her pinkish-brown nipples pouting and hard at the thought of all Javier and Xander might do to her tonight.

Beneath the tight bodice, there was a little leather peplum that ended just above her pussy, leaving it completely open to them. At her hips the little skirt flared lower. London turned and looked at herself over her shoulder in the mirror. The flap of leather covered half her ass. The other half was bare as the day she'd been born, except the fishnet clinging to her cheeks.

After quickly checking her hair and makeup, she slid on a pair of black platform shoes Xander had apparently placed on the counter, then she stared at herself. It was part ghetto streetwalker and part porn star, but unbelievably, she looked . . . wow.

Slowly, she pulled the door open and peeked out. They both stood just outside, waiting impatiently, their eyes gleaming. Any of her remaining uncertainty withered under their hot stares.

"No hiding behind the door, little one," Javier said. "Come out."

Her fingers trembled as she flipped off the bathroom light, then stepped into the bedroom. They groaned. A quick glance revealed they'd both changed into leather pants and now sported healthy bulges.

Xander palmed her breast, dragging his thumb over her nipple. "You look gorgeous."

"She does," Javier agreed, sliding a hand under the peplum and over her hip.

"Hmm," Xander leaned in to kiss the swell of her breast. "You make my kinky heart go pitter-patter."

London had to giggle at that.

Javier handed her a sleek black trench coat, and she slipped it on. Okay, so they weren't staying in the room, but going somewhere. Where this mode of dress was acceptable? Where would *that* be?

After they both slipped on tight black T-shirts, the brothers ushered her out the door. Xander had called ahead to claim the car, and they rocketed onto the softly lit streets toward the unknown. Curiosity nipped at her, but she didn't ask all the questions pelting her brain. She'd soon find out. For now, she trusted them to keep her from being arrested or mistaken for a prostitute.

She sat silently beside Javier, who suddenly reached around to blindfold her. Once the little padded mask was in place, he grasped her hand. Nerves jangled her stomach, but just his touch soothed her.

In a handful of minutes, the car stopped, and they helped her out. Inside, Xander greeted someone named Sweet Pea, who had a Betty Boop voice. He teased her a bit because apparently she'd dyed her hair purple. Then they headed through what sounded like another door, into a bar or lounge area. Low voices mingled. Glasses clinked.

After they threaded their way through the room, Xander gently pulled on her arm to stop her. "I'm going to lead you down these stairs. Follow my lead and trust me. I won't let you fall."

"I know." She flashed a little smile at him. The expression probably looked as nervous as she was, but he didn't mention it. Thanking God that no one could see her under the coat, she reached out for his hand.

Javier took her other arm and assisted. Slowly, they made their way down together. The sounds of slaps and moans combined with the smell of leather. Something musky permeated the air. Sweat?

Arousal? Sex? Whatever the heady scent was, it filled her nostrils and made her nipples tighten. This had to be some sort of sex club.

Just as she had the thought, they reached the bottom of the stairs, and Xander removed the blindfold. She blinked a few times to adjust to the lighting.

"It's so bright." She squinted. "I expected something to set the mood."

Xander shook his head. "It has to be well lit. If a Dom is going to spank his sub, tie her up, drip wax on her, or perform all the other deviant acts his mind can conjure, he must be able to see her to make sure she's getting adequate air and blood flow."

Good point. And looking around, she was hardly seeing the kink equivalent of candlelit dinners. Subs restrained over benches, on tables, on some giant X in the corner, most being spanked, flogged, or whipped. One Dom was carefully securing clothespins to his sub's breasts in a decorative pattern. Another was decorating his sub's back by threading ribbon in a corset pattern into the little metal rings he'd pierced into her skin. *Yikes!*

London jerked her gaze away, and Xander laughed.

"It's not funny. I hate needles or anything piercing flesh."

He sobered instantly. "You've had too much experience with injury. We won't do any of that, *belleza*. I'm sorry."

Javier palmed her nape and rubbed soothingly. "He's sorry for being an ass. Sadly, it happens all the time."

Xander punched his brother, but blocked her view of most of the scenes as they made their way down the hall, her heels clicking on the stained concrete floors.

"I heard a nasty rumor that you were here." A man emerged from the doorway in front of them with a grin, holding out his hand. Tall and lean, with penetrating gray eyes. Though he wore an elegant suit that could have made him look scholarly, the man put off a vibe like he was carefully reining in a motherlode of power.

"Thorpe, man! How are you?" Xander stuck out his hand.

The two shook and bumped shoulders as he answered. "I'm all right. Keeping busy. You still finding trouble?"

"Every minute I can." Xander turned toward her and his brother. "Thorpe, you remember Javier."

Thorpe scowled. "I do. Are you sober?"

London sucked in a breath. *Wow, that was direct.*

Javier narrowed his eyes, looking as if he was trying to keep his expression polite. "Yes."

"Glad to hear it." When Thorpe turned those gray eyes on her and studied her intently, she tried not to shiver. "Who is this sweet little sub?"

She couldn't make herself meet his gaze, so she dropped it to the floor. Was she supposed to answer? A flush crawled up her cheeks as she looked to Xander for direction.

"This is London. She's the cousin of one of Logan's extended family." He nudged her. "It's okay, *belleza*. You can speak to him."

Grabbing her fortitude with both hands, she made herself look up. She focused on Thorpe's brown hair, graying a bit at the temples. His direct gaze was too intense. "Hi."

He smiled gently. His imposing factor didn't go down that much, but at least she felt comfortable that he wouldn't be unleashing whatever dark side he had on her.

Thorpe took her hand between both of his. "Your first time to a club like Dominion?"

"Yes, it is."

"I recognized that wide-eyed look." His smile deepened, and under his close-cropped beard, she saw a hint of dimples. "Have fun and make them earn every ounce of your submission. Xander deserves a challenge."

"Don't listen to him," murmured a vixen who sauntered by in a lacy blue corset that showed off her lush breasts and tiny waist.

The woman's black hair swept across her shoulders. She wore a little black ribbon around her neck and a saucy smile on her face. She was centerfold beautiful.

"That will get you a red ass. Not that you won't enjoy it." The minx winked.

Thorpe raised a brow at her, thunder rolling across his face. "Callie . . . You're being disrespectful. Apologize now."

"Sorry, Xander," she tossed out lightly, lacking any sincerity. "You know how I am."

"A brat through and through. A million spankings won't cure you."

"Nope. But you're welcome to try." She laughed.

London shouldn't have liked her for propositioning her man, more or less. But she instantly liked the woman's humor and admired her moxie.

"Callie!" Thorpe's expression was nothing short of a rebuke.

She rolled her startlingly blue eyes, rimmed in dark kohl. "I'm going. I'm going." The other woman flipped her gaze at London. "Seriously, watch this one. I'm sure he and the devil share a gene or two. Ta-ta!"

Callie stuck out her tongue at Thorpe, then sauntered off. The man watched her go with clenched fists. The moment she turned her back, a stark, hungry longing spread over his taut face, startling London. If he wanted Callie, why did he hide it from her?

With a laugh, Xander turned to Thorpe. "Damn, she's taken bratty to a whole new level."

"Particularly since this Dom who recently moved to Dallas put a training collar around her neck. He's being far too lax with her." Thorpe clasped his hands behind his back, looking entirely without levity.

Wiping the smile off his face, Xander stared at Thorpe in shock. "You removed your protection and let another Dom take your place?"

Judging from Xander's tone, that was a big damn deal. And London understood. Thorpe obviously wanted the beautiful brunette fiercely.

Thorpe drew in a sharp, controlled breath. "I did."

Xander shook his head as if he still couldn't quite believe that. Then he turned to his brother. "Would you take London down the hall? Third door on the right." He handed Javier a card key. "I'll be right there."

Javier nodded, then slid his arm around her waist. "Let's go, little one."

London didn't want to leave. Curiosity as to why Thorpe would relinquish a woman he wanted lingered. Still, she followed Javier down the hall, into a private room.

He opened the door and admitted her, flipping on the light on the wall behind her and illuminating the wide array of BDSM implements inside. Whips, clamps, and restraints were coiled and gleaming all around the room. There was even an old-fashioned stockade inside. Suddenly, other people's sex lives took a backseat, and she started worrying about her own. She was a woman with little experience in a sex club with not one—but two—Doms. London swallowed. Was she in way over her head?

Chapter Sixteen

"ARE you out of your fucking mind?" Xander asked.

Thorpe cut a furious stare over to him. Yeah, yeah, so the big Dom on campus didn't appreciate his tone. His time with London was running short, and Xander wanted to make sure the guy knew that he—and likely a bunch of others around here—thought he'd lost his sanity.

"It's best for Callie," Thorpe said stiffly.

"Really? Or easier for you? If she's not under your protection or in your bed, then you don't have to try so hard not to care."

"I do care, and she knows that."

"Does she know that you love her?"

Thorpe reared back. "Now who's lost their fucking mind?"

"I'm not blind, man. I see the way you watch her, the way you shelter her. Remind me who paid for her education?"

"She wanted to go to college and couldn't afford it." Thorpe bristled. "She learned a lot of skills that she's brought to her job here."

"Are you really thinking about skills she picked up in a classroom when you fuck her?"

The other Dom gritted his teeth, looking like he wanted to rip

Xander limb from limb. "You'd know *far* more about fucking her than me. I've never had that privilege."

So that's what had Thorpe's panties in a twist. "Me, either. The one time I had the opportunity, when Logan was trying to tame her . . . I suspected you were lurking around. Hell, you could have been watching for all I knew. I've always known how you feel about her. I wasn't going to stab you in the back."

The visible relief on Thorpe's face would have been comical if he didn't understand how territorial a man in love could be. And the fact that he understood that after just a few days with London blew his mind.

"Thank you."

"You never touched Callie, not once?" Xander couldn't imagine the fortitude Thorpe must have to covet a woman for years yet never claim her.

"I've worked with Callie during a lot of training sessions, especially with new Dom/sub education classes. But that's public. Alone with the intent to . . ." He sucked in a shaky breath. "Just once. I stopped it quickly and I have no intention of going down that path again. She's twenty-five. I'm almost forty. She could do better."

Xander shook his head. Love was love. Why did anyone think age mattered that much? "I doubt that, and I know you're not fucking anyone else. Man, you ought to go after her. I think she's got deep feelings for you."

Dominion's owner had squared off against some other big bad Doms. He'd once chased down a would-be rapist and beat the crap out of him. Now the guy flinched. So Callie's feelings weren't news to him. That others had noticed was, however. "She's with someone else now, so drop the subject. Besides, when have you ever been a card-carrying member of love and fidelity?"

"Since London." Xander shrugged. "Maybe I'm being naïve because I haven't known her long. But I only know that I used to look at the world through jaded eyes and couldn't care less about tomorrow. Somehow, I see everything as she does now. I think of tomorrow with hope. I'm actually excited. Something just . . . clicked. You can go ahead and laugh."

Thorpe looked closer to crying, but he held it together with a manly grimace. "I'm happy for you. Treat her well and don't ever let her go."

Or you'll live to regret it. Xander heard Thorpe's unspoken words.

A moment later, the cell phone in Thorpe's pocket chirped. He answered, raising his hand with a wave as he walked away. The stupid fuck had let Callie go for some misguided principle. Xander shook his head at the stupidity of that, determined not to make the same mistake.

He started down the hall when he caught sight of Callie peeking around the wall. She'd been watching his discussion with Thorpe. Given the distance and the background noise, she wouldn't have heard a word, but the longing on her face spoke volumes. She wanted Thorpe just as badly. Knowing Callie, she'd done her very best to persuade him, too. That girl didn't give up easily.

Another man stopped behind her, wrapping a possessive hand around her small waist and dropping a kiss on her bare shoulder. Tall, dark, and blue-eyed—and clearly smitten with Callie—he palmed her nape with a proprietary grip. The girl greeted him with a warm smile and allowed him to lead her away after one more lingering glance at Thorpe's retreating figure.

Xander shook his head, feeling more than a little sorry for the lot of them. He'd never thought much about their mutually suppressed feelings before. He'd noticed them, but never cared much.

Maybe because, before London, he hadn't really believed in love.

Hell, what a difference a week and one incredible woman could make.

There was a bounce in his step as he made his way to the room in which she waited with Javier. Amazing that a week ago, he'd wanted to throttle his brother, and now he saw perfectly how essential Javier was—they all were—to this crazy, beautiful relationship. She made them both better men. And they challenged one another in subtle ways to raise their game, too. It was always about London. Any good D/s relationship was about giving the sub what she needed, but this . . . talk about a whole new level of wanting to protect and cherish.

If all went well, tonight would ratchet it up again. And cement their intimacy. He couldn't wait.

Xander stepped inside. He found London pacing on the far side of the room, the trench coat gone. She chewed on a ragged thumbnail. Javier watched her like a hungry, impatient predator.

When his brother's gaze fell on him, a smile stretched across Javier's face. Yeah, they were both more than ready to test the limits of her trust—and hopefully earn the opportunity to see every inch of lovely London naked, scars and all.

Xander approached her with a slow but relentless gait, stepping directly in her path. He gently grasped her shoulders, and she lifted her gaze to him. Anxiety tightened her face.

"London?"

"I don't know if I'm ready for . . . all this." She gestured to all the equipment around the room, giving a second nervous glance to the stockade.

He cradled her face in his hands. "Tonight isn't about all the stuff in this room, *belleza*. It's about us. Javier and I will be watching you carefully. You're so precious." He curled one palm around her nape. "We'd never do anything to truly hurt you. You always have your safe word, and we will always respect it. If I didn't, Thorpe would kill me," he joked. "He might look all sophisticated in a suit, but under that . . . He wouldn't be anyone's friend in a dark alley."

She sent him a lopsided little smile.

"That's our girl. What's your safe word?"

The smile fell. "Ford."

The word sounded raspy and uncertain, and Xander's heart clenched. "Right. Don't be afraid to use it if you need it. But tonight is about reaching what's here." He pointed to her head. "And here." He laid a hand over her heart. "Just breathe and relax and remember that we want everything you can give."

Javier joined him and took her hand in his, bringing it to his lips. "Exactly, little one."

London gave them both a shaky nod. Usually, she was stunning and nearly fearless. She submitted with aplomb and a natural grace that sang from her soul like a haunting ballad. Tonight, she seemed to be a clash of incongruent notes.

Apprehension niggled at Xander as he cast his brother a glance, silently asking if maybe they should wait or relent altogether. Javier gave a small shake of his head. He was right, Xander realized. They'd discussed this. London needed to unburden herself. Sometimes, necessary lessons were the hardest to learn, and trusting in such a case could be especially difficult. She had ample reasons to be worried— surrendering to a womanizer and a seemingly high-functioning alcoholic. But she had one big reason to put herself in their hands: her heart.

Xander prayed what she felt in there would be enough.

"Ready?" he asked her.

She hesitated, then nodded. "Yeah."

Javier raised a brow at her. "London? Is that how you address us?"

"Yes, Sir." She swallowed.

Repressing an indulgent smile, he took her elbow and led her to the St. Andrew's Cross. Eventually, he'd be tougher and insist that she put herself where and how he wanted her. But this would be her first big show of submission. In an unfamiliar place with exotic new equipment . . . challenging her too quickly wouldn't prove productive. He'd rather pick his battles.

As they reached the cross, he pulled one of her claw clips from the bag Javier had set at his feet, tacked the heavy strands of her hair to the back of her head, then backed her against the wooden X. Javier followed, grabbing one of her wrists and securing it in the attached cuff. Xander restrained the other, then they each knelt and attached an ankle at the bottom of the apparatus. Though subs were most often faced toward the cross, he wanted her to feel secure that her back was protected and hidden—for now.

She trembled, looking vulnerable and beautiful. Javier cut a glance his way, and his own feeling was mirrored in his brother's eyes. They had to be careful with this treasure. She'd granted them so much trust—been their strength, the bridge to span the chasm between them. They needed to build her up now and free her from this worry that they would discard her or care less if they saw all of her.

London looked like she wanted to ask a million questions, but stayed silent. Xander smiled at her tenderly. "You're doing great. We have some plans for you tonight. Remember to breathe. Don't think too hard. Just feel and know we're going to be here to catch you."

Xander didn't wait for a reply, but turned to find Javier ready and waiting, their first tool in his fist—a small, deadly sharp knife.

The second she saw the little blade, her eyes flared wide with panic. "Javier?"

"Relax, little one. Trust."

She swallowed, and they stood frozen, breath held. Finally, she gave them a jerky nod.

"That's not enough," Xander murmured. "Tell us you consent."

"I don't know what you're going to do," she argued.

"That's the point." He crossed his arms over his chest.

A long moment later, she drew in a shaky breath. "I either trust you two or I don't. That's what you're saying, right?"

"Precisely," Javier answered.

"Then yes, Sir. Go ahead."

London wasn't without reservation, but she was giving them some trust. Tentative, yes, but still beautiful. It both pleased and made him feel powerful to know that she literally put her safety in their hands.

Javier stalked closer, staring at her like he wanted to ravish her from head to toe. He probably did, and Xander understood perfectly, edging to the side to allow his brother to get closer to London. Javier lifted one of the webs of the fishnet away from her skin with the tip of the blade and pressed the flat of the cold metal between her breasts. She drew in a shaky gasp. Her entire body tensed. He paused again, waiting to see if she would use her safe word. But she remained quiet.

Leaning in, Javier slanted his lips over hers, the kiss looking somewhere between hungry and reassuring. Slowly, he coaxed her to open for him bit by bit until he completely dominated her mouth. Holding her chin in his free hand, he tilted her face to suit him and dove in even deeper, making her take him with a kiss so thorough and intimate, Xander got damn hard just watching.

Finally, his brother swept the very tip of her tongue with his own, brushed his mouth across her yielding lips, then eased away. She whimpered. Above the leather bustier, her nipples were hard. Her skin had flushed a sweet pink.

Javier looked into her eyes and turned the knife on its side, pressing it ever so gently into the soft valley between her breasts. When she gasped into his last kiss, he yanked back on the blade and sliced his way through the fishnet.

Relief relaxed her expression, and Xander smiled. He sidled closer on her right and spread his palm over her leather-clad torso. Her zipper cut cold into his skin, but when he molded his body against hers and seized her lips, everything inside him turned molten. Like goddamn candy, so sweet and pure, pink and delightful. London yielded to him utterly, the starch in her muscles softening as he felt his way up her body, fingers gripping the edge of the snipped fishnet. He pulled the tear wider, away from one breast, then the other, and cupped them, taunting her nipples with his thumbs. She'd look so fucking sexy adorned with clamps.

Xander fished a jeweled pair from a nearby drawer, alternately sucking both nipples until he secured the little jeweled bits, their alligator steel teeth biting into her tender nubs. And still he couldn't stand leaving her in merely a heightened state of sensitivity. Xander needed her attention, her pain, her desire. Her everything—especially her love. He tightened the clamps.

London's head fell back with a cry. Her fingers curled into fists, as if she wanted to grab him and hold on. The restraints didn't allow for that. But he had no doubt she was enjoying this little bite of pain.

"You look stunning, *belleza*," he crooned in her ear. "Do you like knowing that Javier and I are both looking at every exposed inch of you, dying to watch you come for our pleasure? Taste you? Fuck you?"

"Yes . . ." she mewled, looking at him with slightly dazed, pleading eyes.

"But not yet. I've got more surprises for you."

Javier neared her again, blade in hand. This time, she didn't even flinch when he rested the sharp edge just above her nipple, then slowly scraped upward. He didn't draw blood. In fact, he barely disturbed her skin at all. But the sight of her growing trust dazzled him. And it gave him hope. Maybe this plan would work.

The sound of the knife gently abrading her skin blended with her soft pants. He'd become teeth-grittingly hard. Xander ached to fuck her now, but her surrender couldn't be rushed.

"Is your heart racing, little one?" Javier pressed a kiss to her collarbone.

"Yes, Sir."

"Does your skin tingle?"

She nodded, pale hair caressing her shoulders. "Yes, Sir."

"Are you wet for us?"

London sent them the most inviting, beguiling stare. "I am, Sir."

Javier didn't even try to resist. He lowered his hand between her legs and rubbed gently. She moaned. Her lids drooped over increasingly glassy eyes. Her chest rose and fell quickly as she thrust her hips forward toward his touch.

Xander watched with a rapt stare as Javier thrust his fingers into her cunt, fucked her with them slowly once, twice, then withdrew, lifting his fingers high. They were drenched.

"Good girl." Javier sucked his fingers clean. "Very sweet."

A bolt of envy pierced Xander. Damn it, he wanted a sweet taste, too. *Soon*, he vowed. They still had so much to accomplish with London.

Javier twisted his wrist, and the blade that had scraped against her skin now tunneled under the spaghetti strap of her body suit. With a flick, it sliced in two, the little bits of material dangling. He shoved them away from the under-curve of her breast and kissed her pale skin.

Xander held his breath as he tightened his grip on her leather corset. A ball of anticipation sat in his abdomen and swirled energy all through his cock as he waited impatiently. Seconds later, Javier used the blade to cut the other strap. Xander tugged the fishnet completely away from her other breast.

London whimpered, looking sensual, dazed, under their spell. Goose bumps broke out all over her body. The moment dripped of her emotional rapture. She was swept up, eager—almost desperate—to keep giving to them. There was a whole lot more he was dying to take.

It was the perfect moment to grab the zipper of her corset and yank down.

The garment fell away from her body, hitting the concrete with a soft *thunk*. She blinked up at him, looking both hopelessly aroused and utterly lost. She wanted him to save her, and damn if that didn't make him even harder.

Xander grabbed the frayed edges of the body stocking and ripped through every silken joining until he'd torn it clear down to her pussy. The remnants of the garment clung to her thighs. Her torso was beautifully bare of everything except his little jeweled clamps.

Still flushed and panting, her red lips parted with a hovering plea, he skimmed a finger down her body, beginning at the little pool between her collarbones and working down, circling her breasts slowly, letting the dangling clamps swing and pull. London sucked in a shocked breath, and he tugged on the little jewels before fingering his way down her abdomen, slowing up as he stroked down even more. She held her breath. Every inch he descended, she sucked in a bit more until her sigh quivered. Then he slid his hand over her pussy, two fingers swirling over her clit. She cried out his name.

So primed, so perfect. So damn ready. But as much as he wanted to carry her to the bed and fuck her blind, he and Javier had a plan. The short-term orgasm wasn't as important as the long-term trust they were building. But damn it was getting hard to remember that.

Xander stepped away, eliciting a groan of protest from London. He shushed it with a raised brow, then reached for the bag of tricks they'd brought. The first thing he grabbed was the little plastic bag filled with white, fluffy material. It would look like a long, flat strip of simple cotton to her. He grinned. Looks could be deceiving.

He extracted it from the little bag and began to spread it thinly until it looked like the whitest, most delicate cotton candy. Questions ran rampant all over her face, but Xander didn't answer. He simply bent to place a soft kiss on the upper swell of her breast, then affixed a bit of the cotton to her skin, trailing it around her beaded nipple, then down her abdomen, ending just above her mons. He repeated the exercise with her other breast until the thin layer of stretched cotton made a little heart on her body. Javier grinned and knelt to adjust the cotton, centering it right over her pussy. And as long as he was down there, it was no surprise that his brother tongued her slick folds and licked her little candy clit. London's groan zipped thrill through him.

Next test now. Bigger than the last one. Xander's breath shuddered as he dragged it in.

He cupped London's cheek. "How do you feel, *belleza*?"

Her long, sharp gasp told him most of what he needed to know, especially since he could hear his brother making a noisy feast of her pussy below. "C-close, Sir."

"Hold your orgasm, sub. No coming." He infused his voice with command.

London gave a little mewl of protest, but she still managed to nod. "Yes, Sir."

"Javi . . ." he said in warning to his brother, who pulled away from her cunt with a noisy, obviously annoyed sigh. Too bad. Establishing trust was priority one.

Xander turned his full focus back on London. "Do you trust us?"

"Yes, Sir."

The words came without hesitation, and he hoped that she really meant them.

"Remember that."

At her nod, he bent and retrieved the item he needed to really light up this moment. He held it up in front of her face. "What is this?"

Her eyes widened, turning round and wary. "A l-lighter."

"Exactly."

Xander flicked the little igniter with his thumb. A little yellow flame flickered to life between them. He lowered it to the edge of the cotton, hovering near her pussy.

"Do you want to use your safe word?" Javier's stare drilled into her. "We would never damage you, little one, but we understand we're asking a lot."

"This won't hurt?" Her voice shook, and Xander understood. She'd already been through a great deal of trauma. They hadn't been together long enough for him to really understand her limits. She hadn't yet learned to completely give herself over to him and his brother.

But he hoped this would go a long way.

"Just the good kind," he promised.

"I must be crazy," she muttered to herself, then squeezed her eyes shut. "But I trust you."

Excitement roared to violent life inside him with all the subtlety of a volcano. Power and pride mixed, and suddenly all patience flew out the window.

As he reached out to light the cotton, London sputtered in fear, and her heart pounded in a rapid beat visible at the base of her neck. Her entire body trembled, but she still didn't use her safe word.

God, if he didn't fuck her soon, he was going to explode.

With one finger, he lifted her chin, ensuring her brows remained away from the open blaze, then he put the flame to the cotton just above her swollen, slick folds. The thin strips caught fire, flaming quick and bright—a flash of fury . . . then gone. Xander knew the moment the heat registered, and London realized this merely warmed her skin and electrified her senses, rather than singed or charred. She pushed her hips out, trying to meet the sensation. Yes, a burst of heat might put her over the edge, but it wasn't coming. *She* wasn't coming, unless he or Javier gave her the sensation with their hands or cocks.

Crying out for more, she thrust her breasts forward, pleading for something. Idly, Xander wondered if the next sensation would drive her over the edge and give them a reason to punish her for the fun of it.

"That was so good, *belleza*."

"And so brave," Javier added. "Thank you for your trust."

She gave them a shaky nod, her trembling body a plea all its own.

"Relax. If you're good, we'll heap pleasure on you soon."

"Hurry. Please . . ."

Xander gave his brother a glance and a jerk of his head toward London. Javier nodded, and together, they pulled the clamps from her sensitive nipples. In seconds, she screamed as the blood rushed back in. Simultaneously, they bent to lick and gently suck her nipples, giving her just a little bit of succor. London cried out. And even though they'd awakened every nerve ending in her body, she held back her orgasm.

Javier beamed at her, looking every bit as proud as he felt. "Excellent. You're so good."

But now came the biggest test of all.

Xander pressed his body against hers, and she hissed at the contact of his hot chest against her warmed skin. Fresh tears fell, ripping right into his heart. God, if she gave them the chance, they'd make everything all better for her. She'd never have to worry again for a day in her life about being alone or unsure. She belonged with them; he knew it all the way down to his marrow. Hopefully, after tonight, she would believe that, too.

Capturing her lips with his, he ravaged her mouth. The kiss wasn't graceful. It wasn't sweet. But it was raw and needy. That kiss staked a claim. Hoping to fuck she understood and trusted them enough for what came next, he twined his tongue around hers once more, thrusting a pair of fingers over her clit. Javier reached between them to pinch her nipples. She surged against him—her body, her tongue, her need—arching to them as much as her restraints allowed. London was *so* ready.

"Beautiful," Xander crooned. "Do you want to come?"

"Yes!" She couldn't blurt the word out fast enough. "Yes, Sir."

"We want you to. And once you do, *belleza* . . . Oh, baby, we're going to make you do it again with our tongues before we fuck you. You want that?"

London panted. "Y-yes, Sir! Please. Please . . . yes."

He looked over at Javier. His brother nodded back. They were still on the same page. *Excellent.*

Together, they reached up to release her wrists. She sagged against the cross as they knelt to her ankles and freed them as well. Blinking, she watched them, perspiration filming her skin, her eyes pleading.

"We're here for you, little one," Javier vowed, then pointed across the room. "All you have to do is walk to that bed across the room."

* * *

LONDON froze. Cross the floor naked, with *nothing* to cover her scars?

"Less than ten steps, *belleza*," Xander encouraged, holding out his hand. "You can do it. And when you do, we're going to be so proud of you."

She wanted that, along with the pleasure they promised. Her pussy throbbed endlessly. Their beaming smiles always made her glow inside. She'd do anything for their approval—except what they'd demanded. What if she followed their command and, instead of accepting smiles, she saw horrified gapes instead? What if they walked out the door?

Her gaze darted from them to the bed across the room. They flicked up to the bright overhead lights. She shuddered. In her head, she knew they wouldn't be that cruel, at least not to her face. But what if her ugly truth tainted their feelings for her? After all, they wouldn't be the first men who'd been repelled at the sight of her back. She couldn't really blame them; she hated the sight of it, too. And still her clit pounded in need . . .

"Turn off the lights." She knew she wasn't the Dom and had no right to make demands. But they knew her well. They must know how much this terrified her.

"No," Xander answered, his voice so gentle that she wanted to cry.

Maybe they didn't understand her hesitation. "But if I do that, you'll see . . ."

"Your back? Yes, that's the point. I don't get off on knife or fire play usually. And mind fucks that involve fear are never my idea of a turn-on. But tonight, *belleza*, I've been all kinds of aroused by your dazzling trust so far. Don't stop now."

"Think about it, little one," Javier jumped in. "A knife and an open flame have so much more potential to hurt you. We only want to see. Just walk across the room. We won't touch you, if you're not comfortable," Javier added. "We'll want to. But whatever you need, we're here for you."

A pretty speech, but . . . She bit her lower lip, backing up against the cross, fear an icy-hot sear through her blood. If the big X hadn't been sanded and coated in a glossy stain, the move probably would have dug splinters under her skin.

"What's the worst that can happen?" Xander asked softly.

Was he kidding? "You'll know how ugly I am."

Tears brimmed in her eyes, and one rained down her cheek. She wanted to trust them. This was hurting her because she knew how disappointed they were, but couldn't they understand? Of course not. They were beautiful, wealthy, smart, funny, and damn near perfect. She alone had the red, puckered tracks of tragedy raked across her skin.

Xander looked again at Javier, a silent question. Should they back down? Hope buoyed inside London, but Javier dashed it, shaking his head and looking as resolute as ever.

"You'll never be ugly to us, little one," Javier assured. "But we can't let you hide."

"Can I take my hair down?" Her voice trembled, whined. "Please."

Xander looked like he wanted to relent, but finally shook his head. "We can't allow you to keep using that crutch. You won't overcome your fear like that. Off the cross, sub. Walk across the room. Now, or face punishment."

He was probably right. She had to get over this fear. If this relationship was going to last even another few weeks, she couldn't keep hiding from them. If she showed them now and they shrank away in disgust, it would hurt like hell, but she'd know, right?

London drew in a huge shuddering breath and took a half-step away from the cross. She mustered up her determination, clenched her fists.

Pretty justifications, but . . .

"I-I can't." She shrank back.

God, she felt like a coward. Small and weak and every bit as fragile and confused as the girl who'd awakened from that coma to find that her life had utterly changed. Only now, it was worse. She was letting down two men she loved.

Yes, she loved them . . . and she still couldn't expose herself this way. She was going to disappoint them regardless. Why not stay safe doing it?

Javier narrowed those piercing blue eyes at her. "Can't, sub? Or won't?"

"We're deeply disappointed, London." Xander looked ready to tear the big steel door down with his bare hands. Or maybe he looked ready to grab her shoulders and beg. Anger and pain and defeat tightened his features.

That she could reduce these wonderful, proud men to this kind of angst shamed her to the core. And even that couldn't make her give them what they so desperately wanted from her. Was she so damn broken that she shouldn't be wasting their time at all?

At the thought, she ripped out the clip in her hair and let it cover her back as she dropped to her knees and began sobbing.

"London?" Javier asked.

She heard his steps coming closer and shook her head furiously. He couldn't see her. He couldn't touch her. Neither of them could or she would fall apart.

"Ford," she croaked out the word, then looked up to find their faces frozen and stricken.

Hating herself, she backed away from the cross and grabbed the trench coat from the table Javier had placed it on when they'd entered the room. As she donned it, she ached to go to them, let their arms enfold her, feel them around her again. But if she couldn't be the woman they needed, she had to stop wasting their time.

"I'm sorry."

Turning, she wrenched the door open and ran out.

Chapter Seventeen

LONDON had barely run three feet out the door when she bumped into a solid wall of flesh. Heart pumping, tears flowing, she looked up, blinking against the club's harsh lights.

Thorpe towered over her.

"I'm sorry, Sir." She tried not to sniffle and failed. "Excuse me."

When she tried to race around him, he grabbed her arm. He might look elegant, but under that impeccable suit and those cool gray eyes, he was shrewd and far stronger than she expected.

"Did you use your safe word?"

How had he guessed? Though her head was full of landmines exploding with pain and regret, she managed to nod.

He sighed. "Come with me."

She followed because he really left her little choice. When he didn't lead her immediately back to Javier and Xander, but rather down another hallway and through a door he unlocked with a key, then up a flight of stairs, London was more puzzled and relieved than worried.

"You're obviously upset. Would you like to talk about it?"

The room was dim, but she caught sight of a plush chocolate velvet sofa. It invited her to curl up and sob her eyes out, but the man standing in front of her demanded an answer with nothing more than his direct stare and a raised brow.

"No, Sir."

What else could she say? She was a coward who'd failed the two men she loved. She lacked the courage to believe that anyone could overlook her flaws enough to care for her, scars and all. She didn't have the strength to risk seeing the horror on their faces. Maybe she wasn't giving them enough credit. Maybe it wouldn't matter to them. But it mattered to her. She wanted to be perfect for them.

And she never would be.

The thought caved her chest in until she thought she would implode. She curled her arms around herself and couldn't quite stand upright as another sob wracked her.

Suddenly, warm arms wrapped around her, and Thorpe crooned in her ear. God, he even smelled expensive. The inane thought came from nowhere as he led her to a sleek leather club chair near a huge wall of tinted windows that overlooked the interior of the club.

He set her in the chair, then rose and poured a crystal decanter full of an amber liquid. He handed it to her. "Drink."

Clearly, he spent a lot of time in this room, overseeing Dominion.

London clutched the glass. She really wasn't supposed to drink with her medication, but the whole night was irrevocably in ruins, so what the hell? She lifted the glass to her lips and gulped down the contents, barely tasting. It smelled like alcohol, soft spices, with a hint of something floral. It burned gently going down. Best of all, it infused her with warmth right away. A moment later, it made her head slightly fuzzy. And it relaxed her. *Ahhh* . . .

"Thank you." She glanced up at him gratefully.

Thorpe smiled wryly. "You're welcome. Most people savor a glass of Cuvée 1888, but if the cognac calmed you, that's good enough for me."

She winced. Chugging very expensive booze was a no-no. "Sorry, Sir."

He waved her off and looked out the window, into the leather-and latex-clad crowd below with an overseer's stare. "Did they hurt you or force you past your limits?"

"No."

"Good. If you'd rather not talk, I respect that, but for your safety, I can't let you wander the dungeon floor without a Dom at your side or a collar around your neck. You'll be eaten alive."

London flushed and was thankful the room was probably too dark for Thorpe to see. She should have thought of that. It was a sex club, and with this many potential predators roaming about, she should have realized that some Doms might construe her as prey.

"Of course. I wasn't thinking."

"Neither were Xander and Javier. Clearly."

"I ran out and—"

"They allowed it."

Yes, they had. Because she'd disappointed them—probably for the last time. Worse, if she had to make the choice again, nothing would change. A crushing sadness pressed down on her shoulders. It wasn't as if they loved her or anything even close. Somehow, she needed to move on. They would.

And not for anything would she confess all this to the elegant, perfect stranger before her.

"I should go. Would you escort me out?" She rose to her feet on wobbly knees.

Thorpe zipped a pointed stare directly at her. London sat again, and he nodded with satisfaction.

"Would you like me to call a taxi for you?"

She'd left her purse—her phone, her meds, her money—back at the hotel room. *Stupid, stupid, stupid.* "No, thank you. I'll walk." Where to, she had no idea.

"You're not walking alone in this neighborhood." His stern expression backed that up. "And contrary to what you're thinking, Xander and Javier don't appear willing to leave without you."

Whipping her gaze around, she looked out the big, slanted window, to the floor of the club below. Within seconds, she spotted them both, searching the dungeon for her. Xander tried to search unobtrusively, scanning the participants, then creeping past one station after another.

A beautiful blonde made her way toward him on towering silver stilettos. Her mile-long legs gleamed tan and bare under the lighting. The cheeks of her perfect ass were high and firm in a little lacy thong as she approached. The shirt she wore . . . calling it a tank top would be generous, with little glittering straps and a silky, shimmering material that draped elegantly around her slender figure.

The woman slid to her knees before Xander, head bowed, offering herself—and exposing her bare, utterly perfect back from her nape nearly down to the crack of her ass. For a terrible moment, London's heart stopped. She pressed a hand over her lips as more tears burned her eyes. She bit her lip to hold in the sob. Thorpe must already pity her. No way was she going to give him more reasons to feel sorry for her.

When Xander splayed his palm on the crown of the sub's pale head and bent to whisper in her ear, London tore her gaze away. She couldn't watch. The moment was a stark, ugly reminder that Xander wasn't really hers. She'd been something between a convenient distraction and a way to help his brother. The other woman was a beauty Xander would likely welcome, particularly after her own failure. London had to face facts. A gorgeous billionaire who could have—and had—taken any woman he wanted to bed would never choose the scarred, chubby girl. She'd been living in a fantasy world to ever think that was possible for longer than it took for him to have an orgasm or two.

She turned and caught sight of Javier on the other side of the room, still searching for her. Apparently he didn't give a whit for being polite. He barged in on a Dom who towered over three subs on leashes crouched on all fours. After inspecting their faces, Javier ripped away, crowding a Dom who'd restrained a squirming sub to a table wearing only a leather hood that concealed everything but her nostrils. Blond hair cascaded around her, covering most of her breasts.

London knew Javier was going to burst into the middle of the Dom's scene. She didn't know a lot about this world, but she couldn't imagine that behavior would be welcome. It had to be like the doorbell ringing in the middle of sex.

She gasped, and looked to Thorpe, who'd gone tense.

"I can't let this continue," he bit out.

"I understand." Javier couldn't be allowed to act like a bull who'd make a china shop out of his business.

With her heart in her throat, she glanced back over to the spot where Xander had been with the kneeling sub. They were both gone, and knowing him, well . . . he'd soon be inside the perfect blonde, giving her the kind of incredible ecstasy London knew she'd never feel again.

Barely holding in her tears, she whipped away from the window and paced across the room.

"Wait here," Thorpe barked.

Gladly. London didn't dare look out the glass again. But when she turned, the phone on the little coffee table taunted her. She could call Alyssa and plead with her cousin to pick her up. Immediately, London dismissed the idea. Lafayette was six hours away, and she couldn't take the busy woman away from her businesses or her toddler. Alyssa's plate was already full. London knew she had to find her own way out of this mess.

She collapsed onto the sofa, leaning on the soft arm, and sobbed until she felt spent and sick and so wretchedly empty, she had no idea how she'd ever feel whole again. By now, Xander had undoubtedly given the mystery blonde a slew of orgasms. Maybe he would want his brother to join in as well and help him devour their new, unblemished conquest. An ice pick to the chest would hurt less, but the other woman was probably what they both needed.

It certainly wasn't her.

Suddenly, Thorpe opened the door again. "Come with me."

Where? In the end, London didn't ask. She didn't care. She just wiped her tears and rose.

When he offered his arm, she slipped her shaking hand around the hard strength of his biceps.

Without a word, Thorpe led her out of the room, down the stairs, and into his private office. Besides an industrial desk and a sleek laptop, culture abounded here, too. Expensive art. Glass and stainless steel. Within these four walls, sleek, practiced women knelt for Dominant men's pleasure. She wore nothing but a trench coat and smudged mascara. Less than a week ago, she'd been a virgin.

She didn't belong here.

A moment later, the desk chair swiveled, and Javier stood, looking both furious and relieved. He slammed an empty glass on Thorpe's desk and barreled toward her. With a snarl, he grabbed her shoulders, pushed her against the wall, crowded her body with his. He smelled of vodka, hunger, and determination. Her breath caught, and her womb clenched.

Of course she wanted him, but she couldn't be selfish. She'd always love him and Xander with all her heart. Right now, she'd assure them she was fine, then quietly slip out of their lives. But she couldn't, in good conscience, stay when she couldn't be what they needed.

* * *

GRABBING her face in his hands, Javier stared down at London's wide blue eyes. He gripped her possessively, torn between embracing her from now until the end of time and turning her over his knee to blister her ass red.

"Don't you *ever* put yourself in danger like that again. You don't know who the fuck is stalking around a club like this. Sick freaks who devour innocent little girls for dessert."

"I do screen my clients, thank you," Thorpe drawled from the doorway.

Javier turned on the guy. "And your system is foolproof? I notice that you didn't let her alone on the dungeon floor."

"Touché." Thorpe ignored him to regard London. "He's right. This isn't anyplace to be independent. Play nicely, Santiago. I'll send your brother in and leave you alone to . . . talk."

When the man bowed out, Javier watched London drop her gaze to the slick marble tile. His heart ached. He and Xander had pushed her too hard, and Javier kicked himself for not listening to his brother's instincts more. But London's fears went deeper than tonight's fiasco. He didn't know what it would take to reach and reassure her, but whatever it was, he wanted to do it now. As soon as Xander showed, they would talk to her, listen and negotiate, let her know how special she was . . . tell her that they loved her.

"Don't run out on us, London. If you're not ready for everything we've demanded, then okay. But don't leave. Talk to us."

"He's right."

They both turned to find Xander standing in the doorway, his mouth tight, his shoulders tense. Javier sensed that his own anxiety and anger were mirrored in his brother's mood.

"Weren't you busy with the perfect blonde?" London clapped her lips shut as soon as the words left her mouth. "Never mind. You don't owe me anything, and it's none of my business."

"You don't like the thought of me with Whitney? Good. I'm not interested in her. She offered. I refused. She did me a . . . favor a few weeks ago, and it didn't work out as expected." Xander slanted a glance at him, and Javier winced. "I apologized to her. Then I looked for you again until Thorpe sent me here. What the hell are you thinking, running away?"

London's face crumbled into something so sad. "This isn't going to work. Us."

Javier's stomach clenched, dropped. Dread and denial ripped through his system a second later. When he was with her and his brother, it felt so natural, like breathing. He'd never been happier. They'd made her happy, too, goddamn it. He'd seen that on her face, in her radiant smile, the light glowing from her eyes.

"Bullshit." Xander stepped in and slammed the door. "That's utter fucking bullshit. It's fear talking. It's you refusing to believe or trust that we care enough to stay, despite whatever you're hiding. So we didn't get to see your back tonight. I'm disappointed, but I can be patient."

"I don't think I can ever show you." She tried to wiggle from his embrace, but Javier held firm. "You've done everything, given me everything, but that doesn't change who I am. My limitations. What I fear. Let me go. Really, I just can't . . ."

"You're choosing not to," Xander argued calmly.

Javier saw red. "So are you giving us that old line? It's not you, it's me?" The thought that she'd even try that crap on them made his head want to explode. "Don't. I swear, just . . . don't. You're the first person or thing I've given a damn about in years. I'm not letting you go."

"Javier—"

He cut her off with a kiss. No goddamn way was he going to listen to her excuses and self-doubt. She'd pulled him out of a mental hole so deep, he'd been sure he'd never come out. He wanted to do the same for her. Of course he understood that she felt overwhelmed, vulnerable, and scared. But if she'd let them, he and Xander could make her feel so loved that she'd never want to leave.

As if reading his thoughts, Xander merged in behind London, sandwiching her between them. Javier was relieved to see his brother tug the coat away from her neck and lay fiery kisses across her skin, nipping hotly at her lobe. She tore her lips from his and eased her head back on Xander's shoulder. Javier ripped open her coat, and his brother palmed her breasts. She arched into Xander's demanding touch.

Jesus, the sight of London, eyes closed, lips parted in rising desire, with his brother's hands all over her, turned him inside out. Because Xander felt like an extension of his own flesh and blood? Because, like their childhood, he and his brother were in this together, now striving to please the girl they loved? Whatever the reason, it was working for him. Now if they could just reach her, get her to understand that showing them whatever she hid would be all right . . .

"We can't . . ." she gasped. "Not here. Not anymore."

"Fuck that," Xander growled in her ear, then turned her to face him. "We can, *belleza*. Every day. Hell, every hour. That's how bad we want you. Whatever you're thinking about not being pretty or good enough, it's so fucking wrong."

As Xander ground his lips over hers, sinking deep into her mouth, Javier stared at the black trench coat that covered the back London wouldn't reveal. But she hadn't said anything about the rest of her being off limits.

He needed her. They both did. Feeling her skin under their hands and her cries in their ears might calm the terrified, raging beast inside him. Maybe. But more, London needed their reassurance. They had to make her believe that they wanted her in every way, no matter what.

With a gentle shove, he urged the other two across the room. It didn't take long for Xander to raise his head from the silken heaven of London's lips and scowl.

"Sit in the chair, Xander," Javier demanded.

Something—his tone, his expression, the erection about to burst out of his pants—must have communicated to his brother because Xander led her across the room and complied.

London looked down at his brother, who reached for his zipper with a tempting, taunting smile. He lowered the little metal tab, sliding it over almost-silent metal teeth.

She tensed, held her breath, then let it all out in a frustrated sigh. "Stop. It's not that I don't want you. I do. God . . . I just can't be what you need. I'm trying to set you free so you can find her. Don't make this harder on me."

"You *are* her," Xander shot back. "We're going to help you see it." His brother pulled back the front flaps of his leather pants and stroked his straining erection, thumb sliding over the ruddy tip.

Javier pressed his body against London, pushing his own hard cock into the small of her back and nipping at her lobe with his teeth. "You're going to feel how much we need you, little one, just the way you are. Get on your knees."

"But I . . ." She shook her head as if trying to collect her thoughts, and Javier helped her along by sliding his fingers into her pussy, caressing her clit. Under his fingers, the little nub turned hard almost instantly. She gasped.

"You're not going anywhere," Javier assured her. "We're not done with you."

"And we're not scening anymore, so we won't try to peek at your back. Will we?" Xander asked pointedly.

As much as he ached to see it so the healing could begin, he knew his brother was right. Now wasn't the time, and revealing herself had to be her choice.

He shook his head, continuing to pet her cunt. "No. We'll be patient. But we want the rest of your body now. On. Your. Knees."

London melted against him and her voice turned weak. "This is Thorpe's office. He . . ."

"Isn't stupid enough to come back for a while," Xander assured. "Listen to your Doms, and get on your knees."

"Otherwise, there won't be any orgasms in your future, and you want us to give you those, right?" Javier wasn't above using dirty pool to get them what they all needed.

She hesitated an instant before she braced herself on the arm of the chair and lowered herself to the tile floor, one knee at a time. Javier caught glimpses of her thighs and the bottom curve of her ass, and it fired his desire up all over again.

God, she was so beautifully submissive, and he needed her in his life. For the first time in forever, he wasn't dwelling on the past, but looking toward the future. And caring about his life, prosperity, happiness. It was completely London's doing. He wasn't letting her slip through his fingers.

"Suck his cock." Javier stood over her, watching and waiting.

London glanced over her shoulder and met his gaze. Her eyes had gone dark and soft. She liked being commanded. And she liked the specific command he'd given her.

She crawled into the space between Xander's open legs and splayed her hands over his thighs. His brother stroked his cock roughly now, and as she leaned in, he fed it into her mouth, one slow inch after another.

Her mouth dipped down the hard length. Xander snapped his head back with a groan. He'd had hundreds—maybe thousands—of blow jobs in his life, Javier was sure. But London's mouth on Xander was special because he cared about her. Javier knew that as well as he knew his own name.

Watching them together revved him up to a throaty growl. Funny, but when Xander had first dragged him to Lafayette, he'd been beyond furious. But the move had brought London into their lives. They needed her light and warmth. She'd not only saved him, but his relationship with Xander. Now, the connection they shared ended decades of cold solitude in his heart. Because of London, they were mending their bond again—and adding to it. If she'd let it, their future could be even happier than their distant past.

Xander's fingers tunneled through her long, golden tresses, rescuing them from the floor as he gathered them up in his grip and watched her worship his cock. In that moment, she served his brother with her heart, and he accepted her gift with reverence. They weren't two people merely engaged in a sex act, but lovers communicating their feelings for one another without a word. The sight moved him.

"That's it, *belleza*. That's perfect. Your slow strokes are killing me, and that tongue . . . Yeah, baby, lick my cock like— Oh, fuck, that's hot. More. Yes," Xander hissed out as she worked slowly down his stiff cock again. "I need you."

Xander's electric groan pulsed down Javier's spine. If he didn't touch London and seek his pleasure in her soon, he'd lose his sanity. But more, if he and Xander didn't claim her now, he'd fucking die.

Sinking to his knees behind London, he lifted the coat up the backs of her thighs, over her ass—stopping when she froze.

"It's okay," he promised, folding the coat over so that it covered the top of her ass and bunched thickly over her lower back. "I won't go any higher than this. I promise. Just let me inside you."

Xander tugged on her hair, lifting her mouth from his erection and forcing her to look right into his eyes. Javier wished he could see London's face himself, but the lovely ass he caressed more than held his attention.

"It's what we all need, *belleza*. The contact. The closeness." Xander cupped her breast and pinched her nipple. "Feel how right this is."

At his brother's words, Javier sighed in relief. Xander understood perfectly.

London's body jerked at Xander's touch. She gasped. Javier took the opportunity to plunge his fingers into her pussy. So wet . . . She needed their touch every bit as much as they needed hers. If she'd just take that last wall down around her heart, they could prove they loved her, flaws and all.

"Touch me," London whimpered

She hadn't even finished the words when Xander grabbed her head again and raised his hips, filling her little mouth with his hungry cock. She mewled around him and arched her back. The action thrust out her ass at Javier. Tension ripped through him. He could almost feel his brother's pleasure. Frantically, he shoved his hand in his pocket and withdrew the item he'd placed there earlier, then set it by his knee. He hoped to hell London accepted him with the same openness with which she took Xander now.

Tearing into his zipper, Javier lowered his pants, letting them puddle on the floor. The hard tile wasn't kind to his knees, and he didn't give a shit. The only thing that mattered was getting inside London and sharing this experience with Xander. Together, they'd blow her little sheltered world wide open. But they'd always protect her with everything they had.

He ran a hand across that lush ass of hers, then grabbed the tube on the floor. With shaking fingers, he unscrewed the cap and dribbled lube down the crack of her cheeks, then squirted a bit more on his fingers. He rubbed her untried entrance, slowly sinking his fingers inside her until he had two in just as far as they could go. She tensed and moaned around Xander's cock.

"Shh," Javier coaxed her gently, leaning over her body to whisper in her ear. "You've taken the plugs well. I'll go easy on you, little one, but don't shut me out. Let me show you this pleasure. Let me make you feel so good."

Pulling her cheeks apart, he positioned his cock against her little rosette, fighting the urge to slam inside her. His patience was running thin.

"Take her!" Xander growled.

Javier planted his palm in the curve of her back and nudged down gently. London arched even more for him. God, that was one of the most beautiful sights, her open and accepting. Her trusting him not to cause her pain.

"Push out," he demanded, then began to ease inside her. "Good. Open yourself for me."

Slowly, London did as he demanded, and he sawed inside her

tight ass just a fraction. Back and forth, he pushed at the tight ring of muscle a few times before he finally popped past it and he slid down, down, into the tightest silken depths of her body. She gasped, then cried out in a high-pitched whine that was half pleasure, half pain. He slowed, but she still closed around him like a hot velvet glove. A groan tore from his chest at the mind-bending ecstasy. He'd never felt anyone so right. That Xander could feel her with him only made the moment more perfect.

"You in?"

"Yeah," Javier croaked.

Xander tore off his mental leash and started plowing into London's mouth in long, brutal strokes, holding her head exactly where he needed her. "That's it, *belleza*. Open your throat. Take everything. Feel how much we want you. Holy fuck!"

London dug her fingers into Xander's thighs, then shrieked when Javier pulled back slowly before sliding home in a slow thrust that scraped every nerve in his body. The explosion brewing at the base of his spine didn't feel like mere fireworks. No, he was going to blast inside her like a supernova, a violent cataclysm that would be unlike anything he'd ever felt. Her hot, slick flesh against his bare dick—crap, he'd forgotten a condom—was like finding heaven balanced on the knife's edge. Dangerous, painful . . . and the most wonderful sensation ever. But they were both disease free, and it was too late now. No way could he let her go.

"Are you sucking his cock, little one?" he demanded.

She nodded frantically, bobbing up and down on Xander's dick.

"Good girl. Feel me? Am I filling you up?"

Her moan was something between a squeal and a sigh. His cock tingled. So damn sensitive. He gritted his teeth, grabbed a fistful of her coat, then tossed his head back with a growl of pleasure. He couldn't remember the last time he'd fucked a woman's ass. College? It didn't matter. Whoever she'd been, the incident had been erased from his memory bank. Now there was only London and the pure, sharp bliss of her tight grip dismantling his brain with sweet, destructive need.

"Am I hurting you?" he managed to growl out.

Frantically, she shook her head and threw her hips back at him, matching his rhythm. What he'd thought couldn't get any better just had. Javier gripped her waist and plowed harder into her. He knew he'd come soon . . . just like he knew that wouldn't sate him from needing her again. Most likely, he would come somewhere inside her body again in an hour. Then once more later tonight. But no matter how many times he had her, he'd never sate this hunger. She was under his skin, in his blood, burrowed in his heart. He didn't want it any other way.

"Is he filling you full, baby?" Xander asked.

London could only answer with a mournful howl.

She was on the edge and wanted more. Perspiration filmed her body. Every muscle worked in glorious harmony to increase the friction, to get him deeper. She was a thing of beauty as she reached for the pinnacle, writhing between them, her hair falling all around her. Why had he never known how fulfilled love could make him? Why had he ever thought he could settle for less than the flood of devotion now in his heart?

He looked up to find Xander's concentration on her lips absolute. His brother was sweating—temples, shoulders, chest—whispering to London as he shuttled his cock past her lips. Javier stared, feeling his energy flowing through London, then to Xander. Then his brother raised his gaze. And yes . . . the energy surged back. They both felt love for this woman, and being here with her together only multiplied it to something so big, he almost couldn't process it.

The swirl of emotion was a sublime fucking pleasure like nothing he'd ever felt. It seared all the way down his spine, shooting down into his balls until they felt heavy and tight. He tingled as the sensations built.

"Can't last, Xander," he panted out. "You need to claim her, too."

His brother sent him a rough nod, then he caressed London's cheek. "Can you come for us, *belleza*?"

To help her along, Javier leaned over London, encircled her waist, and petted her clit. She jolted, gasped—then she screamed as he caressed her little button. Under his fingers, it swelled, turned harder than steel, and she pulsed around him, gripping, milking, killing his restraint. Javier let loose with a long, loud cry, plundering into her furiously with every ounce of her strength as Xander held back, easing into her tight mouth with carefully controlled strokes. London took everything they gave her, so open, so beautiful.

In her, Javier had not only found his brother again, but he'd found his forever.

The thought zipped lightning down his spine where it pooled in his gut and cooled into contentment. Love wasn't just the stuff of greeting cards, but rightness, belonging, and certainty that made his heart fly. For the last year, he'd been dead inside. Now, because of her, he felt like he could soar for the rest of his life.

Caressing her thigh and kissing the crown of her head, Javier carefully withdrew, then glanced at Xander, who nodded and lifted London's mouth from his cock.

"My turn, *belleza*." Xander stood, then took hold of her arm. "Help me get her on the chair."

Scrambling for his pants, Javier lifted his zipper with a quiet hiss, then assisted London, knees first, into the chair, facing the back. When she tried to turn to sit, he grabbed her hips until Xander came around, rolling on a condom.

"Stay, little one. You're Xander's, too. He's also going to fuck that pretty, perfect ass."

Her breathing hitched as she clutched the back of the chair with white knuckles. "Hurry."

"Right fucking now." Xander ran a palm up her thigh, blanketed her body with his own, the coat rustling between them. He gripped her hips and positioned himself, shoving desperately into her soft, wet cunt. As he buried himself to the hilt, he clenched his jaw, baring his teeth. He swiveled inside her slippery folds and slid his fingers over her clit. London rewarded him with a gasp. Her pale skin flushed as she moved back to take more of him. Watching them together was a thing of beauty—special, intimate—and Javier couldn't stand not being a part of it.

He walked around behind the chair and took her soft oval face in his hands, slanted his lips over hers, and took her mouth in a possessive kiss that he hoped staked his claim every bit as much as being deep in her body had. Javier was gratified when she latched onto his shoulders for dear life and fell heart-first into the kiss.

"Arch your back, *belleza*. Push out for me." Xander snapped the command at her gruffly.

Javier ripped his lips from hers. "Do as he says."

Without pause, she did, and he watched over the length of her body as she slowly accepted Xander's thick, slick cock in her ass. Those gorgeous shrieks of her pleasure-pain filled the air again, and London lifted her stare to him, somewhere between lost and drowning.

"He's inside you, little one, isn't he?" At her frantic nod, he smiled. "So deep, just like I was. Claiming you, just as I did. Take all of him, as you took all of me. Because we want all of you. Every lovely inch, even the scars you're hiding."

"No." She shook her head. "You don't under—"

"I understand perfectly." Javier gripped her hair. "You're afraid and you don't have to be."

Xander groaned as he pushed in again, obviously staving off the need to come by sheer force of will. "Fuck, yes. *Belleza* . . . Oh, baby. So tight. Hot. Fucking perfect. Javier is right. Surrender now. Come and take me with you."

Xander's voice was damn near a plea, and his strokes picked up pace, gone from a smooth slide to a ferocious shuttle in and out of her body. She'd feel well used and a bit sore tomorrow, but Javier knew Xander would care for her, and he vowed to, as well—just as they'd take care of her for the rest of her life if she'd let them.

Life before her hadn't felt important because he hadn't filled it with anything meaningful. How was it possible that she'd cast a bright ray of sunshine into their lives in a handful of days and taught them just how dark their existences had been? Javier didn't know or care. He just seized her mouth again, promising her with every brush of his lips and every sweep of his tongue that she belonged to them.

Suddenly, she screamed into his kiss and stiffened. He looked up in time to see Xander tossing his head back, sweat covering his chest as he gripped London and froze. The snapshot of mind-bending ecstasy made Javier hard all over again. Damn, she could turn them inside out, and he'd do anything to prove that, no matter what she thought, she was the most beautiful woman to him ever.

Javier gripped her tightly as she shuddered in his arms with the shattering force of orgasm. Her cries gave way to soft pants, and Xander pulled free but held her tight, wearing an expression of contentment that had to be identical to his own.

As euphoria and harsh breathing gave way to sated lethargy, London sagged between them. Javier eased to London's side and sat on the cold tile, his back against the side of the desk as he drew her limp body into his lap, wishing it was her soft skin, not the starchy coat, against him.

After zipping up, Xander turned and came to his knees in front of her, cupping her cheek in his hand. "You okay?"

She bowed her head. "Fine."

Her assurance should have made him feel better. It didn't. London was right here between them . . . but he already felt her pulling away.

Before he could ask her to tell them what was on her mind, a knock sounded at the door. If that was Thorpe, the bastard had terrible timing.

"Go the fuck away," Xander demanded.

The door opened anyway, and Callie stepped in with a wry smile. "At least I waited until all the grunts and groans stopped. Imagine if I'd come in a few minutes earlier."

Xander growled out a creative threat, tinged with a few choice curses. Javier couldn't agree more.

"I'm serious, Callie. Go the fuck away or I'll tell Thorpe—"

"He's the one who told me to check on your girl." Callie stepped farther into the room, her black stilettos clicking along the tile. She bent to London, ignoring them both, and smiled kindly. "Need a trip to the ladies' room?"

Translation: Callie was giving London an escape from her lovers in case she needed a few moments away. Javier had never been violent, but right now, he wanted to punch Thorpe for his interference, no matter how well meaning.

"She's fine," Xander insisted. "Now go the fuck away."

"This is one time I don't have to do anything you say, *Sir*," Callie returned tartly, then looked at London with a soft, seeking gaze. "You want a moment to freshen up and put yourself back together?"

Javier tightened his arms around her, willing her to stay with them. But London nodded and pushed back, rising to her feet and tying her coat shut. Xander stood. Javier followed suit, reaching for London's hand.

"Go ahead, little one. But if you're upset or unsure, be prepared to talk to us when you return."

She shrugged, not quite meeting his gaze, then turned away. Javier feared he'd look like an overly possessive caveman if he followed his instincts and grabbed her against him. A glance at Xander told him that his brother was having similar thoughts. Usually after sex, London was soft and happy, cuddly, warm. Now, she was distant. Some mood rolled off her that he didn't like. Regret? Sadness?

"It doesn't matter to us. Your back," he blurted. "I adore you as you are."

Those words, meant to reassure her, seemed to have no impact at all. London didn't turn around. Instead, her shoulders shook. So did her voice. "It matters to me."

Before he could reply, she was out the door. The little click behind them was like a hatchet to the heart.

He charged forward. Fuck what Callie thought. So what if he was a caveman? But when he opened the door, he caught only a glimpse of Callie with her slender arm around London's heaving shoulders. Thorpe blocked the doorway—and the rest of his view. Xander stood beside him, looking like he wanted to punch Thorpe now and ask questions later, but they both knew that would only get them tossed out on their asses.

"It's a trip to the ladies' room, not a hangman's noose, so stop looking like someone died." Thorpe stepped in and shut the door, then made his way to sit in the chair behind his desk. "Give London a few minutes. Whatever's happened here tonight, she's shaken. Did you push past her limits?"

Xander raked a hand through his hair and paced. "She's hiding from us. We're trying to reach her. She can't be free until she accepts herself and believes that we accept her, too."

"And you can't force that. You should know that can take months or years. If she's not ready, she's not ready."

Tell him something he didn't know. Javier rubbed his jaw in frustration.

"Give her time," the big Dom insisted.

In his head, Javier knew Thorpe was probably right. Trust couldn't be forced; it had to be earned. On the other hand, he couldn't turn off the dread. He had a feeling time had just run out.

The seconds dragged into minutes, one after the other. Xander still paced, staring at the door. Javier wanted to dismantle it with his bare hands and find London now. His instincts screamed that he was fucked.

As Thorpe poured himself a drink, Javier kind of wished the bastard would share. But he needed a clear head to deal with London now. No way would he risk her to numb himself.

Thorpe frowned. "The two of you are strung tighter than a symphony orchestra. Relax."

A cell phone beeped. Javier automatically reached for his, as did Xander. But Thorpe was the one reading his screen with a frown. "Well, apparently your girl needs a little more time."

Javier resisted the urge to tear the phone from the other man's hands. "Meaning?"

"London asked to leave Dominion. Callie is taking her somewhere safe and will stay with her until she's ready to return."

The fury that fired through Javier's veins didn't make it to his tongue quite as quickly as Xander's. "Callie has no right to do that. London is *ours*."

"So you married her? Or put a collar around her neck?" Thorpe asked sharply.

No, but in that moment, Javier wished to fuck he'd done both. He loved her. Further, he genuinely believed that she loved him— even if she was afraid to admit it. He couldn't afford to panic. He'd dig up his patience and coax her tenderly, convince her that, with him, she was safe. A glance at Xander said he felt precisely the same.

In the long silence, Thorpe sent them a chilly smile. "I didn't think so. We don't condone anything nonconsensual here at Dominion. Ever. That includes keeping someone against their will. You know that, Xander. Don't worry. Callie will take care of your girl until she sorts out her thoughts."

"It's not Callie being with London that we're worried about. Please tell us where to find her. She's confused and probably overwhelmed. She needs comfort and reassurance. We can't give it to her from here," Xander argued.

Thorpe shrugged with faint regret. "She doesn't seem to want it just now. She gave you her safe word. You fucked her anyway. And it wasn't to make *her* feel better. It was about you. So now you get to back off and pay the price."

A glance at Xander proved that his brother wanted to hit the club owner as badly as he did. Javier had a good idea what might be running through London's head, all of it wrong and terrible. And at the end of all this thinking? Javier dreaded her conclusions. As she'd walked out the door, the desolation in her tone had sounded a little too marked to mean anything more than good-bye.

Chapter Eighteen

SHE'S gone. Those two words resounded in Xander's head over and over. Thorpe stared. Javier looked somewhere between inconsolable and volatile. What the hell were they going to do now?

Fight for her.

"Goddamn it, tell us where she is!" Xander insisted. "She's shutting us out and she needs—"

"Space, obviously." Thorpe reached for his chirping phone, and Xander saw Callie's name flash across his screen. "You love her, I get it. I think she has deep feelings for you, as well. But sometimes, that's not enough. That old saying, 'If you love someone, set them free . . .' That applies here. If she doesn't come back, it wasn't meant to be."

"You know fucking nothing!" Javier stormed across the room at Thorpe, and Xander had to restrain his brother by the collar to hold him back. Even as he struggled against the hold, Javier kept screaming. "That's what cowards tell themselves to make themselves feel better about their loved ones slipping through their fingers. But I know the truth. I let my own fucking wife go because I thought it would make her happier than I could. It was my excuse for not trying harder, for not caring enough. And she's *dead* because of it! Setting someone free is only an indication that you were too weak to fight."

In that moment, Xander couldn't have agreed more. "If you want to pretend you don't give a shit that Callie is giving her devotion and her pussy to someone else, I can't stop you. But you're lying to yourself. And I sure as hell can promise that we won't share your delusion. Tell us where the hell to find London right now."

"Leave Callie out of this and calm down," Thorpe shot back coldly.

The man clenched his jaw so hard, Xander was surprised it didn't shatter. No doubt, challenging Thorpe about Callie had pissed him off, but just because the club owner didn't want to see what was in front of his face didn't mean that Xander was willing to bury his own head in the sand. A decade and a half and thousands of women later, he *finally* knew what—who—he wanted. He wasn't letting her get away.

"We're only pissed off at you. With London, we'll be as calm and gentle as a lullaby."

Thorpe rolled his eyes. "You don't get it. Even if you did, what the hell could you possibly say to her to change her mind? You wouldn't be in this position if she trusted you. She ran because she doesn't, and you should be taking long looks in the mirror and asking yourselves why."

Pivoting on his heel, Thorpe turned away and strode out the door. He restrained himself from slamming it, though Xander was sure he wanted to. Instead, he closed it with a precise click. The resulting silence resounded like a mournful wail in his head.

"He's right," Javier said, sounding hollow, almost defeated. "She's only known me as an undisciplined drunk. I interviewed her drunk. I got so trashed her first day on the job that she had to take care of me. I fucked her for the first time hung over. Why would she trust her body or welfare with someone who has so little self-control?"

A week ago, Xander probably would have agreed with Javier. All that drowning his guilt in vodka had nearly destroyed him—and everyone who loved him. But London had also made him see parts of himself he hadn't wanted to look at too closely.

"It's my fault, too." Xander frowned and clenched his fist, restraining the urge to punch a wall. "I had no fucking purpose in life, so I made it my purpose to fuck. It was the one thing I was good at. You've only been losing yourself in booze for a few months. I've been drowning in pussy for more than half my life. I didn't know what else to do. No one needed me." Tears sprang to Xander's eyes, and it was the most unmanly fucking thing he'd ever endured, but he couldn't hold this in anymore. Exposing his scars might not bring London back, but at least he'd take a step toward healing and maybe be a better man. "Least of all you. I lived in your shadow. I spent years just wanting to be important to you again, like when we were kids. When I wasn't, I became everything you despised just to see if you'd notice."

Answering tears sprang to Javier's eyes. "Sharing London with you . . . I've seen past your playboy-without-a-cause routine. I've seen your pain. I shared it. Because I couldn't control it, I sank deeper and deeper into responsibility until I didn't care about anyone or feel anything, especially after I married Francesca. I knew I didn't love her. She knew it, too. I hid behind my job. I left you both to your own devices. She paid the ultimate price for my neglect because she would have never been with her killer if she'd been getting the attention she needed from me. And I can never change that. Never fully atone. I have to live with that fact for the rest of my life. It was easier to blame you for not training her than for me to accept responsibility for her unhappiness. It was shitty." Javier reached out and grabbed his shoulder. "This week has shown me how important you are—to me, to London. To the business, even. I'm sorry for everything, especially being so distant for so long."

"Apology accepted." Xander grabbed his brother and hugged him. They gave one another a hearty backslap, as if to make up for the tears flowing freely. He turned and tried to surreptitiously wipe his eyes, but Javier had to have seen. "I knew you used to grit your teeth every time one of the L.A. news outlets picked up on my escapades and splashed them all over the page. I'm sorry for being an out-of-control asshole."

"Yeah." His brother swiped his eyes with his sleeve, then tried to grin. "I accept your apology, too, but I'm sure you'll have to apologize again at some point for being an asshole."

Xander laughed, their sudden banter lightening the mood and his heart. "Fuck off."

Javier collapsed into the chair London had graced only a few minutes before and nodded. "Yeah, you fuck off, too."

The ensuing silence quickly filled with gravity. They'd repaired their rift, but London was still gone, still out there alone thinking that she wasn't beautiful enough for them, and not trusting their words otherwise. That hurt Xander most of all. She didn't need to be alone now. She needed to know they loved her. She needed to see that the flawed men they'd been before were better because her sweet spirit and her love had changed them.

"We have a choice," Javier said. "We either let her go and be the men we once were—"

"Fuck that!" Xander didn't want to be that douche anymore. He'd been miserable and lonely. Despite the fact that he'd fucked thousands of women, he'd been intimate with no one until London.

"My thoughts exactly. There's a bottle right there, and I could drink it all and forget for a while . . . but my need for London would be there when the buzz wore off. I can't drink her away."

Not like he had Francesca. Xander understood perfectly. Loneliness could be medicated and masked until a man had something so real that nothing would ever make him forget. "I'm sure I could find Whitney again and fuck her in every way known to man in the next few hours. If she wasn't enough . . . there are others in the club. But I'm not interested and I'm not letting London down. She needs us to be stronger and better so she can heal, finally give herself fully and be free."

"Exactly."

"What do we do? If she's left Dominion, there seems no point in staying," Xander pointed out.

"Have you tried calling her?"

"Her phone is back at the hotel room. Even if she had it, I doubt she'd answer."

Javier nodded. "You don't happen to know where Callie lives?"

"No. That brat was always off limits to me because I knew how Thorpe felt about her, even if the ass is too stubborn to admit it. Besides, Callie wasn't up my alley. She is a serious handful. I kind of feel sorry for her Master, whoever he is. He was probably taken in by her baby blues and lush curves, and is just now figuring out that she's going to make him insane."

"Then . . . I guess we head back to the hotel. Maybe she'll show up there? We've got all her stuff. If not, well . . . she knows how to call us if she's ready to talk."

True. And the fact their phones weren't ringing scraped every bit of his composure raw. His mood bled, and he wasn't going to feel right again until he had London in his arms, between him and Javier, making her feel both so good and so loved.

As they headed out of Thorpe's office and grabbed their belongings from the playroom, they headed back into the main part of the dungeon. Xander spied Callie's Master and Thorpe arguing with gestures as sharp as the crack of a whip. Idly, he wondered if Thorpe realized that his unrequited need and jealousy were making him a real asshole.

With Javier beside him, they headed out into the sweltering night. Ignoring the fact that it was nearly ninety degrees despite being after midnight, he kept his grumbling to a minimum and hopped into the car, speeding through the night back to the Mansion.

The opulence and elegance of the Turtle Creek hotel didn't

register with Xander at all. He prowled through the lobby, fishing out his key, then slamming it into the slot once he reached the door. The moment he pushed it open, he realized the trench London had been wearing when she left the club was strewn across their bed, along with the shoes she'd been wearing. Stomach clenching with anxiety, Xander touched the coat. It was still warm. Her clothing and her purse were nowhere to be found.

"She's gone," Javier said into the awful silence, scrubbing a hand across his terrified face. "I pushed her too hard."

Desolation swamped him. "She has to let go of that hurt and worry. We've got to help her."

"How? We have no idea where she's gone. I doubt very much that she's going to take our calls or show up to the office on Monday. She's not going to pretend that nothing has happened."

Javier was right. "One thing we do know is that she has no reason to come back here. But I have a trick to track her down . . ."

"Oh?" His brother looked intrigued.

"She had problems with her iCloud account one day, so I helped her. She gave me her e-mail and password. With that, I can track her iPhone. Let's see where she's gone." With a few clicks of his own phone, he tried to locate her device, but the app wasn't finding her. Cursing, he tried two, three, four times. Nothing. "Damn it! She's turned off her phone."

With a heavy sigh, Javier sat in a plush chair. "Could anything say more eloquently that she doesn't want to hear from us?"

No, but that couldn't be the end. "Too bad. I'm not letting her fester in self-doubt. I'd bet money that, right now, she wants familiar people and comforts around her."

"Agreed. Somehow, someway, she's headed back to Lafayette."

Xander nodded. "Let's pack up and follow."

His brother began gathering his stuff into a pile, shoving it into bags without a scrap of organization or care. "What do we do when we find her?"

"Convince her that we'll do anything for her and that we're never letting her go."

The words had barely cleared his lips when Xander's phone rang. He yanked it from his pocket, praying London was on the other end, that she missed him, that she wanted to talk—something. When Xander glanced at the screen, he froze.

"Who is it?" Javier demanded.

"Someone I hired to help us with the security issue surrounding the log-ins Maynard was bitching about. He's more than qualified. Former military special forces. He's especially good with industrial espionage. If he's calling in the middle of the night, it's not good." Xander hit the button to answer his phone. "What's up, Decker?"

"Hey. I followed the trail of those IDs down to their last access point near Cancun. I found a guy by the name of Albert Carlton. That name mean anything to you?"

"Not to me," Xander answered, then looked at his brother. "You know an Albert Carlton?"

"Yeah. He's an employee. In R & D. He's Sheppard's work bitch, follows him around from meeting to meeting like a dog in heat."

"You hear that?" Xander asked Decker.

"Yep. And Sheppard is . . .?"

"The head of R & D."

Decker grunted. "That puts a few things into place."

Maybe for Decker, but Xander was confused as hell. "If he's an employee, what's he doing accessing proprietary information in Mexico? Is he working on his vacation?"

"If he was, the vacation is now permanent," Decker drawled.

"What do you mean?"

"I went out there to spy on the guy. Instead, I found a body. My guess is that someone professional whacked him."

"Professional? Like an assassin?" Xander tugged his fingers through his hair. "You're sure?"

"Yep. Carlton wasn't in a hotel room in the tourist area, but in a house on the seedy side of town, so normally I'd think robbery or drugs. But no one took his wallet, phone, credit cards, passport, or his baggie full of coke. His printer, fax, and mouse were all sitting on his desk. His computer, however, was missing. I suspect the killer waited until evening rolled around and Carlton opened his window to the breeze so there'd be no sign of forced entry or struggle. He finished Carlton off before the poor fuck ever had a clue."

"Think the neighbors heard the gunshots?"

"In that neighborhood, they're used to drug dealers taking one another out. If anyone had heard anything, they wouldn't talk. But Carlton wasn't shot. He was strangled. The ligature around his neck is brutal and obvious. Rough rope, about two inches thick. This killer is strong. Carlton died quickly and without mercy."

Those words rattled around in Xander's had. Strangled. By a pro. Who liked fat ropes. Like Francesca. What were the odds of that?

"The good news is," Decker went on, "I did some digging on the vic's phone. I found a list of his passwords. He paid for an online backup service, so I grabbed a fresh computer and put a mirror of Carlton's computer on that. It should be done now, so let me see what we've got, then I might be able to tell you what got him killed."

"Sounds great," Xander said, even though it didn't. It sounded like corporate spying had ratcheted up a notch if dead bodies and professional assassins were involved. And death by strangulation.

But what was the connection to Francesca? She hadn't known a damn thing about the company, nor had she cared.

Fuck, he and Javier didn't need this right now. They needed to be focused on London. But they now had a murdered employee. They needed to get back in town ASAP and start getting some answers to their questions. He gestured to Javier, and together, they gathered their luggage and ran out of the hotel, making their way to the valet stand. His brother barked for the valet, handing over the claim ticket, and waiting with an impatient tapping of his foot.

"You're a lousy liar." Decker laughed.

"Fine. It sucks hairy, ripe monkey balls. Don't pros usually shoot their victims?"

"Most often, yeah. Not always. They might use other methods if they're trying to keep quiet. And some just like a certain MO. Like serial killers, they get off on it."

But in a neighborhood where gunshots were common and no one would tattle, why not kill Carlton by squeezing a trigger rather than his neck? It was such a specific way to kill, and maybe he'd be less suspicious if Francesca had died any other way, but . . .

"Did the cops take any crime scene photos of Carlton's body?" Xander asked as the valet brought the car, and his brother threw the luggage in the trunk as he slid behind the wheel.

"The Mexican police hadn't discovered the crime yet when I was there. And don't worry, I removed all trace of myself so when they come into the crime scene, it will look pristine. But I snapped a few photos on his phone in case they came in handy. I'll forward them."

"Thanks." Xander couldn't help but suspect that what Carlton had known because of his job had gotten him killed. But who would want him dead?

Xander's phone chirped with a message a moment later, but he didn't put Decker on hold to look at them while speeding away from the hotel. He wanted to study the pictures before he showed Javier. Unless the need arose, Xander could see no sense in sending his brother back to the edge of his sanity with pictures of a strangulation. His resolve to give up booze was too fresh.

In Xander's ear, Decker was quiet for a long minute, tapping away at the keyboard. "You told me to look for a Chad Brenner in all this?"

Xander gripped the phone tighter. "Yeah. You got something?"

"A whole bunch of somethings." The other man was quiet for another unbearable stretch of silence. "Ready for this? Carlton worked for you until last Friday. For the past few years, it looks like he's been secretly stealing information from Sheppard and your internal drives and selling it to the highest bidder. Oh, look. He even sold some secure log-ins so other creeps could crawl through your databases. How handy that he documented where he mined all the data from, who he sold it to, and for how much." Decker whistled. "Damn, no wonder he left his job. He'd gotten fucking rich."

"How does Chad Brenner play into this? For a long time, he developed our new technology. He's brilliant. He could invent anything we did, probably faster or better, so I doubt he'd want our secrets."

"There's a long string of e-mails between Carlton and someone calling himself the 'Face of Revenge.'" Decker scoffed. "That shit sounds like a seventh-grade boy making up his screen name for fucking Call of Duty."

Pretty much. Brenner had wanted revenge against S.I. Industries for its perceived theft of his intellectual property since walking out in a huff and suing. Was that silly handle his? "What do the e-mails say?"

"Carlton sold the information to this Face of Revenge character." Decker flipped through the laptop. "All kinds of information, dating back a little over eighteen months. Your information. The most recent sale involved something called Project Recovery."

Which explained exactly how the competition had been beating them for months—by buying stolen advancements in technology and passing them off as their own.

"Fuck me. Any idea who this Face of Revenge is or what he's been doing with the information he bought? One of our competitors had come forward with a product that's suspiciously like ours recently—and that's not the first time."

"Well, it looks like Carlton was having second thoughts about blindly doing business with the Face of Revenge and started digging. He's been compiling information about the identity of his contact. After working his angles for a bit, he surmised it was Chad Brenner. Is the competitor you're talking about United Velocity?"

Decker was good. Xander was always impressed. "The very one."

"Well, whaddya know? Brenner owns a shitload of United Velocity stock, according to Carlton's research."

Yeah? That might be the Holy Grail of information they needed to finally prove that Brenner hadn't given up seeking his pound of flesh after the courts had sided with S.I Industries and affirmed that the release-of-intellectual-property waiver he'd signed meant that everything he'd developed while employed with them belonged to the corporation. Because he'd been unable to take it with him, he'd been stealing everything the company had developed since and funneling it to the competitor—then bought stock to earn an extra buck.

"Amazing." Xander's voice dripped sarcasm. "So why kill Carlton? I mean, your guess. Think Brenner had something to do with it? Maybe he was getting suspicious that the guy was onto him."

"Maybe. More likely Carlton quitting S.I. Industries meant he was both useless in the future and a loose end Brenner wanted to tie up."

Made perfect sense. "Anything else?"

Decker clicked around a bit more, then some truly terrible music blasted through the phone.

"What the hell? That sounds like karaoke at its worst." Xander held the phone away, but the music played on, violating his ears and making him grimace.

"This fucker was weird. He's got a bottle of rum in one hand and seems to be making his own homemade music video. Wow, he looks wasted." Decker laughed, then turned dead sober. "Oh, shit!"

"What?" Xander went on alert.

"Stupid bastard was filming himself singing when his killer sneaked into the room, holding a rope. Carlton saw him in the camera, but didn't turn around in time to fight. As soon as the killer gets the rope around Carlton's neck, he flips the lid of the computer shut."

"And the online backup saved that?"

"Yep." Decker affirmed.

"Did the camera catch the killer's face?"

"In shadows, but you can see some of his features."

That was hard evidence that could be used to solve the murder . . . and maybe make a few other breakthroughs. Was this the same professional strangler who'd murdered Fran? If so, he wondered again what the connection between corporate espionage and a bored housewife was. If Brenner was behind all this, what had he hoped to accomplish?

Revenge.

Xander's heart chugged in his chest. He didn't want to jump to conclusions, but his thoughts—and his hope—raced. Maybe this would give Javier the closure he needed.

"Send me what you've got. I'll look at it as soon as I get it."

"Will do. I'll shout if I find anything else, but I think we're onto something." Before Xander could say a word, Decker hung up.

He sighed, gripping the wheel. The hair on the back of his neck stood up in warning. The day had started badly. London gone. His heart in shambles . . . Carlton strangled. Now this? He didn't like it one fucking bit. Then he glanced at the still pictures Decker had sent of Carlton's neck. He liked everything even less.

The ligature marks on Carlton's neck looked precisely like those around Francesca's corpse. Carlton's home movie hit his inbox next, and watching the final frames of it raked an icy shudder down his spine.

With his heart stuttering, he turned to his brother.

Javier frowned. "You look like you've seen a goddamn ghost. What's wrong?"

Not a ghost exactly, but something far worse.

"Recognize the face creeping up on Carlton?" Xander held up the phone, displaying the frame where the victim realized that he had an intruder in his house and a rope around his neck. It was the best picture of the killer in the video. In Xander's head, it matched the security footage of Fran's lover from the hotel in Aruba where she was last seen alive.

"Valjean the assassin," Javier breathed, then frowned.

Bingo. Xander pressed his lips together grimly and pushed on the gas pedal. Every minute they were in the car was another minute wasted.

Javier looked decimated. "Oh my God. And he killed Carlton?"

"Looks like." Xander dropped the phone on his lap. "We should be asking ourselves why." The more he thought about it, the more Brenner having contact with Carlton and being offed by the same assassin who'd killed Francesca seemed too coincidental. Brenner had to be the connection. "Did you say you'd hired someone to look into Fran's death?"

Looking shell-shocked, Javier nodded. "Private investigator. His name is Nick Navarro."

"Get him on the phone. Brenner had a vendetta against us. He used Carlton to get to us until his usefulness was at an end. Good chance he paid to have Carlton killed. Doesn't it make you wonder if this is the first time Brenner hired this hit man?"

* * *

CALLIE was kind enough to drive her as far as Shreveport, despite the fact that it was the middle of the night. She checked in frequently with her Dom, a Scotsman with a deep, sexy brogue. Thorpe, her boss, called too. Both seemed more than a tad territorial. London stared at her own phone, which she'd powered down as soon as she'd taken it from the hotel room. She wasn't ready to talk to Xander or Javier. They'd tell her that her failure was nothing, that she was overreacting, that she'd merely panicked during the scene. Maybe she had. Missing all the milestones of maturity between fifteen and twenty-five had, at times, left her both confused and scared. Bottom line, she'd allowed herself to sink into the fantasy that they could accept her, scars and all, just as they'd claimed. That they could love her. But when push came to shove, she hadn't been able to risk seeing the revulsion on their faces that she'd seen on Brian's. And they'd never said anything about love. She'd believed it because she'd wanted to, because she'd been surrendering her own heart to them . . . but that didn't make it so.

Now she had to face the fact that Javier was too tormented by his past and Xander simply too wild to be hers forever. Time to get out now before it hurt too much to do the right thing. Alyssa had tried to warn her, but no . . . She'd had to feel this terrible, wretched fear and pain herself before she'd understood that she couldn't possibly help to either heal or hold them. Pressing sadness suffocated her, and the years of being alone stretched out. The accident had made her a freak in so many ways—a scared girl in a woman's body—but for this one week, she'd felt normal. And loved. She'd always treasure that.

Refusing to impose on Callie, despite the woman's repeated assurances, London had swallowed her pride and called her cousin. Alyssa's husband had groggily answered the phone, listened between her tears, and agreed to meet her and Callie halfway between Dallas and Lafayette. Every mile she'd put between herself and the Santiago brothers was a fiery stab burning down her heart. Only ashes remained now. They'd move on. But London knew she'd never be the same again.

"You're awfully quiet," Luc said beside her.

"Thank you for coming to get me. I'm sorry. I know it's incredibly bad timing."

"You've already apologized twice." He sent a dark glance her way as the morning sun poured in through the windshield as they headed southeast. "Tell me what happened."

"Nothing."

"That's crap," Luc said. "Tell me what Xander and Javier did to you. I need to know how painfully they should die."

"Don't even joke about that!"

Luc raised a brow. "Who said I was kidding?"

She glared at him, then rolled her eyes, feeling a bit like a teenager talking to her dad. "It's not their fault."

"Really?" Skeptical would be a kind description of his scoffing tone. "So they were the innocent ones at the beginning of the relationship? They completely gave their hearts to you? But you pushed them too hard, too fast?"

London gaped at him. "How did you . . ."

"Oh, come on. I could have written this script without any imagination at all. You had absolutely no experience with men, did you?" When she shook her head, he went on. "So you fall for a bad boy and a tortured drunk."

"Don't call them that! They're way more. They can be so tender and—"

"To get what they want, of course. They're your first loves. I get it. You fell hard, but they're still playing whatever games they always play. It could only end one way."

"You have it all wrong. I'm the one who walked out. They've been demanding, yes." She blushed and squirmed in her seat, knowing that Luc could read between the lines, but she pressed on. "They've also done their best to take care of me and make me feel good about myself. I'm just not ready to open up in every way they want. I can't show them my scars. They weren't going to accept that."

"Because they're perfect?" He rolled his eyes.

"Of course not. They wanted trust I couldn't give them. That I can't give anyone. They deserve happiness, and I love them enough to let them find it without me."

"At the expense of your own? Don't you think you're being a little rash? You had to have been more than a tad overwhelmed by the speed of this relationship. Trust doesn't develop overnight."

"It doesn't change the facts."

He sighed. "I've been against this relationship from the beginning, but I tried not to stand in your way. You're an adult and you need to experience real life, so I let you. Their problems are pretty damn real. But if you really love them and you're sure this is more than a hit-and-run on their part, then we should talk about this. Sweetie, because of the accident you haven't had past relationships to learn from like most women. That's a lot of growing up to miss. You're overwhelmed, and it's understandable. They are light-years ahead of you."

"They deserve someone who can keep up. Besides, it was probably stupid to think I could handle one man, let alone two. I mean, it didn't work for you, Deke, and Kimber."

"You heard about that, huh?" Luc tightened his jaw. "Different circumstances. Deke wasn't going to heal with me willing to be his crutch. Kimber didn't love me. Everything worked out for the best. Do you love Xander more than Javier? Or vice versa?"

"No!" The idea was preposterous.

"If not for your fears, would you want to try living without one or the other?"

London saw where Luc was going with this logic. "No. And I know you'll probably tell me that I should get over the scars and take the risk that they might accept me as is. But what if they don't? I don't know if I'd survive the hurt, Luc." She buried her face in her hands. "God, if anyone could hear me now, I'm sure they would tell me to get over myself."

"You're right. Some people wouldn't understand, but they obviously can't admit to ever feeling in over their heads and must be absolutely fabulous at conquering their fears. I hope they enjoy their perfect lives. The rest of us mere mortals deal."

She smiled at Luc's sarcasm. "Yeah, it's always easier to judge someone else, isn't it?"

"Exactly. For all intents and purposes, you're a girl in a woman's body. You've got to cut yourself some slack."

London wanted to, but . . . "At the end of the day, I'm doing them a disservice if I can't get over my anxiety and fully trust them. Besides, they never said it was more than a fling. Javier only hired me for five weeks. I think I've let everything mean far more to me. It's time to get out before they break my heart."

Luc hesitated a really long time. "If that's really want you want, I support you. But I'm going to say that I've wondered more than once if Lys can really love me as much as she claims to, even though I probably can't give her more children. I could doubt her, sure. It would be easy. And her assurances are just words, right? And those are simple, both to speak and to blow off when they're spoken. But if it's truly love on all sides, do you really want to give that up? Think about it. Don't make decisions too quickly."

London sighed, his words sinking in. There was some truth to what he said. Maybe she should talk to them. At least she should think about it.

The rest of the drive was spent primarily in silence until Luc's phone began ringing shortly after seven. When he slanted a glance over to her, she looked down at his phone's display. Xander. Her heart stuttered.

"I'll bet Lys gave him my number, damn it," Luc groused with a grim face as he answered the phone. "Yes, I have her. Yes, she's safe. Sweetie, do you want to talk to them now?"

She wanted to. Ached to. Hearing their voices . . . nothing ever made her feel better than being close to them. But this wasn't about soothing her. She had to get her head on straight first. "Not now."

"Sorry, guys. She needs a little more time."

"Please!"

London could hear Xander's frustration through the phone and winced. If she let them in her ear now, even to tell them that she wasn't angry and that she was all right . . . it would be so easy to let them talk her into burying her fears and opening her arms to them again. But they'd run into this brick wall of her insecurities again and again until they got sick of them and broke it off. How much more would it hurt then?

Luc looked at her expectantly. She shook her head.

"Not going to happen, Xander. And pleading with me won't work. She was innocent and struggling just to start life. I don't have any illusions that she's innocent anymore, and this relationship has heaped a lot of emotional shit on her shoulders that she's trying to process. Find some fucking patience. She'll call you if she wants to talk."

Luc was more than a little harsh with Xander, and when Luc disconnected the call, she knew Xander wouldn't try to reach her again through her cousin or her husband.

"I wanted a lover, you know." The confession croaked out. London felt her face flame, but she needed to get this off her chest. Alyssa would comfort her, no matter what she said. But Luc was proving to be a straight shooter. "I wanted not just to be alive but to *feel* alive."

"Sex isn't a life."

"But sex is a part of life, and I've experienced so little in mine. I just wanted . . . everything. A job, friends, independence. I can say I had those briefly, I guess. At least, I can check a broken heart off my list now," she tried to joke.

He sighed and looked at her with such understanding she nearly cried. "Sweetie, you'll have all the experiences you need. I understand that you lost ten years and it's made you anxious to catch up. But there's a reason parents try to protect their teenagers from experiencing everything too fast." When she would have opened her mouth to object, Luc held up a hand. "I know you're not a teenager anymore. If you had been, your ass would be grounded now. But I'm just saying that you have to understand that not every experience is good. And those that are aren't always easy. Be patient with yourself. And while you're at it—God, I can't believe I'm going to say this— but maybe you should be patient with them. If they're calling all over hell this early in the morning, they care."

That was probably good advice. Could she really put it to good use? Her natural inclination was to want to settle problems and questions as soon as they cropped up. But this one was too important to rush.

"Thanks. I really do appreciate you."

"Glad to hear it. You can stay up and spend time with Chloe. I'm going back to bed when we get home."

At first, she tensed. She shouldn't be alone with the toddler, and Luc knew it. But he'd be in the next room. She had to start trusting herself. Then she'd see about trusting others.

She laughed at him. "You're on."

They arrived in Lafayette midmorning. Alyssa hugged her tightly the second she walked in the door. "We'll talk when I get home. About anything you want. As long as you want."

But her cousin's demeanor said she was late for work, so London shoved her out the door. "Go. Luc is going back to bed. I got this."

Alyssa smiled, looking as beautiful as ever in a black ruffled blouse, a short cream-colored skirt, and two-toned peep-toe stilettos. London sighed in envy when Alyssa gave Luc a lingering kiss. She could feel the love between them. Luc had embraced her cousin's terrible past. Lys accepted his shortcomings. They shared a great life, a wonderful house, a beautiful baby. Instead of asking if it was enough, they just went with it and took life as it came.

Maybe she had overreacted to Xander and Javier being so insistent about seeing her back. No, she wasn't ready today, but tomorrow?

Chloe cuddled up in her arms when Alyssa bopped out the door with a wave. Luc locked up behind her, then stumbled back to the bedroom. With a smile, London nibbled on a late breakfast, watched the toddler, and tried to clear her head.

When Luc woke a few hours later, London handed his daughter to him with a grateful smile. Then she grabbed her phone and turned it on, just in case. Ignoring the four voice mails and umpteen missed calls, she shoved it in her pocket, palmed her keys, and let herself out for a walk. It was damn hot, and she'd soon swelter, but she had to keep training for her 5K. And she needed some peace and quiet.

London wandered for a while, wiping the perspiration from her brow, and found herself in front of the office building she'd shared with Javier and Xander. A bittersweet pang wrenched her chest. She should just keep walking. If she wanted a clear head, being in the space in which the men she loved had seduced her, body and heart, wasn't smart. But she wasn't quite strong enough to resist the temptation.

She let herself into the lobby, halfway thankful that the copy and postage facility on the bottom floor dictated that the building remain open seven days a week. With shaking fingers, she called the elevator, then proceeded to the office door, letting herself inside with the key Javier had given her on day one.

Pushing inside the dark room, she turned to flip on the lights.

Before she could, a hard body barged in behind her, shoving her into the room. As she stumbled to find her balance, London heard the door close almost silently. The intruder—a man, based on his grip—grabbed her arm and threw the lock home. She turned to stare at him over her shoulder, and he covered her gasp with his gloved hand.

With her heart pounding, London peered up into his cold dark eyes. Without a word, she knew he was a predator of the worst kind. He had no soul.

"So sorry, love," he muttered with a French accent.

London didn't understand his apology—until he lifted a length of rope between them and brought it toward her neck.

Chapter Nineteen

"Happy seven a.m. This fucking better be good," Nick Navarro growled in his ear.

Javier bit back a pointed reply. He had to stay on task. Shit was hitting the fan. He didn't need to include a breakdown with it, no matter how strung out he felt or how much Nick deserved it. He needed to stop the panicky slide to blackout he'd experienced in the past. London needed him.

"This *is* fucking important." That was as nice as Javier could manage. "You've been keeping tabs on Chad Brenner, right?"

"Yeah. He hasn't left Florida in weeks. Seems to be a workaholic house hermit with a serious Chinese and pizza delivery habit."

"I don't give a shit what he's eating. Have you kept tabs on his bank accounts?"

"There hasn't been anything unusual as of yesterday afternoon."

"Look again."

Navarro groaned, and Javier could hear him rustling sheets as he pushed out of bed. A feminine moan of protest carried across the line, and he forced himself not to care. He paid Nick handsomely to give up some beauty sleep or sex when big stuff happened.

Thirty seconds later, Nick whistled. "How did you know?

Brenner is fifty thousand poorer. He took ten of it out in cash three days ago. The rest just before the bank closed yesterday evening."

"That's what I thought. Have you been tracking Valjean?"

"I've always got a tracker on that fucker's whereabouts. I know some real helpful folks at Interpol, and we trade information now and then." He clicked the keys of his computer a few more times. After a pause, he sighed. "Why the fuck would he be in Mexico?"

"Because he just killed one of my former employees."

"No shit? And you think Brenner is the money man?"

"That's exactly what I think. Look back through Brenner's financials. Can you go back about a year? Do you see any significant cash outlays last June?"

"That will take a few minutes . . ."

Minutes that were going to make Javier insane. He muted the call and turned to his brother. "What the hell should we do if it turns out that Brenner paid Valjean to kill Francesca? Kill the fucker?"

"I'm sure you'd like to but . . ." Xander dragged in a deep breath and shook his head. "We'll go to the police. I don't know if we have enough evidence to prove anything, but we have to try."

"Agreed, but why would Brenner have paid someone to murder Francesca?" Javier had been coping—barely—with the fact that his neglect had driven her into the arms of the man who'd killed her. But Brenner's possible involvement now cast a different light on this.

"Revenge. That's the hand he played with Carlton."

Javier's eyes slid closed as something terrible—final and painful—filled him. It had been wrenching enough to know that he'd starved Francesca for attention so badly that she'd sought a killer. But to know that she'd been targeted because he'd created a terrible enemy in Brenner only made his guilt weigh that much heavier.

"But why not come after *me*?" he argued.

"I think he did," Xander pointed out. "If something happened to you after such a public dispute, wouldn't it have looked suspicious? Besides, if you were dead, then Brenner couldn't watch you suffer all the ways he was fucking with you. He stole all our innovations for the last year or so just to have the pleasure of watching you and the business slowly go down the toilet since Fran's death."

Revenge. The motive was so simple that Javier had overlooked it. Yes, there were lots of layers and sharp complexities to the events that had nearly destroyed him. Fran's resentment, Xander's refusal, his own disregard, Brenner's arrogance. But at the end of the day, the situation boiled down to mere retribution.

"Gotcha!" Nick shouted over the phone.

A moment later, Nick returned. "Last June, I show two large cash withdrawals from Brenner's account, one for ten thousand on the first. The second was for another forty K four days later. At the time, that was every dime the fucker had."

A down payment, followed by a payoff for services rendered the day after Francesca's murder. The evidence was circumstantial at best, but it was a start.

"Fuck." Javier raked a hand through his hair. "Do you have any idea where Valjean is now?"

Nick paused, pounding a bit on his computer. "He's not in Cancun anymore. He was there less than twenty-four hours according to the intel I'm getting. As soon as Mexican police were onto him, he disappeared. They surmise that he hired a charter boat and sailed out, bypassing customs. But he can't go far on a vessel like that."

"How far?" Javier barked.

"Another destination in Mexico, Belize, Cuba. Those would be the easiest. Wait!" A few more clicks later, Javier could almost hear Nick's frown over the line. "The FBI is reporting a possible sighting of Valjean."

FBI only handled domestic matters. Was Valjean on U.S. soil? "Where?"

"Port of New Orleans."

Only a few hours from Lafayette. Had Brenner sent Valjean to kill him finally? Let him. Let the fucker try. He was ready. They'd give all this over to the police, but they'd be slow to turn the wheels of justice, and even then, it might not be enough. Javier was ready to have it out with Brenner. If the fucker wanted to play hardball, fine.

"Another ten grand disappeared from Brenner's account this morning."

The words dropped like a boulder. So this was it. "Brenner's sending someone to end me, then."

"Would he?" Xander questioned. Nick asked basically the same thing in his ear.

"Look at it this way," Navarro added. "If all he wanted to do was kill you, why bother setting the elaborate scheme of selling your information out from under you? Why kill your wife? I don't think he wants you to die, man. He wants you to suffer."

"Just like *he* did." The pieces snapped into place for Javier. Some of Brenner's parting words had been about not resting until he'd destroyed everything Javier had ever cared about. By killing Fran, it had fucked up his head so badly, he'd almost run S.I. Industries into the ground. But he'd been so much better since coming to Louisiana. And he had London—

"Where is she?" Javier turned to his brother, panic tearing through his veins in a fiery chill. Fear threatened to explode him. If Brenner had paid Valjean to hurt one hair on her head . . . the engineer better pray for death because Javier vowed to deliver it, slowly and painfully. He didn't give a shit if he went to prison for the rest of his life. *No one* threatened to end the existence of that beautiful girl who'd struggled so much just to begin a new life after her accident.

"With Luc, I assume." But Xander's face showed that he was starting to think and piece things together. "Fuck! They would have reached Lafayette already."

"I'll call Luc. You see if you can find London's phone now. Nick, keep tracking Valjean."

"You got it. I'll call the second I've got anything."

The line went dead, and Javier didn't waste a second. But Luc's phone just rang and rang. That sent a new bout of panic chugging the fiery chill through his veins and tearing into his gut.

Beside him, Xander called out, "Found her! She's at the office."

"On a Saturday?"

Xander frowned, silently acknowledging that was out of the norm. He dialed London's number. No answer. He repeated the action three times, and her voice mail picked up every time.

Dread gnawed on him. Javier wiped a hand over his face. He was breathing, but it felt as if everything stood still—time, his respiration, even the car rolling down mile after mile of road, still an hour away from Lafayette.

As Xander stabbed his finger into the phone to end the call, Javier felt panic sear an icy path through his veins. "Still nothing?"

Javier shook his head, mind racing. "If she's at the office, she's not with Luc."

"If she's at the office, Valjean might find her there. Fuck!"

He tried to think rationally. "Why would Valjean think to look for her there during the weekend?"

"I don't know, but better safe than sorry." Xander grabbed his phone and dialed quickly. Someone answered right away, and Javier had to hope that whoever it was could help them. "Logan. We need help now."

Quickly, Xander explained the situation. Javier only knew Logan by reputation, but from the sounds of things, the Navy SEAL sprang into action. He said he'd call the police as backup on his way over to the office. Hunter, his brother, happened to be sitting next to him, so they'd tag-team the fucker and save London.

Xander pressed his foot to the accelerator, now going more than a hundred. Javier didn't say a word. Nothing was more important than getting to their girl and saving her. In the meantime, he could only think of one other call that might save London before Valjean struck.

He rifled through his contacts, thankful that he never bothered to remove this one. He prayed the number hadn't changed. Knowing his number would have been blocked, Javier grabbed his brother's phone and dialed.

"This is Brenner."

"Javier Santiago. Don't hang up! I want to negotiate."

"I have no idea what you're talking about," the engineer drawled, as if the sound of his panic was highly enjoyable.

"Your assassin Valjean. I know he killed my wife. I know he killed Albert Carlton. I know he's on his way to kill my assistant, London."

"I'm sure I have no idea where you get these crazy ideas," Brenner denied, but his tone was playful. The fucker was definitely enjoying his anxiety. "I have seen pictures of your assistant. Pretty thing. Since my wife divorced me over the loss of all my intellectual property and income potential after our court case, I know how terrible it is to lose the woman . . . Oh, silly me. I'm assuming you're in love with her. You are, aren't you? I've heard whispers. You know how people talk. There's a whole lot of chatter that you're not only fucking your pretty assistant, but you're sharing her with that manwhore brother of yours. I must say, I'm surprised."

Every minute he let Brenner bait him was another minute that Valjean had to find London. "No more games. What do you want to call Valjean off? I'll give you everything. I'll sign over the entire company to you if you'll call him off London."

Brenner dragged in a breath, and Javier could hear the happy vindication in his sigh. He gritted his teeth, swallowed his pride, and said nothing. "You sound so . . . humble. I don't think I've ever heard you be any less than totally in control. Arrogant, even. I have to say, I'm enjoying this side of you."

The fucker was toying with him. "What else do you want? My life? It's yours. I'll show up any place you want at any time you want so you can have me killed in any way you please."

Xander leaned into the phone. "Me, too. If you want us off the planet and our family gone, it's done. Just tell us when and where. We'll be there."

Javier glanced at his brother in a moment of true understanding. He didn't have to guess what Xander was thinking; he knew. Neither of them would be happy or worth a damn without London. She'd given them both hope, direction, and a reason to be better men.

"Well, that's no loss," Brenner drawled. "What has Xander ever done with his life, except spread his sperm far and wide? That's certainly no contribution to society. But it's interesting that both of you are willing to die for this girl. I guess you're both—gasp—in love with her. That presupposes that you're capable of loving another human being, Santiago, which I'm pretty certain your late wife didn't believe."

"I was a terrible husband," Javier admitted, both to appease Brenner and because it was the goddamn truth. "I'm sorry if I was a lousy boss. I swear, you can have the whole company if you'll just bring London safely back. I'll sign it over as soon as you can have the paperwork drawn up. Just call off Valjean."

Two generations of Santiago sweat and innovation down the toilet. The business he'd devoted his life to. The legacy he'd hoped to someday pass on to a son or daughter. Gone in exchange for a woman he'd met a week ago.

But he wouldn't make any other choice. A glance at Xander told him they were still on the same page.

"Well, as tempting as that sounds, I have no idea who Valjean is," Brenner said. "I have no idea how your overactive imagination dreamed up this tale. Drinking again?"

"Just tell me what you want from us! You believe I took your life's work, so I'll give you mine. No strings. Just return my assistant to me." *My savior, my beloved.*

"I don't want your company, Santiago. Anything I invented when I worked for you is now on the verge of being outdated and I

can innovate again. That's what I do. Thankfully for me, United Velocity is more than happy to pay me in both cash and stock for all the
genius I give them."

Javier gripped the phone tighter, his nerves strung so tight, he
could feel every beat of his heart as a pounding in his head. His
world narrowed as he focused on the nearly empty road in front of
him and the sound of Brenner's voice.

"Do you want money? A public apology? I've offered to die for
her. What else do you want?"

"Oh, you've given me everything I could want now." His voice
sounded just shy of gloating laughter. Normally, that would rub Javier like industrial sandpaper, but his pride didn't matter at all now.
"There's really nothing more you can give me. I hope you find your
girl before it's too late. I'll be thinking of you and watching."

There was a click, and the call went dead in his ear. A cold panic
rushed through his veins. He'd failed. London was innocent of all
wrongdoing. Her only crime had been in not trusting their love. He
froze. No, the crime had been his. How could she trust in a love he'd
never professed to her? God, she couldn't pay with her life and die
thinking he didn't love her all the way down to his soul. He and
Xander would suffer guilt and anguish for the rest of their miserable
fucking existences. In the back of his mind, he was already lining up
the bottles he'd consume—and mentally taking in hand the .38 he'd
hidden from Xander in the back of his closet. For a year, guilt over
Francesca had raged through him, hollowing out his life until he'd
become a shell of his former self. Grief for London would end all will
to live. But before he ended it all, he'd hunt Brenner down like a dog
and kill him slowly, with maximum pain.

"The fucker hung up?"

"Yes." His voice sounded almost calm, and Javier didn't know
how he managed when everything inside him was panicked, railing,
screaming . . . dying. His breath started coming too fast. He fought

the urge to hyperventilate, to allow his thoughts to disintegrate into chaos.

With one hand on the wheel, Xander used the other to slap his thigh. "Stay the fuck with me. No checking out, brother."

The stinging pain burned his skin and brought him back to focus, and Javier nodded gratefully. "Thanks."

"You're welcome. Saving her is going to take both of us."

His brother was right again. "We're in this together."

Xander grabbed his phone back and tried Brenner's number again. It went immediately to voice mail. The engineer was done talking. The man he felt was responsible for all his suffering would now suffer with no recourse, so he'd had his revenge. In the most poetic way, it was an eye for an eye.

"Fucker!" Xander looked like he wanted to throw his phone, but he didn't dare. "Try London's number again. Maybe she'll answer."

Javier's stomach tightened. They were still about thirty minutes out of town. In thirty minutes, it might all be too late. Hell, it might be too late now, but he had to keep hope.

Maybe Valjean hadn't gotten to her yet. Maybe they could save her. Maybe . . . One ring, two, three, four—voice mail. He barked into the phone, hoping she listened to this message, even though he'd keep trying to call. "London, call Luc. Get to safety. Someone is coming after you. He means to—" Javier couldn't say it. The words would make it all too real. "He means to hurt you. Please stay safe for us. I love you."

"I love you, too, *belleza*," Xander shouted into the phone.

Given no choice, they ended the call. A painful two minutes later, they tried again. One ring, two, three, four . . .

* * *

LONDON blinked in the shadowy room at the stranger as her phone buzzed again in her pocket. She couldn't quite reach it, and couldn't try with her assailant bearing down. As that rope came closer, she *knew* that if he got it around her neck, she was as good as dead. With her keys still biting into her palm and her heart pounding, she jabbed them into the killer's stomach.

He anticipated her movement and jumped aside just in time to avoid her.

She reached for the door and grabbed the handle, but he fastened a cruel grip around her arm and yanked her back. As she stumbled, he jerked the keys from her hand and tossed them across the floor.

"Leaving so soon?" His accent was thick.

Looking around for a weapon, she swayed on her feet. A telltale light-headed feeling crept up, and she gasped. With everything that had been going on, she'd missed her last two doses of medicine. What if she passed out?

She'd have no way to put up a fight, and he'd kill her without compunction.

No! Her life had been so short already, having lost so many years to injury, rehab, and pain. She was finally living, damn it.

All because of Javier and Xander.

No way she'd let herself go down now. They were probably somewhere thinking she was a coward. Or worse, not thinking about her at all. But as blackness began to claim her vision and her knees buckled, London couldn't stand the thought that the Santiago brothers might move on before she'd been brave enough to tell them that she loved them. Damn it, she should have stayed with them, shown them her back. Maybe they wouldn't have run screaming. Maybe they would have still wanted her. She could be cuddled in bed between them now, sated and smiling.

Instead, she was fighting for her life.

As London fell, she stumbled into her attacker. He tripped and grunted before landing on the industrial carpet with a thud. He cursed, and London sucked in a breath, struggling to find her feet, and stumbled forward. She had to keep herself conscious, use all her energy and will to fight.

Digging her nails into her forearm and focusing on the pain, she felt her consciousness floating. A dizzy haze swam in her head. She lurched a step, hoping it was toward the door, but her sense of direction was gone, and she nearly took a nosedive into her desk.

London latched onto the edge, desperate to keep herself upright. Her fingers bit onto something cold and metallic. Behind her, she vaguely registered her attacker wrap his hand around her ankle and tug, trying to pull her to the ground. The feel of him, the malice in his touch, made her scream. But no one was here. The only business open today was the copy and mailing place three floors beneath her. No one would hear her. No one knew she was here.

Blackness tugged at her again. London resisted, yanking her leg to pull it free from her attacker. She kicked and kicked, finally striking something solid. She glanced back and saw him cupping his cheek, glaring up at her as he scrambled to his feet. He muttered something, and while every word sounded beautiful in French, his tone didn't sound lovely at all. Anger resonated from that growl, and she knew that once he lost his temper and gained his footing, he'd come at her, overpower her, strangle her with the rope in his hands . . . and what little life she'd enjoyed since the accident would be over. She'd never feel the sun again. Never learn to drive. Never accomplish her goal of finishing a 5K alone. Worst, she'd never get the chance to tell Javier and Xander that she loved them. She'd been hiding, hedging her bets, living in a safe little bubble, and not stepping too far out of her comfort zone. How did she expect to live an extraordinary life if she didn't take some extraordinary risks?

Gumption rose along with bile as her attacker gripped her arm and yanked her around to face him. His intent to kill her shot up her arm, frying her skin. Adrenaline and pure terror juiced her bloodstream with something cold and terrible. London knew she had seconds left if she wanted that extraordinary life. Otherwise, he'd make death inevitable.

Gripping the edge of the desk, the wooden corner biting into her fingers, she forced herself to look across the surface for any advantage, anything that might buy her a few seconds to get the hell out of here, or at least slow him down. There, just beyond her grasp, lay her savior.

London grunted as she hurtled herself across the desk and kicked back at him with all her might. He loosened his grip on her, and she grabbed at her weapon—and missed. Before she could try again, he gave a vicious tug on her ankle and jerked her back toward him. But she wasn't giving up.

As she twisted around, London only had a split second to line up before she slammed the pointy edge of her elbow into his temple.

He toppled sideways, and she was sure she'd only managed that because she'd taken him by surprise. She wouldn't get the same opportunity twice. It was now or never. Yes, her plan might kill him, but he'd had no compunction about killing her, so she had to put away her squeamishness and keep fighting.

Behind her, a purely male roar sounded. He hadn't expected her to be any trouble. He'd simply believed that she'd die like a good little girl. She'd almost done that once. Overrated. She'd already lost years of her youth. Damned if she was going to lose the rest of life's remarkable journey because she wasn't willing to fight hard enough for it. The irony of that hit her just as she reached for her weapon.

Metal dug into her fingers, cold and heavy, as she picked up the big three-hole punch and whirled around. She was only going to have one shot at this, then she'd lose her element of surprise . . . Her attacker barely had time to widen his dark eyes before she rammed the bottom of the heavy device into the side of his severe face.

He stumbled back and fell on his ass. London forced herself to take another step toward him, even as dizziness swarmed her head once again. She stepped up between her attacker's sprawled feet, then reared back and kicked him in the balls as hard as she could.

Clutching himself, he tossed his head back, dark hair doing little to cushion him against the thin industrial carpet. London had no remorse as he rolled to his side, still cupping his family jewels. A big part of her wanted to grab his wrist and use it to drag him to her desk, then tie it to him using his own rope. She didn't dare stay that long or give him a chance to get his hands on her again. It wouldn't take him long to recover from his pain to the gonads, then he'd come after her with a roaring fury and kill her with punitive thrill. Best just to get the hell out of here.

Heart drumming, she tripped over her attacker and stumbled for the door, fumbling for the handle. He'd locked it behind him, and her shaking fingers couldn't quite turn the lock. Panic poured in, then nearly drowned her when she heard him rise behind her, call her something most likely foul in French. His arctic growl sent a chill down her spine.

"Bitch. I will kill you with my bare hands now with pleasure," he translated for her.

No, no, no! She screamed with both fear and frustration at the lock, but it didn't give. Knowing that she was out of options, that he was just a second behind her, she flipped on the office lights, praying it momentarily blinded him. He made an annoyed huffing sound, and to her ears, it seemed that he backed up a step, but London didn't dare look.

Her fingers wrapped around the lock again. This time, she took a deep breath and tried to calm herself, willing her trembling fingers to still enough to do the job. Finally, it worked and she lurched out into the hall—only to fall into a stranger's arms.

Her murderer hadn't come alone?

London gasped and tried to wrest away from the man who stood in the shadowy hallway and held her in strong arms, but he shoved her behind him. He clutched a nasty gun in one hand. He set a finger over his lips, motioning to her to be quiet. His blue, blue eyes looked so intense, just like his chiseled face made almost severe by his military-short blondish hair. Hunter.

And she nearly sagged with relief.

Against the wall beside him crouched another man she recognized because of his incredibly blue eyes. Logan. Like his older brother, he possessed a vicious-looking weapon and the expression of a predator on the hunt. Logan grabbed her and put her on the wall beside him, shielding her body with his own. He held one hand out, indicating that she should stay put.

Trembling and restraining the urge to cry in mad relief, she watched, breath held, as her attacker suddenly stumbled out of the office, looking around the darkened halls for her. He nearly plowed into Hunter, who instantly tackled him to the ground, rolled him to his stomach, and shoved his arm behind his back, his hand somewhere between his shoulder blades. The French bastard started squealing.

"Pipe down," Hunter demanded. "I'm not going to break your arm or dislocate your shoulder. Yet. But if you won't tell me what I want to know . . . we'll have problems."

"I tell you nothing," the Frenchman spat.

"Then get ready to cry like a girl." Logan squatted next to the guy. "See, you apparently think it's all fun and games when you sneak up on a girl who's done absolutely nothing to you." He picked up the length of rope the killer had dropped and held it up to her with a questioning glance. She nodded. "I don't think you meant to play fun bondage games with London."

"No," she choked. "He put it around my throat. He meant to strangle me."

Hunter narrowed his eyes at her assailant as he trained the gun on the guy's head. Logan reached for the man's free hand and, along with the one Hunter held, tied them together using his own rope.

"Wrong way to use a rope, asshole," Hunter muttered. "Grab the phone off my belt, London."

She did as he bid and waited for instructions. Her instinct was to call the police now, but she shook so hard that her teeth chattered.

"Good. Scroll down my contacts to find Jack Cole. Call him, tell him you're with us, and there's a situation. He'll deal with the local sheriff."

Jack answered immediately and assessed the situation in a few sentences, pausing to tell her to calm down and control her breathing. Passing out wouldn't do any of them any good.

Moments later, sirens wailed, coming closer and closer. Trembling overtook her body as a cold relief poured in. She had no idea who this man was or why he'd wanted to kill her, but it was over. She would live.

The fashion in which she did it was now up to her.

Chapter Twenty

ALYSSA sat beside her hospital bed in the ER, looking anxious and stressed. With taut faces, Logan and Hunter in the corner conferred with Luc in low tones, rehashing the conversation she'd had with the police the instant the doctors had cleared her to talk. None of the guys claimed to have any idea why she'd been attacked, but she didn't believe them. Logan had been on the phone almost nonstop since taking down the bad guy. No idea whom he was talking to, or even why he and his brother had been at the office to help her out. But he knew something.

"God, they're tense," she told her cousin. "Something is wrong."

As Chloe played with a stuffed animal in her lap, Alyssa looked over her shoulder at the men, then back at her with a tight smile. "They're just being protective. It's what they do best."

And she had a feeling that when Xander and Javier showed up, protective would rise to new heights. Xander seemed laid back, but that was part of his playboy act. And Javier was high-strung even on a good day. Her phone was still in the pocket of her jeans, which had been discarded for a hospital gown as soon as she'd arrived, but she had no doubt that they were staying on top of the situation somehow. She'd barely hit the door of the emergency room before she'd been shown to a private room with a dedicated nurse. A doctor and a battery of tests had followed. It had taken no time at all to find out what she'd tried to tell everyone all along—there was absolutely nothing wrong with her except that she was scared and shaky, and she knew she'd be dealing with nightmares about strangers bearing ropes for some time.

Alyssa squeezed her hand. "Don't worry. The guys will figure this mess out."

"If they haven't already. I wish they'd tell me what they know."

"Back to that being-protective thing." She shrugged. "You'll get used to it."

Logan's phone beeped, and he glanced down at the screen. He typed a quick message back. Hunter's cell started ringing a moment later. He swiped his thumb across the screen and marched into the hall with ground-eating steps, barking into the little device.

"I doubt that. They're making me jumpier." London tried not to shiver. She was lucky to be alive. Thrilled . . . but troubled. Why had the killer targeted her?

Logan must have bionic hearing because, despite his phone dinging and the monitors attached to her beeping, he turned and pinned those blue, blue eyes on her. "Try to relax. No one is going to hurt you. *No one.* I promise you that."

"And we'll do whatever we have to in order to ensure that," Xander stated from the open door, striding into the room and straight for her bed. Javier followed, moving toward her other side. They both looked exhausted and anxious and so damn relieved to see her alive.

London felt herself come alive the second she saw them. For terrible moments today, she'd thought she'd never lay eyes on them again. Her joy at having them here and near filled her almost beyond her ability to contain it.

Xander didn't hesitate. The moment he skidded to a stop beside her, he grabbed her face in his hands, tilted her up to him, and swooped down to plaster his lips over hers, kissing her as if he'd never been more worried or desperate in his life. London opened for him gratefully, trembling against him. She drank in the sweet relief in the frantic press of his mouth. If something had happened to her today, it would have mattered to him. And on the heels of that kiss, a nip of her lower lip—a promise of punishment later for running away. She shivered.

He released her and gave her a nudge in the opposite direction. Javier stood waiting, staring with burning eyes and clenched fists. "I'm so sorry, little one."

Before she could ask exactly what he was apologizing for—shouldn't she be the one saying sorry?—he bent and pulled her against his broad chest as if his life depended on it, heedless of the wires and machinery hooked up to her. With his heart beating madly, Javier's lips swept across hers—and paused. He didn't shove his way into her mouth or try to deepen the kiss. He merely pressed his lips to hers and breathed her in, his entire body shaking. Clearly, he wanted to comfort her, but she knew right away that he needed reassurance far more. She feathered her fingers softly through his hair and touched his cheek, searching his lips with her own for a response. Barely an instant later, he delved into her mouth. He was everywhere inside her, pleading, taking, his body shuddering with need. He gripped her arms, pressed his body to her as if he never wanted air between them again, and owned her with that kiss. London let him take everything he needed, drowning in the demand of his possessive touch.

At her back, she felt Xander blanket her and press kisses to the top of her head. "We've been terrified, *belleza*. We're so relieved you're safe. We want to hold you and keep you from harm's way and—"

"Ahem," a dark, dangerous interloper interrupted from the doorway, brow raised.

Jack Cole. London had only met him once or twice, but that sense of power kept barely in check oozed from his very pores. She resisted the urge to shrink back like a guilty child.

The Santiago brothers both glared across the room as if they'd like to pull Jack apart one limb at a time and cause a whole lot of pain. Alyssa paid Jack no mind, instead giving London a pointed look, reminding her a bit of a mom discouraging PDA with one's boyfriend. Luc smiled wryly, holding his wife's hand. Logan's eyes twinkled as if he was amused, while Hunter's demeanor was somewhere between watchful and blank. London felt heat flame its way up her face. Funny how every time she was sandwiched between Xander and Javier, she completely forgot the outside world.

"Sorry," she murmured to them all.

"Fuck that." Xander wrapped his arm around her tighter. "You shouldn't be sorry. I'm not."

"What a shock," Logan drawled.

"Don't sidetrack him, water boy," said Jack. "We've got business to clear up."

"You're a buzzkill, ground pounder. And Army Rangers will never be better than Navy SEALs."

Alyssa groaned. "This argument again?"

"I think all that water has affected your brain," Jack quipped. "But enjoy your delusion."

"Can we continue this incredibly pointless argument later?" Xander snapped. "Logan said you've been working with the police. And . . . ?"

All levity in Jack's expression disappeared. "Right. Buckle your seatbelts. Here's where we're at, and it's bumpy." He walked in the room and shut the door behind him. "The Mexican police found Carlton's body after a little tip-off—" Jack cleared his throat. "And they're investigating, but McConnell already found everything you needed to know, right?"

At Xander's nod, London frowned. "Who is Carlton? How are the Mexican police involved? What does this have to do with whoever attacked me?"

Jack shot Xander and Javier expressions that seemed to ask their permission. To finally tell her what the hell was going on? Xander cursed under his breath.

"Oh, no. If you know something, I want to know, too. I deserve to know, damn it."

"You do." Javier sat on the bed beside her. "What happened today . . . It's why I apologized, little one. You did nothing to warrant this attack, except be meaningful to me. Carlton is a former employee who was selling me out to another man who once worked for me, Chad Brenner. He invented some of our most lucrative products, then sued us when he wanted more money for his intellectual property than his employment contract allowed. He left bitterly, lost his lawsuit, and decided to get revenge." He grabbed her hand and sighed heavily. "But I swear, if you'll let me, I'll do everything to—"

"We," Xander cut in.

"We." Javier nodded. "Yes. We'll do everything in our power to keep you safe. But it's largely my fault you're in danger, London."

"*Were* in danger," Jack was the one to correct Javier this time.

Everyone turned to him, hanging on his every word.

"Explain," Javier growled at Jack.

"I was getting there. When the police arrived at your office to arrest Valjean—"

London gasped and whirled to Javier. "Valjean, the assassin who killed your wife?"

He nodded tightly. "The same, yes. I just found out myself."

Shock ricocheted through London's system. "Brenner hired this Valjean to kill me in order to get back at you? The same way he did Francesca?"

"You got it," Jack said. "And the moment the police took him into custody and started grilling him, he was all too happy to give up details. Of course their threat to turn him over to the FBI might have had something to do with it."

"So he confessed?" Javier demanded.

"He did. And he gave up Brenner's name pretty easily." Jack

sighed, and London knew that what followed wouldn't be good news. "Then when they tried to transfer Valjean to a higher-security facility, he jumped his guards and killed one of them. So the others had to shoot him. He's dead."

"Fuck!" Javier jumped to his feet, every muscle tense, looking like he restrained himself from hitting the wall. "So he can't testify, and Brenner will probably walk. No doubt he'll hire someone else to come after London. She's not safe."

"I'm not done with the story." Jack crossed his arms over his chest. "It takes another turn. The Lafayette PD called the FBI. Interestingly enough, Brenner had been a 'person of interest' for some time. They liked Valjean's taped confession and sent local Florida cops in to arrest Brenner. He went without a peep. I'd say he's looking at several consecutive lifetimes for all the illegal shit he's done. And just to make it more fun, the government is seizing all his funds. Apparently the CIA wants to talk to him, too. Seems they've got proof that he's been developing some nuclear ideas for the Iranians."

Hunter whistled. "And depending how deep he is, that might be construed as treason."

"The feds will bury him for the rest of his miserable life." Logan nodded. "Awesome!"

"So it really is over?" London heard her own voice trembling.

Jack crossed the room to her and sat on the other edge of her bed, taking her hand in his with an incredibly gentle grip. He was almost painfully handsome. She was completely in love—times two—and didn't want anyone else. But no denying that he made her damn nervous.

"Yes. Valjean is dead, and Brenner will never see the light of day again. Take a deep breath. That goes for you two, as well." Jack eyed Xander and Javier. "She's safe."

"Beautiful. Thank you." Xander wedged in between them. "Now get your hand off our woman."

Jack rolled his eyes and stood. "If you're going to be that territorial, man, you need to put a ring on that finger. That's what I did when I realized that I didn't want anyone else touching Morgan."

London wished a big hole would open up in the floor and swallow her up. They were not going to marry her after knowing her for a week, especially when she'd closed part of herself off from them.

But she wasn't going to let them slip through her fingers without trying to show them how much she wanted and loved them.

"Thank you for the update, Jack," she rushed to say. Something had to cover up that awkward silence. She turned to Alyssa. "Did the doctor say when I could leave?"

"They're getting your discharge papers now," her cousin said.

"Shouldn't be too much longer, sweetie." Luc sent her a reassuring smile.

As if on cue, the nurse appeared and cut through the small crowd with a disapproving frown. She handed London her discharge papers. "You're free to go. The doctor advises a day or two of taking it easy. Keep up with the meds your doctor in California prescribed. *All* of them. Call your doctor if you become disoriented, have trouble with your balance, or if those cuts on your fingers become infected."

She nodded. "Thank you. I will."

"No. We will." Javier took the papers from her hands and scanned them before addressing the nurse again. "We'll take care of her."

The salty older woman took in Javier's proprietary stance and Xander's possessive hand on her shoulder, then shook her head as if she didn't want to know. "See that you do."

"We'll be here for her," Xander insisted as the nurse left.

"You already got my advice if you want to keep it that way." With a mocking salute, Jack ducked out the door and disappeared.

As soon as Jack had gone, Hunter shrugged. "Being a ground pounder, he's often wrong, but not about this. I married Kata the night I met her. When you know, guys, you just know." He hitched a thumb in Logan's direction. "He's the dumbass who took almost fifteen years to marry the right girl."

"Hey! I knew at sixteen. It's not my fault that everything got fucked up. I won her back and married her, didn't I?" He punched his older brother in the arm.

If the thought wasn't so futile, she would love the chance to strangle all three of the big, testosterone-laden warriors going on and on about marriage. How embarrassing . . .

London cleared her throat. "Thank you both very much for the rescue."

Hunter waved her words away.

Logan grinned. "That was fun. Any time you need help out of a scrape—"

"There'd better not be a next time," Javier growled.

"We'll be there," Xander vowed.

London ignored her men and faced the Edgington brothers. "How swell that you enjoyed it, guys. And I'm glad you're both happily married, but enough already!"

Hunter and Logan frowned, finally having the good sense to look a little self-conscious.

"Yeah, okay," Logan drawled. "Me and my big-mouth brother will, um . . ."

"Go home to our wives." Hunter grabbed Logan by the shirt and hauled him out the door.

London watched them go with a shake of her head. They were both crazy wonderful, emphasis on the crazy.

"Why don't we give you a few minutes to get dressed so we can all get out of here," Alyssa suggested to her. "Do you need any help? If you'd rather, I can send a nurse in."

"I can manage, but thanks." She just wanted to get out of there . . . and plan the best way to get on with her life.

Alyssa stood with a smile. "Let me know if you need any help."

Luc wandered closer and patted her shoulder. "I'm relieved that you're okay. Your cousin and I will always be here for you."

"Thanks." She swallowed back tears. She was overwrought. God knew it had been an eventful day, and it wasn't over. So much unsettled . . .

Especially her heart.

"That means the world to me." She smiled up at Luc.

He smiled back, then turned to Xander and Javier. "Give her a few minutes to get dressed, guys."

Neither moved a muscle. Both looked like it was going to take an act of Congress to make them leave.

"Please," she whispered. She wanted to put her clothes on, gather her thoughts. Find her goddamn courage. Figure out how to say what needed to be said. She had so much on her mind, so much unspoken . . .

Javier cursed under his breath and sent her a look that warned her not to step a single toe out of the room without him before he stormed out into the hall.

Xander looked like he wanted to argue. Or plead. It was a close call. Instead, he growled, "Fine."

He followed his brother out the door, and suddenly she was alone. As she slipped into her pants, the silence should have soothed her. Now that the adrenaline had worn off, weariness tugged at her, all the way to her bones. As she wrestled into her bra and grappled with her shirt, everything felt wrong. She'd spent years alone—in a coma, isolated by her injuries, prisoner of her fears. It hit her that she couldn't really live as long as she was afraid. She was going to get hurt. Not everyone was going to like or understand her. She might find people who were horrified by her scars. *They* were the injured ones. The shallow. The ones unable to look past the surface to see her heart underneath.

Once, she'd thought Xander and Javier might fall into that category. But would the men she knew—and loved—reject her for the roadmap of red lines carved into her back? Maybe . . . but probably not. The relationship might not last forever, but she couldn't know its potential if she didn't take a chance. Wasn't risk part of life?

She donned her shoes and tossed her hair out of her face. Then stared at the closed door separating her from them. She was going to have to step out of her comfort zone. London wanted to come to Xander and Javier rested and whole, not coated in her own fear and another man's violent intent. She wanted them to know that she wasn't running on leftover nerves or fear. They could have no doubts about what was in her heart. If they rejected her then . . . well, she'd have the comfort of knowing she'd truly tried.

Crossing the floor, she pulled the door open with a breath, then stepped into the hall. Her men stood in front of her, a wall of protective males looking ready to do anything to keep her safe and whole. She smiled faintly. "The door is going to hit me in the ass when I let go if you don't back up."

A few steps away, Luc chuckled until Alyssa elbowed him in the ribs.

Javier's eyes narrowed with warning. If they'd been alone and today hadn't been traumatic, he'd be plotting exactly how to spank her, then torture her by arousing her unbearably and delaying her gratification. It kind of sounded wonderful.

Xander merely snagged her by the wrist and jerked her against his body. "Now it won't. You'll be safe with us, *belleza*. Always."

"I didn't doubt that." She managed to pry herself out of his embrace.

Looking on, Javier frowned. "Little one, don't run again. Come with us. Talk to us. We're sorry for what happened last night in Dallas—"

"There's nothing to say." London shook her head, not wanting him to apologize for asking for the trust he needed from her. She'd simply been too afraid to give it, and she would have to work through that before she could come to them whole. "I understand. Just . . . I need some time before I can discuss it. Can you give me that?"

Xander stiffened, looking ready to protest. He whipped his gaze to his older brother, who went just as tense. Some sort of silent communication passed between them, and she stifled a grin. Whatever happened from here out, these two men had one another, and she could think of nothing more important. They might have been out of step for years, but they'd never been truly separate. It warmed every corner of her heart to see them now on the same page.

Finally, Xander's shoulders dipped as he let out a frustrated sigh. Then Javier nodded. "Whatever you need, little one, you just tell us. Whatever it is, however you need it, no matter what you think we might say, please communicate."

London nodded.

"Promise us," Xander prompted. "Day or night, rain or shine . . ."

They cared for her. It seemed so obvious. She suddenly understood what having the warm fuzzies felt like. "I promise."

She stepped between them and pressed a soft kiss to Xander's lips. He grabbed her and tried to keep her tight against him. His revving heart and the taut desperation of his hold nearly had her melting and whispering reassurances in his ear.

London sent him a pleading expression. "A little time. I won't take too much."

Reluctance ripped across his face. He wanted to argue, but shook his head. With one last brush of his lips on hers, he gritted his teeth and stepped back. And she turned to Javier, his blue eyes drilled a million questions into her.

"I don't blame you for being angry with me about Brenner and Valjean and—"

"I'm not." She frowned as if the notion was absurd. Because it was. "You had no idea Brenner was *that* vindictive. Sad to be that petty and cruel, but . . . It's behind us." She drew in a shuddering breath. "It's over."

Javier grabbed her hair in his fists and pulled enough to snap her head back, pulling her mouth under his. He devoured her for a long moment, taking sweeping possession of her entire mouth—and with it, her body—before he grudgingly let go. "Don't forget us."

She looked into his eyes and grabbed Xander's hand, making them a promise. "Never."

* * *

AS the late morning sun slid in, Javier paced the living room, looking at his watch for about the millionth time. A fucking Sunday morning, so he couldn't bury himself in work very successfully. Xander, leaning indolently on the nearby couch, didn't look inclined to try at all. Javier glanced at the bottle of Cîroc on the nearby wet bar. The smooth, clear alcohol no longer held the lure of escape it once had. He didn't have to work so hard to drown out the voices of his guilty conscience. London had shown him a new path, a real love. And without her now, he was crawling out of his skin. How could Xander look so fucking calm?

"You're wearing a path in the carpet," his brother drawled.

"Your ass is making a dent in the couch. Are you not worried?"

A little hesitation, then he shook his head. "London may or may not be ready to commit, but she's not done. She won't give up on us without talking to us first. You did your part, right?"

Javier patted his pocket, both worried and comforted by its contents. "You know I did. I'm ready if she walks in the door now. You have your stuff?"

He patted his pocket. "Got it." Then a Cheshire cat grin spread across his face. "And I got the call this morning. All's clear." Then his smile faded. "Last chance to back out."

"Fuck no!" Was Xander crazy? He'd given up on a lot of things in life: a normal adolescence, his late wife, very nearly the company that had been his birthright. But he'd never give up on Xander again. Or on London. "What about you?"

"Not happening, big brother."

He swallowed. "That's what I want to hear. Now if we just knew when she might want to see us and talk—"

The doorbell chimed, clanging off the arched ceiling of the living room. He ran for the door just as Xander darted off the couch and nearly hurdled the end table to reach the portal. Together, they wrenched the door open. And there London stood.

She was a goddamn vision, her long hair drifting around her in pale curls, swaying on the light morning breeze. Her eyes, trimmed in a thick fringe of dark lashes, fluttered to her cheeks uncertainly before she met their gaze again. Her mouth was drawn into a pensive frown. She wore a sweet white sundress with matching wedges. A twinkling silver bracelet and lip gloss gave her the only hint of sparkle.

"Is this a bad time?"

Her soft voice made Javier instantly hard. He couldn't push the memories of her breathy pants and feminine cries out of his head. The way her skin turned pink and she unconsciously spread her legs wider as she approached orgasm. Afterward, the way she held him so tight . . . he felt like he'd always have a heart to belong to. Now, he just prayed that feeling wasn't wrong.

"Of course not." But he didn't move, couldn't. He just stared at her, trying to wrap his head around everything he had to say to convince her to stay.

"Are you going to keep her on the porch while you stand like a statue and gawk at her?" Xander grumbled in his ear, prying the door wide open to London. He took her by the hand and let her in. Javier could tell that Xander wanted to draw her into his arms, but he knew that they had to hear what she needed to say first. And they had a few things to say themselves.

"Come in, *belleza*. Talk to us."

Javier shut the front door and locked it, then turned his undivided attention to the two people who'd so quickly become his world, following them to the living room.

"Will you sit and just let me talk for a minute?"

The question fell softly from her sweet pink lips, and Javier sensed that she had drawn together every bit of her courage to come here and say whatever was on her mind. Was it what they wanted to hear? Had he misunderstood yesterday? Had her farewell at the hospital been a prelude to good-bye?

"Of course," Javier assured, sitting on the edge of the sofa.

Xander sank down beside him with a frown. "Tell us what's on your mind."

Still standing, she drew in a trembling breath. "I wanted to apologize for Friday night at Dominion."

"It's all right. We asked for too much too fast, little one." Javier fought the urge to take her in his arms and assure her that he understood, even if her lack of trust chafed.

London started to nod, then shook her head. "You asked me for a lot, true. But I panicked and ran like a little girl when I should have trusted you and explained my fears."

"You behaved like a woman who's learning her way through relationships. We all make mistakes. I've made more than my fair share. Xander has made even more—" His brother elbowed him. "But if you're ready to talk now, we're eager to listen."

"Thank you." She wrung her hands together.

Javier wanted to leap up from the sofa and hug her tightly, but she had an invisible wall between them. She wanted to get whatever was in her head out in the open before she let either of them touch her.

So he simply nodded her way. "Before you say anything, I want you to know we're not angry that you left. Yes, we should have discussed your fears, but everything is all right."

"Really?"

"Absolutely everything, little one. Even S.I. Industries."

Xander jumped in. "Yep. We received a call this morning from the Department of Justice. Federal prosecutors are going after Brenner and the executive scum from United Velocity who bought his information, knowing that it came from our R & D department. It's all in black-and-white on the computers law enforcement nabbed in the raid on Brenner's house. We've been assured that more military contracts are coming our way. And the cherry on top? One of their most important researchers was so appalled to find out what his employer had done that he reached out to us. He's left United Velocity, saying that he'll fully cooperate with prosecutors. He's offered to come work for us."

"Which is great because he's every bit as smart as Brenner and seems to have a lot more scruples. With Xander on board and me back to one hundred percent, this company will turn around so quickly." Javier sat back on the sofa like a man content because he was. Well, almost. Just one more possible—albeit beautiful— obstacle. Javier gave London a reassuring gaze. "And then there's you. As sorry as I am for the danger I unwittingly put you in, I'm glad that sordid business of revenge and espionage is behind us. You will never be in danger again, I promise."

"We'll make sure of it," Xander assured.

"Sounds like everything is working out for you two." London sent them a wan smile.

"For *us*," his younger brother insisted. "We want to talk to you, *belleza*. None of this works without you."

"*We* don't work without you." Javier had no trouble being emphatic; he spoke the truth. "The three of us have a . . . symbiotic relationship. Neither Xander nor I were doing well without you, little one. I was well on my way to drinking myself to death and—"

"Were you pining for Francesca?" London frowned.

She ought to know better, and Javier had to look London in the eye. He couldn't be less than honest. "No. I felt guilty. All the 'ifs' assailed me constantly. If I'd been more interested in her, if I'd been more attentive, if I could have scraped together enough feeling to truly care, if I'd divorced her when I should have, would she be alive today? Maybe. Probably. I will never know the answer for sure. But I know you've helped to heal me, taken away my shame, and replaced it with something so pure and wonderful." He smiled wryly, then looked at Xander. "And we all know that, before we met you, he was drowning in boobs and pus—"

"I wasn't making the best use of my time." Xander sent Javier a pointed look.

"An understatement," he grumbled.

"Shut it, big brother." Xander leaned forward and reached for London's hand. "What Javier is trying to say by throwing me under the bus is that we all work better together. And we don't want to lose you."

"Work better? Of course." She drew in a shaky breath and pulled her fingers from Xander's. "I won't quit until after we unveil Project Recovery. We've got more than three weeks—"

"Fuck Project Recovery right now." Javier stood and glared. "United Velocity won't be launching one, so we have time to bring our new research on board and do it right, before we unveil the project. The pressure is off for the moment, little one. Work is the furthest thing from my mind right now."

"It is?" Hope entered those blue eyes again, and he hadn't realized that she still sincerely doubted their feelings until that moment. "You said work, so I—"

"Because he can be a fucktard," Xander groused and stood on her other side, caressing her arm—and looking like he wanted to touch a whole lot more. "He means us." He grinned. "And work is the furthest thing from my mind, too."

Clearly, Xander was hoping there would be a sex portion to the day and that they could skip to it now, but first things first.

Javier sent his brother a heavy stare. "London has come to say something. Let's let her speak."

Xander surprisingly didn't balk. He sat back and studied London. "Go ahead, *belleza*."

She paced a little, her pale curls swaying across her back. As she spun, he saw the determination on her face. "When I came out of my coma just before the rest of my high school class was graduating,

I was told I'd never walk again. I'd been a cheerleader, an athlete, a dancer. I couldn't imagine . . . I refused to believe it. I think the doctors humored me by letting me do physical therapy. It took a few years, but I slowly resumed some motion and feeling in my legs, regained some muscle tone. But it was really slow. I was depressed a lot. I 'medicated' some of it with food. I gained a lot of weight. Then I didn't know what to do. I thought my life was over at twenty-one."

Javier's heart hurt for her. "You're beautiful as you are, little one. Don't believe any different."

"I love your curves," Xander seconded.

"Thank you. I've lost some of the weight. I'd like to lose a bit more to be happy."

"We want you happy," Javier assured with a smile.

London sent him an absent smile in return. "About a year ago, I got a new physical therapist. He helped with muscle strength and fine motor skills in particular. Brian was smart, patient, funny, gorgeous. He didn't feel like just a therapist, but a friend. He asked me out. I'd just turned twenty-four and was going out on my first date. It sounds crazy, but I'd devoted so many years to just trying to be 'normal' again. Our first date went really well. He kissed me, told me he liked me and wanted to see me again. I was like a teenage girl, so giddy."

Javier didn't know exactly where this story was going, but he knew it couldn't end happily or ol' Brian would still be in the picture. "Naturally. Despite your age, you'd never had the normal teenage experiences."

She nodded. "Everything was great until, after a swimming session, I went to change back into my clothes. I got into my bra and panties, then realized that, since I'd used my T-shirt as a cover-up, I'd left it by the pool. I ran out there to get it, certain he'd gone."

She bit her lip, and Javier knew exactly what she was going to say. He wanted to kill Brian, but didn't dare interrupt London. She needed to get this out.

Xander had a little less restraint and growled beside him. "Stupid motherfucker."

Totally true, but Javier elbowed him anyway. "Let her finish."

"I'm sure you can guess. He saw my back. We had this super awkward conversation about my accident and the surgeries afterward. It was . . . clinical. And the day of our next date, he texted me to say that he didn't think it was professional to date clients. When I showed up to my next training session, I'd been reassigned to this beautiful brunette who looked great in a bikini. I found out later that Brian started dating her shortly after he dumped me."

Javier clenched his fists. Questions perched on the tip of his tongue. Maybe Brian hadn't thought it smart to date clients after all, but he wasn't going to give the asshole the benefit of the doubt. He would simply make London feel better by loving her.

"He wasn't worth you, *belleza*." Xander rose and approached her slowly.

Standing as well, Javier circled the other side of the coffee table and closed in on her. "If he couldn't see the lovely woman underneath—"

"Stop! You think you like me. You think my face or boobs or whatever is nice. I've only let you see the best, but you seem to want to see it all. Fine, but don't say another word until you've seen my worst." She looked on the verge of tears, her nose reddening, her lips pressing together as she tried to hold them back. "Not even a sound. If you heap kind words on me and then decide you can't handle all of me, it will hurt so much worse."

That was never going to happen. And a part of Javier wanted to be angry that she'd cast him and Xander into Brian's mold, but he reminded himself that she had no other experience. She'd met a shallow boy. Now, he intended to make sure she knew the difference between that and the men who loved her. A glance confirmed that he and Xander were absolutely on the same page.

Shoving down the reassurances he wanted to speak, Javier simply nodded. Beside him, Xander did the same.

"Thank you." London drew in a bracing breath that shuddered instead. Then she walked to a patch of sunlight slanting through the window, glowing into the room, and reached for the zipper at her side.

Slowly, she drew it down, the zipper a soft hiss in the otherwise quiet air. Anticipation clawed Javier's insides. His heart pounded. When it reached her hip and gaped open over the lush indentation of her waist, she brushed one strap off her shoulder. The other followed, and she pushed the dress beneath her breasts, revealing a lacy white demi-bra with clear straps. She unbuttoned the wrap-around bottom at her waist, and the white eyelet parted to reveal her thighs and the delta between. Javier swallowed, his mouth watering. He clenched his fists to keep himself from touching her. She needed to get this out, and he had to let her.

She pushed the dress down over her hips, revealing the fact that her white panties were small and inviting, and he hoped like hell it was a thong because he loved her ass. Next, she stripped off her shoes, setting them aside efficiently. A long pause followed. London gathered air and courage. Javier sent her an encouraging stare. He could see her body tensing, her heart beating madly at the base of her neck. Silence strangled the room.

Reaching behind her, she unhooked her bra and slid it down her arms. The instant her breasts came into view, Javier had to hold himself back. It had been less than two days since he'd been inside her, and it felt more like ten years. Beside him, Xander clenched his fists and stared at her as if he couldn't wait to eat her up.

The panties came next as she hooked her thumbs in the waistband and drew the scrap of white fabric down over her thighs, past her knees, letting them puddle at her feet. London kicked them aside, and Javier zeroed in on the pink flesh of her slit, wanting his fingers there, his mouth. His cock. Yes, right there—always.

"You're gorgeous." Xander's voice cracked. Not much rattled his brother, but Javier had no doubt he meant every word.

"More than beautiful," he added. "I know you don't want us to say that, but I can't help telling you how lovely you are to me."

"Please . . . let me finish." Fear throbbed just under the surface of her façade. She tried so hard to be strong and brave, and he admired her for it.

And she would never believe that they would gladly lend her their strength every day for the rest of their lives until they passed this test.

"Sorry, little one. Go on."

London took another long pause. "If you're not ready or willing to accept this part of me, do one thing for me? Don't give me any excuses. I can't handle platitudes. Just leave the room and shut a door behind you. Then . . . I'll know."

Chapter Twenty-one

JAVIER blinked in shock. She imagined for a moment that either of them were going to abandon her without a word? Never. That would fucking never happen, ever. Beside him, Xander's eyes widened. He was clearly grappling with the shock of that request every bit as much as he was.

But Xander had been telling him for months that being a Dom was about giving a sub what she needed. Right now, that was reassurance that he could be sensitive to her request, her fragility. That didn't make him a patient man, however.

"If that's the way you want it, fine. But no more hesitation, little one. Show us what's ours now and let us . . ." *Make you feel every bit as beautiful as you should.* "Let whatever is going to happen, happen."

Her gaze dropped to the floor. So automatic, it had to be unconscious. If Javier hadn't already been so hard just seeing her naked and soft in front of him, that would have stiffened him instantly.

"Yes, Sir."

Another deep breath. A willful lift of her shoulders. A trembling of her chin. Javier ached to touch her so badly.

With two steps she turned around, and he could see every inch of her bare back. She knelt, head bowed, exposing not just her body, but her soul. And, breath held, she waited.

Her skin bespoke the tragedy and pain she'd suffered. Deep gouges in jagged patterns zigzagged across her lower back, most a puckered pale pink. Other scars heaped on top, fresher, straighter. Surgery. Judging from the amount of incisions, more than one. Javier would ask her for details later, when she felt comfortable that the answers didn't matter to them. Now wasn't that time.

A glance at his brother showed tears glossing his eyes. *Oh my God,* he mouthed. And he ached for her agony. Javier wished he could take that from her, endure it for her. Xander obviously wished the same. But London's past was part of what made her the woman who knelt before them now.

He nodded at Xander, agreeing with all the silent promise in his brother's gaze to finish her healing and make her whole. They'd do it together.

As one, they dropped to their knees behind her. He couldn't wait another moment to touch her. Neither of them could. She'd been broken and unsure, adrift and afraid. Now they had to put her together, lend her their conviction, and help her find her way home.

Cupping her left hip, he braced himself over her, breathing across her shoulders. Xander did something similar, and London's breath caught on a little gasp. God, she'd really expected them to leave her. Eventually, they'd paddle her ass for that, once she was more secure. Once they could tease her about being so wrong. Now, she needed to know they were here for her.

He brushed his hand down her back, fingers slowing as he closed in on her injuries. He lingered over the tracework of her scars. One bisected another. He didn't look, just felt. The one he followed now with a gentle touch had been deep and probably caused at least temporary nerve damage. A quick mental picture of her trapped in twisted metal, bleeding, crying, so young . . . Fuck, that hurt. He pressed his lips between her shoulder blades.

"On your hands and knees, *belleza*," Xander demanded, his voice low but gentle.

Her shuddering cry tugged at his heart, but she did it, giving them a better angle to access the damage to her body. He saw it even more clearly as the sun illuminated her, bathing her in golden light. All he saw was the pain she'd endured and skin he wanted to kiss. He might not be able to make it better, but he could assure her that her heart mattered to him more than her scars.

Xander grabbed both her hips, angling directly behind her and lowered his lips to a deep gouge directly above her right cheek. Javier did the same on the left, brushing his lips across her pink and red scars, his tongue tracing one that must have bled so much and hurt so deep. London let loose another gasp, trembling, and he glanced around her to see her fingers digging into the beige carpet. She'd hung her head and squeezed her eyes shut.

And tears slid down her angelic face.

Javier's heart squeezed in his chest. "Little one, don't cry. You're still so beautiful to us. You're always going to be beautiful."

"Forever," Xander promised in between kisses. "These aren't scars. They're a testament to your strength. We're so amazed by you. And so grateful for you."

Damn, he was proud of his brother. Javier couldn't have said it better himself.

London sobbed, her body shaking with each breath. And he'd had enough waiting. She'd spilled everything she needed to. Now it was their turn.

Still on his knees, Javier turned her around to kneel in their waiting arms. She raised stormy, vulnerable eyes to him, so wet and lost. He kissed her forehead. "Look at me and don't look away."

She nodded, clutching his shoulder with one hand and his brother's with the other. "Yes, Sir."

God, every time she said that was even more arousing than the last.

"I don't need to see your scars. They aren't important. They're nothing. What I value—what I need—is your heart. Your soul. I love you."

Her mouth fell open with a shocked, silent gasp.

Xander wrapped firm fingers around her chin and brought her gaze to him. "He took all the pretty words, rat bastard, but I think I looked at you dancing so freely on the stage just for the joy of being alive and realized what I'd been missing for years. I love you, too."

Her chin quivered again, then a smile broke across her face. Joyous tears fell this time. Her fingers dug into him, then she brushed her gaze over his face. Her lips followed gently, a whisper. A silent promise. She gave Xander the same attention. "I didn't know who I was or where I was or what I needed until you came and showed me the way. I love you both."

So goddamn perfect, everything about her . . .

Together, he and Xander crushed her naked body against them. His brother quickly shed his T-shirt, then used his lips to climb wild kisses up her neck, her jaw, over to her lips. But Javier was doing the same, and they took turns caressing her lips, delving into her mouth, showing her with their kisses how much they worshipped her.

As Xander stole her succulent mouth away again, he nipped at London's lobe. "Unbutton my shirt, little one."

Her moan sprang free, but she raised her hands to his buttons as arousal began to undo her, and she touched his skin while she lost herself in Xander's embrace.

The feel of her fingers on him nearly turned him inside out. He quickly lost patience, ripping the shirt open. Buttons pinged everywhere, and he didn't give a shit. All that mattered was that he peeled the garment off, threw it across the room, then pressed his skin to hers, his fingers sweeping all the way down her back, from shoulder to hip, over smooth skin and scars, until he held the sweet handful against him.

"I feel so lucky," she said finally when Xander let her up for air.

"So do we," his brother assured.

London blinked, then shook her head. "You're rich and gorgeous, sophisticated and charming. Powerful . . . You could have anyone."

"He has," Javier ribbed."

"Shut the hell up," Xander growled.

"Exactly. So why me?" She sounded so uncertain, and Javier knew only time and love would change that. And maybe a few other things they had up their sleeve.

Xander grabbed her face in his hands. "Everyone else was recreation. A way to pass time and kill boredom. They wanted my money or prowess or for me to look good at their side. They didn't care about me. Or my brother. I didn't look at them and finally understand the concept of home. Of family. I didn't look at them and know where I belonged. Only you did that, *belleza*."

Xander stole her lips again and sealed his bond with her. Reverent and urgent, until she pulled away panting, eyes glazed. Javier held in a grin, figuring that he'd better get his words out before they just didn't care about talking anymore.

"And you thawed me, love." He caressed her jaw, nudging her gaze back to him. "Our father was a cold bastard who embraced only duty and money, and he drilled that philosophy into me ruthlessly. I'd always believed that if I followed those, I'd have what I needed. Francesca was a mistake, and I knew it immediately. But it was my duty to stay married. I'd made a vow. After she was dead, I saw that she had everything money could buy, but not the one thing she truly craved. Fran was a needy creature. She wanted a love I didn't know how to give, and once she was dead, I could only think that my ineptitude might as well have been the rope around her neck."

"And you drowned in guilt and booze," she finished softly. "Oh, Javier. You *do* have a big heart. You gave an inexperienced girl a job, trusted me with your secrets, helped me see what it was to truly live. Give yourself some credit."

Sweet to the very end. "You opened my eyes, little one. I'll be grateful to you forever."

"Before this gets too much sappier, we need to ask you something," Xander piped in.

London giggled. "Gosh, we are sounding a little greeting cardish. What is it? If it's about staying on the job beyond the initial five weeks, yes."

"It wasn't, but good to know." Javier winked, then nerves attacked him as he dug into his pocket. This was it. He was going to say these words for the second time in his life, but mean them for the very first. He fished out the little square inside and withdrew it. "I love you more than mere words can say. Marry me."

As he opened the box, she gasped. She would be seeing the platinum ring, channel-set with diamonds and topped with a one-carat stone, that nestled against a thinner band adorned with a nearly flawless five-carat colorless diamond.

Her eyes widened almost impossibly. "Oh my . . ."

"And me." Xander pulled the other part of the wedding set from his pocket, a mirror of his own band, a row of diamonds set in platinum that would curl around the large center stone. "There's a stone to represent each of us. But you're in the middle, as we'll always want you to be. So you'll always feel surrounded and loved."

Javier expected a lot of reactions, but he hadn't expected sobbing. London buried her face in her hands.

He and Xander glanced at one another, both wearing identically lost expressions.

"*Belleza*, if you don't like the setting—"

"I love it," she gasped and lowered her hands, looking at them both with tear-drenched eyes. "I love you. You're sure you want to marry me after only a week?"

"'Want' might be the wrong word, little one." Javier raised a brow. "'Insist' might be closer."

"I'd go with 'demand,' personally," Xander kicked in.

Javier nodded. "You know, he's probably right. I like 'demand.'"

She laughed and threw her arms around them again. "Then yes. A huge, I'm-the-luckiest-girl-in-the-world yes."

Javier tore the rings out of the box and took her hand in his, sliding them down her finger. Xander took his turn next, easing the final band into place. Three pieces all entwined perfectly.

When he would have moved in for a kiss, Xander elbowed him in the chest. "Wait. There's more."

"Can't we cover this ground later?"

"Nope." Xander sounded like an immovable mountain. "I want to get it all out there now."

Sighing, Javier shook his head. Little brother was probably right, but damn, he wanted to get to the part of the day where they took her to bed and used every part of their bodies to show her just how important she was to them.

"There's something else?" Incredulity lilted her voice.

Javier gave up the notion of having sex right now. London needed to know all they had in mind. "We each wanted to give you something. Since you've never been to your namesake, we wanted to honeymoon there . . . on our way to soak up some sun on the French coast, then take in the beauty of Tuscany. We've all earned some time to just be together."

He scrambled up to retrieve the travel documents on the end table by the sofa, then handed them to her.

She scanned them, her face lowering to a frown. "These tickets are for the first week of September, guys. That's in less than two months. There's no way we can pull off a wedding that quickly."

"There is when you've got money." Javier smiled.

"And we need to make this a quick wedding. For one thing, I don't want to wait until even tomorrow, but I guess you want to have time to explain us to your mother so we can meet her."

"Uh . . . yeah. That's going to be fun." Her sarcasm said otherwise. "But she'll come around. She just wants me to be happy and loved."

"We'll make sure of that," Xander promised. "But the second reason . . ." He fished an envelope out of the back pocket of his jeans and pressed it into her hands. "You can open it here if you want, but this is a fax from the hospital. They did my blood work last night. I knew I was clean because I was always meticulously careful, but I wanted you to see it in black-and-white."

"O-okay." An adorable frown crossed her face. "That's good news."

"It's *great* news," Xander corrected. "I've missed out on years of family. My brother was always busy being groomed for success. I squandered all that time being a dumbass."

"A skirt-chasing dumbass," she teased him.

"Yeah." He had the good grace to flush. "But I don't want to wait anymore. The three of us will marry and be a family. I want to expand it. And I want to start now."

London blinked, jaw dropping. "Like, right now?"

Xander nodded. "I wanted you to know that I'm clean so we'd never need any barriers between us again."

Happiness lit her blue eyes before a crushing frown showed her misery. "I think it's only fair . . . I have to be honest. The doctors say that my blackout spells may never stop. It's much better with my meds, but I can't ever be alone with a child, at least not a very young one. I'm not sure I'll ever be fit to be a mother—"

"Stop there." Those words inflamed Javier. "Hear this and understand it, London. You will make a wonderful mother. You will give our children comfort, love, and guidance. If you're unable to be alone with children . . . well, that's another benefit to there being three of us. We can all pitch in. We can hire any help you need. We'll support you in every way we can."

"We want a family with you, *belleza*," Xander murmured, stroking the soft hair at her crown and looking deeply into her eyes, willing her to understand.

"I feel so blessed." She smiled with all the love shining in her heart.

"Is that a yes?"

His brother was so pushy, but Javier understood. The thought of London under their roof, with their rings on her fingers, her belly swelling with their children as they shared all the years and their love . . . nothing sounded more perfect.

"Yes." She kissed Xander gently. "But you're talking like you want me pregnant before the wedding."

"Tonight, if possible. I've wasted most of my life. I don't want to waste another moment to start our future."

Javier kissed her neck. "I have to agree, little one. I wasn't really living until I met you. It seems only fitting that we create life together."

She bit her lip, then nodded. "You're right. I know firsthand that you never know how long life will last. Why wait? Come love me."

Neither one of them wasted a moment before tearing into their zippers and shoving their pants down and tossing them aside. Javier was already painfully hard and took himself in hand, slowly stroking, wishing to fuck it was her hand around him. Xander looked every bit as ready to be inside her as he was.

Together, they helped her to the carpet, onto her back. London looked a little nervous, and it was natural. They'd made a lot of big decisions today, life-altering ones. This was the first of the wheels they'd set in motion. Maybe it was a bit of the cart before the horse, but they all knew what they wanted and saw no reason to wait.

Javier scooted up to kiss her lips, take her mouth, entwine their tongues. Under him, she gasped, her back arching. He lifted away and looked down to see Xander with his mouth fastened on her pussy, eating feverishly, his tongue working her clit.

A flush quickly spread across London's fair skin. Her breathing picked up pace. God, he wanted to fuck her.

Tucking a hand under her head, he grabbed a handful of hair and pulled until she opened to him. He dove into her mouth, taking everything, stamping himself on her, forcing her to taste how much he wanted her. Under him, she tensed. Her breathing grew erratic. He loved watching her arousal grow, loved adding fuel to the fire.

"Does Xander eating your pussy feel good, little one?" he murmured against her breast before he nipped at the sensitive flesh, then sucked her nipple into his mouth, drawing hard on her flesh.

"Yes . . . yes!"

He took her other nipple and lapped at it, bit at it with his teeth until she hissed, and began muttering incoherent cries. London was so close.

"Yes what?" he growled in her ear, watching as Xander lifted his head from her cunt.

"Yes, Sir."

His brother licked his wet lips, then crawled up her body, between her legs, cock in hand. "I've never done this bareback, *belleza*."

It stunned Javier that Xander hadn't once forgotten a condom during his multiple female, big-party life. But the sincerity radiating from his expression made Javier believe every word.

London spread a bit wider, bending her knees in welcome. Javier pressed kisses to her nipples, watching his brother ease his naked cock into their fiancée.

Once he'd slid in to the hilt, Xander closed his eyes with a low groan. "Fuck, that's the best thing I've ever felt. I never want anything between us ever again."

Wrapping her legs around him, she lifted to him and nodded. "Never."

Poised on his knees above her, Xander pumped her in a slow, strong rhythm. Javier sucked her nipples one after the other, alternating and feeling them harden a bit more with every pass. With his free hand, he stroked her clit lazily.

"When did your last period end?" Xander demanded.

"God, that's so good, I-I can't think."

"Try, little one. For us." But he didn't let up his stroke of her hard little pearl.

"Um . . . I think—" she panted. "Ten days ago. Two weeks. Something like that."

"Likely fertile," Javier pointed out to his brother.

"Yee-haw," Xander drawled and fucked her harder.

London flushed and swelled. Her body tensed all over as she held her breath for the explosion that was moments away.

"She's going to come."

"Good," his brother panted as he thrust faster into her swelling pussy. "We'll do it together."

Around him, the air thickened, rose, waited in anticipation. London gasped. Then she screamed in release. Under his fingers, her clit turned rock-hard. Her whole body bucked. And Xander shouted out in satisfaction, pushing into her strong and fast as he deposited his seed deep inside her.

Then he collapsed on top of her, and the two of them lay limp and still for a moment, a tangle of arms, legs, breaths. Hearts.

And Javier felt ready to explode. He wanted—needed—to be inside her, coating her womb with his semen, filling her up with everything he had to give.

Xander suddenly looked up at him and grinned. "That was amazing. You need some of that."

"Right now," he growled.

"You got it. Get on your back."

Javier wondered why, then he realized what his brother had in mind. And a huge smile spread across his face. He scrambled into place, then gathered London's body against him, slowly bringing her to straddle him. He slid his cock into her soft, drenched pussy, and the feel of her walls closing in on his bare cock made a shudder roll down his spine. "Jesus!"

"Isn't it amazing?" Xander asked as he made his way above London's head, then grabbed her chin. "Open your mouth, *belleza*. Suck me hard. I'm going to fuck you again. Go slow, Javi."

Slow? "Are you out of your mind?" Already he felt moments from explosion, and the sight of their girl opening soft lips to Xander and curling her tongue around his spent cock grabbed him by the balls.

"We had a plan," Xander reminded with a low rumble.

They had, and he needed to stick with it. He nodded and eased into London's cunt again, this time more slowly. He wanted her to come again, this time with him. He wanted her to associate pleasure with their touch for the rest of her life.

Her breasts hung in his face as he raised his hips and filled her with his cock again, so he wrapped his lips around her nipples and sucked. Every time he did, she clamped down on him. Her soft breaths and pants around his brother's cock were getting to him. But it wasn't long before the little berries hardened on his tongue. Her skin took on that rosy glow he knew so well.

And as he found and mercilessly plied that one spot inside her pussy, London tensed. "Javi!"

"Yes, that's our good girl. Feel the pleasure. We're always going to give this to you. The night we're married, as you're swelling with our children, with every anniversary we celebrate, with every year that passes, it's going to be like this for us, love."

"Please . . ." she whimpered, tightening on him again.

"Xander," he warned his brother. Time was running out.

Little brother pulled from her mouth with a soft pop. She cried out in wanting, then gasped when he appeared behind her. Xander fished around in his pants for the tube of lube. In seconds, he'd unscrewed the cap, coated his fingers with the stuff, and rimmed her back entrance. Another dollop and a rub of his fingers, and the lube coated his cock.

"Hold still, Javi."

He gritted his teeth and fought the urge to tell Xander to make it quick.

"Arch your back, baby. Push out at me and let me in."

"Both of you at once?" she whispered.

"Oh, yeah," Xander drawled.

Javier nipped at her breast again. "Every day."

She sighed happily, then did as Xander demanded. Javier felt his brother sliding into place, a thin membrane separating them. Together, they filled the woman who would soon be their wife, the mother of their children. Together, they created the future, alternating slow pumps into her, whispering assurances, checking her comfort, spreading kisses all over her.

The crest rose up quickly again, and to his surprise Xander was with them. His brother held London's hips. She pressed her breasts to his chest, ravaged his mouth with hers, tightening and screaming as orgasm washed over her. Javier felt the tension grab him by the balls. They were heavy, loaded, and as pleasure shimmied down his spine, converging right in the head of his cock, blood filled him. His heart pumped furiously. Fantasies of London pregnant and naked, love shining in her eyes as she waited for them, filled his thought.

God, this orgasm was going to blow him away. But he didn't try to control it. He simply let go and gave everything to her. He growled out his release, his spine melting with ecstasy. Xander joined him with a harsh cry.

Then they fell into a heaping tangle of pants and perspiration. Between them, London giggled. "Clearly, you boys are going to be devoted to this baby-making thing."

"You have no idea." Javier brushed another kiss over her mouth and smiled up into her eyes.

"But we'll be happy to show you," Xander vowed, sliding his left hand over hers and looking at their rings on her finger.

Finally, they rose together and helped her into the shower. It was a cramped press, and Javier made a mental note to make sure that whatever house they settled into had a really big bathroom.

As Xander washed her back with gentle strokes and Javier lost himself in the sweet heat of her kiss, she stiffened. "Wait, guys . . ."

Reluctantly, Javier lifted his head. "What, little one?"

"I-I don't really want to move back to Los Angeles. I know you're from there. I know your business is, too." She sighed. "But there's so many bad memories for me there, and my mom . . . she would mean well, but she would hover and—"

"It's all right," he assured her as he turned her to face his brother, then slid a hand over her cunt again. Still swollen. Still wet. Always perfect.

He took hold of her hips, then turned her, bending her slightly. He slid into her from behind. She gasped and met his gaze over her shoulder. In that stare, he saw surprise . . . with a lingering bit of worry about her scars.

"Shh, I see *all* of you and you're beautiful, London. You always will be. Wherever you want to live is fine. We'll work the business around it, but this—" He eased into her pussy, up to the hilt. "This will always be home."

"For both of us," Xander added. "Damn, I love to watch him fuck you, *belleza*. Take his cock, take our love. That's it."

"I want to stay here." The tension was rising in her voice, then she began to cry out and push back, demanding more.

Javier gave it to her. "Who knew that when my brother shanghaied me to what I considered the ass crack of America that I'd actually find everything I could ever want."

"Thank you for doing that, Xander," she breathed. "Thank you both."

"See, I was right." Xander grinned at him. "I hate to say I told you so, but . . ."

"No, you don't. But in this case, I have to thank you, too."

"You're welcome. Now, shut up and fuck her faster."

"Piss off. You just want me to finish so you can have her again."

"Damn straight," Xander cried, as if he'd voiced the obvious.

Between them, London laughed. "At this rate, we're going to have to get married damn quick."

"Is tomorrow too soon?" his little brother suggested.

"Hmm . . ." The sound was more pleasurable moan than thoughtful musing. "I can't fly my mother out here that quickly and . . . oh God, that feels *so* good. Yes!" She tensed, and he noticed that Xander had a hand between her legs, no doubt helping her orgasm along.

"Then next weekend," Xander insisted. "That gives us a few days to stay in bed. Alyssa, Tara, and Kata will no doubt be happy to plan a wedding. All you'll have to do is show up and say 'I do.'"

London dug her nails into Xander's thighs as she tightened around Javier's cock. The swell of arousal reached a crest, this one less desperate, but a deep, powerful roar that rose up and crested inside him as he filled her with his seed again. God, he'd never get tired of that. It might be primitive, but it eased something inside him to know that he could make her his again and again.

He and Xander all but carried a limp London out of the shower and tucked her into bed. He kissed her softly, contentment like the thickest elixir sliding joy through his veins.

Xander had other ideas. The second she was on her back, he was inside her again, making love to her with his whole body, every slow, hard thrust of his cock making her body writhe. Making her whimper.

"Happy?" Javier asked her.

She nodded, her face an incoherent mask of pleasure, her eyes dazed and drunken with all the arousal they'd heaped on her all morning. And the day was still young.

"Yes," she finally managed. "Very happy, Sir."

Damn it, now he wanted to fuck her again, too. He sighed. They probably needed to give her a break. And they would . . . eventually.

"Me, too, love."

"Oh God, count me in. So fucking happy." Xander gripped her and hammered into her pussy like a man possessed.

"See the way she's turning rosy for you?" Javier said to his brother. "The way she's lifting her lips to you? Go on, Xander. You know what to do."

"You just want her again."

"Always," Javier bantered back, then looked London in the eyes. "You saved me, little one. You both did. And I love you two for it. Thank you."

"I love you, too," she whispered, then panted toward orgasm.

"You're welcome," Xander drawled, then grinned at Javier. "Now fuck off."

About the Author

Shayla Black (aka Shelley Bradley) is the *New York Times* and *USA Today* bestselling author of more than thirty sizzling contemporary, erotic, para-normal, and historical romances for multiple print, electronic, and audio publishers. She lives in Texas with her husband, munchkin, and one very spoiled cat. In her "free" time she enjoys watching reality TV, reading, and listening to an eclectic blend of music.

Shayla's work has been translated into approximately a dozen languages. She has also received or been nominated for the Passionate Plume, the Holt Medallion, the Colorado Romance Writers Award of Excellence, and the National Reader's Choice Award. RT Bookclub has twice nominated her for Best Erotic Romance of the Year, and awarded her several Top Picks and a KISS Hero Award.

A writing risk-taker, Shayla enjoys tackling writing challenges with every book. Find Shayla at www.ShaylaBlack.com or visit her on her Shayla Black Author Facebook page.